At certain moments in history it is a simple incident which sets off a whole series of events, which causes wheels to begin turning—faster and faster.

This time the moment began with Lucie Devaud's attempt to kill Guy Florian, the President of France. . . .

"AN ACTION-PACED POLITICAL THRILLER . . . ROUSINGLY EFFECTIVE."
—KIRKUS REVIEWS

"A WINNER . . . A SUSPENSE STORY IN WHICH THE PACE NEVER LAGS."
—ERIE (PA.) TIMES-NEWS

"ONCE AGAIN, COLIN FORBES HAS SHOWN HIMSELF TO BE ONE OF THE OUTSTANDING STORYTELLERS OF HIS TIME."
—ALFRED COPPEL,
author of "Thirty-four East"

Fawcett Crest Books
by Colin Forbes:

THE HEIGHTS OF ZERVOS

THE STONE LEOPARD

TARGET FIVE

TRAMP IN ARMOR

YEAR OF THE GOLDEN APE

THE STONE LEOPARD

Colin Forbes

A FAWCETT CREST BOOK

Fawcett Publications, Inc., Greenwich, Connecticut

For Jane

THE STONE LEOPARD

THIS BOOK CONTAINS THE COMPLETE TEXT OF
THE ORIGINAL HARDCOVER EDITION.

A Fawcett Crest Book reprinted by arrangement
with E. P. Dutton & Company, Inc.

ISBN 0-449-23129-1

Printed in the United States of America

10   9   8   7   6   5   4   3   2   1

PART ONE

THE LEOPARD

December 8–December 16

1

"After Giscard came de Gaulle . . ."

The dry comment was made by a British Foreign Office undersecretary off the record. A spokesman at the American State Department put it more grimly. "After Giscard came a more brutal de Gaulle—de Gaulle magnified by the power of ten." They were, of course, referring to the new President of the French Republic, only a few hours before the first attempt to kill him.

It was his anti-American outburst at Dijon which provoked these two descriptions of the most powerful political leader in western Europe. Understandably, the real sorrow in certain Washington circles at the news of the attempted assassination of President Florian was that it had failed. But on that wintry December evening when Florian left the Elysée Palace to walk the few dozen metres which would take him to the Ministry of the Interior in the Place Beauvau he was within seconds of death.

The rise to power of Guy Auguste Florian, who succeeded Giscard d'Estaing as President of the French Republic, was spectacular and unexpected—so unexpected that it caught almost every government in the world off balance. Tall, slim and agile, at fifty-two Florian looked ten years younger; exceptionally quick-witted, he was impatient of minds which moved more slowly than his own. And there was something of de Gaulle in his commanding presence, in the way he dominated everyone around him by sheer force of personality. At eight o'clock on the evening of Wednesday, 8 December he was at his most impatient when Marc Grelle, Police Prefect of Paris, warned him against walking in the streets.

"There is a car waiting. It can drive you to the Ministry, Mr. President . . ."

"You think I will catch a chill?" Florian enquired. "Maybe you would like a doctor to accompany me the two minutes it will take to get there?"

"At least he would be available to stop the blood flow if a bullet finds you . . ."

Marc Grelle was one of the few men in France who dared to answer Florian back in his own sardonic coin. Forty-two years old, a few inches shorter than the six-foot one president, the police prefect was also slim and athletic and a man who disliked formality. In fact, Grelle's normal dress for most of his working day was a pair of neatly pressed slacks and a polo-necked sweater, which he was still wearing. Perhaps it was the informality, the ease of manner which made the prefect, widowed a year earlier when his wife died in a car crash, attractive to women. His appearance may have helped; sporting a trim, dark mustache which matched his thatch of black hair, he had, like the president, good bone structure, and although normally poker-faced, his firm mouth had a hint of humour at the corners. He shrugged as Florian, putting on a coat, prepared to leave his study on the first floor of the Elysée.

"I'll come with you then," the police prefect said. "But you take foolish risks . . ."

He followed Florian out of the study and down the stairs to the large hall which leads to the front entrance and the enclosed courtyard beyond, slipping on his leather raincoat as he walked. He left his coat open deliberately; it gave easier access to the .38 Smith & Wesson revolver he always carried. It was not normal for a prefect to be

armed but Marc Grelle was not a normal prefect; since
one of his prime duties was to protect the president inside
the boundaries of Paris he took the responsibility personally. In the carpeted lobby a uniformed and bemedalled
usher opened the tall glass door and Florian, well ahead of
the prefect, ran down the seven steps into the cobbled
yard. Still inside, Grelle hurried to catch him up.

To reach the Ministry of the Interior, which is only
three minutes' walk from the Elysée, the president had to
leave the courtyard, cross the rue Faubourg St Honoré,
walk a few dozen metres to the Place Beauvau where
he would turn into the entrance to the Ministry. He was
starting to cross the street when Grelle, saluting the sentries briefly, came out of the courtyard. The prefect
glanced quickly to left and right. At eight in the evening,
barely a fortnight before Christmas, which is not cele-
brated with any great enthusiasm in Paris, it was dark
and quiet. There was very little traffic about and on his
face Grelle felt spots of moisture. It was going to rain
again, for God's sake—it had rained steadily for weeks
and nearly half France was under water.

The street was almost empty, but not quite: coming
towards the Elysée entrance from the Madeleine direction,
a couple paused under a lamp while the man lit a cigarette. British tourists, Grelle guessed: the man, hatless,
wore a British warm; the woman was dressed in a smart
grey coat. Across the road was someone else, a woman
who stood alone close to a fur shop. A moment earlier
she had been peering into the window. Now, half-turned
towards the street, she was fiddling inside her handbag,
presumably for a handkerchief or comb.

A rather attractive woman—in her early thirties so
far as Grelle could see—she wore a red hat and a form-
fitting brown coat. As he headed for the Place Beauvau,
crossing the street diagonally, Florian was passing her at
an angle. Never a man to fail to notice an attractive
woman, the president glanced at her and then moved on.

All this Grelle took in as he reached the sidewalk kerb, still a few metres behind his impatient president.

No detectives were assigned to accompany Florian when he went out: he had expressly forbidden what he called "an invasion of my privacy . . ." Normally he travelled in one of the black Citroën DS 23s always waiting parked inside the courtyard, but he had developed this irksome habit of walking to the Place Beauvau whenever he wanted to see the Minister of the Interior. And the habit had become known, had even been reported in the press.

"It's dangerous," Grelle had protested. "You even go out at the same time—at eight in the evening. It wouldn't be difficult for someone to wait for you . . ."

"You think the Americans will send a gunman?" Florian had enquired sardonically.

"There are always cranks . . ."

Grelle had stepped off the kerb, was still catching up with Florian, his eyes darting about, when something made the president glance back. He was hardly more than a metre away when the woman took the gun out of her handbag. Quite coolly, showing no sign of panic, her arm steady, she took deliberate, point-blank aim. Florian, twisted round, froze in sheer astonishment for only a matter of seconds. In another second he would have been running, ducking, doing something. The sound of two shots being fired in rapid succession echoed down the street like the drumbeat backfire of a large car.

The body lay in the gutter, quite inert, quite dead. The complete lack of movement is always the most disturbing thing. Grelle bent over her, the .38 Smith & Wesson still in his hand. He felt shocked. It was the first time he had killed a woman. When the Forensic Institute people examined the corpse later they found one of Grelle's bullets in her heart, the second one centimetre to the right. A moment earlier the prefect had hustled the president back

inside the courtyard, gripping him tightly by the arm, taking no notice of what he said, ushering him back inside
the Elysée like a felon. Now guards with automatic weapons were flooding into the street. Far too late.

Grelle himself removed the automatic from the hand
of the dead woman, lifting it carefully by the barrel to
retain fingerprints. It was a Bayard 9-mm short made by
the Belgian small-arms factory at Hertal. Small enough
to go inside a handbag, it was by no means a lady's gun.
Fired—as it would have been—at point-blank range,
Grelle had no doubt the result would have been fatal. A
few minutes later his deputy, Director-General André
Boisseau of the Police Judiciaire, arrived in the cordoned-
off street in a police car with siren screaming.

"My God, is it true?"

"Yes, it is true," Grelle snapped. "His would-be assassin, a woman, is just being carried into that ambulance.
Florian is unhurt—back in the Elysée. From now on
everything will be different. We will have tight security
on him twenty-four hours a day. He is to be guarded
wherever he goes—I'll see him in the morning to get his
approval . . ."

"If he doesn't agree?"

"He'll receive my immediate resignation . . ."

The press had arrived now, the reporters were trying
to force their way through the churning crowd of gendarmes, and one of them called out to the prefect. "The
hyenas are here," Grelle muttered under his breath, but
it was important to set them right immediately. They still
had time to file their stories for tomorrow's banner headlines. He ordered that they be let through and they
swarmed round the slim, athletic man who was the calmest
person present. It was, of course, the reporter from
L'Humanité—"that Communist rag," as the prefect called
the paper—who asked the question. "You say the assassin
was a woman? Did the president know her?"

The implication was crude and clear, bearing in mind

the rumours about Florian's strained relations with his wife, about his relationships with other women. *L'Humanité* scented a juicy scandal of international proportions. Grelle, who detested politicians, understood politics. He paused to get everyone's close attention, to build up a suspense he could deflate.

"The president did not know this woman. He had never seen her in his life. He told me this when I was hustling him back into the Elysée . . ."

"He saw her clearly then?" the reporter insisted.

"He happened to be looking straight at her when she aimed the weapon at him . . ."

Soon after this exchange he shut them up, had them sent back further down the street behind the cordon, knowing they would soon have to rush off to phone their offices. The ambulance had gone now. Police photographers were taking pictures of the sidewalk section where it had happened. Leaving a superintendent in charge to complete the formalities, Grelle got inside Boisseau's car and his deputy drove them back to the préfecture on the Ile de la Cité.

On the way the prefect examined the dead woman's handbag he had slipped inside his raincoat pocket. The usual equipment: lipstick, powder compact, a ring of keys, comb and one hundred and fifty-seven francs in notes and coins, and an identity card. The woman who had tried to kill the president of France was a Lucie Devaud. At this time Grelle saw no significance in the name. Nor did he see any significance in the fact that she had been born in the department of Lozère.

At certain moments in history it is a single incident which triggers off a whole series of events, which causes wheels to begin turning in several continents, wheels which move faster and faster. Lucie Devaud's attempt to kill Guy Florian was just such an incident. It came at a critical moment in the history of Europe.

The airlines were carrying an ever-growing number of tourists to distant and exotic places; the world stock markets were climbing rapidly—Dow Jones had passed the 1500-line—and the terrors of inflation were now only a memory. And, as the Hudson Institute, the American think tank, had predicted, France was leading the world with a great economic surge. For various reasons France had become the most powerful nation in western Europe, overtaking even West Germany; so, the President of the French Republic, Guy Florian, was the most powerful statesman between Moscow and Washington. On the political front the scene was less reassuring.

During the economic blizzard Soviet Russia had made vast strides. Portugal was now a Communist state, the Communist party there having seized power by rigging the elections. In Greece a Communist *coup d'état* had taken over the government. And Spain, after a long period of chaos, was now in the grip of a Communist-dominated coalition government. Soviet warships were in the Piraeus harbour of Athens, were anchored off Barcelona, and were using the facilities of Lisbon as a naval base. The Mediterranean had become almost a Russian lake. Added to this, the last American troops had left Europe as the American Congress retreated further and further into isolation.

It was all this—plus her growing economic power—which made France the key state in western Europe. Allied with western Germany, she provided the key element which barred any further Soviet advance. This was the situation when the news reverberated round the world of Lucie Devaud's attempt to kill President Guy Florian. The Frenchwoman failed to pull the trigger on her 9-mm automatic, but inadvertently she pulled a different kind of trigger.

Very shortly her death was to affect the lives of Alan Lennox, an Englishman based in London; of David Nash, an American living in New York; of Peter Lanz, a German based in Bavaria; of Colonel René Lasalle, ex-assistant chief of army counter-intelligence, now living in exile in Germany; and of certain other people at the moment residing in Czechoslovakia. The first reaction came from Col René Lasalle who made yet another inflammatory broadcast over the radio station Europe Number One, which transmits from the Saarland in Germany.

"Who was this mysterious woman, Lucie Devaud?" he asked in his late-evening broadcast on 8 December. "What was her secret? And what is the secret in the past of a leading Paris politician which must not be discovered at any cost? And why is Marc Grelle clamping down a security dragnet which overnight is turning my country into a police state? Is there a conspiracy . . ."

Extracts from the broadcast were repeated in television news bulletins all over the world. Lasalle's broadcast—his most venomous yet—had all the elements to stir up a ferment of speculation. "The secret in the past of a leading Paris politician . . ." The phrase was seized on by the foreign correspondents. Was there, they speculated, somewhere in Paris a key personality—even a cabinet minister —who was secretly working against President Florian? If so, who was this shadowy figure? The wildest rumours were spread—even one to the effect that a right-wing group of conspirators headed by the unknown cabinet minister was behind the assassination attempt, that they had tried to kill Florian before he made his historic visit to Soviet Russia on 23 December.

In an apartment on the eighth floor at an address on East 84th Street in New York, David Nash dismissed the conspiracy rumour as rubbish. Nash, forty-five years old, a small and well-built man with shrewd grey eyes and thinning hair, worked for a special section of the State Department which no congressional committee had yet penetrated and so rendered useless. Officially, he was concerned with policy—"the vaguest word in the dictionary," as he once commented; in fact he was involved with counter-espionage at the highest level. And since he made a point of rarely appearing in the capital, the press corps was hardly aware of his existence. In the afternoon of the day following Lasalle's outburst over Europe Number One he sat in his apartment studying a transcript of the broadcast. Round the table with him were seated two men who had just flown in from Washington.

"The way things are," Nash commented, "it sends shivers up my spine how close Florian came to death. If France were plunged into chaos at this particular moment, God knows how Russia might try to take advantage of the situation. We've got to find out who was behind that attempt . . ."

Andrew MacLeish, Nash's nominal superior, a thin, austere fifty-year-old, broke in irritably. He hated New York and counted every minute spent there as time out of his life. "You think this nut, Lasalle, has any idea of what he's talking about? For my money he's got his knife into Florian and just enjoys twisting it at random. By my count this is his tenth anti-Florian broadcast in six months . . ."

"The tenth," Nash agreed. "Incidentally, I've accepted his invitation to meet with him."

"What invitation?" MacLeish demanded. "This is the first I've heard you've had any contact with that psychopath . . ."

"Even psychopaths sometimes know a thing or two," Nash remarked. "Col Lasalle approached me through the Brussels embassy late this morning, our time. He says he has some vital information about what's really happening inside Paris but he'll only talk to a representative from Washington—face to face. And we have to keep very quiet about this . . ."

"I don't think we ought to get mixed up with psychopathic exiles," MacLeish repeated. He looked out of the window where he could just see a section of the Triborough Bridge through the skeletal framework of a new high-rise. They argued about it for over an hour, but in the end Nash wore them down. It was Washington which was becoming psychopathic in Nash's view; with the military and most of the administration against the troop withdrawal from Europe which Congress had forced on them, it was becoming even more important to know what was really happening in Europe, to warn their ex-allies of any dangerous development they could uncover. On the following day Nash flew to Europe to meet the man Guy Florian had ruined.

Col René Baptiste Lasalle, ex-assistant chief of French military counter-intelligence, had recently been called "an extinct volcano" by Guy Florian, but for a man whose career was abruptly ended when it seemed almost certain he would soon be promoted to the exalted rank of general, the volcano remained remarkably active. Certainly the rumbling of Col Lasalle was heard clearly enough in Paris.

Six months before Lucie Devaud tried to shoot Guy Florian in Faubourg St Honoré, Lasalle had quarrelled violently with the president and had to flee France overnight; it was rumoured he was about to be arrested for conspiring against the president. Driving his own car, Lasalle crashed through a frontier control post east of Metz at four in the morning and took refuge in West Germany. From the moment of his arrival in the Federal Republic he set about organizing a campaign of rumours to discredit the man who had ruined him. As his instrument he chose Europe Number One, the independent radio station with its transmitters in the Saarland.

At the time when David Nash flew from New York to meet him secretly, Col Lasalle was fifty-five years old. Small, compact and lean-faced, he now made his way through life with only one arm: his left arm had been blown clean off his shoulder by a landmine in Algeria in

1962. At that time a captain in army counter-intelligence, Lasalle had proved himself the most brilliant officer in the French Army when it came to rooting out Arab underground leaders. Within twenty-four hours of his arm being taken away from him, his family was also taken away: a terrorist threw a bomb into the living-room of his villa, killing his wife and seven-year-old son. Lying in hospital, his reaction was typical when he heard the news.

"Since my private life is finished I shall devote the rest of my time to France—to help preserve her way of life. It is the only thing left to me . . ."

Immediately his convalescence was over, he returned from Marseilles to North Africa. The convalescence in itself was remarkable. Finding his sense of balance faulty, Lasalle took to walking in the Estoril mountains with a stick, leaping over deep ravines to find a new balance. "When survival is at stake," he said later, "the body adjusts itself wonderfully . . ." He went back to Algeria just in time to detect and foil the most determined effort up to date to assassinate General de Gaulle. Then, years later, came the clash with Florian.

Now, exiled to the Saarland, living in a farmhouse close to Saarbrücken—close also to the French border—Lasalle broadcast regularly over Europe Number One, the radio station on German soil listened to by millions inside France. And the loss of one arm seemed to have increased the electric energy of this small man who boasted he had never been idle for a day in his life. The target of his virulent broadcasting campaign was Guy Florian.

"Why is he going to visit Soviet Russia on 23 December? What is the real motive behind this visit? Why is he going there of all places at a time when Europe is threatened by the looming shadow of the Red Army as never before. Who is the cabinet minister about whom whispers are spreading in Paris . . .."

Never once did Lasalle refer to Florian by name. Al-

ways he referred to "he", to "this man", until gradually
it dawned on Paris that Lasalle was not only an expert
counter-intelligence officer; he had now become a master
of poisonous political propaganda who was threatening
to undermine the foundations of Florian's régime. This
was the man who had quietly indicated to the Americans
that he wanted to speak to a trustworthy intelligence
official.

On the night of Thursday, 9 December, the same day
when in New York David Nash informed MacLeish that
he would be flying to Europe to interview Col René
Lasalle, a short, grizzle-haired man in shabby clothes
arrived in the Faubourg St Honoré and took up a position opposite the Elysée Palace. He was standing at
the exact spot on the kerb where, twenty-four hours
earlier, Lucie Devaud had fallen into the gutter when
Marc Grelle's bullets hit her in the chest. No one took
any notice of him, and if the uniformed garde republicaine
on duty outside the Elysée gave him even a moment's
thought he must have assumed that this was just another
voyeur, one of those macabre people who delight in
goggling at the scene of an attempted crime.

The shabbily-clothed man arrived at 7.30 p.m. when
it was dark. In his middle sixties, his face lined and worn
and with a straggle of grey moustache, he was still standing there at 8.30 p.m. when, as if in a daze, he suddenly
stepped into the street without looking. The car coming
at speed only a few metres away had no time to pull up;
the man must have loomed in front of the driver's windscreen without warning. The vehicle hit the pedestrian
a terrible blow, drove on over him and accelerated down
the street, disappearing in the direction of Madeleine.
Fifteen minutes later an ambulance with siren screaming
rushed him to the Hotel-Dieu on the Ile de la Cité. On
arrival a doctor examined the patient and said he would
be lucky to last the night.

On Thursday, 9 December, having got rid of his visitors
from Washington, David Nash consulted a road map of
western Europe, checked distances and promptly decided
to fly across the Atlantic the same night. If he caught
Pan Am flight 92 leaving New York at 5.45 p.m. he
could be in Brussels early next day, which should give
him time to drive to Luxembourg—where he had arranged
to meet Lasalle—and back again to catch another night
flight from Brussels to New York. He boarded flight 92
by the skin of his teeth and then relaxed in his first-class
seat as the Boeing 707 climbed steadily towards thirty
thousand feet above the Long Island coast.

Nash had a tight schedule ahead of him. He was not
only going to meet Lasalle on the neutral ground of
Luxembourg; he had also arranged to meet his German
counterpart, Peter Lanz, with whom he maintained a
close and cordial relationship. After all, the French fugitive colonel was residing in Germany and it had been
one of Lanz's more delicate duties to keep an eye on his
electric visitor who had fled from the territory of Germany's closest ally.

The German authorities had very mixed feelings about
the arrival of Col Lasalle in their midst. They gave him
refuge—no specific charges had ever been levelled against
him by Paris—and the local police chief in Saarbrücken
was instructed to maintain a distant surveillance on the
fugitive. Lasalle himself, fearing an attempt to kidnap him,
had asked for police protection, and this was granted on
the understanding that it was never referred to publicly.
With the passage of time—Lasalle had now been in
Germany for six months—the surveillance was relaxed.

Peter Lanz had visited Lasalle several times, requesting
him to tone down his broadcasts, and always Lasalle received the German courteously and said he would consider the request. Then he would get into his car, drive

to the radio station and blast Florian all over again with a fresh series of innuendoes. Since he was breaking no law, Lanz would shrug his shoulders and then sit down to read carefully a transcript of the latest outburst.

Lanz, at thirty-two, was exceptionally young to occupy the post of vice-president of the *Bundesnachrichtendienst*, the West German Federal Intelligence Service. He owed his rapid promotion to his ability, and to the fact that a large number of older men were suddenly swept out of the organization when the new Chancellor, Franz Hauser, was elected three months after Guy Florian's own rise to power. "I don't want intriguers," Hauser had snapped, "I want young and energetic men who can do the damned job . . ."

This very young second-in-command of the BND was a man of medium height, slim build and thinning brown hair. "In this job I shall be bald at forty," he was fond of saying. "Is it true that women go wild over bald men?" Normally serious-faced, he had one quality in common with Guy Florian: when he smiled he could charm almost anyone into agreeing with him. His job was to try foresee any potentially explosive situation which might harm the Federal Republic politically—to foresee and defuse in advance. The arrival of Lasalle on German soil was a classic case. "Not one of my outstanding successes," he once admitted, "but then we don't know where it's going to lead, do we? Lasalle knows something—maybe one day he will tell me what he knows . . ."

Nash met Lanz at Liége in Belgium. Earlier in the morning, landing at Brussels at 8.30 a.m., the American had hired a car at the airport in the name of Charles Wade, the pseudonym under which he was travelling. Arriving in Liége, Nash spent half an hour with Lanz in the anonymous surroundings of the railway station restaurant, then he drove on south to Clervaux in the Ardennes. The secret rendezvous with Col Lasalle had been chosen carefully—Clervaux is neither in Germany

nor in Belgium. This little-known town is high up in the
hills of northern Luxembourg.

The secrecy surrounding Nash's visit was essential to
the survival of Lasalle as a credible public figure; once
Paris could prove he was in touch with the Americans
he could so easily be discredited as a tool of Washington.
At the quiet Hotel Claravallis in Clervaux, inside a room
booked in the name of Charles Wade, Nash and Lasalle
talked in absolute secrecy for two hours. Afterwards,
Lasalle left immediately and drove back to Germany.
Nash had a quick lunch at the hotel and then drove
straight back to Belgium where he reported to Peter
Lanz who had waited for him in Liége. Half an hour later
Nash was on his way back to Brussels where he caught
the night plane to New York. During his lightning dash
to Europe, travelling under a pseudonym, Nash had gone
nowhere near the American Embassy in Brussels. He was
eating dinner on the plane while he doodled animal pictures and then erased them. Pictures of the head of a
leopard.

2

David Nash was somewhere on the road between Brussels
and Liége, driving to keep his first appointment with
Peter Lanz, when Marc Grelle in Paris received what
appeared to be a routine phone call. The large office of
the police prefect is on the second floor of the préfecture;
its walls are panelled, its windows overlook the Boulevard du Palais; and to ensure privacy the windows are

masked by net curtains. As usual, Grelle was wearing a pair of slacks and a polo-necked sweater as he sat behind his desk, going through the morning's paperwork, which he disliked.

Grelle, born in the city of Metz, was a man of Lorraine. In France the Lorrainers are known as the least French of the French. Sturdy physically, not at all excitable, they have a reputation for being level-headed and dependable in an emergency. Grelle had travelled a long way to reach Paris from Metz. At the time of Florian's election as president eighteen months earlier, Marc Grelle had been police prefect of Marseilles and would have been quite content to complete his career in that raffish seaport. "Look where ambition gets you," he had a habit of saying. "Look at any cabinet minister. They take pills to help them sleep, they take stimulants to keep them awake at the Wednesday cabinet meetings. They marry rich wives to further their ambitions, then spend their wives' money on mistresses to keep themselves sane. What is the point of it all?"

It was only with the greatest reluctance that Grelle accepted Florian's strong plea for him to come to Paris. "I need one honest man close to me," Florian had urged. His face had creased into the famous smile. "If you won't accept I shall have to leave the post vacant!" So, Grelle had come to Paris. Sighing, he initialled a paper and was turning to another document when the phone rang. The call was from André Boisseau, his deputy.

"I'm at the Hotel-Dieu, chief, just round the corner. I think you ought to get over here right away. A man is dying and there's something very odd about him . . ."

"Dying?"

"He was knocked down by a hit-and-run driver in the Faubourg St Honoré yesterday evening opposite the Elysée —at the very spot where Lucie Devaud died . . ."

Boisseau didn't want to say any more on the phone, so putting on his leather raincoat, Grelle left the build-

ing and walked the short distance to the large hospital
which overlooks the right bank of the Seine. It was
pouring with rain but he hated driving short distances—
"Soon, babies will be born with wheels instead of legs,"
was one of his favourite sayings. Boisseau was waiting
for him on the first floor of the gloomy building. "Sorry
to get you wet through, chief, but he won't speak to
anyone except the police prefect. The man's name is
Gaston Martin. He's just back from Guiana—for the first
time in thirty years, for God's sake . . ."

Later, Grelle pieced together the bizarre story. Guiana is
the only overseas department in South America which
still belongs to France. Known once to the public mainly
because this is where the notorious penal settlement
Devil's Island was situated, it had remained for years out
of the world's headlines, one of the sleepier areas in the
vast Latin-American continent.

Gaston Martin, a man in his late sixties, had spent all
of his life since the Second World War in this outlandish
place. Then, for the first time in over thirty years, he had
returned home aboard a freighter which docked at Le
Havre on 9 December, less than twenty-four hours after
the attempted assassination of Guy Florian. Travelling to
Paris by train, he dumped his small bag at the Cécile, a
seedy Left Bank hotel, and went out for a walk. Eventually he turned up outside the Elysée where, at exactly
8.30 p.m., he had been run down by a car as he stepped
off the sidewalk. Grelle knew nothing of this as he followed Boisseau into a room occupied by only one patient.
The prefect's nose wrinkled as he smelt antiseptic. A fit
man, he detested hospital odours.

Gaston Martin lay in the single bed attended by a
nurse and a doctor who shook his head when Grelle
asked how the patient was. "I give him one hour," he
whispered. "Maybe less. The car went right over him . . .
lungs are pierced. No, it makes no difference if you

question him, but he may not respond. I'll leave you for
a few minutes . . ." He frowned when Boisseau made his
own request. "The nurse, too? As you wish . . ."

Why were so many wards like death cells, Grelle
wondered as he approached the bed. Martin, his head
covered with wispy grey hair, had a drooping moustache
under a prominent hooked nose. More character than
brains, Grelle assessed as he drew up a chair beside the
bed. Boisseau opened the conversation. "This is the police
prefect of Paris, Marc Grelle. You asked to see him . . ."

"I saw him . . . going into the Elysée," Martin quavered.

"Saw who?" Grelle asked quietly. The man from Guiana
reached out and held the prefect's hand, which gave
Grelle a funny feeling, a sensation of helplessness. "Saw
who?" he repeated.

"The Leopard . . ."

Something turned over inside Grelle, then he remembered something else and felt better. In the few seconds
before he replied his memory spun back over God knew
how many files he had read, trying to recall exact details.
He knew immediately who this man must be referring to,
and when he recalled the second detail he realized Martin
must be raving.

"I don't know who you mean," Grelle said carefully.

"Communist Resistance leader . . . the Lozère." Gripping the prefect's hand tightly, Martin struggled to heave
himself up on the pillow, his face streaked with sweat.
Boisseau tried to stop him, but Grelle said leave him alone.
He understood the desperate reaction: Martin was trying
to stay alive just a little longer, feeling he could only do
this by getting himself out of the prone position.

"Communist wartime leader . . ." Martin repeated. "The
. . . youngest . . . in the Resistance . ."

"You couldn't have seen him go into the Elysée,"
Grelle told him gently. "There are guards, sentries on the
gate . . ."

"They saluted him . . ."

Grelle felt the shock at the pit of his stomach. Despite the effort he made a slight tremor passed through his hand, and Martin felt it. His rheumy eyes opened wider into a glare. "You believe me," he gasped. "You have to believe me . . ."

Grelle turned to Boisseau, whispering the order. "No one is to be allowed in here—not even the doctor. On my way in I saw a gendarme near the entrance—go get him, station him outside this door, then come back in yourself . . ."

He was with the dying Martin for twenty minutes, knowing that his questioning was hastening the poor wretch's death, but also knowing that Martin didn't mind. He just wanted to talk, to pass on his dying message. Boisseau returned to the room a few minutes later, having left the gendarme on duty outside. At one stage a priest tried to force his way into the room, but Martin indicated he was an agnostic and became so agitated the priest withdrew.

For Grelle it was an ordeal, trying to get the man to talk coherently, watching his skin become greyer under the film of sweat, feeling Martin's hand gripping his own to maintain contact with the living, with life itself. At the end of twenty minutes what Grelle had extracted was mostly incoherent babbling, a series of disconnected phrases, but there was a certain thread running through the feverish ramblings. Then Martin died. The hand in Grelle's went limp, rested quietly like the hand of a sleeping child. The man who hadn't seen Paris for over thirty years had returned to die there within forty-eight hours of landiing in France.

Returning to his office in the préfecture with Boisseau, Grelle locked the door, told his secretary over the phone that he could take no more calls for the moment, then went over to the window to stare down into the rain-swept street. First he swore his deputy to absolute secrecy.

"In case anything happens to me," he explained, "there must be someone else who knows about this—who could carry on the investigation. Although I'm still praying that Martin got it wrong, that he didn't know what he was talking about . . ."

"What was Martin talking about?" the diplomatic Boisseau enquired.

"You know as well as I do," Grelle replied brutally. "He was saying that someone who visited the Elysée last night, someone important enough to be saluted—so he has to be of cabinet rank—is a top Communist agent . . ."

On Grelle's instruction, Boisseau sent off an urgent cable to the police chief at Cayenne, Guinna, requesting all information on Gaston Martin, and then between them they sorted out the broken, often-incoherent story Martin had told them.

He had stood in the vicinity of the Elysée Palace for about one hour—between, say, 7.30 p.m. and 8.30 p.m., sometimes standing at the edge of the kerb where Lucie Devaud had been shot, sometimes wandering up towards the Place Beauvau, and then back again. At least they were sure of 8.30, the time when a car had knocked him down, because this had been witnessed by one of the Elysée sentries. "Partially witnessed, that is," Boisseau explained. "I phoned the inspector in charge of the case while you were coming to the hospital and the fool of a sentry isn't even sure of the make of car which knocked down Martin . . ."

And at some moment during this approximate hour Martin swore he had seen the man he had once known as the Leopard walk into the Elysée courtyard and be saluted by the sentries. It was this brief statement which so disturbed Grelle. "They saluted him . . ." Martin's description of the man had been vague; by the time Grelle got round to asking this question the dying man had been slipping away fast. And often he had rambled off in another direction, forgetting the question Grelle had asked him.

"But according to Martin this man was very tall—over six feet," the prefect emphasized. "He said that three times—the bit about his great height."

"This goes back over thirty years to the wartime Resistance," Boisseau protested. "That is, if Martin is to be believed at all. How on earth could he recognize a man he hadn't seen all that time? People change like hell . . ."

"He was very insistent that he saw the Leopard. Said he hadn't changed much, that the first thing he noticed was the man's walk—then I couldn't get him to describe the walk."

"It doesn't sound at all likely . . ." Boisseau was tieless by now, in his shirt-sleeves. Coffee had been brought in to them and the room was full of smoke as Grelle used up cigarette after cigarette. The rain was still lashing the windows.

"It doesn't," Grelle agreed, "but I was the one who heard every word he said and he frightened me. I think I can judge when a man is telling the truth . . ."

"This Leopard then—you think he was really telling the truth about that?" Boisseau, small and heavily-built, with almond-shaped eyes and thick eyebrows, had made no attempt to keep the scepticism out of his voice. "Personally, I have never heard of him . . ."

"But you are younger than me." The prefect lit another cigarette. "The Leopard is on file, a very old and dusty file by now. And yes, I do think Gaston Martin was telling the truth—as he believed it to be."

"Which could be a very different thing . . ."

"Quite true. You see, there's something you don't know. The Communist Resistance leader known during the war as the Leopard is dead."

On Saturday morning, 11 December, David Nash, who

had just returned from Europe aboard the night flight
from Brussels, flew from New York to Washington for an
emergency meeting with Andrew MacLeish at the State
Department. The two men locked themselves away in a
a small room on the second floor and MacLeish listened
without saying a word for fifteen minutes; it was one of
his strong points, that he could absorb a verbal report
without interruption, soaking up information like a sponge.

"And Lasalle gave absolutely no indication of the
identity of this alleged cabinet minister who could be a
secret Communist agent?" he enquired eventually. "This
man he calls the second Leopard—because he has
adopted the pseudonym of the dead wartime Communist
Resistance leader?"

"None at all," Nash replied promptly. "He played the
whole thing very close to the chest. What he did tell me
was that he believes he was on the verge of uncovering
the agent when he had his titanic row with Florian—
which ended in his flight from France. Since then he
hasn't been able to carry his investigation any further
and he's worried stiff that a *coup d'état* is planned to take
place while Florian is in Moscow on this coming visit. He
suspects that the Russians invited the president to Russia
to get him out of Paris at the crucial moment. The attempted assassination decided Lasalle—to make contact
with me. He's pretty certain that if it had succeeded the
coup d'état led by the second Leopard would have taken
place at once."

"So he wants us to complete the investigation he
started . . ."

"He has this list of three witnesses who worked closely
with the original Leopard during the war . . ."

"A list he wouldn't give you," MacLeish snapped.

"I'm not sure I blame him for that," Nash countered.
"He's very security-conscious and that I like. He'll only
hand over the list to the agent we provide to go inside
France to meet these people . . ."

"What the hell can these three so-called witnesses tell us?" MacLeish demanded irritably. "If the original Leopard is dead I don't see the connection . . ."

"Lasalle believes someone who was in the Leopard's wartime Resistance group cleverly took over his name as the code-name the Russians would know him by. So to find this top Communist agent we have to dig back into the past, to find who could fit. Find out who he was in 1944 and we'll know who he is today."

MacLeish, whose other strong point was his ability to take a quick decision, drummed his thick fingers on the table like a man playing a piano. "So the deadline is 23 December when Florian takes off for Moscow, which gives us exactly eleven days. You're going to have to move damned fast . . ."

"So I can send someone in?" Nash interjected.

"You can send someone in," MacLeish decided, "but not an American. If Florian's security apparatus got hold of him the French would have a field day. I can hear Florian's next anti-American speech now—Yankee agent discovered trying to smear Paris cabinet minister . . . That we can't risk. An agent yes, but not an American," he repeated.

"But not an American . . ."

It was still Saturday morning when Nash gave the instruction to his assistant, Ward Fischer, in the suite of offices on the third floor which housed his staff. Normally everyone except Fischer would have been at home on a Saturday, but before boarding his New York flight to Washington Nash had phoned ahead and the suite was now occupied by men recalled hastily while Nash was airborne.

"Kind of narrows the field," Fischer remarked.

"Narrow it to zero. Find the man," Nash snapped. "Inside two hours," he added.

Fischer went into the next office and within five minutes

his staff was searching through the files, looking for a name. The specification for the man who would go into France to interview Lasalle's witnesses was stringent. He had to have top security clearance; to be fluent enough in the language to pass as a Frenchman; to be experienced in the security field; and he must be a man with a cold, careful temperament who could be relied on in an emergency, operating entirely on his own. As to nationality, he must not be an American, nor must he be a Frenchman.

It was Nash himself who added this final qualification which caused Fischer to swear colourfully the moment he left his boss's office. "The God-damned specification screams for a Frenchman," he complained to one of his staff, "so now you've got to find a Frenchman who isn't a Frenchman. Get on with it . . ." Nash had a very good reason for adding this last qualification. Because France is a very special place and many of its people are highly political, Nash felt it would be dangerous to choose a Frenchman to spy on the French. He also felt pretty sure Col Lasalle would have the same doubts.

While Fischer and his staff were searching, Nash went over the file in his mind of people he had known—or known of. One name came to him quickly, but he rejected it: he could never persuade this man to do the job. Sitting at his desk, his chubby hands clasped behind his neck, he checked back in his mind, rejecting candidate after candidate. As Fischer had said, the specification certainly restricted the field. In the end he came back to the man he had first thought of.

At 1.30 in the afternoon Fischer came into his office carrying two files. "These are the only two people who fit," he said wearily. "We ate at our desks and we've been working since I left you. Cancelling out the French made it that much tougher . . ." Nash looked at the two files. One of the names was Jules Beaurain, a Belgian. "Belgium isn't France," Fischer said hopefully. The other was the name Nash himself had thought of.

"It will take pressure to get this man," Nash said reflectively. "I may have just hit on how the pressure could be applied. Get me details of all overseas bids for security contracts inside the States. Get them now . . ."

"It's Saturday . . ."

"So the calendar tells me. Phone people at their homes, get them behind their desks fast. Tell them it's an emergency—and give them my compliments . . ."

"They're going to appreciate that," Fischer said and went out of the office to phone his wife. She also was going to appreciate it, he felt sure.

Left alone in his office. Nash took a ballpoint out of his pocket and indulged in his liking for doodling portraits. He drew from memory a head-and-shoulders sketch of a man he had once known well, a man he had liked and respected despite disagreements. When he had finished the sketch he added a caption underneath. Alan Lennox. Security expert. British.

Three thousand miles across the Atlantic in London it was Saturday evening as Alan Lennox turned the key in the doublelock Chubb, checked the handle of the door to his office, and stood for a moment staring at the plate on the wall. *Lennox Security Company Limited*. On the stock exchange the shares had climbed to £3.50 and it looked as though they were going higher; security companies were enjoying a minor boom. God knew why, but recently they had become a City cult. Probably because they were "export-orientated" as the little wise men who sent out brokers' recommendations phrased it. All over the world large industrial concerns were employing Britons to organize their security because, it was alleged, they were incorruptible. Another cult. Lennox thought maybe it was a good time to sell out—once he had obtained the big American oil combine contract he was bidding for. With that under his belt the shares should go through the roof.

The only man in the building—managing directors

worked alone on Saturdays—he went down in the lift to Leadenhall Street and out into the storm which had broken over London. Collecting his Citroën DS 23 from the underground garage, he drove home through sheets of blinding rain to his flat in St James's Place, reflecting that it wasn't a Saturday night to encourage a man on his own to dine out. Arriving inside the flat, which he had furnished with antiques, Lennox took off his two-hundred-guinea coat and poured himself a large Scotch. The next problem was to decide whether to eat out or grill himself a steak from the fridge.

Thirty-five years old, managing director of the most successful international security company based in London, Lennox was a well-built man of medium height who moved with a deceptive slowness; in an emergency he could react with the speed of a fox. Dark-haired, the hair cut shorter than the normal fashion, his thick eyebrows were also dark. The eyes were his most arresting feature; brown and slow-moving, they looked out on the world warily, taking nothing for granted. "It's in the nature of my job to be suspicious," he once said. "A man called Marc Grelle told me in Marseilles that I had the mind of a policeman; I suppose he was right . . ."

Born in Paris, Lennox's mother had been French, his father a minor official at the British Embassy in the Faubourg St Honoré. The first ten years of his life had been spent in France and Lennox was fluent in French long before he mastered English at school. Disliking his father's idea that he enter the diplomatic service—"after eighteen I found we had nothing to say to each other"—he joined a large international oil company. Because of his fluency in English, French, German and Spanish he was attached to the security department. Five years later he was directing it.

"I was lucky," Lennox recalled. "The timing was right. Security had become the key to survival. You can buy tankers, drill new oilfields—but where's the profit if people keep dynamiting them?"

Lennox's career soared at the time when Arab terrorists were turning their attention to blowing up non-Arab oilfields—to increase the economic power of the Middle East fields. In an emergency boards of directors turn to the man who can save them; they turned to Lennox. Travelling widely, he organized new systems to protect oilfields, tankers and refineries in four continents. He soon decided that defensive measures were not enough; if you are to win you must carry the war into enemy territory.

Disappearing into the twilight world of counter-espionage, often for months at a time, Lennox penetrated the terrorist groups, locating their camps in Lebanon and further back in Syria. At this time he was employing all sorts of dubious people, paying them large sums in tax-free cash—which drove prim accountants at headquarters crazy. One of his most successful anti-terrorist teams was recruited from the Union Corse—the French Mafia—who were annoyed because Arab money had bought up certain Parisian protection rackets they had previously controlled. "The Red Night of July 14" was splashed across the world's headlines.

Lennox waited until he was ready, waited patiently for months while he built up an intimate knowledge of the terrorist gangs. On 14 July he struck. The Union Corse team—speaking French, the second language in Lebanon —landed by helicopters and came ashore from boats on isolated beaches. In eight hours they wiped out three major terrorist gangs, killing over two hundred men. Only Corsicans could have killed so swiftly and mercilessly. From that night the sabotage of oil installations dropped to five per cent of its previous volume.

It was during these years that Lennox came into contact with leading security and police chiefs from Tokyo to Washington, including men like David Nash and Peter Lanz, and organizations like the FBI and the Sûreté

Nationale, all of whom provided discreet and unofficial help to a man who could take the ultimate measures they were not empowered to employ. At a later period he spent four years with an American company, including hazardous months along the Mexican border where terrorists were infiltrating with Mexican peasants coming into the United States to find work. Then, without warning, he resigned to set up his own outfit.

His private life was less successful. Married twice, he lost both wives to other men who came home each night. "To my home," he said sardonically. In both cases he divorced his wife despite the urgent plea of one that he assume the role of guilty party. "You knew what my life was like before we married," he said bluntly. "I warned you time and again—and the one thing I can't stand is people who break contracts . . ." At the moment Lennox was consoling himself with his third girl friend without too much enthusiasm. He knew what the trouble was: three years after the foundation of his own company he felt that once again he had done what he had set out to do, so he was losing interest. "I'm bloody bored," he told himself as he drank his Scotch. "I need something new . . ." He raised his glass to the telephone. "Ring," he told it, "ring from some faraway place . . ."

He had finished his Scotch and was taking the steak out of the fridge when the phone rang. Knowing it had to be a wrong number, he picked up the receiver. The international telephone operator had a seductive voice. "Mr. Alan Lennox?" she enquired. "Overseas call for you. Person-to-person. From Washington . . ."

Two men stood talking in the walled Paris garden, their overcoat collars turned up against the chill December wind. One of them was tall and slim, the other short and powerfully-built, and the language they conversed in was French. The Leopard, tall and slim, shook his head doubtfully as his companion repeated the same argument forcefully.

"We believe it is essential to eliminate Col Lasalle. We have people who can make it look like an accident, people waiting at this moment for the order to proceed . . ."

"It could be a mistake . . ."

"It could be a mistake to do nothing, not to take action. These people who would deal with the matter are competent, I assure you . . ."

They went on discussing the problem as darkness fell and beyond the walls the Paris rush-hour traffic built up to a peak. Not a score of metres from where the two men stood the life of the capital proceeded in its normal mundane way and some people were even buying presents for Christmas.

3

Carel Vanek drove the Citroën DS 21 forward at high speed, heading for the bulky figure standing in the middle of the concrete track. The light was bad; it was late in the afternoon of 11 December, just before dark. Through the windscreen Vanek saw the figure rush towards him, blur as the car hit it at 90 k.p.h., elevate under the impact, then the whole vehicle wobbled as he drove on, passing over the body. A dozen metres beyond he pulled up with a scream of tyres, looked over his shoulder, used the reverse gear, then backed at speed.

The body lay still in the dusk, a vague hump as he

backed towards it, accelerating. Vanek never enjoyed
himself more than behind the wheel of a car; he felt he
was an extension of the mechanism, that the gear lever
was another arm, the brake a third foot. It was exhilarat-
ing. He went on backing at speed and his aim was perfect.
For the second time he felt the wobble as the Citroën's
wheels passed over the hump lying in the roadway. Then
he went on, backing into a sharp curve, stopping, driving
forward again, turning the wheel until he was moving
away at speed in the opposite direction.

"Thirty-five seconds," the quiet man in the back of
the car said as he clicked his stop-watch.

Vanek braked with a jerk that nearly threw the passenger in the seat beside him through the windscreen,
laughing as Walther Brunner cursed. "Do you have to be
quite so dramatic?" Brunner demanded as he sagged back
in his seat.

"Reaction—reaction . . ." Vanek snapped his fingers.
"It's what this is all about. On the day when we visit
Lasalle I might have to do just that—you must be ready
for it . . ."

They got out of the car and walked back up the
abandoned race-track which lies just outside the Czech
town of Tábor forty-five miles south of Prague. Little
more than a bulky shadow in the distant gloom, Michael
Borisov, the Russian in charge of the training centre, was
bending over the form in the road, a form constructed
of sacking and straw for the limbs, the body and the
head. A powerful spring had held the make-believe man
upright until Vanek had hit him. "Good?" Vanek enquired as he reached Borisov. "No delay at all on the
second run—I went straight back and straight over
him . . ."

Borisov, thick-bodied and muffled in a fur coat and
hat against the intense cold—a snow warning had been
broadcast over the Prague radio—regarded the Czech
sourly. Vanek was too sure of himself, too arrogant for

him ever to like the man, and the trouble was Vanek was right: it had been a perfect run. The bloody Czech trained to perfection in everything he did. "We run back to the centre," he said abruptly. "I'll send someone to collect the car . . ." Borisov had spoken in French; ever since training had begun all conversation had been carried on in the Gallic language.

They ran down the track through the chilly dusk which was almost darkness now and Vanek deliberately kept a few paces in front of the other three men to demonstrate his fitness. As they went inside a concrete cabin huddled under a copse of fir trees a wave of warmth from a boiling stove met them. Borisov, the oldest and the last of the four men to enter the building, slammed the door shut to keep in the warmth. Taking off their coats, they lit cigarettes—Gauloises—and sagged into chairs round a table. A large-scale map of France and Germany covered one wall; on another hung a map of Paris. Various guidebooks, including time-tables, Michelin and the *Guide Bleu* occupied a wooden shelf. Most prominently displayed was a large photograph of Col René Lasalle.

"That's enough for today," Borisov announced as he poured French cognac from a bottle. "You're improving," he added grudgingly.

With typical bravado Vanek raised his glass to the photograph on the wall. "To our meeting, my dear colonel . . ."

Carel Vanek was thirty-one years old, a tall, lean and bony-faced man with very dark hair and a neat dark moustache. A natural athlete, his quick-moving dark eyes stared back insolently as the Russian studied him. Vanek knew that he was good at his job, that the Russian disliked him but also recognized his ability, which made everything so much the better; and the way to keep Borisov in his place was to push the training even harder than the Russian wished. "We'll repeat the night exercise,"

Vanek said abruptly. "Running a man down in the dark is even trickier."

In Russia they have a word for the Czechs which means "the smart people, too clever by half . . ." And this summed up the Russian trainer's opinion of his protégé. On the other hand, Borisov was thinking, Vanek was definitely the man to lead this Soviet Commando; he had all the qualifications. Five years earlier Vanek had been attached to the security unit at the Czech Embassy on Avenue Charles-Floquet near the Eiffel Tower in Paris. Like so many Czechs, Vanek was an excellent linguist; he spoke French, German and English fluently. And when the three-man team was given the signal to leave for the west they would travel as Frenchmen, speaking that language and equipped with French papers.

Vanek had other useful skills, too—besides those of the trained assassin he had perfected at the training centre. A handsome man, bold and confident in manner, the Czech was attractive to women, which at times proved highly convenient. After all, the way to a man was so often through his woman. And finally, Borisov thought as he smoked his Gauloise, Vanek had a cold streak which enabled him to kill a man and sleep well after the act. This had been proved when he had travelled to Istanbul to kill a Soviet cipher clerk who had developed an appetite for American dollars. Vanek had choked the man to death and then thrown him from a balcony into the Bosphorus one dark night.

Much as it went against the grain, Borisov the Russian had to admit that the three Czechs, led by Vanek, made an ideal assassination Commando. And although Borisov could not have known it, the specification for the Commando leader was not at all unlike the specification David Nash had laid down for choosing a man to go into France. Fluency in French, knowledge of France, the ability to pass as a Frenchman—and whereas Nash had insisted on a non-American, so the three members

of the Russian Politburo who had sanctioned the mission
had added their own proviso: the men who made up the
Commando must be non-Russian. If anything went wrong
the real power behind the operation must never be
exposed.

"When the hell are we going to leave to visit this Col
Lasalle?" Vanek demanded.

"Soon," Borisov replied, "the signal will come soon . . ."

On the same evening when Alan Lennox in London
received the phone call from David Nash, two hundred
miles away in Paris Marc Grelle sat up late in his bachelor apartment on the Ile Saint-Louis reading an old and
dusty file. It was the file on the Leopard.

André Boisseau, who lived in the rue Monge, spent
the earlier part of the evening with the prefect, and since
he had read the file earlier they compared notes. In the
Second World War every single member of the Resistance
had worked under a false name—to protect his family
and his friends. Normally another French surname was
chosen at random; sometimes a man would be known
by a false Christian name; and certain high-ranking army
officers labelled themselves with geometrical symbols
such as Hypoteneuse. But the Leopard was different: he
had taken the name of a savage animal as though to stress
his uniqueness.

"I think the choice of the name indicates a supreme
self-confidence," Boisseau remarked. "One of those people
who kids himself up he's a man of destiny . . ."

The Leopard had certainly had a remarkable—although
brief—career. In his earliest twenties—one of the few
facts known about this elusive figure—he had commanded
one of the most powerful Resistance groups in the Massif
Central, operating in the departments of Lozère and
Haute-Loire. He distinguished himself from other Resistance leaders by his brilliance and ruthlessness; there
had been something almost Napoleonic in the way

he had descended out of nowhere on the enemy, destroyed him, and then vanished again.

The Leopard's extraordinary success was based on a widespread intelligence system. He had agents everywhere —in the Vichy police, in the telephone exchanges where operators plugged in to enemy calls, on the railways where the staff reported on the movement of munition and troop trains, and inside the *Milice,* a Vichy organization of vicious thugs and collaborators. He had even planted someone inside the *Abwehr*, the enemy counter-intelligence organization.

"Perhaps we ought to be looking for someone who is an expert on intelligence and security apparatuses," Boisseau suggested.

The prefect grunted and continued reading. The thick file went on endlessly describing the Leopard's achievements, but the weird thing was there was hardly a hint of what he looked like. There were reasons for this. The Communist leader had gone to extraordinary lengths to ensure that no one—not even his close associates—had any idea of his personal appearance. There was one exception: a deputy, code-named Petit-Louis, had gone everywhere with him, issuing instructions while the Leopard stayed out of sight.

"He was over six feet tall and not much more than twenty at the time, which would put him in his early fifties now if he had survived," Grelle pointed out. "And that's all we do know about this ghost . . ."

"Petit-Louis probably knew what he looked like," Boisseau remarked.

In the autumn of 1944 events took a more sinister turn. At the time of the second Allied landing—in August in the south of France—the Midi was practically under the control of the Resistance for a short period. It was a period no one talked about much in later years: the prospect had been too frightening. This was when the Communists came within an inch of establishing a Soviet

Republic in the south of France.

All the plans were laid. The signal for setting up the Soviet République du Sud was to be the capture by the Communists of the key cities of Limoges and Montpellier. It was calculated that, presented with a *fait accompli* while the Allies were still fighting the enemy, the Soviet Republic would have to be accepted. The mastermind behind this plan was the Leopard himself. Only de Gaulle's swift and sudden descent on the region smashed the plot. Soon afterwards the Leopard died.

His death was carefully documented in the file. He had been shot by an enemy sniper in the streets of Lyon on 14 September. Full of anguish at the death of their leader, worried that a gang of Vichy thugs might desecrate the grave, a small party of Communists had carried the body away and quietly buried it in the middle of a forest. Petit-Louis, the Leopard's deputy, had not been present at the burial. Near the end of the file an appendix noted small details which Grelle found interesting. The Leopard had always been guarded by a huge and ferocious wolf-hound called César which kept even trusted friends at a distance.

"To make sure they never knew what he looked like," Grelle commented. "I wonder what happened to the hound?"

The *Abwehr*, the enemy intelligence service, had also apparently compiled a detailed file on their mysterious enemy. The officer who had undertaken this task was a certain Dieter Wohl, who had been thirty at the time. "So he would be in his sixties now," Grelle observed. "I wonder whether he survived?"

Grelle received the shock after Boisseau had gone home to his wife and two children. At the end of the file he found a worn and tattered envelope with a photo-graph inside of the Leopard's deputy, Petit-Louis. At first he couldn't be sure, so he took the faded sepia print over to his desk and examined it under the lamp. The print was better preserved than he had feared and out of it stared a face, a face recorded over thirty years earlier. Age changes a man, especially if his life has been hard, but if the bone structure is strong it sometimes only makes clearer features which always existed. The face of Petit-Louis was the face of Gaston Martin, the man from Guiana.

4

For the second time in less than seventy-two hours David Nash had crossed the Atlantic. Disembarking from Pan Am flight 100 at Heathrow Airport at 9.40 p.m. on Sunday night, 12 December, only ten days before Guy Florian was due to fly to Moscow, Nash took a cab to the Ritz, left his bag in his room and walked to Lennox's flat in St James's Place. On arrival he presented the Englishman with a bottle of Moët & Chandon.

"When the Greeks come bearing gifts . . ." Lennox greeted him cynically as he slipped the bottle inside the fridge. "We'll open that later—I presume we're going to be up half the night?"

"At the very least," the American assured him. "We're up against a deadline which is ten days from now . . ."

"You are up against a deadline," Lennox corrected him. "I warned you on the phone—your kind of business is something I can do without . . ."

They talked until 3 a.m. while Nash used up two packs of cigarettes, telling the Englishman about his recent visit to Peter Lanz and Col Lasalle, about the enormous anxiety in Washington that some great Communist coup was imminent, that René Lasalle might possibly—just possibly—be able to provide the key which would unlock the identity of the unknown Soviet agent in Paris. "He's convinced the crunch is coming when Florian flies off to Moscow," Nash said at midnight as he sipped his champagne. "So we have no time at all to check out these three people inside France Lasalle believes may come up with the answer . . ."

"I had the quaint idea that Washington hates the guts of President Guy Florian," Lennox observed.

Nash's mouth tightened. "That's as maybe. The hell of it is we're stuck with him—just as we were stuck with de Gaulle. In politics you may not like your bedmate, but you have to sleep with her all the same. President Florian of France and Chancellor Hauser of Germany are all that stand between Soviet Russia and the Channel coast now that Congress has opted out of Europe—your Channel coast too," he added.

"So where does the Leopard come into it? None of what you say makes much sense," Lennox remarked bluntly. "The Leopard is dead—he was shot in Lyon in 1944. I think Lasalle is just trying to stir up some muck, hoping it will stick to his old enemy, Guy Florian. Your French colonel is a fanatic."

"Even fanatics get to know things," Nash persisted. "We don't entirely go along with his Leopard story but we do think he stumbled on something six months ago just before Florian threw him out of France. He got a sniff of some highly placed underground link with the Soviets—and don't forget that Lasalle was the best army counter-intelligence chief the French ever had . . ."

"But he won't give you this list of so-called witnesses, if it exists . . ."

"I'm certain it exists," Nash flared. "He's very security-minded so he only gives that to the man who goes into France to interview them . . ."

"So why come to me?"

Nash swallowed the rest of his champagne, taking his time over replying. "Because of who you are," he said quietly. "These witnesses may well only speak to a Frenchman. Lanz has agreed to supply cover papers. To avoid the security apparatus the man who goes in must merge with the landscape. You qualify, Alan. You were born and grew up in Paris. We gave you top security clearance while you were in the States. You're experienced in underground work, God knows. The Red Night in Syria proved that. You're made for the job," the American went on. "We need you. You need us . . ."

"And just why do I need you?" Lennox asked quietly.

"Because you need American government approval of that bid you put in for a major security contract with an American company, a company which, incidentally, handles certain Defence Department projects. Confidentially, I understand your bid was the lowest and is acceptable—providing you get Washington's rubber stamp . . ."

It was at this point that the explosion came, that Lennox started talking non-stop, refusing to allow Nash to interrupt while he told him what he thought about politics and politicians. "Your own people do the same thing . . ." Nash interjected and then subsided under the torrent of Lennox's words. "It's pressure," Lennox told him savagely, "bloody pressure tactics, and you know how I react to that . . ." The verbal battle went on until close to three in the morning as the atmosphere thickened with smoke, as they drank Scotch, as Nash, tieless and in his shirt-sleeves now, fought back against Lennox's onslaught. Then, without warning, the Englishman switched his viewpoint.

"All right," he said as he refilled the glasses, "I'll go and see Lasalle and talk to him—but on the clear understanding that I make up my mind when I get there whether it's worth going into France . . ."

"That's great . . ."

"Wait a minute, there are conditions. If I go in, you'll personally guarantee my American contract is approved. You'll also guarantee that only MacLeish will know I've agreed—the security on this thing has to be ironclad tight. Finally, you'll pay me a service fee of twenty thousand dollars . . ."

"For God's sake," Nash protested, "you'll be getting the contract . . ."

"Which is the least I deserve since my bid is lowest. The twenty thousand dollars is danger money. You think it's going to be a picnic going undercover into France now?" Lennox demanded. "For Christ's sake, before you arrived I was listening to the news bulletin—since the attempt on Florian's life French security is buzzing like a beehive. I'll risk tripping up over Grelle's mob, the counter-espionage gang, maybe even the CRS thugs. MacLeish is getting himself a non-American messenger boy on the cheap at twenty thousand."

"Who said anything about a non-American?" Nash enquired mildly.

"You did when you phoned from Washington and then flew over here by the seat of your pants . . ."

Shortly after three in the morning they came to their agreement. Nash swallowed a final gulp of neat Scotch, checked over certain details with Lennox and then walked back through the rain to the Ritz, quite satisfied and grimly amused at Lennox's insistence on the service fee. MacLeish could damn well shell out the twenty thousand and trim his budget elsewhere. Back in his flat Lennox washed dirty glasses and then started packing. Like Nash he was a night bird, and like Nash he was satisfied. From the moment the proposition had been put to him he had been interested because it suited him. It gave him something new and interesting to poke his nose into; it made the American contract secure; and he had just concluded a hard-fought deal. Extracting the twenty thousand from

MacLeash was a bonus which lived up to his main principle: never do anything for nothing.

In Paris on Monday morning, 13 December, Grelle and Boisseau were no nearer clearing up the mystery surrounding Gaston Martin's strangely coincidental arrival only hours after the attempt on Florian's life. Detectives had visited the Hotel Cécile where Martin had dumped his bag after getting off the boat train from Le Havre and his few miserable possessions had been brought to the préfecture. They consisted of one small suitcase of clothes. "And this is all he had to show for sixty years of living," the prefect commented. "It's pathetic, the way some people live—and die . . ."

"This newspaper we found in his room is interesting," Boisseau replied. "It clears up the riddle of why he was standing at the spot where Lucie Devaud died . . ."

The copy of *Le Monde*, dated 9 December, the day after the assassination attempt, had carried one of those "scene of the crime" diagrams newspaper editors are so fond of inserting; this one was a street plan of a section of the eighth arrondisement with a cross marking the spot where Lucie Devaud had been shot. Martin's copy of the paper, purchased at Le Havre when he came off the freighter, had been folded to the diagram, as though he had used it as a reference. "They even showed the fur shop in the diagram," Boisseau explained, "so it was easy for him to find the spot . . ."

"Which tells us nothing about any connection he may have had with the Devaud woman," Grelle snapped. "We've traced her to an expensive apartment in the Place des Vosges but no one there seems to know anything about her . . ."

At nine in the morning the telex came in from Cayenne, Guiana—in response to Grelle's earlier request for information. It was a very long message and Grelle later supplemented it by a phone call to the Cayenne police chief. The story it told was quite damnable. During the war Gaston Martin had fought with the Resistance group commanded by the Leopard in the Lozère. He had, according to his own account—told to the Cayenne police chief only a few weeks earlier—worked closely with the Leopard, acting as his deputy. He even mentioned the savage wolfhound, César, who guarded the Communist leader wherever he went.

At the war's end, still a dedicated Communist, Martin had reported to party headquarters in Paris where he was placed under the control of a special political section. Then, in July 1945, only two months after the war's end, Martin was entrusted with a mission: he was to go to Guiana in South America to organize a secret cell inside the union of waterfront workers. "Control the ports of the west," he was told, "and we shall rule the west . . ."

Martin had set off with great enthusiasm, taking a ship from Le Havre bound for Cayenne, proud to be chosen for this important work. Landing in the tropical slum which is Cayenne had somewhat tempered his enthusiasm, but soon he plunged into a world of intrigue and underground activity. He took his orders from a man called Lumel; of mixed French and Indian blood, Lumel had been born in Guiana. Then the blow fell. Overnight his world was shattered. Drinking in a waterfront bar one evening before going home, he witnessed a drunken brawl and an American seaman was knifed to death. The police, tipped off by an anonymous call, came for him the next day. They found the murder weapon hidden at the back of a cupboard in the shack where he lived.

Lumel supplied Martin with a lawyer, who muffed his defence at the trial. He was sentenced to twenty years' hard labour on Devil's Island. For the first few months in this dreaded penal institution Martin was sustained by the belief that Lumel would find some way to free him; hope died with the passing of the years, with the non-arrival of any message from Lumel, who seemed to have abandoned him. When Devil's Island was closed in 1949 he was transferred to another equally sordid penal settlement.

With good behaviour—and he was a model prisoner—Martin should have been released in 1963. But late in 1962 there was an incident in the prison to which Martin had been transferred. A warder was knifed in the back and died. The murder weapon was found in the holdall Martin used to store his wooden eating implements. It was a repetition of the Cayenne murder sixteen years earlier. And should have immediately been suspect, Grelle thought grimly as he went on reading.

Reading between the lines, the governor of the prison had been an unsavoury character who wanted the matter cleared up quickly. Martin was accused, tried and sentenced to another twenty years. It was about this time that Martin became finally convinced that someone was trying to keep him in prison for ever. He served the greater part of his new sentence and then something odd happened. Lumel, knocked down in a street accident by a hit-and-run driver, called the Cayenne police chief as he lay dying. "That car knocked me down deliberately," he alleged. "They tried to kill me . . ." Before he expired he dictated and signed a confession.

The order to put Gaston Martin out of circulation reached Lumel in 1945 even before Martin disembarked at Cayenne. "It came from Communist party headquarters in Paris," Lumel explained in his statement. "I could have had him killed, of course, but they didn't want it done that way . . ."

"I know why," Grelle said to Boisseau, who was smoking his pipe while the prefect read the report. "Too many people who could identify the Leopard had already been killed . . ."

"You're guessing, chief."

"I'd bet my pension on it . . ."

Lumel admitted organizing the frame-up of Gaston

Martin for the bar-room killing, admitted that years later
he had paid a large sum of money to arrange for the
killing of the warder inside the prison Martin had been
transferred to. After Lumel died Martin was personally
interrogated by the Cayenne chief of police, a decent man,
Grelle gathered from the tone of the report. Bitterly
disillusioned by his long years in prison, by Lumel's confession, Martin had told the police chief everything. "I
think he realized that his entire life had been thrown
away for an illusion—the illusion of the Communist ideal,"
the Cayenne police chief commented in his report. "I
arranged for his immediate release. It will probably always
be a mystery why Gaston Martin had to be condemned to
the life of an animal for nearly all his days . . ."

Grelle dropped the report on his desk. "The bastard,"
he said quietly. "To go on concealing his identity he had
people killed, a man imprisoned in that black jungle hell
for life. God knows how many other poor devils died
for the sake of the cause—in the report I read of the
Leopard I noticed a number of his closer associates came
to a sticky end before the war was over. It's a trail of
blood this man has left behind him . . ."

The prefect was walking round his office with his hands
shoved down inside his slacks pockets. Boisseau had rarely
seen his chief so angry. "Remember this, Boisseau," Grelle
went on. "Do a job but never devote your life to a so-
called cause. You will find yourself in pawn to scum . . ."

"All this to protect the Leopard? A man who is dead?"

"We'll see about that." Grelle was putting on his leather
raincoat. "I'm going to the Elysée. If anyone asks for me,
you don't know where I am."

"I still don't understand it," Boisseau persisted. "The
record shows the Leopard died in 1944. Gaston Martin,
who we now know was Petit-Louis, the Leopard's right-
hand man, says he saw him walk into the Elysée . . ."

"When you get a conflict of evidence, you test it. I'm
starting to test it," Grelle said brusquely.

The direct route to the Elysée would have led along the rue St Honoré and the Faubourg St Honoré beyond, but because of the one-way system Grelle drove via the Place de la Concorde, along the Avenue Gabriel, which took him past the American Embassy, and then up the Avenue Marigny, passing on his right the large walled garden which lies behind the Elysée itself. Arriving at the palace, he waited while a guard lowered the white-painted chain and then drove into the courtyard beyond. Getting out of his car, he went straight to the guard-house.

"Can I see the register of visitors?" the prefect asked casually.

The officer showed him the book which records the date, time of arrival and identity of everyone visiting the Elysée. It was the page for Thursday, 9 December, the day when Gaston Martin had stood outside the Elysée which interested Grelle. He checked the entries for visitors who had arrived between 7.30 and 8.30 in the evening; then, to throw the duty officer off the scent, he looked at one or two other pages. "Thank you," he said and went out into the courtyard and up the seven steps which led to the plate glass doors of the main entrance.

Not even a cabinet minister could have called as casually as this, but Marc Grelle was held in especially high regard by Guy Florian. "He has no political ambition," the president once informed a cabinet minister he knew to be excessively ambitious. "I had to drag him away from Marseilles to Paris. Sometimes I think he is the only honest man in France. I would trust him with my life . . ."

In fact, Guy Florian had entrusted Grelle with his life. While the president is inside the department of Paris the responsibility for his security—and that of cabinet ministers—is in the hands of the police prefect. On the morning after the assassination attempt Florian had ordered that from now on his personal safety was to be in the hands of Marc Grelle throughout the whole of France. With one stroke of his pen Florian had made the prefect the most powerful figure in the French Republic after himself—if he chose to exercise that power.

"The president will receive you," a uniformed usher informed Grelle as he waited in the marble-floored lobby which is carpeted only down the centre. The interview took place in the president's study on the first floor at the rear of the Elysée, a room with tall windows which overlooks the walled garden laid out with lawns and gravel paths. Facing the president as he sits at his Louis XV desk is a Gobelin wall tapestry of "Don Quixote Cured of his Madness by Wisdom," and there are two telephones on the desk, one black and one white. A third instrument stands on a side table close to his right hand. As the door was closing behind Grelle he heard the chiming of one of the hundred and thirty-seven clocks which furnish the Elysée. 11 a.m. A large Alsatian dog bounded across the room, reared up and dropped its forepaws on the prefect's shoulders.

"Kassim, get down, you brute," Grelle growled affectionately. The prefect himself, who was fond of dogs, had personally found the animal when requested to do so by Florian soon after his election. It was said in the Elysée that only two people dared touch the animal: Grelle and the president himself. Removing the forepaws, the prefect bowed and then sat down opposite the most powerful statesman in western Europe. Typically, Florian waited for him to speak.

"I was very disturbed to see that you again walked back from the Place Beauvau on the evening of 9 December," Grelle began. "And only twenty-four hours after the appalling incident . . ."

Florian lowered his lean, intelligent head like a small boy caught in the farmer's apple orchard. It was the kind of gesture, coming from a president, which would have disarmed most men, but Grelle's expression remained grave. "It will not happen again," Florian assured him. "You saw the pictures in Friday's papers, of course?"

"I was thunderstruck."

"But you are no politician, my friend. The street was swarming with detectives—at a discreet distance so the photographers would not include them in the pictures! But it is good politics, you see—the president walks the streets again only one day after the incident!" Florian grinned impishly. "It is all nonsense, of course. Tell me, am I forgiven?"

Grelle returned to the préfecture reassured that from now on the president would stay behind the security fence erected to guard him. Only one question remained: was the security fence foolproof?

"Come in, close the door and lock it," Grelle told Boisseau as he settled himself on the edge of his desk. It was a habit of the prefect's when disturbed to perch his buttocks on the edge of a desk or table so he could start pacing about more easily if the inclination took him. Boisseau sat in a chair, took out his pipe and relaxed, waiting. With less nervous energy than his chief, he had the look of a patient squirrel, and behind his back that, in fact, was what his staff called him. André the Squirrel.

"I checked the visitors' register at the Elysée for the evening of 9 December for the hour 7.30 to 8.30," Grelle said abruptly. "Before I go on remember that the only physical description we have of the Leopard concerns his height—over six feet tall . . ."

"You have found something?" Boisseau suggested.

"Someone—more than one, as it happens. Florian himshelf arrived back on foot at eight o'clock from the Place Beauvau—that won't happen again, incidentally. The interesting thing is three other ministers also arrived on foot—they had come from the meeting at the Ministry of the Interior . . ."

The two men exchanged cynical smiles. Normally

everyone would have returned from the Place Beauvau in his own ministerial car, but because the president had walked back they had felt obliged to adopt the same form of locomotion. "And, of course, they hoped to get their own pictures in the papers," Grelle observed, "knowing there were photographers in the Place Beauvau."

"Who else came came back?" Boisseau asked quietly.

"Pierre Rouget for one—we can dismiss him, of course." They smiled again. Rouget was the nominal prime minister, the man the reporters called "Florian's poodle". An amiable man—"with a backbone of rubber" as Grelle sometimes remarked—no one took much notice of him and it was rumoured he would soon be replaced. In any case, he was no taller than five feet eight. "Between 8.15 and 8.30," Grelle continued, "two other men arrived and walked into the Elysée—and they came back separately, a few minutes apart. One of them was my own boss, the Minister of the Interior, Roger Danchin. The other was the Minister of National Defence, Alain Blanc. Both of them as you know are the tallest men in the cabinet, both of them are over six feet tall . . ."

Boisseau took the dead pipe out of his mouth and stared at the prefect. "You don't really believe this? Danchin, Blanc—the two strong men in the government? Martin must have been having hallucinations."

"I don't really believe anything," Grelle replied coolly. "All I do is check the facts and see where they lead—as we do in any investigation. But as we have agreed, I'm telling you everything however absurd it may seem."

"Absurd? It's unbelievable . . ."

"Of course." Grelle picked up a report off his desk, talking as he scanned the first page. "Something else has happened. David Nash, the American, has just been spotted arriving at Roissy airport this morning by a Sûreté man. And I have received a pressing invitation to a reception at the American Embassy this evening. You believe in coincidence, Boisseau?"

André the Squirrel did not reply. He was gazing into the distance, as though trying to grasp a fact so great it was beyond his comprehension. "Danchin or Blanc?" he murmured.

It had been Roger Danchin's aim to become Minister of the Interior since he had been a youth, spending endless hours over his studies at the Ecole Normale d'Administration, the special school founded by de Gaulle himself to train future leaders of the French Republic. And while Guy Florian and Alain Blanc—at the Ecole Polytechnique—were the hares who forged ahead because of their brilliance, Danchin was the tortoise who got there in the end because he never stopped trying. Sometimes it is the tortoise which outlasts the hares.

By the time he was offered the post of Minister of the Interior, Roger Danchin, an intelligence expert, probably knew more about the French security system than any other man alive. Like Alain Blanc, over six feet tall, he had developed the stoop which tall men sometimes affect. Fifty-two years old, he was thin and bony-faced, a man with a passion for secrecy and a man who loved power. Blanc, who disliked him, summed up Danchin in a typical, biting anecdote. "Danchin would interrogate his own grandmother if he suspected she had changed her will—and after three hours under the arc lights she would leave him all the money . . ." Danchin was at the height of his power when he summoned Grelle to see him just after the prefect returned from checking the Elysée register.

When the prefect entered the Minister's office on the first floor Danchin was standing by the window which overlooks a beautiful walled garden at the rear of the building, a garden the public never sees. "Sit down, Grelle," Danchin said, still staring down at the garden. "I hear from Roissy that David Nash, the American, has just arrived in Paris. What do you think that implies?"

"Should it imply something?" Grelle enquired. By now

he had grasped how this devious man's mind worked; rarely asking a direct question, Danchin tried to catch people out by encouraging them to talk while he listened.

"Something is happening, Grelle, I sense it. Strange also that he should arrive here so soon after the attempt on the president's life . . ."

"I don't see the connection," Grelle stonewalled. "But I have an invitation to the American Embassy this evening . . ."

"You are going?" Danchin interjected sharply.

"Why not, Minister? I may pick up something interesting. At least I should be able to answer your question as to why he has come to Paris . . ."

"And this woman, Lucie Devaud—has Boisseau found out something more about her? She couldn't be connected in any way with the arrival of Nash, I presume?"

"Surely you can't suspect the Americans were behind the attempt?" Grelle protested. "They do some strange things but . . ."

"Probing, Grelle, just probing . . ." Danchin suddenly returned behind his desk, moving so quietly Grelle was not aware he had left the window. It was another disturbing habit of Danchin's which his assistant, Merlin, had once complained about to Grelle. "He turns up without warning like a ghost, standing behind you. Did you know that when people go out to lunch Danchin creeps into their offices to check the papers on their desks—to make sure they are not doing something he has no knowledge of? The atmosphere inside this place is terrible, I can tell you. Terrible!"

Grelle got out of Danchin's office as soon as he could, mopping his brow as he went downstairs and out into the fresh air. I wouldn't work in this place for a million francs a year, he told himself as he got behind the wheel of his car. He drove out with a burst of exhaust as though to express his relief. Not for ten million francs!

Alain Blanc was born to a world of châteaux and money, of vintage wines and good food, possessed of a brain which in later years could absorb the details of a nuclear test ban treaty in a third of the time it would have taken Roger Danchin. With the family land and vineyards behind him Blanc, who came from the Auvergne, need never have worked for a day in his life. He chose to ignore the chance of a life of idleness, plunging instead into a life of furious activity.

A man of enormous vitality and appetite for work, he became one of the key political figures in Florian's régime, the man whom ambassadors quietly consulted when they could not get Florian's ear. An "X", which stands for the crossed cannons symbol of the Ecole Polytechnique, a school where money is no substitute for brains, he was one of the five top students the year he graduated. His close friend, Guy Florian, passed out first among a galaxy of brilliant men. Years later, well entrenched in the political bedrock of France, it was Alain Blanc, the manipulator, who masterminded Florian's rise to the presidency.

Over six feet tall, fifty-four-year-old ex-paratrooper Blanc was heavily built; plump-faced, his hair thinning, his head was like a monk's dome. A man of powerful personality, he was reputed to be able to talk anyone into agreeing to anything with his warmth and jovial aggressiveness. Women, especially, found him attractive—he was so lively. "He doesn't take himself seriously," his mistress, Gisèle Manton, once explained, "but he takes women seriously—or pretends to . . ."

His relations with Marc Grelle were excellent: the prefect understood the Minister of National Defence and never let Blanc overwhelm him. When they argued, which was frequently, it was with a fierce jocularity, and Blanc knew when he was beaten. "The trouble with you, Grelle," he once told the prefect, "is you don't believe in politicians . . ."

"Does anyone?" Grelle replied.

Blanc came to see the prefect in the afternoon shortly after Grelle had returned from his brief interview with Danchin. It was typical of Blanc to drive over to the préfecture in his Lamborghini rather than to summon Grelle to his ministry, and even more typical that he flirted with Grelle's secretary on his way up. "I shall have to abduct you, Vivianne," he told the girl. "You are far too appetizing for policemen!" He came into the prefect's office like a summer wind, grinning as he shook hands. "What are the political implications behind this assassination attempt?" he demanded as he settled into a chair, drooping his legs over the arm.

"We nearly lost a president," Grelle replied.

"I'm talking about this Devaud woman," Blanc snapped. "If it can be proved she ever knew the president—even if only briefly—the press will rape us. Can they?"

"You'd better ask the president . . ."

"I have. He says he had never seen her before. But he could be wrong. Over the years God knows how many people he has met—or known slightly. What I'm saying is—if your investigation turns up a connection, could you inform me?"

"Of course . . ."

Blanc left soon afterwards and the prefect smiled grimly as he watched the car from the window moving off too fast towards the right bank. Strictly speaking, anything which came to light should be reported only to his chief, Roger Danchin, but everyone knew that Blanc was Florian's eyes and ears, the man who fixed a problem when anything awkward cropped up. Boisseau, who had come into the office as Blanc left, watched the car disappearing. "It's quite impossible to suspect a man like that," he remarked.

"If the Leopard exists," Grelle replied, "it's because he has reached a position where people would say, 'it's quite impossible to suspect a man like that . . .' "

One 9-mm Luger pistol, one monocular glass, three forged driving licences, and three different sets of forged French papers—one set for each member of the Soviet Commando. Walther Brunner, the second member of the team, sat alone inside the concrete cabin at the edge of the race-track wearing a pair of French glasses as he checked the cards. The equipment they could carry was meagre enough but the time was long since past when Soviet Commandos travelled to the west armed with exotic weapons like cyanide-bullet-firing pistols disguised as cigarette cases. The craft of secret assassination had progressed way beyond that.

Brunner, born at Karlsbad, now known as Karlovy Vary, was forty years old; the oldest member of the Commando he had hoped to lead until Borisov had selected Carel Vanek instead. Shorter than Vanek, he was more heavily-built and his temperament was less volatile; round-headed, he would soon be bald and he felt it was his appearance which had persuaded Borisov to give the leadership to the younger man. At least he ranked as the second member of the three-man team, as Vanek's deputy, the man who would take over operations if something happened to Vanek while they were in the west. Rank, oddly enough, is an important factor in Communist circles.

Brunner was the Commando's planner, the man who worked out routes and schedules—and escape routes—before the mission was undertaken, the man who arranged for the provision of false papers, who later, when they arrived at their destination, suggested the type of "accident" to be applied. "You must make three different plans," Brunner was fond of saying, "then when you arrive at the killing ground you choose the one best suited . . ." Beer was his favourite drink and, unlike Vanek, he regarded women as dangerous distractions. His most distinctive feature was his large hands, "strangler's hands," as Vanek rudely called them. There was some justification in the description; if Col Lasalle had to die in the bath Brunner was likely to attend to it.

This was the nub of the training at the abandoned race-track outside the medieval town of Tábor; here the three Czechs who made up the Commando perfected the skill of arranging "accidental" deaths. Death by running someone down with a car was trainer Borisov's favourite method. The research section, housed in a separate cabin and which worked closely with the Commando, had studied the statistics: more people in western Europe died on the roads than from any other cause. Accidents in the home came next. Hence Brunner's special attention to drowning in the bath, which had been practised in a third concrete cabin with an iron bath-tub and live "models".

A fact largely unknown to the outside world is that an assassination Commando never leaves Russian-controlled territory without the express sanction of three members (who make up a quorum) of the Politburo in Moscow. Even in 1952—when the power of the Committee for State Security was at its height—the Commando sent to West Berlin to kidnap (or kill, if necessary) Dr Linske, had to be approved by Stalin himself and two other Politburo members (one of whom was Molotov).

The reasoning behind this policy is sound. If a Commando's actions are ever detected the international image of Soviet Russia becomes smeared—because one thing the western public does know is that nothing happens inside Russia without government approval. The Politburo is aware of this, so a Commando is only despatched where there is no other alternative. Vanek's Commando had been fully approved by the First Secretary and two other Politburo members; now it only awaited the signal to proceed, travelling on French papers which would easily pass inspection inside Germany. Brunner had just completed his inspection of the identity cards when

Borisov came into the cabin with the news.

"The execution of Lasalle has been postponed . . ."

"Damnit!" Brunner was furious. "And just when we were all geared up . . ."

"Have patience, my impetuous Czech," Borisov told him. "You have to stand by for a fresh signal. You may be departing at any time now."

5

On the morning of Monday, 13 December, when Marc Grelle received his telex from Guiana about Gaston Martin, Alan Lennox was flying to Brussels. Travelling aboard Sabena flight 602 he landed in the Belgian city at 10.30 a.m. Earlier, from Heathrow Airport, he had phoned his personal assistant at home to say an urgent enquiry had come in from Europe and he was flying there to get the contract specification. During the brief conversation he made a vague reference to Denmark. "You'll be back when, if ever?" Miss Thompson asked him gaily.

"When you see me, I'm back . . ."

It was time to sell out, Lennox thought as he boarded the Sabena flight. He had organized the company so well that now he could go away for long periods and the machine ran itself. So I've worked myself out of a job again, he told himself as the Boeing 707 climbed up through the murk and broke through into a world of brilliant sunshine which was always there, even over England, if only the inhabitants could see it. The reference to Denmark was a precaution; if anyone enquired for him at the office Judith Thompson would be close-mouthed, but if someone clever did make her slip up, then they were welcome to search for him in Copenhagen.

At Brussels airport he hired a Mercedes SL 230. Offered a cream model, he chose a black car instead; black is less conspicuous, less easy to follow. Driving first to Liége, Lennox kept a careful eye on his rear-view mirror, watching for any sign of a car or truck keeping persistently behind him. It was unlikely but not impossible; since David Nash had walked from the Ritz to his flat in St James's Place and back again he could have been followed, and the follower might have turned his attention to the man Nash had crossed the Atlantic to meet.

At Liége, where only three days earlier Nash had twice met Peter Lanz of the BND in one day, Lennox took a further precaution. Visiting the local Hertz car-hire branch, he invented a complaint about the performance of the Mercedes and exchanged it for a blue Citroën DS 21, his favourite car. Then he turned south-east, heading for the Ardennes, which is not the direct route into Germany. Sometimes it is possible to follow a man by remote control—observing the route he is taking and then phoning ahead. It takes a team of men to carry out the operation, but at the last count Lennox had heard the French Secret Service was employing over a hundred full- and part-time operatives in Belgium. If the main routes out of Liége were now being checked for a black Mercedes the watchers were hardly likely to take much notice of a blue Citroën.

Eating a sandwich lunch on the way while he drove, Lennox arrived in Saarbrücken as a cloudburst broke over the German city. The windscreen wipers almost gave up the job as hopeless while he was threading his way through the traffic. Rain cascaded down the glass, beat a tattoo on the cartop while he went on searching for the main post office. On the continent post offices provide the most useful means of making a call you don't wish to be overheard.

From the post office he called Col Lasalle's number which had been given to him by Nash. When Lennox asked for the colonel the man who answered the phone in French said he would take a message. "You won't," Lennox snapped. "Put me through to the colonel. Edmond calling . . ."

"Edmond who?"

"Just Edmond. And hurry it up. He's expecting the call."

The man at the other end—probably Captain Paul Moreau whom Nash had mentioned as Lasalle's assistant —obviously did not know about all the colonel's activities, which was reassuring. It suggested the ex-chief of military counter-intelligence had not lost his touch. The code-name Edmond, provided by Nash, put him through to Lasalle and the Frenchman said he could come at once. "I will be waiting for you," he replied crisply and put down the receiver. No waste of words, no questions, and the voice had been sharp and decisive.

It took him an hour, driving through rain squalls, to find the remote farmhouse, and it was dark as his head-lights picked out an old lodge beside a closed gate. There had been lights inside the lodge when he first saw it, but now the place was in darkness. He kept the engine running and waited, then got out cautiously when no one appeared. He was walking past his own headlights when a shutter in the lodge banged open. The muzzle of a Le Mat sub-machine-gun poked out of the aperture.

"Stay where you are—in the lights," a voice shouted in German.

"You're expecting me," Lennox shouted back in French. "I rang you from Saarbrücken. For God's sake open the bloody gate before I get soaked . . ."

"Come in on foot . . ." The voice had switched to French. "Come through the gate . . ."

Opening the gate, Lennox went up to the lodge, tried the door, opened it, stepped inside and stopped. A man in civilian clothes faced him, still holding the sub-machine-gun which he aimed point-blank at the Englishman's stomach. A smooth-faced individual with a smear of moustache, a man in his late forties, Lennox assumed this must be Capt. Paul Moreau. "I'm Edmond," Lennox said after a moment. "Do you have to keep pointing that thing at me?"

"Some identification—on the table . . ."

"The colonel is going to be happy about this?"

"On the table . . ."

Lennox extracted his passport carefully from inside his dripping raincoat and then threw it casually on the table. To reach for the document with his right hand the man with the gun had to cradle the wire stock under his left arm; as he did so Lennox suddenly knocked the muzzle aside, grasped the barrel and wrenched the weapon out of the man's grip. "I don't know who you are," he remarked as the Frenchman recovered his balance and glared, "but you could be someone who just knocked out the real lodge-keeper . . ."

"Lodge-keeper? I am Capt. Moreau, the colonel's assistant." Bristling with anger, the man examined the passport at much greater length than was really necessary. "You could end up dead—taking a crazy risk like that," he grumbled.

"Less of a risk than facing an unknown man with a gun in this God-forsaken place."

Lennox insisted on seeing Moreau's own identity card before he returned the weapon, first folding the projecting magazine parallel to the barrel so the weapon became inoperative. When identity documents had been exchanged the Frenchman told him curtly to leave his car and walk up to the house. "Why don't you get stuffed?" Lennox suggested. Going outside, he climbed into his car, drove through the gateway and on towards the house.

Moreau was using a wall phone when he left the lodge, presumably to call up the colonel.

As he drove slowly up a long curving drive Lennox saw how neglected the place was. Wet shrubbery which gleamed in the headlights had grown out over the drive, in places almost closing it so the car brushed past shrubs as he approached Lasalle's refuge. The farmhouse, a long, two-storey building which came into view round a bend, was in the same state. Unpainted, with tiles missing from the roof, it hardly looked habitable. Shortage of money, Lennox assumed: fugitive colonels are hardly likely to be sitting on fat bank accounts.

Col René Lasalle met him at the entrance, then closed, locked and bolted the heavy door before leading the way into a large rambling living-room crammed with old-fashioned furniture. In the hall Lennox noted there were new and modern locks on the door; in the living-room locks had been attached to all the windows. Theoretically safe inside Germany, the colonel had sealed himself off inside a minor fortress.

"They will come for me one day," Lasalle remarked crisply. "Shabby little Corsican thugs with knives in their pockets. They may try to kidnap me—they may come to kill me. But they will come."

The one-armed colonel, his left sleeve flapping loose like the broken wing of a bird, was small and spare, and as he fetched drinks from a sideboard he moved with a springy step. Lennox immediately had an impression of enormous energy, of a strong-willed personality likely to dominate any group of people he might be a part of. Fifty-five years old, Lasalle's features were sharp and gaunt, his eyes large and restless, his thin moustache little more than a dark slash. He still had a full head of dark hair and his most prominent feature was a hooked nose. In some ways he reminded Lennox of a miniature version of Charles de Gaulle himself. The colonel handed him a large brandy, raised his own glass. "To the destruction of the enemies of France!"

"I'll drink to that . . ." Lennox was watching the colonel carefully. "Whoever they might be."

"The Soviet faction inside Paris—led by the Leopard. But first I need to know something about you, about your background . . ."

For fifteen minutes he grilled the Englishman. It was the most shrewd and penetrating interrogation Lennox had ever experienced, with a lot of cross-questioning, a lot of jumping backwards and forwards as the Frenchman swiftly absorbed the details of Lennox's life and probed deeper and deeper. "You have met Marc Grelle?" he said at one point. "You are a personal friend of the police prefect then?" Lennox assured him that this was not so, that they had met only once for an hour in Marseilles during the planning of a counter-terrorist operation. At the end of fifteen minutes Lasalle pronounced himself satisfied.

"You can go into France for me," he said as though conferring a high honour.

"I'm glad I pass inspection," Lennox replied ironically, "but what you may not realize is I haven't made up my mind about you . . ."

"That is necessary?"

"That is essential. You see—it's going to be my head laid on the block . . ."

Leon Jouvel. Robert Philip. Dieter Wohl.

These were the names of the three witnesses, as Lasalle persisted in calling them, which he wished Lennox to visit and quietly interrogate. "I'm convinced that one of these three people—all of whom were involved with the Leopard during the war—can tell you something which will lead us to the Communist agent inside Paris today," the Frenchman said emphatically. "In any case, as far as

I know, they are the only survivors, apart from Annette Devaud—and she is blind . . ."

"Devaud?" Lennox queried. "That was the name of the woman who tried to shoot Florian . . ."

"A common enough name." Lasalle shrugged and made an impatient gesture with his right hand. "I see no reason for a connection. And in any case, Annette Devaud, who must be over seventy now, has been blind since the end of the war. A blind person can identify no one positively. Now . . ."

It had started eighteen months earlier—a year before the climactic row with President Florian which ended in the colonel's flight from France. Lasalle had been interrogating a known Communist agent who had infiltrated inside a French army barracks near Marseilles. "That area is infested with the vermin," the colonel remarked. Lennox gathered the interrogation had been preceded by a physical session which had reduced the agent, a man called Favel, to a moaning wreck. "While trying to escape from the barracks," Lasalle explained, "he accidentally shot a sergeant. The men who questioned him before me were the sergeant's friends. So . . ."

An hour after Lasalle had begun his own interrogation just before midnight Favel had started rambling on about the wartime Resistance. At first Lasalle had thought this was a trick to veer the interrogation into other channels; later he had become interested as the prisoner made repeated references to the Leopard. At intervals—the interrogation had continued for over twelve hours—the broken man had told a strange story about a man who would one day rise from the dead to liberate France from the capitalist yoke. This man, had, in fact, already risen from the dead and was walking the streets of Paris.

"It seemed absolute nonsense for a long time," Lasalle explained. "I thought I was dealing with a religious maniac —which seemed odd for a dedicated Communist—and then he told me he had been hiding in the barracks . . ."

"Hiding?" Lennox queried.

"Hiding from his own people," Lasalle said impatiently. "I had got it the wrong way round—instead of trying to spy for the Communist cell in Marseilles he was fleeing from them. What better place to hole up than in a military barracks—or so he thought. They were trying to kill him—I think because he knew too much."

"But he did know something?"

"He said it was no common spy he was talking about—a civil servant who photographs documents at dead of night and passes over microfilm inside a cigar or some such absurdity. No, Favel was referring to a highly placed mandarin close to the centre of power. To a man who for years had waited and worked his way up steadily—without having a single contact with any Communist organization. That is the genius of the idea—with no Communist contacts it is impossible to detect him."

"Favel named the man?"

Lasalle made a gesture of resignation. "He did not know who he was—only that he existed. What finally convinced me was a tragedy. The day after I completed my interrogation, Favel escaped from the barracks—twenty-four hours later he was found at the bottom of a cliff with his neck broken."

"His so-called friends caught up with him?"

"I'm convinced of it," Lasalle replied. "I started my own investigation and eventually I came up with those three names on the list. I visited one of them—Leon Jouvel in Strasbourg—but I think my position frightened him. I came away feeling sure that he knew something. Shortly after that I had my great confrontation with Florian and had to flee my own country . . ."

Lennox asked other questions. Both Jouvel and Philip, the two Frenchmen on the list of witnesses, lived in Alsace. Was it a coincidence? "Not at all," Lasalle explained. "The Leopard favoured men from Alsace in his Resistance group—he believed they were more reliable than the more excitable men from the Midi." The colonel smiled sarcastically. "He was, I am sure, a realist in everything."

"But the Leopard is dead," Lennox pointed out. "He died in Lyon in 1944 . . ."

"Which is the clever part of the whole thing. Don't you see?"

"Frankly, I don't," Lennox replied.

"The man has to have a code-name for the few occasions when he is referred to in Soviet circles. So they chose the name of a man known to be dead. What is the immediate reaction if the name ever slips out? It must be nonsense. He is dead! My God, what was your own reaction?"

"I see what you mean," Lennox said slowly. "You're saying there is . . ."

"A second Leopard—who was in some way connected with the Leopard's original Resistance group. This unknown man would easily think of using this name—if he once worked with the man whose name he has stolen. One of those three witnesses on that list should be able to clear up the mystery . . ."

"Who is this Dieter Wohl?" Lennox enquired. "I see he lives in Freiburg now. He's a German, of course?"

"Dieter Wohl was the Abwehr officer who tried to track down the Leopard during the war. He knew a great deal about the Resistance in the Lozère . . ."

Lasalle had thought more than once of approaching Dieter Wohl himself; unable to get back into France to interview the two Alsace witnesses he could easily have travelled to Freiburg. He had decided against the idea in case the BND heard of the visit. "They might have said I was interfering in German affairs," he remarked. "I cannot afford to be thrown out of the Federal Republic at this stage. Now, answer me one question quite simply. With those names and addresses, will you go into France?"

"Yes."

While Lennox was talking to Col Lasalle near Saar-brücken, two hundred miles away to the west in Paris Marc Grelle was arriving at the American Embassy on the Avenue Gabriel. As he walked through the gateway at 6 p.m. he was well aware he was being photographed by agents of the Direction de la Surveillance du Territoire —political counter-intelligence. He even knew where the camera with the telescopic lens was situated, hidden inside the large blue Berliet truck parked by the sidewalk oppo-site the Embassy. Uniformed gendarmes lounged round the truck, giving the impression they were a reserve force, standing by in case of trouble. By the following morning the photo would lie on the desk of the Minister of the Interior. Attached to the print would be a form filled in to show the details. *1800 hours. Visitor: Marc Grelle, police prefect of Paris.* Later, the time of his departure would be duly recorded.

Going inside the embassy, Grelle signed the visitors' book and went upstairs where he was relieved of his rain-coat by a girl with a Texan accent. "I was once in Dallas," he told her, "on the day President Kennedy was assas-sinated." He went into the large room overlooking the Place de la Concorde where the reception was being held. The room was a blaze of lights, a babble of voices, and the curtains were drawn, presumably to mask the room against the probing telephoto lens inside the Berliet truck. Grelle hovered at the edge of the crowd, getting his bearings and noting who was present.

"That computer-like mind of yours must have listed all the guests by now," a voice behind him suggested, "so why don't we slip away into the library where the real stuff is kept?" David Nash grinned and shook hands when the prefect turned round. "I had to come to Paris, so . . ."

"You thought we could chat? Or, you came to Paris so we could chat?" Grelle enquired in English.

"That policeman's mind of yours!" Nash led the way

out of the reception room and across the corridor into another room lined with books. Shutting the door, he turned the key which was already on the inside. "Now we won't be disturbed . . ." Pouring a large Scotch, Nash handed it to the prefect, ushered him into an armchair and perched himself on the arm of another chair as he raised his glass. "Here's to France. May she survive for ever, including the next two months . . ."

"Why shouldn't she?" Grelle peered at the American over the top of his glass. "Or is it a state secret? You still hold the same post as when we last met, I presume?"

"The same post," Nash leaned forward, keeping his voice low. "I come here as a friend, not as an agent of my government. As a friend of France, too. Marc, have you ever heard of the Leopard?"

Aware that Nash was studying him, Grelle sipped his Scotch and kept his face expressionless. He mopped his lips with a silk handkerchief before he replied. "The leopard? An animal with a spotted coat which can be dangerous . . ."

"This one is dangerous," the American agreed. "He's sitting behind a government desk not a mile from where we are at the moment. Let me tell you a story . . ." Nash told the story well—about a Russian defector who had arrived in New York only a week earlier, who had been rushed from Kennedy airport to a secret camp in the Adirondack mountains where Nash himself had questioned the man. The following morning—before the interrogation had been resumed—the Russian had been shot by a long-distance sniper with a telescopic rifle. "It happened while I was walking beside him," the American went on. "One moment he was walking beside me, the next he was sprawled on the track with a bullet through his skull . . ."

Grelle went on sipping his Scotch, listening with the same expressionless face as the American related how the high-grade Russian had told him about a French Communist agent—adopting the name of the wartime Resistance leader Leopard—who for over thirty years had worked himself up to become one of the top three men in France. "The Leopard could be any one of your top cabinet ministers," Nash concluded. "Roger Danchin, Alain Blanc . . ."

Grelle drank the rest of his Scotch in two gulps, placed the empty glass on the table and stood up. His voice was crisp and cold. "The lengths to which the American government has gone recently to smear our president have been absurd, but what you have just suggested is outrageous . . ."

Nash stood up from the chair. "Marc, we don't have to blow our tops . . ."

"Your so-called story is a tissue of fabrication from beginning to end," Grelle went on icily. "Clearly you are trying to spread a lying rumour in the hope that it will damage the president because you don't like his speeches . . ."

"Marc," Nash interjected quietly, "I'll tell you now that you are the only man inside this embassy who will hear what I have just told you . . ."

"Why?" Grelle snapped.

"Because you are the only Frenchman I really trust with this secret—the only contact I have come to warn. I want you to be on your guard—and you have ways of checking things out, ways that we couldn't even attempt . . ."

"You'd get chopped if you did!" Grelle, his face flushed, moved towards the door, then seemed to calm down and for a few minutes he chatted with the American about other topics. It was, Nash told himself after the prefect had gone, a very polished performance: outrage at the suggestion and then a brief relaxation of tension to indicate to the American that they would remain friends in the future. Lighting a cigarette, Nash wandered back across the hall to the reception, satisfied with the result of his trip to Paris. Because despite what he had said, Grelle would check. Grelle was the policeman's policeman. Grelle always checked.

To give himself time to think, Grelle drove round in a circle to get back to the préfecture. On his way he passed the Eliseé and had to pull up while a black Zil limousine with one passenger in the back emerged from the palace courtyard. Leonid Vorin, Soviet ambassador to France, was just leaving after making one of his almost daily visits to see Guy Florian. Since the trip to Moscow on 23 December had been announced, the Soviet ambassador had consulted frequently with the president, driving from his embassy in the rue de Grenelle to the Elysée and back again. Inside the limousine Leonid Vorin, short and stocky with a pouched mouth and rimless glasses, sat staring ahead, looking neither to right nor left as the car swung out and drove off towards Madeleine.

The uniformed policeman who had halted Grelle, saluted and waved him on. Driving automatically, the prefect had half his mind on what Nash had told him. Up to half an hour ago his suspicions had been based on Gaston Martin's strange story and what he had heard from the Cayenne police chief, all of which was disturbing but by no means conclusive. Now the same story was coming from Washington, and soon rumours might start sweeping through the European capitals. As Grelle told Boisseau later, "I don't believe a word of that fairy-tale Nash told me about a Soviet defector—he was protecting his real informant—but this is something we are going to have to investigate in the greatest secrecy . . ."

As he crossed the crowded Pont Neuf on the Ile de la Cité Grelle shivered, a nervous tremor which had nothing to do with the chill night air now settling over Paris. For the police prefect his world had suddenly become unstable, a place of shifting quicksands where anything might lie under the surface. "Roger Danchin . . . Alain Blanc . . ." he muttered to himself. "It's impossible."

Leaving the isolated farmhouse at about the same time when Grelle was returning to the préfecture, Lennox drove back to Saarbrücken through slashing rain with the distant rumble of thunder in the night. The storm suited his mood; he also was disturbed. At one point in the conversation he had asked the colonel who had typed out the list of names and addresses he now carried tucked away inside his wallet. "Capt. Moreau, my assistant, of course," Lasalle had replied. "He was the only officer who came with me when I left France and I trust him completely."

"You didn't trust him with my real name until shortly before I arrived," Lennox had pointed out. "When I phoned from Saarbrücken he had no idea who I was . . ."

"That was to protect you until you arrived safely. I called Nash in London at a certain time and he gave me your name, but I withheld it from Moreau. If my assistant had been kidnapped while you were on the way he couldn't have identified you under pressure. For the same reason Moreau does not know I am in touch with the Americans . . ."

Under pressure . . . As he peered through the rain-swept windscreen Lennox grimaced. What a life the colonel was living since he had fled France. Locked away inside a German farmhouse, guarded at the gate by a man with a sub-machine-gun, ready at any time for the intruders in the night who might arrive with chloroform— or something more lethal. And tomorrow Lennox himself would cross the border into France—after first meeting Peter Lanz of the BND.

While Alan Lennox was driving through the night to a hotel in Saarbrücken, Marc Grelle had returned to the préfecture from the reception at the American Embassy where he dealt with the paperwork which had accumulated in his absence. "There are too many typewriters in Paris," he muttered as he initialled minutes from Roger Danchin and ate the sandwich brought in from the local brasserie. He was just about to leave when the phone rang. "Shit!" he muttered, picking up the receiver. It was Cassin, one of the phone operators in the special room at Sûreté headquarters.

"Another message has come in from Hugon, Mr Prefect."

"Routine?"

"No. There has been a development . . ."

Grelle swore again under his breath. He would have liked to ask the operator to relay the message over the line, but that was impossible—he had personally issued strict orders that this must never be done. Phones can be tapped: all you need is a post office communications expert who knows how to leak off a private phone. Never mind about exotic electronic bugs; splicing the right wires will do the trick. "I'll come over," Grelle said and put down the receiver.

Rush hour was over as he drove along streets gleaming wetly under the lamps and turned into the rue des Saus-saies where Sûreté headquarters forms part of the huge block of buildings centred round the Ministry of the Interior. In the narrow street he waited while a uniformed policeman dropped the white-painted chain and then drove under the archway into the courtyard beyond. The room was on the fourth floor and at that hour he met no one as he climbed the gloomy staircase, walked down an ill-lit corridor and used his key to open the locked door. Closing the door on the inside, Grelle stared down at Cassin, the night man. The room smelt of garlic, which meant the operator had eaten a snack recently. A half-filled glass of red wine was on the table beside the tape-recorder which was linked to the phone. "Well?" the prefect asked.

"Hugon phoned at 6.45 p.m. . . ." Cassin, a lean, pasty-faced man of thirty, was reading from a notebook in a bored tone. "I recorded the message as usual and it's on tape."

"How did he sound?" Grelle perched his buttocks on the edge of the table. He would hear what Hugon had said in a minute, but the recording was inclined to iron out a man's voice, to drain it of emotion, and Cassin had listened while the tape recorded.

"A bit excited, nervous, agitated—as though he hadn't much time and was afraid of being interrupted."

"That's a precise analysis."

"He's sending something through the post—a list of names and addresses. He didn't want to transmit them over the phone. Said it would take too long . . ."

"Or he was being careful," Grelle suggested. "Did he say when he would post this list?"

"He'd already done it. He was in the post office."

"You look as though you could do with a bit of fresh air, Cassin. Come back in fifteen minutes—I'll stay and listen to the tape . . ."

Alone, Grelle listened to the operator locking the door from the outside, then sat down in the chair and lit a cigarette. The room was sound-proofed and was checked daily for bugging devices, so every possible precaution had been taken to protect Hugon. Grelle pressed the re-play button.

The tape which had recorded Cassin's conversation with Hugon was waiting on the machine. The man whose voice he was going to listen to had phoned one of the special numbers reserved for the Sûreté Nationale's private use, numbers unlisted in any directory. If anyone called the number by mistake, without giving the correct name, the operator informed him that he was the exchange, that the number had been disconnected. The machine crackled.

"What number are you calling?" Cassin enquired.

"Hugon speaking. Is that the Polyphone Institute? Good, I haven't much time . . ."

"Where are you calling from?"

"The Saarbrücken post office. Look, I told you . . ."

"Take it easy. I'm listening. Don't babble," Cassin snapped.

Grelle was standing up now, perched against the table edge, watching the spools turn slowly, recording each word in his brain as the machine replayed them. And Cassin had been right: Hugon's agitation came through even the recording.

"The colonel had a meeting this evening with an Englishman. Name Alan Lennox . . ." Hugon spelt out the name. "Thirty-five, dark-haired, clean-shaven, wearing . . ." A description of the clothes followed. "They talked alone in the farmhouse . . ."

"How did this Lennox arrive? By taxi? By car?"

"In his own car . . . I can't stay here long. It's dangerous, you know. The car was a blue Citroën DS 21. Registration number BL 49120. Lennox came by appointment. I was able to get back to the farmhouse and overhear just a few words, but it was dangerous . . ."

"So you keep saying. Who is this man Lennox?"

"I've no idea. Stop interrupting me. For God's sake *listen!* When I heard them talking Lennox was asking about a man called the Leopard . . ."

Grelle stiffened, stopped the machine. Gabbling on, Hugon had blurred the words. He played it back again, listening carefully. Yes, for Christ's sake, Hugon had said "the Leopard". The recording continued.

". . . and there was something about a list of witnesses. Yes, witnesses. If you don't let me get on I'm hanging up. Yesterday morning the colonel dictated to me a list of three people's names and addresses. I think this is the list they were talking about. I think the colonel gave Lennox this list . . ."

"We need those names and addresses," Cassin interjected.

"Shit!" Hugon spoke the word with venom. "I was just going to tell you—I made a carbon copy when I typed out the list. I put this in an envelope and sent it off yesterday to the address you gave me. And yes, Lennox has left. No! I have no idea where he has gone. I got the idea he's going to see the people on the list . . ."

"Which country are these people in?"

"Two in Alsace, one in Germany. Goodbye!"

The prefect stopped the machine, still perched on the table with a forgotten Gauloise smoking at the corner of his mouth. It was Guy Florian himself who authorized Marc Grelle to conduct the operation which penetrated Col Lasalle's farmhouse refuge in the Saarland. Normally such an assignment would have been handled by the Sûreté, but the president had told Danchin he wanted Grelle to deal with it. "I trust Grelle," he remarked casually, watching the minister wince.

The penetration operation had not been too difficult. Capt. Moreau, who had been given the code-name Hugon, had fled France with Col Lasalle on an impulse; later, as the months went by, as he found himself acting as housekeeper to the colonel, which even included preparing the meals and keeping the house clean, his enthusiasm for exile had waned. Seeing nothing ahead but an empty future, Moreau had snapped up Grelle's secret offer of four thousand francs a month paid into a Paris bank account. "With indecent haste," as the prefect had remarked at the time.

When Cassin returned from his breath of fresh air, Grelle left the Sûreté to drive back to his apartment on the Ile Saint-Louis. The next step would be to circulate Alan Lennox's description to all French frontier checkpoints.

6

Leon Jouvel. Robert Philip. Dieter Wohl.

The list of names and addresses meant nothing to either Grelle or Boisseau when the envelope containing the typed sheet reached the préfecture on Tuesday morning, 14 December. The envelope arrived in the prefect's hands by a somewhat devious route. As instructed earlier if he had anything to send by post, Hugon-Moreau had sent the envelope to an address in the rue St Antoine near the Place de la Bastille. The rue St Antoine is one of the many "village" districts which make Paris one of the most complex and varied cities in the world. The envelope was addressed to the owner of a small bar who lived over his business; an ex-police sergeant, he supplemented his income by acting as a post-box for the Sûreté. Under the circumstances, it would hardly have been discreet for Moreau to send a communication direct to the rue des Saussaies. Warned of its imminent arrival, the bar-owner phoned the Sûreté when it arrived, who in turn phoned the préfecture. A despatch rider delivered the envelope to Grelle's desk by ten in the morning.

"These people mean nothing to me," Boisseau told Grelle as they checked the list together. "Do you think Hugon is inventing information to justify his four thousand francs a month?"

"No, I don't. Look at the German name—Dieter Wohl. I read about him in the file on the Leopard. He was the Abwehr officer in the Lozère during the war. I seem to

77

remember he compiled a dairy on the Leopard's activities . . ."

"In any case," Boisseau said, sucking on his extinct pipe, "the Leopard, as I keep reminding you, is dead . . ."

"So, Boisseau, we have two facts which contradict each other. First, the Leopard's deputy, Petit-Louis, whom we now know to have been Gaston Martin, stated quite categorically that he saw the Leopard walk in through the gates of the Elysée five days ago. That is a fact—he made the statement. Fact two, the Leopard is dead—the record says so. How do we reconcile these two contradictory facts?"

"We check them . . ."

"Precisely. I want to know everything there is on file about the burial of the Leopard in 1944. I want to know where the grave is, whether a priest attended the funeral, whether he is still alive, who the undertaker was, whether he is still alive—every little detail that you can dig up. Phone my friend Georges Hardy, the police prefect of Lyon. But tell him to keep the enquiry just between me and him . . ." His deputy was leaving the office when Grelle called him back. "And Boisseau, I want the information yesterday . . ."

The prefect next called in his secretary and dictated a confidential memo to Roger Danchin telling him the contents of the latest message from Hugon-Moreau. When the memo was typed he initialled it and a despatch rider immediately took it to the Place Beauvau. And as has been known to happen before when a subordinate reports to his superior, Grelle censored the report, omitting any reference to the Leopard. Danchin was reading the memo before noon.

Earlier, as soon as he arrived in his office, the prefect started the machinery moving which, in a few hours, would have circulated to all French frontier checkpoints the name and description of Alan Lennox. "It's odd," he said to Boisseau, "I once met a man with this name when I was in Marseilles. Get someone to phone the right

man at our embassy in London and try to check him out
—with particular reference to his present whereabouts.
Alan Lennox—he was an international security expert . . ."

The headquarters of the BND, the German Federal Intelligence Service, is located at Pullach in Bavaria, a small
town on the banks of the river Isar six miles south of
Munich. On the morning when Grelle received the list of
witnesses from Hugon, Peter Lanz called in at his office
in the two-storey building which houses senior staff at
the unearthly hour of 5 a.m. Rising so early did not
bother Lanz who could easily get by on four hours' sleep
a night. As he collected papers from his desk and put
them inside a brief-case his secretary, Frau Schenker, a
pretty girl of twenty-seven and the wife of an army officer,
came into the room.

"The car has arrived, Herr Lanz. They say the airfield
is fogged in . . ."

"They have a flare path, for God's sake!" Lanz grinned
to take the edge off his outburst. "I haven't had coffee
yet, so you must excuse me. You can phone me in Bonn
up to nine o'clock—if you must!"

"I shall forget you have gone to Bonn," Frau Schenker
replied. She was half in love with her boss, but sensible
enough to know that this was really because she spent all
day with him and he was so considerate. At least it helped
to dispel the feeling of isolation working at Pullach en-
gendered; none of the people who worked at the BND
were able to let their friends know their real job. As Lanz
went down to the car, she checked her watch. He would
be airborne within thirty minutes.

As Lanz had foreseen, they had to light the flare path
before his executive aircraft could take off, then it was
climbing steeply through grey murk which was always
disturbing: you couldn't rid yourself of the feeling that
a large airliner might be heading direct for you. To sup-

press the fear, Lanz pulled out the table-flap and read the transcript of Col Lasalle's latest broadcast over Europe Number One. The Frenchman had excelled himself.

"The Hawk in Paris is getting ready to take flight . . . Soon he will alight in the city of the new Tsar whose shadow falls over the ancient and famous cities of Athens, Rome and Lisbon . . . Is Paris to be the next city to fall under the darkness of this barbaric shadow?"

Which was as good as saying that Paris might soon fall to a Communist *coup d'état*. *Ridiculous*. Lanz scribbled the word in the margin. Chancellor Franz Hauser, whom he was flying to see at Palais Schaumburg, would be furious at this latest outburst. Every Tuesday morning Lanz flew to Bonn to brief Hauser on the latest international developments as seen by the BND. It was really the job of the BND president to attend this meeting, but the president was now no more than a figurehead. "That empty old beer barrel," as Hauser rudely called him, only to correct the description even more rudely. "I'm wrong, of course. He's always full of beer—that's the trouble . . ."

Finishing the Lasalle transcript, Lanz checked his diary. After seeing the chancellor he would then fly straight back to Frankfurt, take a car from the airport and drive straight over the Rhine bridge to Mainz on the west bank of the river. The previous evening Alan Lennox had phoned him at the number provided by David Nash from Saarbrücken. At ten o'clock in the morning Lanz was due to meet Lennox at the Hotel Central in Mainz.

The meeting did not take place at the hotel. When Lanz arrived at the Hotel Central reception desk and enquired for Alan Lennox he was handed a note inside a sealed envelope. *The Hauptbahnhof second-class restaurant*, the note read. Lanz hurried across the square and found the Englishman sitting reading a copy of the *Frankfurter Allgemeine Zeitung*. "I prefer the anonymity of railway stations," Lennox explained in German. "How are you?"

The Englishman spent the next fifteen minutes telling the BND chief about his visit to Lasalle, but when he mentioned the list and Lanz asked to see it, he shook his head. "If I'm going to see these people, the fewer who know where I'm going the better. As you know, I always work on my own—that way I can only betray myself."

"I'm relieved," said Lanz. "It suggests you haven't lost your touch since the Syrian days. And yes, we are going to provide you with cover papers—identity card, driving licence, and so on. In the name of a Frenchman, you said?"

"Jean Bouvier," Lennox replied. "A reasonably anonymous name. Your documents section can put me down as a journalist—a useful profession for someone who wants to go about asking questions . . ."

Leaving Mainz Hauptbahnhof, Lanz drove the Englishman in his own car back over the river Rhine and then accelerated along the main highway to Frankfurt. "There are speed-traps near the Rhine bridge," he remarked as the speedometer needle climbed. "It wouldn't do for me to get caught by the cops!" On the way to Frankfurt he talked in English, always glad of the chance to practise another language. Reaching the city, he slowed down, went past the Frankfurt Hauptbahnhof and then crossed a bridge over the river Main into the ancient suburb of Sachsenhausen. The shoe-box buildings of glass and concrete which are modern Frankfurt changed into *weine stube* going back to the days of the first Rothschild. "We are there," Lanz announced.

The shabby photographic studio was on the first floor of an old building with a cake shop below, a building containing a number of small firms with single offices. "If anyone has followed us," Lanz explained as they climbed the twisting staircase, "they won't have a clue as to which office we have visited. And I don't think anyone has followed us . . ."

The taking of the photograph occupied less than five

minutes. "Too good a print on an identity card would at once arouse suspicion," the old photographer with horn-rim glasses commented with a dry smile. He promised Lanz that the false papers would be ready for collection within two days. Lennox, who had been watching the old man sceptically, asked him sharply to make a note of his vital statistics. "You are going to need them for the papers," he pointed out. The old man grinned and tapped his forehead. "I've noted them up here. Eyes brown, hair black, your height I checked when you stood close to that vertical rule . . ."

They were driving away from Sachsenhausen when Lennox asked the question. "I thought you had your own sections for producing convenient papers—or has Hauser cut your budget?"

"He has increased our budget most considerably. And we do have our own documents sections, as you suggest. But yours is a delicate undertaking and I have received orders to take you nowhere near a BND department. Joachim, whom we have just left, and his younger brother, probably produce the best documents in Germany. Even if the Sûreté examine your papers I am sure they will be quite satisfied with them. Now, I know an excellent place for lunch . . ."

Lennox refused the invitation, saying he had things to do, and Lanz drove him back to Mainz, giving him a Frankfurt number he could phone before they parted company. As soon as he was on his own, Lennox went to the garage where he had parked his Citroën, registration number BL 49120, and drove out of the city, heading back towards the French frontier along the same route he had come from Saarbrücken. On the way he purchased some food and a bottle of beer and he ate his snack lunch as he drove. At exactly three o'clock he reached the French border.

There was no trouble on the way in. The frontier control officials took little interest in him, waving him on after a brief glimpse of his British passport. From then on he drove at speed, keeping just inside the limit until he reached Metz, the nearest large city to the border. As he was parking his Citroën it occurred to Lennox that Metz was Marc Grelle's birthplace.

He spent one hour in Metz, moving quickly from shop to shop, limiting himself to only a few purchases at any one establishment. When he drove out of the city at five o'clock he had a suitcase full of French clothes—nine shirts, two suits, underclothes, ties, handkerchiefs, one raincoat, one heavier coat, a hat, and various accessories including two ballpoint pens, a wallet and a reporter's notebook. He had also purchased toothbrush, toothpaste and a set of French shaving equipment.

Arriving back at the frontier control point well after dark he immediately noticed signs of intense activity. Papers were being checked with great care, the number of officials on view was greater, and a long queue of cars had formed. When his turn came the passport officer studied his document with interest, going through every page, which was unusual. "You are leaving France, sir? That is so?" He was speaking in French.

"I beg your pardon?" Lennox replied in English.

"Un moment . . ." The officer disappeared into a hut, still carrying the passport. When he returned ten minutes later he brought with him another official who spoke English. The second man, who now held the passport, leaned into the car and stared hard at Lennox. "What was the purpose of your visit to France and how long have you been here?"

Lennox switched off the ignition, leaned an elbow on the window and assumed an expression of great patience. Never provoke passport control; they can make life hell for you. "I have been in France for three hours," he explained. "I found myself close to the border and decided to drive over here for the pleasure of some French food. I have not found German food all that interesting," he lied blandly. "Can you understand that?"

"Please proceed!"

And what the hell was that all about, Lennox asked himself as he crossed over into Germany and accelerated. Why the interest in someone with a British passport? It gave him a feeling of relief to have passed through frontier control; he had not particularly wanted his suitcase opened up when it was full of newly-bought French clothes. Must have been a spot check, he thought as he drove on through the night towards Mainz where he had booked a room at the Hotel Central. Within the next two days he would have his second meeting with Peter Lanz to collect the French papers. Then he would cross the French frontier again, this time as Jean Bouvier, newspaper reporter.

Grelle received the summons to the Ministry of the Interior at 6 p.m., just about the time when Lennox was coming up to the frontier control post. "He's getting worse," he told Boisseau. "Soon I shall be seeing him hourly. I'll see you when I get back . . ."

Driving to see Roger Danchin, he ran into the rush-hour traffic, and since it was pouring with rain people's tempers were even shorter than usual. Sitting in a traffic jam, he quietly cursed the minister in barrack-room language. It was 7 p.m. when he pulled into the courtyard behind the Place Beauvau, sighed, and then went inside the building. When he entered the minister's office Danchin was standing in his favourite position, by the window and staring down into the hidden garden with his back turned. "Grelle," he said, "I have the report on my desk of your visit to the American Embassy yesterday. You arrived at six and left at six-twenty. That seems to have been a very brief visit indeed." Then he waited, still not looking round.

Grelle made a very rude, two-fingered gesture behind his trouser-leg and remained standing, saying nothing. He had not yet been asked a question and he was damned if he was going to play Danchin's game, to start babbling on, explaining himself. The silence lasted a minute. "Well," Danchin said sharply. "What happened?"

"I saw David Nash . . ." Grelle, well prepared for the query, spoke in a monotone, almost in a bored tone. "He had come over to try and find out why Florian is making more and more anti-American speeches. Apparently the State Department is getting very worried about it. I fenced with him, told him I knew nothing about politics, that I was a policeman. He didn't seem very satisfied with my reply, so I thought it best to leave, which I did."

"Mm-m . . ." The stooped figure turned away from the window and suddenly stood quite erect. It gave Grelle a slight shock; he could never remember seeing Danchin perfectly erect. "I think you handled the situation well. What do you think Lasalle is up to now? I had your memo this morning."

Again the disconcerting switch to an unexpected topic, a typical tactic of Danchin's to catch the man he was interviewing off guard. Grelle shrugged his shoulders, aware that his casual dress of slacks and polo-necked sweater was being studied with disapproval. "I'm as puzzled as you are, Minister, about Lasalle," he replied. "I've alerted the frontier people about the Englishman, but we may have to wait for Hugon's next report before we learn more."

"Probably, probably . . ." Danchin wandered round the room and then stopped behind Grelle. "Do you think there is any chance that Lasalle is in touch with the Americans?" he enquired suddenly.

Grelle swung round and stared at his interrogator. "So far I have no evidence to suggest that. Are you saying that you have? Because if so I should know of it . . ."

"Just thinking aloud, Grelle. Not even thinking—just wondering. I don't think I need detain you any longer . . ."

On his way back to the préfecture Grelle went into a bar behind the rue St Honoré to calm down. Does everyone hate his boss, he wondered as he got back into his car and drove to the Ile de la Cité. The news Boisseau gave him made him forget the irritation of the trip to the Place Beauvau.

"They've spotted Lennox . . ."

Boisseau came into the prefect's office holding a piece of paper. "They checked his passport at the nearest border control point to Saarbrücken. He was travelling alone in a blue DS 21—registration number BL 49120. It all fits with the data Hugon gave us. The passport simply designates him as business executive."

"Quick work. Have they put someone on his tail?" the prefect asked.

"No. How could they? He was crossing into Germany. The time was 1800 hours this evening . . ."

"Crossing into Germany? You mean he had just left France? What the hell is he up to? According to Hugon he was coming into France!" Grelle walked across his office to study a wall map. "He crosses the border into France and then drives straight back into Germany? It doesn't make sense, Boisseau."

"Perhaps Hugon is not all that reliable . . ."

"He was reliable in telling us the Englishman had visited Lasalle. I just don't understand it." Grelle began pacing backwards and forwards in front of the map, occasionally glancing at it. "It's too much of a coincidence that he should cross over so close to Saarbrücken," he decided. "He must have gone back to see Lasalle. We'll have to wait for the next report from Hugon. I've no doubt he'll tell us that Lennox went back to see the colonel."

"Shall we keep on the frontier alert?"

"Yes. Just in case he comes back again."

The third member of the Soviet Commando was Antonin Lansky, the man they called the Rope. Twenty-eight years old, Lansky had already travelled abroad to track down two Czechs who defected from the political intelligence section in Bratislava. The two Czechs, a man and a girl, had fled across the border into Austria where they sought refuge in Vienna. Their disappearance—on a Friday night in the hope that they would have the weekend to get clear—was discovered by accident within a few hours. Lansky was sent after them.

The Austrian security service reacted too slowly. On arrival the Czech couple applied for political asylum and were temporarily housed in an apartment off the Kärntnerstrasse, which was a mistake because the apartment had been used before and a security official from the Soviet Embassy watching the apartment saw them arrive. He informed Lansky the moment the Czech reached Vienna.

How Lansky talked his way inside the apartment was always a mystery, but it was known that he spoke fluent German. In the early evening of Sunday an official from the Austrian state security department arrived at the apartment to interrogate the Czech couple. Getting no reply to his repeated knocking, he called the caretaker who forced the locked door. They found the man and the girl in different rooms, both of them hanging from ropes. A note—scribbled in Czech—explained. "We could no longer face the future . . ." From then on inside Czech state security circles Lansky was nicknamed the Rope.

Antonin Lansky was a thin, wiry man of medium height with a lean, bony face and well-shaped hands. Blond-haired, his most arresting feature was his eyes, large-pupilled eyes which moved with disconcerting slowness. Reserved by nature, he had spoken least during the training session at the race-track outside Tábor, listening while Carel Vanek, ever ready to express himself on any subject, talked non-stop in the evenings before they went to bed. Even Vanek found the quiet, soft-spoken Lansky hard to understand; if a man won't join you in conversation you can't get a grip on him, bring him under your influence. "You'll have to prattle on a bit more when we go into Germany," Vanek told him one evening, "other- will you'll stand out like raw egg on a bedsheet. French- men are always prattling . . . ."

"That was not my observation when I was in Paris," Lansky replied quietly. "I often sat in bistros where the locals were playing piquet and they hardly spoke a word for hours."

When I was in Paris . . . Subtly, Lansky had needled Vanek again. The older Czech disliked being reminded that Lansky had succeeded him in the security detachment with the Czech Embassy in Paris, that Lansky, too, knew something about France. The truth was that Antonin Lansky was deeply ambitious, that he looked forward to the day when he would replace a man like Vanek, whom he thought too volatile for the job of leader.

It was close to midnight on Tuesday, 14 December, when the Russian trainer, Borisov, burst into the concrete cabin where the three members of the Commando were getting ready for bed. Lansky was already in his upper bunk against the wall while Vanek and Brunner, who had stayed up talking and smoking, were just starting to dis- robe. Borisov came in with his coat covered with snow. For several days snow had been falling heavily east of a line between Berlin and Munich; now it had come to Tábor.

"You will be leaving for the west within forty-eight hours," he announced. "A signal has just arrived—every- thing is changed. Forget Lasalle—you have three other people on the list now—two in France and one in Ger- many . . ." He dropped a sheet of paper on the table which Vanek picked up as Brunner peered over his shoulder. "And you have to complete the job by the night of 22 December," he added.

"It's impossible," was Brunner's immediate reaction. "Not enough time for planning . . ."

"Difficult, yes, but not impossible," Vanek commented as he took the list of names and addresses over to the wall map. "Strasbourg, Colmar and Freiburg are in roughly the same area—on opposite banks of the Rhine. We already have our different sets of French papers, we all speak French . . ." In the background Borisov was watching closely, sure now that he had chosen the right man to lead the Commando: Vanek was adaptable in an emergency. "I think as we're going into France," Vanek went on, "each of us should carry a Sûreté Nationale card— they have some in Kiev and if they get the lead out of their boots they should be able to fly them here by tomorrow night. And a set of French skeleton keys. Then we could leave on Thursday morning . . ."

Brunner exploded. "That gives no time for planning," he repeated, "and only seven days to do the whole job . . ."

"Which means we shall have to move fast and not hang about and that's no bad thing," Vanek replied quietly. "It gives us the whole of tomorrow to plan schedules and routes—which I will help you with . . ." The Czech's normal arrogance and cockiness had disappeared as he continued speaking persuasively, building up an atmosphere of confidence, making the other two men see that it really was possible. Borisov, who had not detected this side of Vanek's character before, congratulated himself again on his choice. Vanek, clearly, was going to rise very high in state security when he added a few more years to his experience.

"And French ski equipment would be useful," Vanek added. "With the snow in the Bavarian and Austrian alps we can travel as tourists just returning from a brief holiday . . ."

"I'll phone Kiev," Borisov promised. "There is one more thing. When you are in the west you have to phone a certain number in Paris I have been given in case of further developments . . ."

"We have enough on our plate already," Brunner grumbled as he reached for a western railway timetable off the shelf.

"You make one phone call each day," Borisov continued, "using the name Salicetti."

Lansky, who had got down from his bunk, looked at the names and addresses on the list.

Leon Jouvel. Robert Philip. Dieter Wohl.

7

"This vast American state which no president can rule effectively . . . where secret government intelligence agencies operate as a second state within the state . . . where senators use their office to increase their private fortunes . . .

"What does Europe want with this terrifying offspring? Or should we finally sever the tenuous links between the Old World and the New—so that our ancient civilisation can go its own way, untainted by the giant Mammon?"

Guy Florian made the new speech at Lille, only eight days after his vicious outburst against the Americans at Dijon, and it seemed to his audience that he was stepping up the tempo, "muckracking with a bulldozer", as Alain Blanc expressed it to Marc Grelle in Paris later that evening.

The police prefect arrived at his office early in the morning of that day, Wednesday, 15 December, and again called his deputy and told him to lock the door. Two closed suitcases lay on his desk. "Boisseau, it's possible this Leopard business could be very serious, something which might well endanger both our careers if we carry on with it. You should now consider your position very carefully—and remember, you have a family . . ."

"What are your orders?" Boisseau asked simply.

"First, to put two top cabinet ministers under close and highly secret surveillance—Roger Danchin and Alain Blanc. Do you still wish to be involved?"

Boisseau took out his pipe and clenched it between his teeth without lighting it. "I'll have to form a special team," he said, "and I'll spin them a story so they won't get nervous. Is there anything else? Incidentally, this surveillance, I presume, is to see whether either man— Danchin or Blanc—is having contact with a Soviet link?"

"Exactly. And yes, there is something else, something rather punishing." Grelle pointed to the two suitcases. "Late last night I collected a whole bunch of wartime files from Sûreté records. You take one case, I'll take the other. Somewhere in those files I think we will find out where both Danchin and Blanc were during the war—because the solution to this Leopard affair lies a long time ago in the past. If either of these men can be positively located during 1944 in an area far from the Lozère—where the Leopard was operating—then we can eliminate him . . ."

Taking a suitcase back to his own office, Boisseau then set up a secret conference. Certain reliable detectives of the Police Judiciaire were detailed to work in relays, to follow Roger Danchin and Alain Blanc whenever they left their ministries. Boisseau himself briefed the chosen men. "You work in absolute secrecy, reporting back to me alone. We have reason to believe there may be a plot to kill one of these two ministers. It could be connected with a recent event," he confided mysteriously.

"We may have to prevent another assassination attempt?" one of the detectives enquired.

"It goes deeper than that," Boisseau explained. "The

plot may involve someone close to January or August . . ." From now on, he had stressed, real names must never be used, so code-names were invented: January for Danchin and August for Blanc. "So," Boisseau continued, "we need a record of everyone these two men meet outside their places of work. One of their so-called friends may be the man—or woman—we are after . . ." By mid-afternoon the surveillance operation was under way.

Grelle himself later approved the measures Boisseau had taken. "We are," he remarked wrily, "in danger of becoming conspirators ourselves, but there is no other way."

"Could you not confidentially inform the president of what we are doing—and why?" Boisseau suggested.

"And risk going the way of Lasalle? Surely you have not forgotten that the colonel was dismissed for exceeding his powers? The trouble is Florian has so much confidence in his own judgment that he will never believe someone close to him could be a traitor . . ."

Shortly after he made this remark, what later became known in Paris circles as "L'Affaire Lasalle" exploded. Grelle's first warning that a potential disaster was imminent was when Roger Danchin summoned him to a secret meeting at the Ministry of the Interior.

It was late in the morning of 15 December—the day after Danchin had asked Grelle whether he believed Col Lasalle was in touch with the Americans—when the prefect was called urgently to the Place Beauvau. Grelle was the last to arrive. On either side of a long table sat all the key security officials including, the prefect noted as he entered the room, Commissioner Suchet of counterintelligence, a man whose methods and personality he intensely disliked. Large and gross, with a plump face where the eyes almost vanished under pouches of fat, Daniel Suchet was a bon vivant who made no bones about it. "I eat well, drink well and seduce well," he once confided to Grelle.

Presiding at the head of the table, Danchin waved the new arrival to a vacant chair. "Everything said at this meeting is absolutely confidential," he instructed in his best ministerial manner. "Not to be discussed with personal assistants unless necessary in the execution of the operation . . ."

"What operation?" Grelle asked.

"You are not involved," Danchin informed him. "Suchet will be in charge. But we need you to give us information about Col Lasalle's daily habits and routines—since you have the link with Hugon."

"Minister, why do you need this information?" Grelle enquired.

"Just give us the information, please, Mr. Prefect . . ." It was Suchet who intervened, clasping his plump hands on the table and leaning forward aggressively. "I do not wish to be discourteous, but there is a question of security. The fewer people who are involved—you know what I mean . . ."

"I have no idea what you mean. Unless I know what you are up to I cannot possibly help—I shall probably leave out a vital piece of information . . ."

"I'll be the judge of that," Suchet rapped back.

"Please, gentlemen," Danchin interjected. "We are all here to help one another . . ."

"Then let him tell me what he is up to," Grelle repeated.

"We have decided to arrest Col Lasalle."

There was a silence and, knowing his reputation, every head round the table turned to stare at the prefect. Grelle requested permission to smoke and Danchin, who was already smoking, nodded impatiently. The prefect took his time lighting the cigarette, staring hard at Suchet whose eyes flickered and looked away. "Is this Commissioner Suchet's mad idea?" he enquired.

"No, it is mine," Danchin said quietly.

"You are going to kidnap Lasalle . . ."

" 'Arrest' was the word he used," Danchin snapped.

"You cannot arrest a man on foreign soil," Grelle said in a monotone. "You can only kidnap him and drag him over the border by brute force. How can we expect the public to respect the police, to obey the law, when the law itself is acting like the Mafia . . ."

"Careful," Danchin warned. "Perhaps you would prefer to withdraw from the meeting . . ."

"Like the Mafia," Grelle repeated. "Horrible little thugs in plainclothes breaking into a man's house at dead of night, grabbing him . . ."

"Lasalle is a traitor . . ."

"Lasalle is living in Germany. There would be an international outcry."

"We've thought of that . . ." Danchin adopted a more conciliatory tone. "It would be announced that Lasalle had secretly entered France of his own free will, that he had been seen and then arrested on French soil . . ."

"De Gaulle got away with it with Col Argoud," Suchet said.

"It's not good enough!" The prefect's fist crashed down on the table. "If you insist on going ahead with this bizarre operation I shall inform the president of my objections . . ."

"The president is aware that this meeting is taking place," Danchin informed him.

"How close is this operation, Minister?" Grelle asked.

"We may act tomorrow night."

"Then I must act now." Grelle stood up. "You invited me to withdraw. May I accept your invitation now?"

The interview with Florian was tense, so tense that Kassim the Alsatian, feeling the tension between the two men he regarded as his friends, slunk away under a couch. Beyond the tall windows of the president's study snowflakes drifted down into the Elysée garden, snow which melted as it landed. On the desk between the two men a sheet of paper lay with the telephones and the lamp. Grelle's hastily penned letter of resignation. Florian slid the sheet across the desk so it dropped over the edge into the prefect's lap.

"I won't be involved in this thing if that's what is worrying you," he stated icily. "Danchin, from what I hear, plans to repeat the Col Argoud abduction technique. Lasalle will be brought from Germany and left a prisoner somewhere in Paris. You will receive a phone call—you will then find Lasalle tied up in a van in a back street. It will be your duty to arrest him."

"It is an illegal act, Mr President . . ."

"Neither of us will be directly involved . . ."

"But both of us will know. President Nixon once tried to play a dubious game—look what happened . . ."

"You are frightened it will not work?" Florian demanded.

"I am frightened it will work . . ."

Florian's expression changed suddenly. Leaning back in his embroidered chair he steepled his hands and stared hard at Grelle, frowning. The desk lamp was on and against a wall Florian's shadow was distorted and huge. "I think you're right," he said quietly. "I'm too much surrounded by politicians. Shall I tear up that piece of paper or will you?"

Within three minutes of Grelle leaving the room, Florian picked up the phone and cancelled the operation.

Grelle left the Elysée in a stunned frame of mind. When he first heard of the plot to kidnap Lasalle he felt sure it was the brainchild of the devious Suchet; then he thought it must be a brainstorm on the part of Roger Danchin. The realization that Guy Florian himself had sanctioned the plan had astounded the prefect. It seemed so alien in character, or had he all along misjudged the

president's character? On an impulse, when he had got
into his car, he drove in a circle round the high wall
which encloses the Elysée garden—following the one-way
system—and this brought him back to the rue des Saussaies. Going inside the Sûreté, he collected two more dusty
files from the records department.

In the German city of Mainz Alan Lennox was waiting
impatiently at the Hotel Central to collect his French
papers from Peter Lanz. At eleven in the morning he
phoned Lanz at the Frankfurt number the BND chief
had given him and the German came on the line immediately. He was apologetic. "I doubt whether the documents
we are talking about will be ready before tomorrow," he
explained. "If you like to call me again at four this afternoon I may have more news . . ."

"What's keeping the old boy?"

"He's a craftsman. He wants the product to be right—
and so do you . . ."

"He's not producing the Mona Lisa . . ."

"But a portrait which we hope will be equally convincing. Alan, trust me . . ."

Lanz put down the receiver and pursed his lips. He was
unhappy about deceiving the Englishman; he even doubted
his success in so doing. He felt sure that Lennox knew
the BND had ways of collecting blank French identity
cards, which they had, and that probably they possessed
a store of such blanks, which they did. The papers made
out in the name of Jean Bouvier, reporter, were in fact
inside a drawer in Lanz's desk as he spoke to Lennox.
What Lanz was waiting for was final approval from the
Palais Schaumburg for the Englishman to proceed into
France.

Chancellor Franz Hauser, whom Lanz had seen once
before he met Lennox on the previous day, and once since
the meeting, was still unsure about the wisdom of probing
into the affairs of his most important ally. "If this English-

man is caught—and talks—we shall be keelhauled by
Paris," Hauser had remarked to Lanz. "Give me a few
hours to think it over—I will take a positive decision tomorrow night. Maybe something will happen to decide
me . . ."

It was in the evening of the night when Franz Hauser
took his decision that Guy Florian made his violent
onslaught on America in his speech at Lille.

As they had done on the previous Saturday night, Grelle
and Boisseau spent the evening in the prefect's apartment,
but this time instead of checking the Leopard's file they
were studying the wartime files on Roger Danchin and
Alain Blanc. It was close to midnight before they completed their reading.

"At least we know a little more," Boisseau suggested.

"Do we?" Grelle queried dubiously.

"Alain Blanc was officially studying at a remote farmhouse in Provence," Boisseau stated as Grelle poured
more black coffee. It had been agreed that Boisseau should
concentrate on Blanc. "He was sent there by his father
to stop him getting mixed up with the Resistance."

"Did it stop him?"

"No! He stayed at the farmhouse, continuing his studies,
and allowed the local Resistance group—which incidentally was wiped out to a man in August 1944 in an
ambush—to use the place as an ammunition and weapons
store."

"So you exonerate him?"

"By no means," Boisseau replied. "The only person
who could have vouched for his presence at the farmhouse
during the critical period was the housekeeper who looked
after him, a Madame Jalade. She died in July 1946 only
a year or so after the war ended. There was an accident
—she was driving her old gazogene-powered car into
town and ended up at the foot of a sixty-foot gorge."

"There were no witnesses?" Grelle asked quietly.

"None at all. She was alone. A faulty braking system was given as the cause of the accident. So she died soon after Gaston Martin was imprisoned in Guiana. It could be a coincidence, of course . . ."

"It could be," Grelle agreed.

The prefect then relayed what he had discovered reading the files which pieced together the wartime career of Roger Danchin. Joining one of the Resistance groups in the Massif Central, Danchin had worked under the cover-name of Grand-Pierre. He had soon become an agile liaison officer between several groups, one of them commanded by the Leopard. "He was a will-o'-the-wisp," Grelle explained. "Keeping in the background, he used a chain of couriers to keep one group in touch with another. Even in those days he had a great grasp of detail, apparently. He was reputed to be the best-informed man in the Midi."

"We strike him out?" Boisseau asked.

"I'm afraid not. His documentation in 1944 is so vague. And he was in the right area—very close to Lozère."

"So it could still be either of them?" Boisseau shrugged. "Like so much police work—a great deal of sweat and then nothing. At least we are finished with these mouldy files."

"Not quite." Grelle balanced two files on his hand. "I decided to check someone else—purely as a theoretical exercise. Gaston Martin said he saw a tall man walk into the Elysée between 7.30 and 8.30, a man saluted by the guards. Remember we are policemen—we go solely by facts. At eight o'clock Guy Florian returned to the Elysée. I have also checked his wartime background."

When Boisseau had recovered from the shock, when he grasped the fact that Grelle was conducting a theoretical exercise, he listened while the prefect briefly outlined the president's wartime career. He had served in a section of what came to be known as the Comet Line, an escape route for Allied airmen running from France across the Spanish border. Stationed in an old house up in the Pyrenees behind St Jean-de-Luz, Florian had escorted escaping airmen into Spain where they were met by an official from the British consulate at Bilbao.

"Two hundred and fifty miles away from Lozère," Boisseau commented, joining in the game, "so he could not possibly be the Leopard."

"Impossible," Grelle agreed. "Except that his brother Charles, who was older but looked like him, also served in the Comet Line. Now, if Charles had agreed to impersonate Guy Florian—remember, escape routes are shrouded in mystery and the operatives rarely appeared . . ."

"I didn't know he had a brother . . ."

"He hasn't any more. In July 1945 Charles set off on one of his solitary swims into the Atlantic and never came back. His body was washed ashore two weeks later."

"I see . . ." Boisseau sucked at his pipe. "A lot of people died young in those days; a lot of them connected with the Leopard. I had the report in from Lyon late this afternoon about the men who buried him and the undertaker . . ."

"Which reminds me," Grelle interjected. "We are flying to Lyon tomorrow. There is only one way to clear up the contradiction between the man Gaston Martin said he saw and the recorded death of the Leopard—and that is to open up his grave. I spoke to Hardy on the phone myself and he is rushing through an emergency exhumation order. Now, what about the men who buried the Leopard?"

"All dead. Shot in an enemy ambush four days after the burial, the bodies riddled with Mauser bullets."

"Plenty of Mausers about in all sorts of hands in 1944," Grelle observed. "And the priest?"

"There was no priest—the Leopard was an atheist . . ."

"Of course. And the undertaker?"

"Shot through the head the morning after the burial. Someone, identity unknown, broke into his house. And there was another curious thing," Boisseau continued. "A young Communist sculptor who had worked with the Resistance group wanted to do something to commemorate his beloved leader. So he sculpted a statue which was placed over the grave six months later. It is still there, I understand, deep inside the forest. It is a statue of a leopard, a stone leopard."

8

On 16 December the Soviet Commando crossed the Czech frontier into Austria. They came over at the obscure border post at Gmünd in the Nieder-Osterreich province where Czech control towers loom over the landscape like gallows. Arriving just before nine in the morning, they presented their French passports for inspection.

The sleepy Austrian official—he had been up all night and was soon going off duty—was already prejudiced in their favour. A few minutes earlier he had seen his Czech opposite numbers giving the three tourists a thorough going-over. The battered old Peugeot had been searched while the three men stood in the road. Their documents had been carefully examined. Anyone who was no friend of the Czechs had to be all right for entry into Austria. He had no way of knowing that Vanek himself had phoned the Czech border post earlier to arrange this charade; nor could he know that their arrival had been timed to coincide with the moment just before he went off duty.

A tired official is unlikely to check new arrivals with any great interest.

"Our papers are foolproof," Vanek had explained to his companions, "but the way to succeed in this life is to load all dice in your favour . . ."

The Austrian official stamped the French documents, the frontier pole was raised, the Peugeot with Vanek behind the wheel drove across the border into the narrow streets of the small Austrian town. If the sleepy official thought about them at all as he kicked snow off his boots he must have assumed they were French tourists returning from a winter sports holiday. The conclusion was easy to draw: Vanek and Brunner, sitting in the front of the car, with Lansky occupying the back, were all clad in French ski-clothes.

"First hurdle jumped," Vanek said cheerfully.

Brunner grunted. "Plenty more ahead of us . . ."

Vanek drove at speed for two hours along the lonely open road which leads to Vienna and where fields spread out across the plain for ever; where the only traffic you meet is the occasional ox-drawn farm wagon. Overhead it was cloudy and grey; on either side the fields were snow-bound; ahead the highway was a pure white lane with Vanek's the first car to leave wheeled tracks in the snow. Beyond the small town of Horn he pulled up in the deserted countryside. Getting out of the car, Vanek burned the French papers the passport official had stamped and then, using a spade which Brunner handed him, he buried the remnants, carefully re-arranging the snow over the shallow hole. Getting back into the Peugeot, he handed round sets of French papers which were duplicates of those he had just burned; duplicates except for the fact that they carried no stamp linking them with Czechoslovakia.

Reaching Vienna at noon, he parked the Peugeot in the Opera Square; later it would be picked up by a minor official from the Czech Embassy. When they had crossed the frontier at Gmünd their car registration number had been automatically noted, so now they severed this second link with their country of origin. With Vanek leading the way, shouldering his skis, the three men walked into the main entrance of the Hotel Sacher and turned through the doorway on the right which opens into a tea-room. They spent the next half-hour in leisurely fashion, drinking coffee and eating cakes while Vanek, chattering away in French, watched every person who followed them into the tea-room.

At 12.30 p.m. exactly the three men left the tea-room by a door leading into a side street, still carrying their skis. The Mercedes waiting for them was parked outside the Hotel Astoria and the registration number confirmed to Vanek that this was their vehicle. The key was in the ignition and nearby a Czech official who had watched the car folded up his newspaper and walked away; when he had picked up the Peugeot waiting in Opera Square his job was done.

With Vanek again behind the wheel, they drove to the Westbahnhof, the terminus from which trains depart from Vienna for western Europe. Brunner—with Vanek's help —had worked out the schedule precisely. Arriving at the Westbahnhof before 1 p.m. gave them nice time to eat lunch in the station restaurant before they boarded the express due to depart at 2 p.m. The train was moving out of the station when a Slovak climbed inside the Mercedes parked outside the Westbahnhof and drove off. The Commando, all links with Czechoslovakia effectively severed, was on its way to Germany.

It was just before noon in the German city of Mainz— four hundred miles to the east the Soviet Commando had now arrived in Vienna—when Alan Lennox again met Peter Lanz of the BND in the station first-class restaurant. The Englishman, who had been sitting at the table for a few minutes, nodded as Lanz took a chair and dropped a copy of the magazine *Der Spiegel* on the chair between them. Lanz picked up the menu. "The papers are inside," he murmured. "Sorry we've taken such a bloody long time over them. But they're good . . ." He ordered coffee from the waiter.

It was impossible for Lanz to tell the Englishman the real cause of the delay, that he had just returned from the Palais Schaumburg in Bonn where Chancellor Hauser had given the go-ahead. "That speech of Florian's at Lille last night disturbed me," the chancellor had explained to Lanz. "If he goes on building up this atmosphere of ferment he may leave behind him in Paris a situation ripe for a *coup d'etat* while he is in Moscow. We must find out whether there is a high-level Communist at work in Paris—and quickly . . ."

"Under that napkin near your hand," Lennox said quietly, "you'll find my British passport. Hang on to it for me until I get back. It wouldn't be very clever if they found that on me when I'm inside France . . ."

Lanz put the folded napkin in his lap, paused while the waiter served coffee, and then pocketed the document. "I suppose you will be driving into France?" he enquired. "It will give you total mobility."

"Probably. I want to be off in about twenty minutes. Is there anything else I need to know?"

"I'm afraid there is." Lanz leaned across the table, smiling as though he were saying something of little consequence. "We've just heard that some kind of alert has gone out from Paris. We've no idea why. But there is increased surveillance at all French frontier crossing points."

"Thanks, I'll watch out." Lennox made no mention of the fact that he already knew this. It wasn't that he distrusted the BND chief, but when he was working alone he made it a point to let no one know what he would do next. He rested his hand lightly on the copy of *Der Spiegel*.

Blan

"The papers seem a bit bulky," he commented, drinking the rest of his coffee.

"We've included five thousand deutschmarks in high-denomination bills—for expenses. We don't expect you to be out of pocket on this thing . . ."

"Thanks again. If I want to contact you, I use the Frankfurt number?"

"No, a different one. In Bonn, actually . . ." Lanz didn't explain that from now on he was staying in the German capital where he could have immediate access to Franz Hauser in case of a crisis. "You'll find the new number written on the inside of the envelope," he went on. "You can reach me at that number at any hour of the day—or night. I shall stay in my office at that number, eat there, sleep there. If you phone I promise you it will be my hand which will lift the receiver."

Lennox stared at the German. This kind of considera-tion he had not expected. "Thanks once more," he said. "But this trip could take anything up to a fortnight if I run into trouble—and you could get pretty stiff staying locked up in one room for as long as that."

"It's the least I can do, for Christ's sake." Lanz spread his hands. "I wouldn't want to take on the job myself, I can tell you. There's something stirring in the French security system, and it may not be healthy. If you get in a jam, call me. I can't promise one damned thing—not inside France—but I can at least try. If it gets hot, get out . . ."

Grelle was airborne in an Alouette helicopter, heading south for Lyon to attend the exhumation of the Leopard's grave, when he made another decision. He had been sitting silently for some time, not speaking to Boisseau who was beside him, staring down at the flooded landscape below. For large stretches it was more like travelling over Asian rice paddyfields than the plains of France.

"Boisseau," Grelle said eventually, "there are two

persons on that list Hugon supplied who live in France—
excluding the man in Germany . . ."

"Two," Boisseau agreed.

"I want you to set up close surveillance on both those
people. It must be very discreet—the two men being
watched must have no idea they are under surveillance."

"They are to intercept the Englishman, Lennox, if he
shows up?"

"No! If Lennox appears I want the fact reported, then
I want Lennox discreetly tailed. But he must not be inter-
cepted."

"I will have to quote your personal authority. It is out
of our jurisdiction, of course."

It was, indeed, out of Grelle's jurisdiction. Normally the
power of the police prefect of Paris ends at the city's
boundaries; he possesses not one shred of authority outside the capital. But Florian had expressly handed over to
Grelle the responsibility for his own security to cover the
whole of France since the asssassination attempt.

"Of course," Grelle agreed. "So you tell them this concerns the safety of the president of the French Republic."

To check passengers travelling from Vienna to Germany,
passport officials sometimes board the train at Salzburg,
but not often; this is one of the more open frontiers of
Europe. The Soviet Commando crossed the Austro-Ger-
man border without any check at all. With their ski equipment in the luggage van, travelling with French papers,
carrying French francs and German marks in their wallets,
the trio were to all outward appearances French tourists
returning home from Austria via Germany.

Even so, Vanek was still taking precautions. Deciding
that two travellers were less conspicuous than three, he
sat with Brunner in one first-class compartment while
Lansky travelled alone in a different coach. As they
moved through the snowbound countryside of Bavaria
beyond Salzburg after dark they caught glimpses in the

moonlight of the white Alps to the south. Later, approaching Munich, they passed close to Pullach, the home of the BND headquarters. Reaching Munich at eight in the evening, Vanek and Brunner took a cab to the Four Seasons Hotel, the most expensive hostelry in the city.

"No one," as Vanek explained earlier, "looks for assassins in the best hotels . . ."

Privately, Brunner had a more simple explanation. Vanek, he felt sure, believed that only the best was good enough for a man of his talents. While they proceeded to their own hotel, Lansky left the station by himself and booked a room at the Continental. To adjust themselves to the western atmosphere they went out in the evening after Vanek had phoned Lansky from an outside call-box to make sure he had arrived. "Don't sit in the hotel room," Vanek ordered his subordinate. "Get out and sniff the place. Circulate . . ." But he did not invite Lansky to join himself and Brunner.

At a beer hall Vanek picked up a couple of girls, using his fluent German to pull off the introduction, and later the four of them ate a very expensive dinner. When Brunner, hurrying after his leader to the lavatory, questioned these tactics, Vanek was brusque. "Don't you realize that two men with a couple of girls are far less conspicuous than two foreigners on their own? In any case," he said as he adjusted his flies, "they are nice girls . . ."

At the end of the evening, drinking absurdly-priced champagne in a night-club, Vanek persuaded his girl friend to take him back to her flat. Outraged, Brunner cornered Vanek in the foyer, saying he was going back to the hotel to get a good night's sleep. "A good night's sleep?" Vanek queried. "My dear comrade, I can spend a little time with a girl, sleep for four hours, and face the morning with the physique of an athlete . . ."

"We are catching the early morning train to France," Brunner reminded him.

"So don't oversleep," Vanek replied.

Lennox, who was always a lone wolf, waited until Lanz
had left the Mainz Hauptbahnhof restaurant, then he
picked up the copy of *Der Spiegel*, went into the lavatory
and locked the door of the cubicle. Sitting on the seat,
he extracted the French papers, put the five thousand
deutschmarks into his wallet, memorized the Bonn telephone number and tore up the envelope which he flushed
down the pan. Emerging from the lavatory, he made no
move to leave the station to collect his car. He had, in
fact, already handed it in to the car-hire branch in Mainz.

At 12.38 p.m. he boarded the Trans-European express
Rheingold which had just arrived from Amsterdam. Finding an empty compartment—there are few people on the
Trans-European express in mid-December—he settled
down in a corner seat and lit a Benson and Hedges
cigarette. He had waited until the last second to board
the train and no one had followed him. The people he
was worried about were the French Secret Service agents
attached to their embassy in Bonn. They would hardly
know about him yet, but the second-in-command of the
BND was an obvious target for them to follow. As the
express picked up speed he took hold of his suitcase and
went along to the spacious lavatory.

The man who went inside was Alan Lennox, British.
The man who emerged ten minutes later was Jean Bouvier,
French. Settling down again in his empty compartment,
Lennox was dressed in French clothes and smoking a
Gitane. He was also wearing the hat he had purchased in
Metz and a pair of hornrim glasses. Normally hatless,
Lennox knew how much the wearing of headgear changes
the appearance of a man. When the ticket collector
arrived a few minutes later and he had to purchase the
TEE supplement, Lennox conversed with him in French
and a little ungrammatic German.

When the express reached Freiburg, the last stop before

the Swiss border, Lennox had a moment's hesitation. One of the three people on Lasalle's list of witnesses—Dieter Wohl—lived in Freiburg. Shrugging his shoulders like a Frenchman, Lennox remained in his seat. At the moment the important thing was to get clear of Germany, to break his trail; Freiburg was just across the Rhine from Alsace and he could visit Wohl later, after he had seen the Frenchmen. Promptly at 3.36 p.m. the *Rheingold* stopped at Basel Hauptbahnhof where Lennox got off. He had now arrived in Switzerland.

Leaving the station he crossed the street and went into the Hotel Victoria where he booked a room for one night only. He had plenty of time then to find the right shop and purchase a second suitcase. Taking it back to his own room, he re-packed, putting his British clothes into his own case; the French items he had purchased in Metz —all except those he was wearing—went into the Swiss case he had just bought. Going out again with the British case, he walked into the Hauptbahnhof and locked it away in a luggage compartment. As he shut the door he knew it was by no means certain he would ever see this case again.

Grelle arrived late for the exhumation of the grave of the Leopard. Involved as he was in three major operations —probing the attempt to assassinate the president; investigating the mystery of the Leopard; perfecting the security surrounding Guy Florian—he needed every spare minute he could find in a day. Already he was keeping going on only four hours' sleep a night while he catnapped during the day when he could—in cars, in aircraft, even in his office when he could snatch time between interviews.

With Boisseau behind the wheel, Grelle was dozing as they turned off the main road into the forest along a muddy track. A gendarme with a torch had signalled them at the obscure entrance, which they would otherwise have missed. Long after dark—the exhumation was being carried out at night to help keep it secret—it was pouring with rain and the rutted track showed two gullies of water in their headlights. The prefect opened his eyes. "If this goes on much longer," he grumbled, "the whole of France will be afloat . . ."

It was a fir forest they were moving into. A palisade of wet trunks rippled past the headlights as the track twisted and turned, as the tyres squelched through the mud and the storm beat down on the cartop. About two kilometres from where they had left the road Boisseau turned a corner and the headlights, shafting through the slanting rain, shone on a weird scene.

Arc-lights glared down on the excavation which was protected with a canvas tent-like erection. Heaps of excavated soil were banked up and men with shovels were shoulder-deep inside the pit, still lifting hard-packed soil. Through the fan-shapes cleared by the wipers Grelle saw they were inside a wide clearing. Parked police vehicles stood around on carpets of dead bracken. Under the arc-lights a deep-scored mud-track ran away from the grave. Following the track with his eyes, Grelle saw a few metres away the blurred silhouette of the stone leopard effigy which had been hauled off the grave. It looked eerily alive in the beating rain, like a real animal crouched for a spring.

"I'll see how they're getting on," said Boisseau, who had stopped the car. "No point in both of us getting wet . . ."

An *agent de la paix*, his coat streaming with water, peered in at the window and his peaked brim deposited rain inside the car. Embarrassed, he took off the cap. "Put it on again, for God's sake," Grelle growled. "Are you getting anywhere?"

"They have found the coffin . . ." The man was boyish-faced, excited at addressing the police prefect of Paris. "They will have it up within a few minutes."

"At least there is a coffin," Grelle muttered. He was

anything but excited. Even if there were a body inside he
was dubious of what this might prove; after all, 1944
was a long time ago. Pessimistic as he was, he had still
arranged for the forensic department at Lyon to be ready
to get to work at once when the remains were delivered
to them. A pathologist, a man with a fluoroscope who
could assess the age of the bones, various other experts.

Grelle followed Boisseau out into the rain, hands tucked
inside his raincoat pockets, hat pulled down. He would
have to get wet sooner or later, and it looked bad for
the prefect to sit in a warm car while the other poor
devils toiled in the mud. He had taken the precaution
of putting on rubber boots and his feet sank ankle-deep
into the slippery mud. He stood under the glow of an arc-
light while a drop of rain dripped from his nose-end,
staring at the stone leopard crouched in the rain.

Above the noise of the pounding rain, the distant rumble of thunder, a new sound was added as they fastened
chains round something in the depths of the pit. The tent
was moved away so a breakdown truck could back to
the brink. The driver moved a lever and the crane apparatus leaned out over the pit. In case of an accident the
men were climbing up out of the pit now, smeared with
mud. A filthy job. Probably all for nothing.

It was a disturbing scene: the wind shifting the tree
tops, the endless rain, the glare of the arc-lights. And now
the men in shiny coats fell silent as they waited expec-
tantly, huddled round the grave. The chained coffin had
been fixed to the hoist; the only man doing anything now
was the truck driver, sitting twisted round in his seat
as he operated levers. The coffin came up out of the
shadows slowly, tilting at an acute angle as the machinery
whirred, as the rain slanted down on the slowly-turning
box. Everyone was very still. Grelle inserted a cigarette
in the corner of his mouth and then didn't light it as he
saw a gendarme glance at him severely. "Bloody hell,"
he thought, "does he expect me to take off my hat?"

Looking to his right again he saw the stone leopard, its mouth open, caught in the arc-light, as though enraged at the desecration. The officer in charge of the whole business shouted an order. The coffin, now above ground, swivelled in mid-air, was carried by the steel arm over to the canvas tent, gently eased and dropped just inside, under cover from the rain. Another shouted order. A man with a power saw appeared, examined the coffin and then began work, slicing the lid above where it had originally been closed. Boisseau made an enquiry, came back to the prefect.

"The screws are rusted in. They were advised not to use chisels and crowbars—the vibrations might have shivered the remains to powder . . ."

Grelle said nothing, standing quite still with the unlit cigarette now becoming soggy in the corner of his mouth. On Boisseau's orders a light was brought closer, shining directly through the tent's mouth on to the coffin.

"It it going to tell us anything, I wonder?" Boisseau murmured and there was a hint of excitement in his voice.

"I wouldn't bet on it . . ."

"They said as far as they could tell it hadn't been disturbed for many years. The earth is packed like concrete."

"What about that damned statue?"

"Well bedded in. Again, not touched for years . . ."

The man with the power saw stopped. They were ready. A couple of men stooped at either side of the coffin, began sliding the lid off with care, out of the tent, so until they had removed the whole lid it wasn't possible to see what might lie inside. They seemed to take an age, bent as they were under the canvas roof, and they had to watch their footing; the ground was becoming a quagmire. Then they had moved aside and under the glare of the arc-light everyone could see. There was a gasp of horror. Grelle stood as immovable as the stone statue a few metres away. "My God!" It was Boisseau speaking.

Inside the coffin was stretched the perfect skeleton of an enormous hound, lying on its haunches, its huge skull rested between its skeletal paw-bones, its eye-sockets in shadow so it seemed to stare at them hideously with enormous black pupils.

"César . . ." The prefect grunted. "Macabre—and brilliant. He couldn't take his dog with him because that would identify him. And he needed something to weight the coffin. So he killed the dog and provided his own corpse."

Boisseau bent over the skeleton, examined it briefly. "I think there is a bullet-hole in the skull."

"I wonder if the bastard shot his own dog?" Once Grelle had owned a British wire-haired terrier which had eventually been knocked down in the Paris traffic. He had never replaced the animal. He spoke in a monotone, then stiffened himself. "Tell them to replace the lid and get the whole thing to Lyon. Come on!"

They left the men in the wood lifting the coffin and its contents into the breakdown truck and drove back along the muddy track. The statue would remain in the wood, close to the grave it had guarded so long. which was already filling up with water. Boisseau, noting the frown of concentration on his chief's face, said nothing until they turned on to the main road. "Surprised?" he asked as they picked up speed.

"Not really—although I didn't anticipate the dog. The whole thing has worried me since I read the file—it was out of pattern. He took all those precautions to make sure he couldn't be identified and then, when it's nearly over, he walks into Lyon and gets himself shot. If he'd survived up to then, he should have gone on surviving—which he did."

"So he's about somewhere?"

"I know exactly where he is. He's in Paris. The trouble is I don't know who he is."

"Danchin or Blanc—according to Gaston Martin. It's a nightmare."

"It will get worse," Grelle assured him.

Grelle remained in Lyon just long enough to make a few more enquiries and to hear the result of the fluoroscope test on the skeleton. "I estimate the age of the bones as being somewhere between thirty and forty years," the expert told the prefect. "That is, they have lain in the forest for that period of time." Which meant the animal could easily have been shot and buried in August 1944.

Flying back to Paris aboard the helicopter, Grelle told Boisseau about his other enquiries. "They gave me the details about the sculptor who made the statue. He was found shot in his house soon after he had finished the statue. The place had been ransacked and it was assumed he had disturbed a burglar. It gives you some idea of the ruthlessness of the man we're looking for. He covered his tracks completely—or so he thought. Until Lasalle resurrected him."

"What the hell are we going to do?" Boisseau asked.

"Track him down."

9

The two men walked alone in the Paris garden, one of them tall and stooping slightly to catch what his much shorter companion was saying. The shorter man was thick-bodied and had short, strong legs. He spoke with respect but firmly, as though expecting opposition he

must overcome. He spoke in little more than a whisper
even though there was no one within twenty metres of
where they walked.

"We must add Lasalle to the list. He is a very dangerous man and at this stage we dare not risk leaving him
alive. Otherwise he will go on ferreting until he digs up
something."

"I think it's unwise," the tall man repeated. "I have
given you three names and that is enough. Every one you
add to the list increases the risk. Something will go
wrong . . ."

"Nothing will go wrong. They are using the best people
available for this sort of work. I understand the Commando has almost arrived in France—and they should
complete their task within six days . . ." The short man
took out a handkerchief and blew his nose. He had a cold
coming on; Paris really was an unbearably damp place.
"You haven't heard even a whisper that anyone knows
about this?" he enquired.

"Nothing. Let them just get it over with quickly," the
tall man said sharply. "And let me know when I can
stop worrying about it. I have enough on my mind at
the moment."

The short man glanced quickly at his companion, sensing the undercurrent of tension. This he understood; he
felt tense himself. "And Lasalle? Since the kidnap operation has been cancelled we really must deal with that
problem, too."

"You can get in touch with the Commando then? Just
in case any other problem crops up?"

The short man hesitated, then took a decision. "They
will make contact with us at regular intervals. So the
answer is yes. I hope you haven't left someone off the list?"

"No one! Now I think we have talked enough . . ."

"And Lasalle?" the short man persisted. "It will look
like an accident, I promise you. The men who are dealing
with this are experts . . ."

"Experts?" The tall man straightened up and his expression showed distaste. "In wartime one took these actions for granted, but in peacetime . . . Still, it has to be done. In a way it is a continuation of the war. As for Lasalle, he must not be added to the list yet. I am sure he has no idea what is going to happen when the president of France leaves for Moscow . . ."

PART TWO

THE KILLER COMMANDO

December 17–December 21

10

It had been the secret nightmare of every major security service in the west since the earliest days of the Cold War —and the later phoney period of so-called "detente"— that in one major country or another a secret Communist would stay dormant until he had worked his way up the ladder of power and reached the summit.

This is the man who is most feared by intelligence chiefs in London, Washington and other capitals—the Rip Van Winkle of Communism who has no contact with Russian agents, who visits no safe houses to pass on information, who is controlled by no spymaster. And because for many years he has no contact with Moscow there is no way to detect him as, by sheer ability, he continues his climb. He is not interested in delivering the details of a guided missile system to Moscow—he hopes to deliver his country.

It was Col René Lasalle who first caught a whiff of conspiracy when he was still assistant chief of military counter-intelligence. Burrowing deeper into the background of the elusive Leopard, he came up against Guy Florian, who dismissed him for crossing the thin line between military and political counter-espionage. By a strange quirk of history it fell to Marc Grelle to take up the trail again where Lasalle had been compelled to lose it.

On Friday, 17 December—the day the Soviet Commando

crossed the border into France—Marc Grelle was distracted from his many duties by what, at the time, seemed a diversion, an incident which would be recorded in the files and forgotten. At ten in the morning he heard of the emergency at Orly airport where Algerian terrorists had just tried to destroy an El Al aircraft on the verge of take-off. "We'd better go and have a look," he told Boisseau. "I thought the security at Orly was foolproof . . ." Grelle had reason to be worried; in only a few days' time Guy Florian was due to fly from Orly to Marseilles where he would make a major speech on the eve of his departure for Russia.

Arriving at the airport, where it was pouring with rain, they found that Camille Point, the officer in command of the Airport Gendarmerie, had the situation under control. In the distance, barely visible in the rain squalls, they could see the Israeli aircraft which had been the target standing unscathed at the end of a reserve runway. Boisseau left Grelle with Camille Point for a moment to check the position with a radio-equipped patrol-car. The whole airport was swarming with armed police.

"One of my men spotted the terrorist just in time," Point explained. "He was aiming his weapon at the El Al machine which was just about to take off with two hundred people aboard. Mouton—the gendarme—fired at him and missed, but he scared the terrorist who ran off and left his weapon behind. Come up on to the roof and I'll show you . . ."

"This terrorist—he escaped?"

There was anxiety in Grelle's voice. It had been known for some time that an Algerian terrorist cell was operating inside Paris and the prefect was anxious to round up the whole gang. He had given orders—which Roger Danchin had approved—that if the gang was cornered the police were to shoot to kill. But one man was not enough. Boisseau, who had run back from the patrol-car, heard the question.

"He got away, yes," Boisseau began.

"Shit!" Grelle said venomously.

"But we have him under observation," Boisseau continued. "Using the new system you have set up for the presidential motorcade drive to Roissy on 23 December, he is being passed from one patrol-car to another at this moment. And he does not appear to realize he is being tailed. I have just heard that he is moving along the Périphérique, heading for northern Paris . . ."

Boisseau broke off as the driver of the near-by patrol-car waved to him. When he came back after taking the new radio report he nodded to the prefect. "He's still under surveillance, still heading north. Do we risk losing him or close in?"

"Don't close in—and don't lose him," Grelle replied.

"That's what I have just told them . . ."

It was worth the risk, Grelle told himself as he followed Point up on to the roof of the building. If they could trace the Algerian to his secret hideout, maybe even then continue to keep him under surveillance, they stood a chance of wiping out the whole cell at one swoop. Reaching the rooftop, Grelle paused and stared. Five uniformed gendarmes were gathered round a bulky instrument lying on a sheet of canvas. The fingerprint man, who had just finished examining the weapon, stood up and addressed Boisseau. "I've got what I want. Pleasant little plaything, isn't it?"

"Grail?" the prefect enquired.

"Yes, sir." It was a young, keen-looking gendarme who replied.

Grail is the NATO code-name for the Russian-made SAM—surface-to-air missile system—of the man-portable variety. It was also the rocket-launcher, quite capable of being carried by one man—which Moscow had supplied in meagre quantities—and quite unofficially—to certain Arab terrorist organizations. Weighing no more than eighteen kilos when loaded with one rocket or *strela* (the

Russian word for arrow) it has a range of between one and two miles.

Only a few years earlier Heathrow Airport, London, had been sealed off while crack troops of the British Army took control in a major anti-terrorist operation. At the time there had been reports that a terrorist group armed with Grail was waiting to shoot down the incoming plane carrying Dr Kissinger. Similar to a bazooka in appearance, the weapon had a heavy stock and a complex-looking telescopic apparatus mounted over its thick barrel. Two rockets lay beside it on the canvas. Point flopped down behind the unarmed launcher and aimed it over the parapet at the stationary El Al plane. "You should look at this," he told the prefect. "It gives me the creeps how close that bastard came to wiping out two hundred people. Buvon here knows the damned thing backwards. He's with the anti-terrorist section . . ."

Grelle was appalled as he took up Point's prone position and gazed through the sight. The Israeli machine, blurred as it was by the rain, came up so close he felt he could reach out and touch it. Flopping beside him, Buvon demonstrated how it worked, even to the extent of inserting a rocket.

"It works on a heat sensor system. There is a device in the nose of the rocket which, once airborne, homes straight on to the highest temperature source within range—in this case, with the Israeli plane just airborne, it would have homed on the heat emitted by the machine's jet engines . . ."

Stretched out in the rain, Grelle listened a little longer. "Can the pilot of the plane take any evading action?" he enquired as he handled the weapon. "Is there any hope?"

"None at all," Buvon replied briskly. "Even if he saw it coming, which is doubtful, even if he changed course— even more doubtful—the heat sensor would simply change direction, too and go on heading for the target until they collided. Then—boom!—it's all over . . ."

Remembering that Florian was due to fly off from this airport to Marseilles in only a few days, Grelle took an immediate decision. "I'm carrying this hideous thing back to Paris myself," he announced. "Have it put in the rear of my car . . ." With Boisseau behind the wheel, they drove to Sûreté headquarters at the rue des Saussaies where the prefect personally watched it being put away inside a strong-room on the fourth floor which itself was isolated inside another room. Demanding all the keys to both rooms, he was handed three and when he asked if these were all he received an equivocal reply. "There were four originally, but one of them was a bad fit. I understand it was destroyed."

"No one, absolutely no one is to be allowed in this room without my permission," Grelle ordered. "When the army people want to have a look at it, they must come to me for the keys . . ."

They had only just returned to the préfecture when Boisseau received a phone call. He went to the prefect's office to report immediately. "The Algerian has gone to earth and we know where. He is inside an abandoned apartment block off the Boulevard de la Chapelle in the eighteenth arrondisement. The address is 17 rue Réamur . . ."

"That stinking rabbit warren," Grelle commented. It was the Arab Quarter in the Goutte-d'Or district, an area which had been an Arab preserve for over thirty years. "Any more of the gang visible?" he enquired.

"There is no sign of anyone else about and we think he is alone. One of the patrol-car men who overtook him thinks he identified him as Abou Benefeika, but that's not certain."

"He can't give us the slip, I hope?" Grelle asked.

"He's safely penned up and we have men watching both front and rear entrances. Also there are good observation points where we can watch him night and day. Do we bring him in or leave him to ferment?"

"Let him ferment," Grelle ordered.

In Basel at the Hotel Victoria Alan Lennox heard the news report of the alert at Orly over his bedroom radio. He thought nothing of it as he sat smoking a cigarette, checking his watch occasionally; terrorist alerts at Orly had happened before. The Englishman was killing time, something he disliked, but there was a right moment to cross the border into France; about eleven in the morning he estimated. Earlier the passport control people would only just have come on duty; they would be irritable and alert as they started a new day; and they would give their full attention to the few travellers passing through.

At 11 a.m. precisely he left the Victoria, crossed the street and went inside the Hauptbahnhof. At Basel Hauptbahnhof there is a French frontier control post unique in Europe. While techincally still on Swiss soil, all French nationals returning home from Basel pass through a special checkpoint quite separate from Swiss passport control. The checkpoint is manned by French officials who deal only with their own countrymen. It was a perfect opportunity to test the false papers Peter Lanz had supplied.

If there was trouble—if the falseness of the papers was detected—he would be handed over to the Swiss police. He could then give them Peter Lanz's name and phone number and he had little doubt that, bearing in mind the discreet co-operation which goes on between the Swiss and German authorities, that Lanz could persuade them to release him into the hands of the German police. Lennox was not a man who had survived so far by taking unnecessary risks. Carrying his Swiss case, he joined the queue which was moving quickly.

"Papers . . ."

It was unfortunate: the examination was conducted by one of the younger officials, a sharp-eyed man whose enthusiasm had not yet been dulled by years of looking at dog-eared passports. The official compared the photograph carefully with the man standing in front of him, then disappeared inside a room. Inwardly tense, Lennox leaned against the counter with a Gitane hanging out of the corner of his mouth, looked at the woman next to him and shrugged. These bloody bureaucrats, he seemed to say. The official came back, still holding the document.

"Which countries have you visited?"

"Switzerland and Germany . . ." It is always best to tell the truth whenever you can. Lennox looked bored as the young official continued examining the passport as though it were the first he had ever seen, as though he was sure there was something wrong. "How long have you been away from France?"

"Three weeks . . ."

Always just answer the question. Never go babbling on, embroidering with a lot of detail. It is the oldest trick in the book, used by officials all over the world; get the suspect talking and sooner or later he trips himself up. The official handed back the passport. Lennox picked up his bag, was waved on by Customs, and walked on to the platform where the train for France was waiting. Within two hours he would be in Strasbourg.

The Munich express was due to arrive at Strasbourg in two hours. In the corner of a first-class compartment Carel Vanek sat reading a French detective novel and the aroma of an expensive cigar filled the compartment as the Czech smoked fitfully. Opposite him the austere Brunner did not approve of the cigar; he had even made the mistake of making a reference to it. "When we get back we shall have to account for our expenditure . . ."

"In a capitalist society an air of affluence opens all doors," Vanek replied and turned the page of his book.

The truth was that Vanek enjoyed the good things of life and regarded Brunner as a bit of a peasant. Now, as they came closer to Strasbourg, he read his novel with only half his mind. He was thinking of Dieter Wohl, the

German who lived in Freiburg. Of the three people on the list the Commando had to "pay a visit"—Vanek's euphemism for terminating a life—the German was closest to them at this moment. It seemed logical that Dieter Wohl should be the first to receive a visit from them.

But the idea had not appealed to the Czech when he had first examined the list, and he found the same objections influencing him now they were approaching the Rhine. The point was Vanek did not wish to risk alerting a second security service—that of Germany—so early on in the trip; just in case the killing of Wohl by "accident" went wrong. And later they would have to return across Germany from France on their way home. No, better leave Dieter Wohl until later. So, for quite different reasons, Vanek had taken the same decision as Alan Lennox—to go into France first.

Closing his novel, he puffed more cigar smoke in the direction of Brunner. Again Lansky was travelling on his own in a separate coach; it was good tactics and it also suited Vanek who disliked the younger Czech. Soon they would reach Kehl, the last stop inside Germany before the express crossed the Rhine bridge into France. He decided they would get off at Kehl—even though it would have been simpler to stay on the express until it reached Strasbourg. Vanek had an idea—which was not entirely incorrect—that the frontier control people cast a careful eye over international expresses. Getting off at Kehl, they could board a more local train to take them on to Strasbourg, and possibly purchase certain extra clothes while they were in the German city. He took out his papers and looked at them. When they arrived in Strasbourg they would be three French tourists returning from a brief winter sports holiday in Bavaria. There was no longer anything to link them with Czechoslovakia.

Leon Jouvel, 49 rue de l'Épine, Strasbourg, was the first name on the list Col Lasalle had handed to Alan Lennox.

Fifty-three years old, Jouvel was small and plump with a bushy grey moustache, a shock of grey hair and a plump right hand which liked to squeeze the knees of pretty girls when he thought he could get away with it. Louise Vallon, who worked in the television shop he owned, found him easy to handle. "He's not dangerous," she confided to a friend, "only hopeful, but recently he's seemed so depressed, almost frightened . . ."

What was frightening Leon Jouvel was something which had happened over thirty years ago and now seemed to have come back to haunt him. In 1944, working with the Resistance in the Lozère, he had been the Leopard's radio operator. Even holding that key position, like everyone else he had no idea what the Communist leader looked like. He had always known when the Leopard was close because the wolfhound, César, would give a warning growl. Jouvel hated the beast, but obeying instructions he always forced himself to turn his back on the animal and wait with his notebook until the Leopard arrived and gave him the message to transmit. Noting down the message—which he immediately burned after transmission— he would hurry away to his concealed transmitter, aware only that the Resistance chief was a very tall man; once, on a sunny day, he had seen his shadow.

But because of his job—and the frequency of these brief communications—Jouvel was more familiar with the Leopard's *voice* than anyone in the Resistance group, and Jouvel had an acute ear for sounds. During the past eighteen months—since Guy Florian had become president—Jouvel had changed considerably. All his friends commented on the change. Normally jovial and talkative, Jouvel became irritable and taciturn, often not hearing what was said to him. It was the frequent appearance of the president on television which had unnerved the plump little man.

A widower, it had been Jouvel's custom to while away the evenings in bars and cafés, gossiping with friends. Now he sat at home alone in his second-floor apartment, watching the news bulletins and political broadcasts, waiting for Guy Florian to appear, to *speak*. During a Florian speech he would sit in front of the television set with his eyes shut, listening intently. It was quite macabre—the similarity in the voices, but it was impossible to be sure.

Sitting with his eyes closed he could have sworn he was listening to the Leopard standing behind him, giving him yet another message to transmit in those far-off days up in the mountains. He studied the speech mannerisms, noted the little hesitations which preceded a torrent of abuse as the president attacked the Americans. At first he told himself it was impossible: the Leopard had died in Lyon in 1944. Then he began to think back over the past, recalling the burial of the Leopard deep in the forest which he had attended. The four men who had handled the coffin—all of whom died a few days later in an ambush —had been in a great hurry to get the job over with. There had been a lack of *respect*. A few months later Jouvel had been terrified by a visit from Col Lasalle, who had arrived in mufti.

"This man, the Leopard," the colonel had said, "if you took down all these signals from him, surely you could recognize his voice if you heard it again?"

"It was so long ago . . ."

Fencing inexpertly with one of the most accomplished interrogators in France, Jouvel had managed not to reveal his crazy suspicion. Like many Frenchmen, Jouvel mistrusted both the police and the army, preferring to go his own way and not get mixed up with authority. But had he convinced the sharp-eyed little colonel he knew nothing? Jouvel sweated over the visit for weeks after Lasalle had gone. And now, only eight days before Christmas, there had been the incident this evening.

Locking up his shop at six, he walked back over the bridge from the Quai des Bateliers into the deserted old quarter. After dark the rue de l'Épine is a sinister street where ancient five-storey buildings hem in the shadows and your footsteps echo eerily on the cobbles. There is no one about and not too much light. This evening Jouvel was sure he had heard footsteps behind him. Turning round suddenly, he caught the movement of a shadow which merged into the wall.

He forced himself to turn round and walk back, and it reminded him of all those occasions when he had once forced himself to turn his back on the Leopard's vicious wolfhound. Jouvel was trembling as he made himself go on walking back down the shadowed street, and he was sweating so much his glasses steamed up. Reaching the doorway where he had seen the shadow move, he couldn't be sure whether anyone was there. Pretending to adjust his glasses, he wiped them quickly with his fingers. The blur cleared and a heavily-built man with a fat face stared back at him out of the doorway. Jouvel almost fainted.

The fat-faced man, who wore a dark coat and a soft hat, lifted a flask and drank from it noisily, then belched. Jouvel's pounding heart began to slow down. A drunk! Without saying a word he walked back up the street to his home. Behind him police detective Armand Bonheur was also sweating as he remained in the doorway. Good God, he had almost blown it! And the inspector's instructions had been explicit.

"Whatever happens, Jouvel must not suspect he is being tailed. The order comes right down the line from Paris . . ."

Turning in under the stone archway of No. 49, Jouvel went across the cobbled courtyard and into the building beyond. Climbing the staircase to the second floor, he was unlocking his apartment door when a red-haired girl peered out of the next apartment. He smiled pleasantly. "Good evening, M'selle . . ." Disappointed, the girl made a rude gesture at his back. "Silly old ponce." For Denise Viron anything over forty was fodder for the graveyard; anything under forty, fair game.

Inside his apartment Jouvel hurried over to the television set and switched on. Brewing himself a cup of tea in the kitchen, he came back, settled in an old armchair and waited. Florian's head and shoulders appeared on the screen a few minutes later. Jouvel closed his eyes. "The Americans want to turn Europe into one vast supermarket, selling American goods, of course . . ." And still Jouvel couldn't be certain. I must be going mad, he thought.

"Mr. Jouvel? He is away today but he is back in Strasbourg tomorrow. The shop opens at nine . . ."

Louise Vallon, Jouvel's assistant, put down the phone and thought no more about the call as she turned to attend to a customer. In a bar close to the shop Carel Vanek replaced the receiver and walked out on to the Quai des Bateliers where Walther Brunner sat waiting in the Citroën DS 23 they had just hired from the Hertz branch in the Boulevard de Nancy. "He's out of town today," Vanek said as he settled himself behind the wheel, "but he's back tomorrow. Which just gives us nice time to soak up some atmosphere . . ."

When the Soviet Commando had arrived aboard a local train from Kehl they split up again as they had done in Munich. Lansky had simply walked across the large cobbled square outside the station and booked a room at the Hotel Terminus in the name of Lambert. After depositing three sets of skis—which would never be collected—in the luggage store at Strasbourg Gare, Vanek and Brunner took two separate cabs at intervals to the Hotel Sofitel where they registered, quite independently, as Duval and Bonnard. Meeting outside the hotel, they went to the Boulevard de Nancy and hired the Citroën.

Before leaving his room at the Sofitel, Vanek had consulted Bottin, the French telephone directory, to check on Leon Jouvel's address. Yes, it was the address given on the list, 49 rue de l'Épine, but there had also been the

address of a television shop in the Quai des Bateliers.
Using a street map of Strasbourg purchased from a newspaper kiosk, Vanek and Brunner had driven round the old
city to locate both addresses before Vanek made his first
call from the bar. He then drove a short distance from the
quai before handing over the car to his companion. For
the rest of the afternoon and most of the evening the
three men would move round Strasbourg on their own,
familiarizing themselves with the city's layout and getting
the feel of being in France.

"Buy a paper, go into bars and cafés, chat with everyone you can," Vanek had instructed. "Start merging with
your background by mixing with it. Take a short bus-ride,
find out what people are talking about. By tonight I want
you to be more French than the French themselves . . ."

Following his own advice, Vanek sampled the flavour
of Strasbourg by working. Unlike Brunner, from now on
he walked everywhere, knowing that the easiest way to get
your bearings in a strange city is to walk. As the street
map indicated, the old quarter of the city was for all
practical purposes an island surrounded by water, the
huge "moat" being formed by the river Il which encircles
the heart of Strasbourg. A series of bridges all round the
perimeter crossed the river into this ancient heart built,
for the most part, in the fourteenth century. It was still
daylight at four o'clock, but only just in the narrow, silent
rue de l'Épine, when Vanek walked in under the archway
of No. 49.

One of the numerous plates at the entrance to the
building registered the fact that Leon Jouvel lived on
the second floor, and he was knocking on the door of the
second-floor apartment when the door of the neighbouring
apartment opened and a red-haired girl peered out at him
speculatively. "He's gone away for the day to see his
sister—back in the morning," she informed the Czech.
"Do you think I could help you in some way?"

Vanek, careful to eye her hips and other parts of her

anatomy with due appreciation, had no trouble at all in extracting from Denise Viron the information he needed. He was, he explained, a market research specialist. "Mr Leon Jouvel is one of the people chosen to answer our questionnaire . . . a survey on pension needs." Within a few minutes he learned that Jouvel was a widower, that he occupied the apartment on his own, that he possessed no animals—here Vanek had in mind a guard-dog—that he was out all day at the shop and only returned at 6.30 in the evenings, that he was no longer a sociable man, so there were few visitors.

"If you would like to come in," the girl said, smoothing her skirt down over her long, lithe legs, "I might be able to help you in other ways . . ."

Vanek, whose appetite for women was healthy, made it a point never to mix business with pleasure. And in any case, the girl had so far not had too close a look at him in the gloomy hall. Explaining that he had five more people to interview that day, he left her with a vague impression he would certainly be calling on her again within a few days. As arranged earlier, at eight in the evening he met Brunner and Lansky at a corner of the Place Kléber as snow drifted down over the huddled rooftops of Strasbourg. Taking them into a crowded bar, he found a table at the back.

". . . and so," he continued a few minutes later, "it is made to order for a quick solution. You visit him tomorrow night, soon after 6.30 when he has returned home . . ." It was Lansky he had chosen to pay a call on Leon Jouvel. "He is a widower and lives on his own. He has a second-floor apartment and the building is quiet. No one about at all except for a red-headed girl who lives next door. She could be a nuisance—she's looking for somebody to keep her bed warm."

"I don't like it," Brunner said. "You're moving too fast. We need more time to check on this man . . ."

"Which is exactly what we have not got," Vanek

snapped. "In five days from now—December 22—we
have to complete the whole job, which includes visiting
three people, one of them in Germany. So, the strategy
is simple—we deal with the first two on the list
quickly . . ."

"If the place is empty, I'd better take a preliminary look
inside it tonight," Lansky said. He stood up. "We'll meet
at the bus station in the Place de la Gare tomorrow at
the time agreed?"

"It's dangerous to hurry it," Brunner muttered.

Vanek leaned forward until his face almost touched
Brunner's, still speaking very quietly. "Think, man! It
will be Saturday night—the body won't even be discovered
until Monday morning at the earliest . . ."

The Rope used the set of French skeleton keys—which
had been flown from Kiev to Tábor with the false Sûreté
cards at the last moment—to open Jouvel's apartment
door. It was a four-roomed apartment: a living-dining
room with a colour television set, two bedrooms, a kitchen
and a bathroom. When he entered the apartment the first
thing he did was to draw the curtains, then he examined
the place with the aid of a pocket torch. Everything was
neat and tidy; Lansky reminded himself he must remember this when it came to setting the stage.

Lansky had brought no rope with him; purchasing a
length of rope can be dangerous if the police institute
a proper check afterwards. Instead he looked round for
something on the premises—a sash cord, a belt, anything
strong enough to hang a man by the neck until he is dead.
Inside an old-fashioned, free-standing wardrobe he found
what he was looking for—an old woollen dressing-gown
with a cord-belt round the waist.

He tested the strength of the cord carefully by tying
one end to the leg of the old-fashioned gas cooker in the
kitchen and pulling hard on it. If necessary, to give it
more strength he could immerse it in water later. Privately,

he had already rejected Brunner's suggestion that Jouvel might drown in his own bath; that involved undressing a man, which took more time. And suicide was always something the police were willing to accept with a widower living on his own. He next tested the handle on the outside of the bathroom door to make sure it was firm. Brunner had told him it was not unusual for people to hang themselves on the inside of a bathroom door; perhaps they felt they could do the job here in decent privacy.

Twenty minutes is the maximum time a burglar allows for being inside a house; after that the statistics show the law of averages moves against him. Lansky carefully timed his visit for twelve minutes. He had re-opened the curtains and was ready to leave when he heard voices in the corridor near by. With his ear pressed against the door panel he listened carefully. Two voices, a man's and a girl's, probably the girl in the next apartment Vanek had mentioned. They were talking in French but Lansky couldn't catch what was being said. He waited until the voices stopped, a door closed, and footsteps retreated along the corridor. When he came out and relocked Jouvel's door the building was full of silence. In less than twenty-four hours, at seven on the following evening, he would return to pay his last call on Leon Jouvel.

He emerged from the archway into the rue de l'Épine with equal caution. But tonight police detective Armand Bonheur was fifty kilometres away in Sarrebourg, sitting cold and depressed inside his car while he watched the house where Leon Jouvel was paying his duty call on his elderly sister. Lansky waited a little longer until the only person in sight, a man walking away towards the Place Kléber, disappeared. The man was Alan Lennox.

At eight o'clock in the evening of Friday, 17 December, at about the time the Soviet Commando went into a bar near the Place Kléber, André the Squirrel made his sug-

gestion to Marc Grelle in the prefect's office in Paris.
Would it be worth while for him to fly to Strasbourg to
interview Leon Jouvel and then go on to see the other
witness in Colmar? "If Lasalle is right and these people
knew the Leopard they might be able to tell me something."

Grelle considered the suggestion and then decided
against it. For the moment at least. The trouble was he
needed his deputy in Paris to help complete the security
fence he was building round the president. "Let it wait,"
Grelle advised.

Travelling up from Switzerland by train, Alan Lennox
had arrived at Strasbourg station while the Soviet Commando was still in Kehl across the river Rhine. Since
there are only two or three first-class hotels in the city, it
was not surprising that he chose the Hotel Sofitel, which
is built like an upended shoe-box and more like the type
of hotel found in America. Registering in the name of
Jean Bouvier, he went up to his fourth-floor room which
overlooked a concrete patio.

His first action was to consult Bottin, the telephone
directory, and like Vanek in the same hotel only two
hours later, he noted that Leon Jouvel had two addresses, one of which corresponded with the Lasalle list,
the other a television shop. Unlike Vanek, he phoned the
shop from the hotel room. The number went on ringing,
but no one answered. In the shop Louise Vallon was
having her busiest time of the day and she was damned
if she was going to attend to the phone as well. In the
Sofitel Lennox replaced the receiver. The obvious next
move was to try Jouvel at home.

Checking the street-guide he had bought at the station,
he found that the rue de l'Épine was only a short walk
from the hotel. Putting on his coat and hat again, he went
out into a world of slow-falling snowflakes which made
it seem even more like Christmas in Strasbourg. Unlike

Paris, the city was full of reminders of the approaching festive season; the Place Kléber was decorated with enormous Christmas trees which lit up at night. In less than ten minutes Lennox was standing at the archway to 49 rue de l'Épine.

Leon Jouvel. The door on the second floor carried the name on a plate beside it. Lennox knocked for the third time but there was no reply. And for once the door of the neighbouring apartment was not opened by the redheaded and enthusiastic Denise Viron; at lunchtime she was still in bed and fast asleep. Leaving the building, he went out to find somewhere to eat.

In the afternoon he visited the shop on the Quai des Bateliers and it was full of customers. The fair-haired girl behind the counter was having trouble coping with the rush and there was no sign of a man in the place. While she was occupied he peered into the back office and found it empty. He decided to go back to Jouvel's apartment in the middle of the evening. If you want to interview a man the place to corner him is at home, after he has finished his day's work and eaten—when he is relaxed. Lennox went back to No. 49 rue de l'Épine at 8.30 p.m.

Denise Viron was just going out for the evening, wearing a brilliant green coat which she felt sure suited her exciting personality, when Lennox stopped in front of Leon Jouvel's door. Eyeing him, wondering whether she really was going out after all, she stood outside her doorway with the light still on so it threw into stark relief her fullbreasted figure.

"He's away for the night," she said. "Was there something I might be able to help you with?"

Lennox, who had his hand raised to knock on the door Lansky had opened with his skeleton keys only a few minutes earlier, took off his hat instead. He moved a few paces towards the girl who took a tentative step back inside her own apartment. Pulling at her long, red hair, she watched him with her lips slightly parted. God, a tart, Lennox thought. "You mean Mr Leon Jouvel?" he enquired in French. "It's rather urgent—you're sure he won't be back tonight?"

The girl puckered her over-painted mouth. "Popular today, aren't we? Jouvel, I mean. I've just had one of those market research blokes asking after him this afternoon. No accounting for tastes."

"Market research?"

"That's right. You know the type—nosey. Personally I think it's an impertinence the way they ask you all those intimate questions . . ."

"Mr Jouvel," Lennox interjected with a smile. "When will he be back then?"

"Tomorrow—Saturday. That market research chap . . ."

"Is there someone I could leave a message with? His wife, perhaps?"

"He's a widower. Not interested in women any more." She gazed past Lennox's shoulder. "Personally I think when you get to that stage life isn't worth . . ."

"No one else in the apartment?"

"No. He lives alone." The girl was frowning, as though making a tremendous intellectual effort to solve a problem. "Funny, I'm having almost the same conversation with you as I had with that other chap. What makes Jouvel so popular all of a sudden? Weeks go by and he sits alone in there glued to the box and now . . ."

"He's home all day Saturday?" Lennox enquired.

"There you go again—same kind of question." Denise Viron was beginning to tire of the conversation. "All day Saturday he's at the shop," she snapped. "And it's not a good time to see him—Saturday is his big day. And you won't find him back here before 6.30 in the evening. Are you another market research chap?" she enquired sarcastically.

"I knew him a long time ago," Lennox replied vaguely

and excused himself. He heard a door slam as he went down the stairs and behind him Denise Viron re-buttoned the coat she had unfastened as they talked. She was going to have to go out, and in this weather, for God's sake.

At 5.30 p.m. on Saturday evening detective Armand Bonheur yawned in the police office and checked his watch. Soon he would be on the bloody night-watch again, taking over from his colleague who at this moment was discreetly observing Leon Jouvel's shopfront on the Quai des Bateliers. Bonheur would then wait on the quai for Jouvel to lock up so he could follow him and keep an eye on who went in and out of No. 49 rue de l'Épine. Already Bonheur was getting to hate this duty. What the hell had Paris got on a man like Jouvel anyway?

It would not have been possible for even Borisov, his trainer, to recognize Lansky easily as he left the Hotel Terminus with a group of people who had just come out of the lift. Wearing a German suit and a Tyrolean hat he had purchased during the Commando's brief stay in Kehl, Lansky was also equipped with a pair of thick-lensed, hornrim spectacles of the type normally only worn by old men. Even his walk had changed as he shuffled across the wind-swept Place de la Gare with his hands deep inside his overcoat pockets, a coat also purchased in Kehl. To complete the transformation he carried an umbrella which he had previously ruffled and dirtied. Muffled up inside a scarf, shuffling across the cobbles, Antonin Lansky now looked more like a man in his late sixties.

Reaching the station, he mooched inside the glassed-in restaurant which fronted on the square, sat down at a table and ordered coffee in German. Occasionally as he sat there amid people waiting for trains he checked his watch. He would be visiting Leon Jouvel somewhere be-

tween 6.30 and 7 p.m., catching him off guard soon after
he had arrived home.

At 6 p.m. Alan Lennox sat at a window table in the café
next door to Jouvel's television shop drinking coffee. It
was well after dark and under the street lamps the cobbles on the quai gleamed from the recent snow flurries.
He had decided to take Denise Viron's advice, to let
Leon Jouvel, whom he had seen at the other side of his
shop window, get his big day over with before tackling
the Frenchman. And since it was Saturday he thought it
highly likely Jouvel would stop off at a bar on the way
home—and what better place to get a man talking than
in a bar?

A trained observer—trained by long experience—Lennox had automatically noticed the man in the raincoat
on the far side of the quai who stood under a lamp reading
a newspaper. Probably waiting for his girl, Lennox sur-
mised: at intervals the waiting man checked his watch
and looked up and down the quai as though expecting
someone. Lennox finished his third cup of coffee. To spin
out the time he had ordered a pot, and the francs for
the bill were already on the table so he could leave at a
moment's notice. At 6.5 p.m. a short, plump figure with
a bushy moustache came out and locked up the shop.

As Jouvel said goodnight to his assistant, Louise Vallon,
and crossed the quai Lennox emerged from the café
and paused at the kerb to light a cigarette. No need to
follow too close in this part of Strasbourg and the shopowner was wearing a distinctive yellow raincoat. Putting
away his French Feudor lighter, Lennox was on the
verge of stepping into the road and then stopped before
he had moved. The man under the lamp had tucked his
paper under his arm and was strolling after Jouvel. A
coincidence: he had got fed up waiting for his girl.

As the traffic stopped against the lights, Lennox hurried
across and then slowed down again. On the bridge crossing

the river Il to the old quarter he saw the man with the
paper and ahead of him Jouvel. The shopowner, who had
crossed the bridge, had stopped to peer in through the
lighted windows of a restaurant as though wondering
whether to go inside. The man with the paper had also
stopped, bending down as he pretended to tie his shoe-
lace. It was now quite obvious to Lennox that Leon Jouvel
was being followed by someone else.

As Jouvel left the restaurant and crossed the road to
turn up the rue de l'Épine—which meant he was going
straight home—Lennox changed direction to approach No.
49 by a separate route. The man with the paper had left
the bridge and followed Jouvel. In that lonely and deserted street a second shadow would be a little too conspicuous. Familiar now with the immediate area, Lennox
walked rapidly up the rue des Grandes Arcades and then
into a side street leading into the rue de l'Épine, arriving
just in time to see Jouvel turn in under the archway.
Lower down the street the man with the paper disappeared inside an alcove as Denise Viron, wearing her
bright green coat, came out of the archway. She stopped
when she saw Lennox.

"You've come back to see me?" she enquired hopefully.

"Another night maybe? There are plenty of nights
yet," Lennox told her.

Their voices carried down the narrow canyon of the
empty street to where detective Armand Bonheur waited,
huddled inside the alcove. His instructions had been complex, too complex for his liking. He must keep Jouvel
under surveillance. He must not let the shopowner know
he was being watched. He must keep an eye open for an
Englishman called Lennox, and the description had been
vague. Hearing the reply to the girl's invitation given in
perfect French, Bonheur did not give a moment's thought
to the Englishman he had been told about. He settled
down to a long wait.

As far as Bonheur was concerned the form of surveillance was very unsatisfactory—it was impossible to station himself inside the building, to keep close observation on Jouvel. The only positive factor in his favour was that the building had no rear exit. Everyone who entered No. 49 had to go in under the archway. It was just after seven—it had begun to rain again—when Bonheur saw a shuffling old man with an umbrella approaching No. 49.

Lennox rapped on Jouvel's door only a minute or so after the Frenchman had arrived home. Lennox's manner was businesslike as he explained he was a reporter from the Paris newspaper, *Le Monde*, which was going to run a series on the wartime Resistance. He understood that Jouvel had been an active member of the Lozère group and would like to talk to him about his experiences. Nothing, he assured Jouvel, would be published without his permission. And there would be, Lennox added casually, a fee . . .

"What sort of fee?" Jouvel enquired.

He was standing in the doorway, still wearing his yellow raincoat, his mind in a turmoil. He had asked the question to give himself a little more time to think. For over a year he had fretted over whether to approach the authorities with his suspicion, and here was a golden opportunity presented to him on a plate. Should he talk to this man, he was wondering.

"Two thousand francs," Lennox said crisply. "That is, if the information is worth it—makes good copy. In any case, I will pay ten per cent of that sum for fifteen minutes of your time."

"You had better come in," said Jouvel.

Sitting on an old-fashioned settee in the living-room, Lennox did most of the talking for the first few minutes, trying to put Jouvel at his ease. The Frenchman's reaction puzzled him. Jouvel sat facing him in an arm-chair, staring

at him with a dazed look as though trying to make up
his mind about something. When he mentioned the Leopard, Jouvel closed his eyes and then opened them again.

"What about the Leopard?" the Frenchman asked
hoarsely. "I worked closely with him as radio operator,
but he is dead, surely?"

"Is he?"

The brief question, phrased instinctively by Lennox as
he detected the query at the end of Jouvel's own question,
had a strange effect on the Frenchman. He swallowed,
stared at Lennox, then looked away and taking a handkerchief out of his pocket he dried the moist palms of
his chubby little hands.

"Of course," Lennox went on, "if you prefer it we could
print your story as being by 'an anonymous but reliable
witness.' Then no one would connect you with it but you
would still get the money . . ."

Something snapped inside Jouvel's mind. The pressure
he had lived under for months became unbearable now he
had someone he could talk to. He told Lennox the whole
story. The Englishman, who for the sake of appearances
had taken out his reporter's notebook, was careful not to
look at Jouvel as he went on talking in agitated bursts. "It
must seem ridiculous to you . . . every time I hear him
on television . . . the Leopard, I know, was shot during
1944—and yet . . ."

As the words came tumbling out it was like a penitent
confessing to a priest, relieving himself. At first Lennox
was sceptical, thinking he was interviewing a lunatic, but
as Jouvel went on talking, pouring out words, he began
to wonder. "The way they handled the coffin at the
burial point . . . no respect . . . brutally . . . as though
nothing was inside . . ."

At the end of fifteen minutes Lennox stood up to go.
The Frenchman was repeating himself. Instead of the two
hundred francs Lennox handed over five hundred out
of the funds Lanz had provided. "You will come back

tomorrow," Jouvel urged, "I may have more to tell you . . ." It was untrue, but the agitated little shopowner, unsure now of what he had done, wanted to give himself the chance to withdraw the statement if, when the morning came, he felt he had made a terrible mistake.

"I'll come tomorrow," Lennox promised.

He left the apartment quickly before the Frenchman could ask for a telephone number or address where he could be reached. Going down the dimly-lit staircase deep in thought, he pulled himself up sharply before he crossed the courtyard: he was travelling with false papers so he had better be on the alert every moment he was in France. Lennox walked with a natural quietness and he was coming out of the archway when he cannoned heavily against an old man stooped under an umbrella. Slipping on the wet cobbles, the man lost his pebble glasses and his Tyrolean hat was knocked sideways half off his head. By the light of the street lamp Lennox caught a glimpse of a face. The man swore in German.

"A thousand apologies . . ."

Lennox had replied in French as he bent down and picked up the pebble glasses, relieved to find they were intact. A gloved hand came out from under the adjusted umbrella and accepted the glasses without a word. Lennox shrugged as the man shuffled off inside the building, then he walked out and went up the rue de l'Épine in the direction of the Place Kléber, still thinking about what Leon Jouvel had told him.

Half-frozen inside his alcove, detective Armand Bonheur continued to do his duty, recording everything that occurred in his notebook with the aid of his Feudor lighter, adding to earlier entries. *6.30.* Jouvel returns home. *6.31.* Denise Viron departs. *6.31.* Viron's friend arrives. *7.02.* Viron's friend departs. (He had assumed from the conversation he had overheard that Denise Viron knew Lennox well.) *7.02*. Umbrella man arrives. *7.32*. Umbrella man departs.

11

The police discovered Leon Jouvel hanging from the inside of his bathroom door the following morning.

"It will be Saturday night—the body won't even be discovered until Monday morning . . ." It was a shrewd and reasonable calculation on the part of Carel Vanek, but the shrewdest plans can be upset by tiny human factors. Sunday, 19 December, was close to Christmas, so before he left his shop on the Saturday evening Leon Jouvel had persuaded Louise Vallon to come in for a few hours on Sunday morning to help prepare for the expected Monday rush of business. "I'll pay you double," he had promised her, "and in cash, so forget the tax man. And I'll be here at 8.30, so mind you're prompt . . ."

By nine o'clock on the Sunday morning Louise Vallon, who had her own shop key, was sufficiently surprised by Jouvel's non-appearance to phone him. There was no reply. She called him again at 9.15 and then, growing worried, at regular ten-minute intervals. At 10 a.m. she phoned the police.

The inspector in charge of the surveillance on Jouvel, a man called Rochat, went to the apartment himself, worried about what the reaction from Paris might be. After talking to the medical examiner and checking the scene of the death, Rochat—initially suspicious—was soon convinced that Leon Jouvel had committed suicide. Pur-

Blan

suing this line of enquiry, he quickly found evidence to back up his opinion. A number of Jouvel's friends told him how the Frenchman had seemed worried for several months, that he had complained of lack of sleep, that he had stopped spending his evenings in bars as had once been his habit. No one could say why Jouvel had been worried but Rochat thought he knew when he discussed the case with his detective, Bonheur.

"A widower living alone—first losing interest in his friends, later in life itself. It forms a pattern . . ."

Rochat's complacent view of the case lasted exactly three hours. It was shattered when he received a call from the Paris préfecture informing him that André Boisseau was already on his way to Strasbourg. Forgetting the recent edict from the Elysée, Rochat protested that the Paris préfecture had no jurisdiction outside the capital. "It is my case," he said stiffly. He then received a further shock when the caller revealed that it was the police prefect of Paris himself speaking.

"And this," Grelle blandly informed him, "does come under my jurisdiction since it may well concern the safety of the president of the French Republic . . ."

Despite his irritation with what he regarded as Parisian interference in a local affair, Rochat had at least had the sense to phone Boisseau and inform him of the apparent suicide before he left to visit Jouvel's apartment. The man in Paris fired a number of questions at him, put the phone down and went straight to the office of the prefect who was working on Sunday—like a juggler trying to keep half a dozen balls in the air at once.

"Leon Jouvel," Boisseau announced, "has just died in Strasbourg. He is supposed to have committed suicide. I don't think that Rochat—the man in charge down there—is too bright. I checked up on him—he's fifty-six and still only an inspector."

"Does the death have to be suspect?" Grelle enquired.

"Not necessarily, but over the years too many people who were connected with the Leopard have died. Now we hear that Jouvel . . ."

"And," Grelle smiled grimly, "since we are getting nowhere at this end you are restless to check something else."

It was true that they were getting no results from their enquiries in Paris. The discreet surveillance on Danchin and Blanc had turned up nothing promising. Danchin, dedicated to his work as always, had hardly left the Ministry of the Interior where he had an apartment on the first floor overlooking the Place Beauvau, so frequently, unlike other cabinet ministers, he didn't even dine out.

Alain Blanc had also spent long hours at his Ministry, but twice he had visited the address in Passy district where he met his mistress, Gisèle Manton. She, also, had been followed, and Grelle had a detailed list of where she had been and whom she had met. For neither of the two ministers did there seem to be any trace of a Soviet link. Grelle, without revealing it to Boisseau, was beginning to get worried. Could he have made a terrible mistake about the whole business?

"You'd better take a look at Strasbourg," he said. "Fly there and back, of course. I need you here in Paris . . ." It was typical of the prefect that after Boisseau had gone he had personally phoned Strasbourg to inform them that Boisseau was on the way. As he put down the receiver he was inclined to agree with his deputy's assessment: Inspector Rochat was never going to set the world on fire.

The proprietor, M. Jouvel, has died suddenly. This shop, therefore will remain closed until further notice.

Lennox stared at the typed notice pasted to the glass door and went on staring beyond it at the girl inside. When he rattled the handle she waved at him to go away and then, as he persisted, came forward glaring and unlocked the door. Taking off his hat, he spoke before she

could start abusing him. "I'm a friend of Leon's—this is
a great shock to me, you'll understand. Can you tell me
what happened?"

Relenting, because he was so polite—and because now
she could see him properly she liked what she saw—
Louise Vallon, who had just returned from being interviewed by Inspector Rochat, let him inside the shop and
told him all the grisly details. Lennox had the impression
that although she managed to bring tears to her eyes, she
was rather enjoying the drama of it all. At the end of ten
minutes he had heard most of the story; he knew that
Leon Jouvel had been found hanging behind his bathroom door, that the time of death was estimated as being
between six-thirty and eight-thirty the previous evening.

"They wanted to know whether anyone normally
visited him at that time," the girl explained tearfully.
"The last words he said to me were . . ."

Lennox excused himself after explaining that he had
been away from Strasbourg for some time and had just
called to have a word. "It wasn't a close friendship," he
went on, aware that this conversation might be reported
back to the police, "but we had business dealings occasionally." Telling her that his name was Zuger, that he had
to catch a train for Stuttgart, he left the shop, walked a
short distance towards the station, and then doubled back
over one of the bridges into the old quarter.

The police patrol-car he had seen earlier was still outside No. 49, so he left the vicinity of the rue de l'Épine.
At one in the afternoon it was still very quiet on Sunday
in Strasbourg as he wandered round the ancient streets
thinking. He found the suicide of Leon Jouvel hard to
swallow. The Frenchman had been followed to his home
by the unknown man with the newspaper only an hour or
so before he had died. He had arranged to meet Lennox
the following morning with the expectation of receiving
more money in exchange for more information. A man
who is contemplating killing himself is hardly likely to

show interest in the prospect of acquiring more money. It smells, Lennox told himself; in fact, it more than smells, it stinks.

Over lunch he wondered whether to go straight on to meet the next witness on the list, Robert Philip of Colmar, and then he decided he would wait until Monday. The local Monday newspaper should carry an account of Jouvel's death, which could be enlightening.

Robert Philip, 8 Avenue Raymond Poincaré, Colmar, was the second name on the list Col Lasalle had handed over to Alan Lennox. It was also the second name on the list Carel Vanek carried in his head. On Saturday evening the three members of the Soviet Commando paid their bills at their respective hotels and left Strasbourg, driving the forty miles to Colmar through a snow-storm. They arrived in the Hans Andersen-like town of steep-roofed buildings and crooked alleyways at 9.30 p.m. and again Vanek took precautions, dropping off Lansky with his suitcase near the station, so that only two men arrived together at the hotel.

Lansky walked into the station booking-hall, enquired the time of a train to Lyon for the following day, and then smoked a Gauloise while he waited for a train to come in—any train. Walking out with the three passengers who got off a local from Strasbourg, he crossed the Place de la Gare to the Hotel Bristol which Vanek and Brunner had entered earlier and booked a room in the name of Froissart. The receptionist, noting he had no car, assumed he had just come off the Strasbourg train.

Upstairs in his bedroom Vanek had followed his usual routine, checking Philip's address in the telephone directory and locating it on the Blay street-guide of Colmar he had obtained from the hall porter. He looked up as Brunner slipped into his room. "This is very convenient —staying here," he informed the Czech. "Philip lives just round the corner . . ."

"If he is home," the pessimistic Brunner replied.

"Let's find out . . ."

Vanek did not use the room phone to call Philip's number; that would have meant going through the hotel switchboard. Instead he went out with Brunner to the car and they drove about a kilometre into the shopping area and entered a bar where Vanek called the number he had found in the directory. The voice which answered the phone was arrogant and brusque. "Robert Philip . . ."

"Sorry, wrong number," Vanek muttered and broke the connection. "He's home," he told Brunner. "Let's go look at the place . . ."

On a snowbound December night at 10.30 p.m. the Avenue Raymond Poincaré was a deserted street of trees and parks with small, grim, two-storey mansions set back behind prison-like railings. No. 8 was a square-looking stone villa with steps leading up to a porch and a gloomy garden beyond the railings. There were lights in the large bay window on the ground floor and the upper storey was in darkness. "I think you can get round the back," Brunner said as the Citroën cruised slowly past the villa and he tried to take in as much detail as he could.

"The next thing to check is whether he lives alone," Vanek remarked. "Tomorrow is Sunday. If we can check out the place in the daytime I think we might just pay a visit to Mr Robert Philip tomorrow night . . ."

"One day you will be too quick . . ."

"Tomorrow is 19 December," Vanek replied calmly. "We have only four days left to visit two people—one of them across the Rhine in Germany. In speed can lie safety. And this will not be a job for the Rope. We have had one suicide, so Robert Philip will have to die by accident . . ."

Earlier on the same day, arriving in Strasbourg by helicopter, Boisseau put Inspector Rochat through a grilling almost without Rochat realizing what was happening. He was well aware he must tread warily: unlike Lyon, Grelle had no particular friendship with the prefect of Strasbourg and the locals were prickly about his arrival. After half an hour he suggested that later Rochat must join him for a drink, but first could they visit the dead man's apartment?

It was Boisseau who extracted from detective Bonheur the information that two men had entered No. 49 between 6.30 and 7.15 p.m., that the second man had shuffled and carried an umbrella, that later the first man had left at 7.2 p.m., followed by the umbrella man half an hour later. "Which was just about the time Jouvel may have died," he pointed out to Rochat.

It was Boisseau who interviewed the other tenants in the building and discovered no one could identify the shuffling man, which meant he did not live there. "Which proves nothing," he informed Rochat, "but why did he come here when we can find no one he visited? And half an hour is a long time for a man to enter a building for no purpose."

It was Boisseau who interviewed Denise Viron, the red-headed girl, obtaining from her a detailed description of two quite different men who had made enquiries about Leon Jouvel the previous day. He made a careful note of the descriptions, observing that neither of them could have been the shuffling man. "Could either of these two men have been English?" he asked at one stage. Denise had shaken her head vigorously, crossing her legs in a provocative way which made Inspector Rochat frown. Boisseau, on the other hand, who was interviewing the girl in her apartment, had noticed the legs appreciatively while he offered her another cigarette.

"Was Jouvel often asked about by people?" he enquired. "Did he have many visitors?"

"Hardly any. The two callers were exceptional . . ."

Boisseau had not blamed Rochat for failing to dig up this information. It was quite clear that his superiors had resented the Paris police prefect's intrusion on their territory and had ordered the inspector to clear up the case quickly. So, once it seemed clear it was suicide, Rochat had enquired no further.

"You are satisfied?" Rochat suggested as he drove the man from Paris back to the airport.

"Are you?" Boisseau countered.

"Technically everything was as it should be—taking into account Jouvel's short stature, the length of the rope, the position of the bathroom chair he had kicked away from under himself. Only an expert could have faked it."

"I find your last observation disturbing," Boisseau said.

Robert Philip, fifty-two years old—the same age as Guy Florian, but there the resemblance ended—rose late from his bed on Sunday morning, and was then annoyed because his companion, Noelle Berger, continued sleeping. Shaking her bare white shoulder roughly, he made his request with his usual finesse. "Get up, you trollop, I want some breakfast . . ."

Separated from his wife, he now consoled himself with a series of fleeting affairs, each of which he took care to ensure did not last too long. As he told his drinking cronies, "Have them in the house for a week and they think they own the place . . ." Of medium height and gross, heavy figure, Philip had a thatch of reddish hair cut *en brosse* and a thick moustache of the same reddish tinge. Grumbling, he went downstairs and pulled back the living-room curtain. At the opposite kerb in the normally deserted street was parked a Citroën with the bonnet up and two men peering inside at the engine. A holdall lay on the pavement with tools spread about. "Serve you right for wasting petrol," Philip muttered, holding his silk dressing-gown round his middle as he went off into the kitchen. A few minutes later, similarly attired, Noelle Berger, small and blonde-haired and with an ample figure, wandered into the living-room in search of a cigarette.

"See the girl," Vanek whispered, his head half under

the Citroën's bonnet. "This is going to be complicated."

"Ideally," Brunner replied, "she should be dealt with away from the house . . ."

"If she leaves the damned place. This is Sunday . . ."

Robert Philip had been the Leopard's armourer during the war, the man in charge of acquiring weapons and ammunition for the Resistance group, a process which normally involved raiding enemy munition stores, and as such he had been one of the key members of the Leopard's staff. Since the war Philip's career had been a success story—if you measure success by the acquisition of a large villa and a sizeable bank account by dubious means. Philip was a gun-runner.

In 1944, while Resistance groups in the Midi were building up huge caches of weapons to support the République Soviétique du Sud the Leopard was on the verge of bringing into existence, Robert Philip was busily diverting some of these weapons to secret hideouts. It must have been a great relief to Philip when the Communist coup failed. Seeing de Gaulle was winning, Philip proclaimed himself a lifelong Gaullist, revealing half of his weapon caches to the General. The other half he salted away as a future investment.

In the years which followed Philip supplied weapons to Fidel Castro in his early days—using the Communist connections he had built up in the Lozère—to Eoka terrorists fighting the British in Cyprus, to Kurdish rebels fighting the Iraqui government, and to anyone hard-pressed enough to pay over-the-odds prices for an inferior product. "I have," as he once boasted to a bar companion, "overtaken my contemporaries." His wife, Yvonne, now occupied an apartment in Paris. "I have pensioned her off," as he was fond of saying. "After all, I do not believe in treating a woman badly . . ."

At two in the afternoon Noelle Berger emerged from the villa alone, well wrapped in a fur coat, and walked the few steps which took her to the station, leaving Robert Philip alone in the house. The Citroën which had been parked opposite to No. 8 had long since disappeared and the only person in sight was a lean, bony-faced individual who stood gazing into a shop window. Noelle went into the station and bought a return ticket to Strasbourg, taking no notice of the man who came up behind her and in his turn purchased a single to the same city.

Vanek's instructions to Lansky had been simple. "I don't think she's his wife—she looked far too young and casual. If she comes out, follow her—unless she has a suitcase, in which case she's leaving, so forget her . . ."

Noelle Berger had decided to go and do some Christmas shopping in Strasbourg to give Philip time to recover his temper. Let him stew in his own juice, she reasoned, and then he'll be glad to see me back this evening. In Strasbourg the shops had opened at two—to scoop in more business since it was so close to Christmas—and Noelle spent quite a lot of Philip's money in the rue des Grandes Arcades. Which damned well serves him right, she told herself. Later she relented and bought him a bright yellow waist-coat. Once, someone nearly knocked her under the wheels of a bus as she waited at a crowded kerbside, but when she looked round she saw only a fat woman behind her. At the end of the afternoon, laden with purchases, she made her way to the quiet district known as Petite France down by the river. She had decided to have a cup of tea with a friend before catching the train back to Colmar.

At the edge of the lonely Place Benjamin Zhia the river Il divides into three different sections before joining up again lower down, and here an intricate network of footwalks crosses the river. There is a lock-gate, a penned-up channel where the water roars through the bottleneck, and sluices which flood out from under a building beyond. The sound of churning river is deafening. Taking a short-cut, Noelle moved out on to the footwalks, quite alone as

far as she knew. She was half-way across, she had heard
nothing above the growling roar of the water, when something made her turn round. Lansky was one step behind
her, both hands upraised. She stared in disbelief as the
hands reached her and shoved. She was half-way down
before she screamed, and her screams were lost in the
boiling sluices which dragged her under and then rushed
her at speed towards the Quai des Bateliers. Bobbing on
the surface of the racing flood her Christmas purchases
had a bizarre, festive look, including a bright yellow
waist-coat which broke free from its wrappings.

   In twenty minutes Lansky was boarding the turbotrain
which would return him to Colmar by seven in the evening. With two people in a house it is too difficult to stage
a convincing double "accident."

12

On the evening of Sunday, 19 December, Grelle waited
in his office for Boisseau to return from Strasbourg, but as
the hours ticked away the police prefect was far from
idle. For a good part of the day he had been immersed in
tightening up the security arrangements for the presidential motorcade drive to Charles de Gaulle Airport—or
Roissy as it was often called—on the morning of 23
December when Florian departed for Russia.

   Marc Grelle had made himself an expert on death by
assassination—on the methods used, on the people who
used them. He had made a particular study of the thirty-
one attempts which had been made to assassinate General

de Gaulle, on the reasons why they might have succeeded, on the reasons why they failed. The list of techniques employed was quite formidable.

Killing by remote detonation of explosive charges under a moving vehicle; killing by sniper armed with rifle and telescopic sight; killing at close quarters—by stabbing, by shooting; killing by imposture—by use of a stolen military or police uniform; killing by motor-bike outrider approaching presidential car; killing by suicidal air collision —one plane crashing into another carrying the president; killing by absurdly exotic methods—using a camera-gun, using explosive-carrying dogs trained to run to a certain spot where the president was due to speak; and killing by *motorized ambush.*

The last method was the favourite, and Grelle could see why. The motorized ambush was most deadly because it used highly-trained thugs at short range, men who could react at the last split second according to circumstances. De Gaulle had, in fact, come closest to death when his motorcade was ambushed by other cars. With this catalogue of assassination attempts in his head Grelle, aided by the tireless Boisseau, set out to counter every one of them. He was still working on the problem when his deputy returned from Strasbourg.

It was nine in the evening and Boisseau, who had had nothing to eat since lunch, sent out to the corner brasserie for food. He ate his meal at the prefect's desk while he went on reporting about the Strasbourg trip. "You see," he continued, "Jouvel's suicide is technically sound, no doubt about that, and few people can fake that kind of death. As you know, they would overlook certain details . . ."

"Unless we are confronted with a professional assassin? Which would give rise to all sorts of unpleasant implications . . ."

"What I don't like," Boisseau remarked, sopping up gravy with a piece of bread, "is those two men who called on the tart and asked her—quite independently—almost the self-same questions about Jouvel. And that when Jouvel normally had no one calling on him or even interested in him. So, who were those two strangers—to say nothing of the man with the umbrella whom none of the tenants recognized?"

"Face it," Grelle advised, "Jouvel may well have committed suicide and these other people are probably irrelevant. At this end we are getting nowhere yet—neither Roger Danchin nor Alain Blanc have made contact with any known Soviet link. We are at that stage we have encountered on so many cases when everything is a blind alley. We have to wait for a development, a pointer . . ." He took out from a locked drawer the list of witnesses compiled by Col Lasalle, glancing at it again. "For all we know the key to the whole thing may be a man we can't even put under surveillance—Dieter Wohl of Freiburg."

"You could phone Peter Lanz of the BND," Boisseau suggested. "He is always very helpful . . ."

"When even here on our home patch we are having to proceed with the secrecy which characterizes conspirators? I dare not start spreading this abroad." Grelle stretched and yawned. "God, I'm tired. No, we must wait—and hope—for a pointer . . ."

In a two-storey house beyond the outskirts of Freiburg, the university town on the edge of the Black Forest, the ex-Abwehr officer, Dieter Wohl, stood by the window of his darkened bedroom as he peered across the fields towards the west, towards France only a few miles away across the Rhine. He was remembering.

A large, well-built man with a strong-jawed face, Wohl was sixty-one years old. As his shrewd blue eyes stared towards Alsace, a faint smile puckered his mouth. It had all been so long ago, so futile. Now there was peace on both sides of the Rhine, thank God; at least he had lived to see that. A retired policeman and widower, Dieter Wohl had plenty of time to think about the past.

It was the banner headline in the *Frankfurter Allgemeine Zeitung* eleven days ago which had first stirred
memories, the story about the attempt to assassinate the
French president. A shocking business. What had intrigued
Wohl had been the name of the woman who had made
the attempt, a Lucie Devaud. Curious. That was the name
of the woman who had died in the sunken car when the
Leopard went into the river. Could there be any connection, he wondered?

After reading the newspaper story Wohl had dug out
one of his old war diaries from the back of his desk. It
had been strictly forbidden by military regulations—to
keep a diary—but many soldiers had broken the regula-
tion; even generals and field-marshals who later made a
pot of money writing up their memoirs. With all the time
in the world on his hands, Wohl read through the whole
of the diary for 1944. As he read, it all came back to him.

As a keen young Abwehr officer stationed in the Lozère
district of France, Wohl had made up his mind to trap
the Leopard. Diligently he picked up every scrap of gossip
about the mysterious Resistance leader and recorded it;
his passion for secrecy, his remarkable network of agents,
his ferocious dog, César—the Leopard's only friend so far
as Wohl could gather.

Once—and only once—Wohl had come close to cap-
turing the Leopard when he received a tip-off that his
adversary would be driving down a certain country road
at a certain time. The ambush was laid on the far side of
a bridge over a river the Leopard would have to cross. At
this point a thick forest came down steeply to the water's
edge and Wohl stationed himself high up among the trees
with a pair of field-glasses. It was close to noon on a
windy day when he saw the car coming behind a screen
of trees, coming at high speed. Through his glasses Wohl
saw an image blurred by foliage—and the speed of the
approaching vehicle.

"God in Heaven!"

A man was behind the wheel and beside him sat a girl, her hair streaming behind her in the wind. This was something Wohl had not anticipated—a woman in the car— and it worried him as the car came closer to the bridge. She must be a Resistance courier, he imagined. He strained to see detail in his glasses and he was excited. This was the first time anyone had actually seen the Leopard. The trouble was he couldn't see the man's face— everything was blurred by the screen of trees and the vehicle's movement. But he would have to slow down as he came up to the river: there was a sharp bend just before the road went over the bridge. Beyond the far end of the bridge was a road-block.

The Leopard made no effort to slow at all. He was reputed always to move at speed to avoid being shot at. With a scream of tyres and a cloud of dust the vehicle careered round the bend and came up on to the bridge. It was a remarkable piece of driving, Wohl admitted, his eyes glued to the glasses. As the car came out of the dust-cloud half-way across the bridge the Leopard must have seen the road-block. He reacted instantly; still moving at speed he drove into the parapet, smashed through it and went down into the river which at this point was eighteen feet deep. Wohl could hardly believe his eyes as he saw the vehicle disappear and a belated burst of machine-gun fire rattled.

As it plunged the car turned turtle and went down roof first. When it settled on the bottom both the man and the girl must have been upside down as the river surged inside. Wohl was quite sure that the Leopard must now be dead but he took no chances. Using a megaphone he barked out orders and the soldiers began to force their way through the thick undergrowth lining the banks. It was three hours later before a breakdown truck equipped with a crane hauled the sunken car slowly to the surface.

Wohl was on the bridge when the car, dripping with

water, was swung over and down. He received another
shock. There was no trace of the Leopard. But the girl
was still there, imprisoned in the front seat, her dark hair
plastered to her skull, an attractive girl of about twenty.
After a few days, using the Vichy police's fingerprint
records, Wohl was able to identify her as Lucie Devaud.
The medical examiner told the Abwehr officer that at some
recent time she had been delivered of a child.

The incident caused a minor scandal among the Resistance forces which split into two opposing views. Some
said that the Leopard had acted correctly, had sacrificed
everything to reach his rendezvous on time. Others were
not so charitable—Lucie Devaud had a courageous record
as a courier—and argued that he could have taken the
girl out with him if he hadn't been so concerned to save
his own skin. But then the surge of war, the later attempt
to set up a Communist République du Sud, smothered the
incident and it was forgotten, particularly when the
Leopard himself was shot dead in Lyon . . .

Over thirty years later all this came back to Dieter
Wohl when he read in the paper the name of the woman
who had tried to kill Guy Florian. And by now Wohl
himself had started to write his memoirs, so it seemed
too good an opportunity to miss—to try and prompt
people who might know something into writing him, to
furnish more material for his book. On Friday, 10 December, he wrote a letter to the *Frankfurter Allgemeine
Zeitung,* referring to his wartime diary and the fact that
he was writing his memoirs, and to give his communication an air of authority he mentioned the name of a certain
Annette Devaud, who had also been a member of the
Leopard's Resistance group, even going so far as to
include her last known address of over thirty years ago.
To make his letter even more arresting he quoted a
sentence from one of Col Lasalle's provocative broadcasts.
"Who is this Lucie Devaud who last night tried to kill a
certain European statesman?" At the conclusion of his

letter Wohl added a question of his own. *Is Annette Devaud still alive in Saverne, I wonder?*

Wohl succeeded in his aim even more swiftly than he could have hoped. The letter was printed in the *Frankfurter Allgemeine Zeitung* on Tuesday, 14 December, and was duly read on the same day by Paul-Henri Le Theule, the Secret Service officer attached to the French Embassy in Bonn. Le Theule, thirty-eight years old and only a child at the war's end, knew nothing about the Leopard, but his eye was caught by the brief reference to Col René Lasalle. Hard up for material to pad his next report, he cut out the letter and added it to the meagre pile waiting for the next Paris diplomatic bag.

The bag was delivered to Paris on Saturday, 18 December, but it was only Sunday morning when Roger Danchin, working his way through a pile of paperwork, came across the cutting, which he showed to Alain Blanc who happened to be with him. Dictating a memo to the Elysée, Danchin sent both memo and cutting across the road and by lunchtime Guy Florian had seen both documents. At three in the afternoon Soviet Ambassador Leonid Vorin, who had lunched with Alain Blanc, arrived at the Elysée, talked briefly with the president and then hurried back to his embassy in the rue de Grenelle.

Returning to Colmar aboard the turbotrain from Strasbourg at seven on Sunday evening, Lansky hurried the few steps from the station across the *place* to the Hotel Bristol where he found his two companions waiting impatiently for him in Vanek's bedroom. He told them how he had dealt with Noelle Berger and Vanek was relieved. "It means Philip is now alone in the house and we may be able to turn his girl's disappearance to our advantage, but we must advance the time of our visit . . ."

"Why?" asked Lansky. "Late on a Sunday night would be much safer . . ."

"Because," Vanek explained with sarcastic patience, "Philip will soon begin to worry about what has happened to her. If we leave him to worry too long he may call the police . . ."

While Lansky had been away in Strasbourg the other two men had continued their research on Robert Philip, each of them taking turns to watch No. 8 from a small park further down the Avenue Raymond Poincaré while they pretended to feed the birds or to be waiting for someone. And it was because it was difficult to keep Philip's villa under observation from a closer point—and a tribute also to their skill—that they escaped the notice of the occasional patrol-car which came gliding along the avenue while the officer behind the wheel checked on the same villa.

At three in the afternoon, throwing bread for some sparrows, Vanek saw Philip emerge from the house, come down the steps and walk to the gate which he proceeded to lean on while he smoked a cigarette. Slipping behind a tree, Vanek used the monocular glass he always carried to study the Frenchman close up. Under the flashy, camel-hair coat he wore Vanek noticed between the railings that the Frenchman was still clad in pyjama trousers. On Sundays Philip rarely dressed; slopping about the house in his night-things was his way of relaxing. And also, he was thinking, that when Noelle returned it would be so much easier to flop her on the bed when all he had to divest himself of was pyjamas. Left alone in the house, Philip was lusting for his latest mistress.

"That could be a bit of luck, too," Vanek informed Brunner later, "bearing in mind the method we shall adopt . . ."

It was close to nine o'clock when Brunner walked up the steps leading to the porch of No. 8 and rang the bell. At that hour on a Sunday the snowbound Avenue Raymond Poincaré was deserted and very silent. Lights were on behind the curtained bay window at the front and Brunner's ring on the bell brought a quick—but cautious—reaction. A side curtain overlooking the porch was drawn back and Philip stood in the window, still wearing his dressing-gown over his pyjamas. Holding a glass, he stared at Brunner suspiciously, then dropped the curtain. A few moments later the door was opened a few inches and held in that position by a strong chain.

"Mr Robert Philip?" Brunner enquired.

"Yes. What is it?"

Expecting to see Noelle Berger laden with packages, Philip was taken aback by the arrival of this stranger. Brunner presented the Sûreté Nationale card he had carried since the Commando had left Tábor.

"Sûreté, sir. I am afraid I have some bad news about an acquaintance of yours, a young lady. May I come in for a moment?"

Worried as he was about his mistress, Philip was a wary man who had not survived all these years in the half-world of gun-running by accepting people or identity cards at face value; in fact, he himself had more than a nodding acquaintance with false papers.

"I don't know you," he said after a moment. "And it just happens that I know most of the police in Colmar . . ."

"That doesn't surprise me . . ." Brunner made an impatient gesture. "I was transferred here from Strasbourg only last week . . ."

"Wait there while I get some clothes on . . ." The door slammed shut in Brunner's face. Inside the hall Philip frowned, sensing something odd about this unknown visitor. He reached for the phone on a side-table and something hard and pipe-like pressed against his back, digging through the silk dressing-gown as a voice spoke quietly. "If you make a sound I shall shoot you. Take your hand away from that phone. Now, face the wall . . ." While Brunner was distracting the Frenchman's attention, keeping him at the front of the house, Vanek had gone round the side-path to the back of the house. He had followed the same route earlier—soon after dark when Philip had drawn the curtains over the front windows—and had found the French doors which were locked and without a key in the hole. Now, using the skeleton keys, he had let himself inside and come into the hall while Philip was talking to his unexpected visitor.

"Don't move . . ." Vanek pressed the Luger muzzle against Philip's back again to remind him it existed, then he turned the key in the front door, drew the bolt and removed the chain. Brunner himself turned the handle, came inside and closed the door quickly. "Fasten it up again," Vanek ordered. "No one saw you? Good . . ."

Prodding Philip up the staircase ahead of him, Vanek waited until they were on the upper landing, then handed the Luger to Brunner and quickly explored the first floor. All the curtains were closed in the darkened bedrooms and he found what he was looking for leading off a large double bedroom at the back—a bathroom. Switching on the light, he studied the room for a moment and then nodded to Brunner who prodded Philip inside his own bathroom. "What the hell is going on?" the Frenchman blustered. "The police station is just round the corner and . . ."

"The Police Nationale headquarters is in the rue de la Montagne Verre which is well over a kilometre from here," Vanek informed him quietly. "Now take off your clothes."

"My brother and his wife will be calling . . ."

"The clothes . . ."

Brunner rammed the Luger barrel hard against him. Philip stripped, taking off dressing-gown and pyjamas until he was standing gross, hairy-chested and naked. Frightened by the coolness of Vanek, he still had some spirit left as he asked again what the hell this was all about.

"Haven't you heard of burglars?" Vanek enquired. "It

is a well-known fact that a man without any clothes on is in no position to run about the streets seeking help—especially on a night like this. And before we leave we shall rip out the phone cord. Standard practice. Don't you read the newspapers?"

Telling him they were going to tie his feet to the taps, they made him lie down inside the bath and then Brunner turned on both taps, mingling the water to a medium temperature. The Frenchman, growing more frightened every second, for the third time asked what the hell was going on. It was Vanek who told him. "We want to know where the safe is," he said. "We have been told you have a safe and you are going to tell us where it is . . ."

"There is no safe . . ."

"If you don't tell us where it is my colleague will grab hold of your feet and drag you under . . ."

"There is no safe," Philip screamed.

"Are you sure?" Vanek looked doubtful, still aiming the Luger at Philip's chest. The bath continued to fill with water at a rapid rate. "We wouldn't like you to lie to us," Vanek went on, "and we shall be very annoyed if we search the place and find one . . ."

"There is no safe! There is money in my wallet in the bedroom—over a thousand francs . . ."

Brunner switched off both taps and stared at Philip who was now sweating profusely. Bending down, the Czech took hold of the Frenchman's jaw firmly, then pushed his face close to Philip's. Vanek moved to the other end of the bath and took hold of both the Frenchman's ankles. Half-sitting, half-lying in the bath, Philip braced himself, prepared to be dragged under, still protesting there was no safe in the house. Suddenly, he felt the grip on his ankles released as Vanek, in a resigned voice, said, "I think perhaps he is telling the truth . . ." Philip relaxed. Brunner jerked the jaw he held in his hand upwards and backwards in a swift vicious movement and the back of Philip's head struck the bath with a terrible crack. "He's dead," Brunner reported as he checked the pulse and then Philip slid under the water and his face dissolved into a wobbling blur.

"The correct sequence," Vanek commented. "The medical examiner will confirm he died by striking his head before he immersed himself. Get finished quickly . . ."

Vanek checked the large double bedroom, looking under the bed, on the dressing-table, inside the wardrobe. The few feminine clothes confirmed to him that the girl who had been followed to Strasbourg by Lansky was only a brief visitor, so he set about removing traces of her presence. Taking a suitcase engraved with the initials N.B., he piled in her clothes, her night things, her cosmetics and six pairs of shoes, her lip-stick-stained toothbrush from the bathroom shelf and two lace-edged hand-kerchiefs from under a pillow. There would still be traces of her presence in the house the police would find, but without clothes they would shrug their shoulders. The last thing Vanek wanted to happen in the next few days was a police dragnet out for a missing woman. He was closing the case when he heard Brunner, who had fetched a pan from the kitchen, scooping out water from the bath and throwing it on the floor. He checked the bath-room before he went downstairs.

"Perfect?" enquired Brunner.

A tablet of soap he had dropped in the bath was muddy-ing the water as it dissolved. Robert Philip had just had a fatal accident, and most accidents happen at home. He had been standing in the bath when he had stepped on the soap tablet, lost his balance and gone crashing down to hit the back of his head. Water had welled over the rim of the bath on the floor, soaking his pyjamas and dressing-gown. "I brought up that ash-tray from the living-room," Brunner remarked. On a stool stood the ash-tray the Czech had carried up in his gloved hand, the burnt-out remnant of the cigarette Philip had left smoking when he answered the door still perched in the lip of the tray.

"Perfect," Vanek replied, being careful to leave on the bathroom light as he followed Brunner downstairs, carrying Noelle Berger's suitcase, then he switched off the living-room light. Left on all night, it might well have attracted attention, unlike the bathroom which was at the back of the house.

They left by the way Vanek had entered the house— by the french door at the back. Once outside, they re- locked the door with the skeleton keys, and then Vanek waited with the suitcase in the little park until Brunner arrived with the Critoën. It took them only twenty minutes to drive to the banks of the Rhine, and on the way they stopped briefly at a deserted building-site while Vanek collected a few bricks to add weight to the suitcase. A few minutes later he watched the case sink into the swift- flowing current, took over the wheel from Brunner, and by 10.30 p.m. they were back inside their bedrooms at the Bristol, ready for a night's sleep. They would be leaving early in the morning—on their way to pay a visit on Dieter Wohl in Germany.

In Strasbourg Alan Lennox woke early on Monday morn- ing, got out of bed at the Hotel Sofitel, opened his door and picked up the local paper he had ordered from the hall porter. He read it in his dressing-gown, drinking the coffee he had ordered from room service. He hardly noticed the banner headline as he searched through the inner pages for a report on Leon Jouvel's suicide, which he found reported at greater length than he had expected; there was a shortage of local news after the weekend. The details it gave were hardly more illuminating than those he had heard from Louise Vallon, Jouvel's assistant, but an Inspector Rochat was mentioned as being in charge of the case and the address of the police station was given.

Finishing his coffee and croissants, Lennox showered

and shaved, dressed and paid his bill. Snow was drifting down from a leaden sky as he took a cab to the station where he deposited his bag in the luggage store; Colmar was only thirty minutes away by train and he confidently expected that in one day he should be able to find and talk to Robert Philip, assuming the Frenchman was not away. He was just in time to climb aboard the 9.15 a.m. turbotrain for Colmar before it began moving south. As the train left Strasbourg and moved across the flat plain with glimpses of the Vosges mountains to the west, Lennox read the banner headline story he had skipped over in his bedroom. Another international crisis was brewing.

The Turkish Naval Command in the Bosphorus had recently received a long signal from their opposite numbers at the Russian Black Sea port of Odessa. The signal informed the Turks that a very large convoy, code-named K.12, would be making passage through the Bosphorus and the Dardanelles *en route* for the Mediterranean. This was in accord with the long-time agreement whereby Soviet Russia always requests formal permission before sending ships through the Turkish-controlled straits.

As always, the Russians specified the make-up of the convoy, and this so startled the Turkish naval commander that he phoned Ankara urgently. The Defence Minister in the Turkish capital was woken in the middle of the night and he immediately reported the signal to NATO headquarters in Brussels. It was decided as a matter of policy to leak the news to the press. What caused the ripple of alarm was the size of the convoy. The Soviet signal had specified six heavy cruisers (four of them missile-bearing), one aircraft carrier, twelve destroyers and fifteen large transports. The size of the convoy was unprecedented. What could the fifteen large transports be carrying? Where was this enormous convoy headed for?

As the train pulled in to Colmar, Lennox folded up his newspaper and forgot about the scare story. After all, it had nothing to do with the job he was working on, and by now his whole attention was fixed on his coming interview with Robert Philip.

By eight o'clock on Saturday night, 18 December, every defence minister in western Europe and north America had received a copy of the Soviet signal, including Alain Blanc, who paid it rather more attention than Alan Lennox. Within only five days the president was due to fly to Soviet Russia and Blanc was not at all happy about the signal. On Sunday morning he had a brief interview with Guy Florian, who took a quite different view.

"Certainly they would never dream of precipitating a world crisis on the eve of my departure for Moscow," he told Blanc. "They are much too anxious to cement relations with us as the major west European power . . ."

Alain Blanc left the Elysée unconvinced and even more disturbed than before he had arrived. Why had Florian suddenly become so complacent about the intentions of Soviet Russia?

Arriving at Colmar, Lennox purchased a street-guide at the station kiosk and found that the Avenue Raymond Poincaré was only a few metres away from where he stood. When he started walking down the avenue he received an unpleasant shock: two patrol-cars with uniformed policemen standing beside them were parked outside a square-looking two-storey villa. He felt quite sure this would be No. 8 even before he drew level with the villa on the opposite side of the street and continued walking. Yes, it was No. 8. It was a repeat of the same scene he had witnessed outside No. 49 rue de l'Épine only the day before. Fifteen minutes later, having walked in a circle—to avoid re-passing the police stationed outside the villa—he walked into the bar of the Hotel Bristol opposite the station.

"What are all those police cars doing in the Avenue

Raymond Poincaré?" he asked casually as he sipped his cognac.

The barman was only too eager to pass on information; in a small town like Colmar the grapevine is reliable and swift. A local bigwig, Robert Philip, had died in his bath the previous evening, he confided. The tragedy had been discovered when his cleaning woman had arrived to find the front door still bolted and chained. "She had a key," the barman explained, "so Philip always undid the bolts and chain first thing and then she could let herself in. The police found him floating in his bath. He won't be running after skirt any more, that one . . ."

Lennox ordered another drink but the barman had little more information. Except that the police had been to the hotel asking a lot of questions about two men who had stayed there for two nights.

"They had a Citroën," the barman went on, "according to the night porter. I didn't see them myself—I don't think they ever came in here. Personally, I can't see the connection . . ."

As Lennox walked out of the bar two uniformed police-men came in, which decided him to leave Colmar as rapidly as possible; there was a fifty-fifty chance the talkative barman might relay to them his recent conversa-tion with the stranger who had just left. Crossing the *place* to the station, he bought a one-way ticket to Lyon and then boarded a train for Strasbourg which had just come in. When the ticket collector came through the train he used the return to Strasbourg he already had in his pos-session. Of the three wartime survivors who were once familiar with the Leopard there was now only one left. Dieter Wohl of Freiburg.

Unlike Inspector Rochat of Strasbourg, Inspector Dorré of Colmar was only forty and he took nothing for granted. Saturnine-faced, impatient, a fast-talking man, he phoned Boisseau two hours after the death of Robert Philip had

been discovered, explaining that there had been no surveillance on Philip after the Frenchman had returned
home apart from observation by a routine patrol-car. "We
are very short of men," he went on, "so I was unable
to obtain personnel for a proper surveillance, which is
regrettable . . ."

At the other end of the line Boisseau guessed that someone higher up had been unhelpful—because they had
resented Paris's intrusion into their backyard. This time
he had neither the necessity nor even the opportunity to
ask probing questions: Dorré went on talking like a
machine-gun.

"According to the medical examiner and my own observation there is no doubt at all that Robert Philip died
by accident when he slipped and caught the back of his
skull on the edge of his bath. He was alone in the house
at the time and there are no signs of forcible entry or
anything which would indicate foul play— although there
had been a woman in the house, but probably only for
a few hours. Philip was like that . . ."

There was a brief pause, then the voice started up again.
"Pardon, but I have a cold and had to blow my nose. So,
technically, it is an accidental death. For myself, I do not
believe it for a moment. I have heard that another man
you also requested to be put under surveillance—a Leon
Jouvel—hanged himself in Strasbourg less than forty-eight
hours ago. I have also heard—I was in Strasbourg yesterday—that my colleagues are satisfied that Jouvel committed suicide. For me, it is too much, M. Boisseau—
two men you ask to have put under surveillance both die
in their homes by suicide, by accident in less than two
days. I tell you, there has to be something wrong . . ."

"Is there anything specific . . ." Boisseau began, but he
got no further.

"Pardon, Mr Director-General, but I have not finished.
A woman who knows—knew—Robert Philip well drove
past his villa yesterday morning and saw a blue Citroën

parked opposite his villa. Two men were trying to repair the car, but she thought they were watching Philip's villa. She reported it to me when she saw the patrol-cars outside this morning, assuming there had been yet another burglary . . ."

"Any registration number?" Boisseau managed to interject.

"Unfortunately, no, but I have not finished," Dorré continued. "It occurred to me to check with all the local hotels and we find that two men arrived at the hotel nearest the station at 9.30 on Saturday night. The hotel, incidentally, is no more than a few metres away from the villa of the late Robert Philip. They arrived in a blue Citroën and we have the registration number. It is being circulated at this moment. Also, the descriptions of the two men. There may be no connection but I do not like this death at all, despite its technical perfection . . ."

"If it were not an accident then," Boisseau hazarded, "it would have to be the work of highly-skilled professionals?"

"They would have to be trained assassins," Dorré said bluntly, "because if I am right—and I do not say I am— then presumably Leon Jouvel's death was also arranged, and again there was technical perfection. You must not think I am a romantic," he insisted, "trying to turn every event into a crime, but I repeat, two men under surveillance dying so quickly does not smell of roses to me, sir. And," he went on, once again preventing Boisseau from speaking, "the geography is interesting, is it not?"

"The geography?"

"It is not so very far to drive from Strasbourg to Colmar. I will let you know as soon as we get information on the car registration of the Citroën . . ."

Vanek, driving at speed, but always keeping just inside the legal limit, reached the Boulevard de Nancy in Strasbourg by nine in the morning, one hour before Inspector

Dorré had circulated the car registration number. Handing back the Citroën to the Hertz agent, he walked out again and went into the restaurant where he had dropped Brunner and Lansky while he got rid of the vehicle.

"We've used that car quite long enough," he told the two men, "and two visits is more than enough by the same mode of transport."

Refusing to allow them to finish their drinks, he took them outside where they again separated. With Brunner he took a cab to Strasbourg station, leaving Lansky to follow in a second vehicle. They joined forces again at the station but they each bought their tickets separately. Boarding the train by himself while the other two men went into a different coach, Lansky put his bag on the rack and lit a cigarette. Within fifteen minutes the train had crossed the Rhine bridge and was stopping in Kehl. The Soviet Commando had arrived in Germany.

13

Monday was a bad day for Lennox, who never forgot that he was travelling with forged papers. Arriving back at Strasbourg station, intending to collect his suitcase from the baggage store and then take another train across the Rhine into Germany, he immediately noticed signs of intense police activity. There was a uniformed policeman on the platform as he alighted from the train, a young and alert man who was obviously scrutinizing all passengers as they walked past him to descend the exit steps.

In the main hall there were more police—some of them

Lennox felt sure in plain clothes—and when he approached the luggage store two gendarmes stood by the counter, checking people's papers as they withdrew their luggage. Lennox walked away from the store and went inside the glassed-in café which fronted on the Place de la Gare. Sitting down at a table he ordered coffee, quite unaware that he was in the same café Lansky had waited in the previous Saturday evening before paying his final call on Leon Jouvel. While he drank his coffee Lennox watched the station and what he saw was not encouraging.

Another police van arrived, disgorging a dozen more policemen who ran inside the main hall. The energetic Inspector Dorré of Colmar had been in touch with his Strasbourg colleagues—Vanek's Citroën had now been traced to the Hertz car-hire branch in the Boulevard de Nancy—and Inspector Rochat's superiors, nervous now of a monumental blunder, co-operated fully. The abandonment of the car logically led them to the assumption that the recent hirers must now be travelling by train or air. A massive surveillance operation was put into action at the railway station and near-by airport. Ironically, the dragnet thrown out to trap the Soviet Commando was endangering Lennox.

It is one thing to slip across a border with false papers; it is quite a different kettle of fish to risk being checked carefully when an emergency dragnet is under way. Lennox paid for his coffee, walked across the Place de la Gare to the bus station, and jumped on the first crowded bus leaving. It happened to be going to Haguenau, a place he had never heard of, so he bought a ticket which would take him the whole route. The earliest he could risk crossing over into Germany would be the following day; dragnets are at their most vigilant during the first twenty-four hours. And the big problem would be where to spend the night: when the police are really looking for someone they check every hotel, even phoning those outlying places they cannot easily reach.

Lennox caught a late evening bus back from Haguenau to Strasbourg, and the first thing he noticed when he alighted at the Place de la Gare was the line of police vans drawn up outside the station. Early that morning, reading through the newspaper to find the report on Leon Jouvel's death, he had noticed a reference to an all-night session of the European Parliament being held in the city. After eating dinner in a back street restaurant, he took a cab to the Parliament building. His papers, which showed him as a reporter, readily gave him admittance and once inside he settled down in the press gallery to his own all-night session.

Before taking the cab to the European Parliament he had slipped into a hotel washroom where he had shaved with equipment he had bought in Haguenau; it might not have been wise to present an unshaven appearance inside the august precincts of Europe's talking shop. The precaution turned out to be unnecessary—there were few other reporters in the press gallery and at times, as the dreary debate droned on and on, Lennox was able to snatch an hour or so of sleep. Checking his watch at frequent intervals, he waited while the night passed on leaden feet. In the morning he would try once again to cross the Rhine into the Federal Republic of Germany.

It was Inspector Jacques Dorré (who in later years rose to the rank of Commissioner), who finally alerted Marc Grelle. When the prefect received Boisseau's report of his conversation with Colmar he personally phoned Dorré, who now had more information. He was able to tell Grelle that the Citroën which had transported two men to the hotel in Colmar had been handed in to the Hertz branch in the Boulevard de Nancy, Strasbourg.

"Yes," he further confirmed, "the description of the man who returned the car tallies with the description of one of the two men who stayed at the Hotel Bristol on the nights of 18 and 19 December—and on the 19th

Robert Philip died in his bath . . ."

"If these two men—Jouvel and Philip—were murdered," Grelle suggested to Dorré, "it has to be the work of a professional assassin then? No amateur could fake both deaths so convincingly, you agree?"

"I agree," Dorré replied crisply. "But it appears there is a team of at least two assassins on the move—maybe even three men . . ."

Grelle took a tighter grip on the phone. "How do you make that out?" he demanded.

"I personally checked the register at the Bristol. Ten minutes after the first two men—Duval and Bonnard—booked in, a third man, Lambert, took a room also. There is nothing to link these three men together—except that they all arrived on the night of the 18th and departed on the morning of the 20th, which is early today, of course. The point is, at this time of the year the hotel was almost empty . . ."

Grelle thanked him for his co-operation and put down the receiver. "There could be some kind of assassination team on the move in Alsace," he told Boisseau. "It's all theory, but if it were true who the hell could they be?"

"Only Lasalle and the Englishman, Lennox, have that list, presumably," Boisseau pointed out. "Surely Lasalle is not wiping out his own witnesses? That doesn't make any sense at all. The only thing which would make sense is if someone employed by the Leopard were doing the job . . ."

"But the Leopard can't have the list . . ."

Grelle stopped and the two men stared at each other in silence. An hour later the indefatigable Dorré was back on the line again. He was working in close touch with his colleagues in Strasbourg, he explained, and at his suggestion Rochat had started contacting every hotel in the city. The names Duval, Bonnard and Lambert had soon been tracked down. The first two had spent the night of Friday, 17 December, at the Hotel Sofitel, while

Lambert had slept at the Terminus, and it was during the evening of 18 December that Leon Jouvel had hanged himself.

"So," Dorré pointed out, "these same three men—and again the descriptions, though vague, tally—then moved down here to Colmar late on the evening of the 18th and were in the town when Robert Philip died. How far do you stretch the long arm of coincidence without breaking it?"

"That's it!" Grelle snapped. "When your descriptions of these three men arrive I'll circulate them throughout the whole of France—and we have their names. I want that trio detained and questioned the moment they surface again . . ."

On the night of 20 December it was dark by six o'clock in the Freiburg area as Dieter Wohl stood looking out between the curtains of his unlit bedroom. Wohl felt quite at home in the dark, possibly a relic of his wartime years when he had so often observed a suspect house from behind an unlit window. Wohl was not a nervous man, even though he lived alone in his two-storey house perched by itself at the roadside three kilometres outside Freiburg, but at the moment he was puzzled. Why had a car stopped just short of his house and stayed there at this hour?

Overnight there had been a weather change; the snow had melted, the temperature had risen, and now the sky was broken cloud with moonlight shining through, illuminating the lonely country road and the trees in the fields beyond. Most people would not have heard the car, but ex-policeman Wohl—he had joined the force after the war—had the ears of a cat. A black Mercedes SL 230, he noted by the light of the moon. One shadowy figure sat behind the wheel while his two passengers had got out and were pretending to examine the motor. Why did the word "pretending" leap into his head? Because although they had the bonnet up they kept glancing at

his house and looking all round them as though spying
out the land. Their glances were fleeting—so fleeting that
probably only a trained observer like Wohl would have
noticed them.

"My imagination is running away with me," he murmured.

Below him in the road one of the men left the car and
made his way into a field alongside the house, his hand
at his files. He's just gone for a pee, Wohl decided. Leaving the front bedroom, still moving around in the dark, he
went into the side bedroom where the curtains had not
been drawn; keeping to the back of the room, he watched
the man perform against a hedge. It was all perfectly
innocent, except that the man relieving himself kept
glancing at the back garden and up at the side of the
house. Well hidden in the shadows, Wohl waited until
the man had finished and returned to the car. A moment
later the two men closed the hood as Wohl watched from
the front bedroom, climbed back inside the Mercedes
and the driver tried the engine. It sparked first time and
drove off towards Freiburg. I must be getting old, Wohl
thought, seeing sinister things where none exist. He went
downstairs to continue work on his memoirs. Half an
hour later the phone rang.

"Herr Wohl? Herr Dieter Wohl? Good evening. This
is the Morgenthau Research Institute, a market research
organization. We are carrying out research connected with
a campaign to increase state pensions. You have been
selected . . . "

The researcher, a man called Brückner, checked Wohl's
status, noted that he was a widower living alone, that
he owned his house, that he never took a holiday, and a
number of other pertinent questions. Thanking Wohl profusely, the caller said he might wish to visit Wohl but
he would first phone for an appointment. Would any of
the next three evenings be convenient? It would? Excellent . . .

Putting down the phone Wohl went back to his desk in the front living-room and settled down again to the arduous task of completing the introduction to his memoirs. But he found it difficult to concentrate; his suspicious mind kept going back to the telephone call.

Only eight hours earlier Vanek had phoned the special Paris number from Kehl. Each day, since arriving in Munich—with the exception of the Sunday in Colmar—he had phoned the number his trainer, Borisov, had given him from a post office—and each day there had been no new instruction passed over to him. Phoning from Kehl, he had anticipated the same dead call. Hearing the same voice and name—Jurgensen—repeat the number at the other end Vanek identified himself.

"This is Salicetti . . ."

"There is a development," the voice said quickly. "At the Freiburg branch you must collect a wartime diary and the manuscript of the customer's memoirs. Understood?"

"Understood . . ."

"Then you must visit another customer—note the address. A Madame Annette Devaud, Saverne . . ." Jurgensen spelt out the name of the town. "It is in Alsace . . ."

"That's a vague address . . ."

"That's all we have. Goodbye!"

Vanek checked his watch. The call had taken only thirty seconds. Quite calm while he had been making the call, the Czech swore to himself as he looked out of the phone booth to where people were queuing up to buy postage stamps. The new development was not to his liking at all; it meant that when they had made the visit to Freiburg they would have to re-cross the border back into France. And it was now 20 December, which gave them only seventy-two hours to complete the job.

Alan Lennox crossed the border to Kehl on the morning of Tuesday, 21 December. At Strasbourg station the dragnet had been relaxed, although still partly in operation. After the initial burst of activity—which brought no result —the resentment felt by the local police at Paris's interference in their affairs began to surface again, especially since there was a terrorist alert—later proved to be unfounded—at Strasbourg airport. Men were rushed to the airport and the surveillance at the railway station was reduced.

Collecting his bag from the luggage store, Lennox boarded a local train, later passed through the frontier control without incident—no one was looking for a man called Bouvier—and arrived in Kehl. He immediately put through a call to Peter Lanz at the special Bonn number he had been given and—in a round-about way—told the BND chief everything that had happened. "The two French witnesses have died suddenly, one might say violently—within twenty-four hours of each other . . . one of them partially identified our animal impersonator . . . by voice alone, I emphasize . . . Guy Florian."

Lanz adopted an off-hand tone, as though discussing something of minor importance. "You would say your witness was reliable? After all, we do have other depositions . . ."

"It is by no means certain," Lennox replied.

"And your next move?"

"Peter, the third witness lives in Freiburg—I didn't mention it before, but I'm going to see him now. Yes, one of your countrymen. No, I'd sooner not mention names . . ."

"In that case," Lanz said crisply, "I will be in Freiburg myself this evening. You will be able to contact me at the Hotel Colombi. Look after yourself. And if that is all I have to go to a meeting which is urgent . . ."

Franz Hauser, recently elected Chancellor of the Federal Republic of Germany, agreed to see Peter Lanz at the Palais Schaumburg at 11 a.m., which was only one hour after Lennox had phoned from Kehl. Immersed in work—Hauser seldom got to bed before midnight—he had now asked Lanz to make his temporary headquarters in Bonn instead of at Pullach in Bavaria. "I need you across the hall from me the way things are shaping up in Europe," he informed the BND chief.

Small, neat and wiry, Hauser had been elected on a platform of taking the strongest measures against terrorists, the urban guerrillas who were still plaguing Germany. He had also preached the gospel that now the Americans had withdrawn from Europe the continent must protect itself. "Combining with our friends, France, Great Britain and our other allies we must build up such strength that the commanders of the Red Army will know Europe can only be their graveyard if ever they make the mistake of crossing the frontiers . . ."

At eleven o'clock promptly Lanz was ushered into his office and Hauser, a man who hated formality, came round his desk to sit alongside the security chief. "Is there information from the Englishman, Lennox?" he enquired. He listened for ten minutes while Lanz explained what had happened, his small, alert face puckered in concentration. "If this links up with the movement of Soviet convoy K.12," he commented, "then we may be on the eve of a catastrophe. The Russians are striking before we can build up our strength."

"You do not really believe it, sir?" Lanz protested. "I mean that Florian could be this Communist Resistance chief, the Leopard?"

"No, that is impossible," Hauser agreed. "But it is no longer beyond the realms of possibility that one of his key cabinet ministers may be. And then there is the fact that the Leopard was not found when his grave was disinterred near Lyon. How did you hear about that, by the way?"

"A contact we have across the Rhine . . ."

"All right, keep your secrets. What disturbs me are the

growing rumours of a *coup d'état* in Paris. Supposing Leopard is Alain Blanc, Minister of National Defence—might he not be planning to seize power while Florian is away in Moscow?"

"That hadn't occurred to me," Lanz admitted.

"Is there some huge conspiracy afoot?" Hauser murmured. "If Moscow is co-operating with the Leopard might they not have asked Florian to Moscow to get him out of the way while the Leopard takes over in France? Why is that Soviet convoy proceeding into the Mediterranean at this moment? Everything seems to be moving towards some climax. We need more information, Lanz. Immediately . . ."

Arriving by train at Freiburg, Lennox left his bag at the station, checked the phone directory to make sure Dieter Wohl was still living at the address given on the list, and then phoned the German. He introduced himself as Jules Jean Bouvier, a reporter on the French newspaper *Le Monde*. His paper was about to embark on a series on the French wartime Resistance, with particular reference to operations in the Lozère. He believed that Herr Wohl had served in this area during the war, so . . .

Wohl was hesitant at first, trying to decide whether seeing Bouvier would help him with his memoirs, then it struck him that a little advance publicity could do no harm, so he agreed. Lennox took a cab to the ex-Abwehr officer's remote house and Wohl was waiting for him at the door. A cautious man, Wohl sat his visitor down in the living-room and then asked for some identification. Lennox produced his papers. "Anyone can get a press card printed," he said easily.

It took half an hour to coax Wohl into a trusting frame of mind, but when Lennox mentioned the Leopard he saw a flicker in the German's eyes. "This is something I am concentrating on," Lennox explained. "I find it excellent copy—the mystery surrounding the Leopard's real identity. It was never cleared up, was it?"

Wohl went over to his desk where part of a hand-written manuscript lay alongside a worn, leatherbound diary. For fifteen minutes he told Lennox in precise detail all the steps he had taken to track down the Resistance leader during 1944. Lennox had filled a dozen pages of his notebook with shorthand, had decided that the German really had no information of value, when Wohl mentioned the incident when he had almost ambushed the Leopard. At the end of the story he gave the name of the girl who had died in the submerged car. Lucie Devaud.

"It was a shocking business," Wohl remarked, "leaving the girl to drown like that. The car was in eighteen feet of water, my men were some distance from where it went over the bridge. I'm convinced he could have saved her had he tried. He didn't try . . ."

"Lucie Devaud," Lennox repeated. "That was the name of the woman who tried to kill Guy Florian. I suppose there's no possible connection?"

"I wondered about that myself," Wohl admitted. "Annette Devaud was very close to the Leopard—she was in charge of his brilliant team of couriers. I understand she went blind soon after the war . . ."

Lennox sat very still, saying nothing. Col René Lasalle had made a passing reference to Annette Devaud, dismissing her as of no importance because of her blindness. Could the French colonel have slipped up here—if Annette had indeed been so close to the Leopard?

"I wrote to the *Frankfurter Allgemeine Zeitung* last week," Wohl continued, "and I mentioned the incident of the drowned girl. I also mentioned that another Devaud —Annette—who was involved with the Leopard, might still be alive in France. I even gave her last-known address, which perhaps I should not have done. Here it is. Annette Devaud, Woodcutter's Farm, Saverne, Alsace. It was a long time ago but some French people stay in one place for ever . . ."

Wohl showed Lennox the address at the back of the war
diary where he had underlined it several times. "Living
alone as I do," he said apologetically, "I get funny ideas.
Only last night I thought some people were watching my
house. And then there was that peculiar phone call from
the market research people . . ." As he went on talking,
Lennox listened.

". . . in fact, Wohl only mentioned it in passing, but con-
sidering what happened in Strasbourg and Colmar, it just
made me wonder . . ." At four in the afternoon Lennox
had met Peter Lanz in a bedroom of the Hotel Colombi
in Freiburg soon after the BND chief had flown there from
Bonn, and now he was telling the German about his meeting with Dieter Wohl. Earlier Lanz had told the Englishman about the opening up of the Leopard's grave in a
forest near Lyon, about how the French police had found
only the skeleton of a hound inside the Resistance leader's
coffin.

"This is what has turned a vague disquiet into alarm
and crisis," the BND official explained. "It now seems
probable that Lasalle has been right all along—that somewhere in Paris a top Communist is working close to
Florian, maybe only waiting for the president to leave the
capital for his visit to Moscow . . ."

"I suppose it's confidential—how you heard about the
exhumation of the Leopard's grave?" Lennox hazarded.

"It's confidential," the German assured him.

He saw no advantage in revealing to Lennox that it
was Col Lasalle who had passed the information to him.
And Lanz himself had no inkling of the colonel's source
which had passed on the news to Lasalle. Georges Hardy,
police prefect of Lyon and Marc Grelle's great friend, had
for some time disagreed violently with Guy Florian's
policies, and to express this disagreement he had been
secretly furnishing Lasalle with information about developments inside France.

Lennox had then reported to Lanz on his interview
with Dieter Wohl, ending by describing the curious inci-
dents of the previous day the ex-Abwehr officer had
described. "I gather he was looking out of a bedroom
window last night in the dark when he saw this car stop
outside," he went on. "It just reminded me of the man I
saw following Leon Jouvel that night in Strasbourg. I
suppose it isn't possible that someone has Dieter Wohl
under observation? Then there was the peculiar telephone
call. After all, two out of the three men on Lasalle's list
have already died suddenly. And it's damned lonely out
there where he lives . . ."

"If by a long chance you are right," Lanz suggested,
"this could be a breakthrough. If we grab hold of someone
trying to put Wohl out of the way, too, we can find out
who is behind this whole business."

"It's a very slim hope," Lennox warned.

"What else have we got?" Lanz demanded. He was
well aware he was grasping at straws, but Chancellor
Hauser had said he wanted positive information immediately. From the hotel bedroom he phoned the police chief
of Frieburg.

The Mercedes SL 230 hired in Kehl pulled in at the kerb
close to Freiburg station and Vanek lit a cigarette as he
watched people coming off a train. Nearing the end of
the Commando's mission, the Czech had become mis-
trustful of hotels and the previous night the three men
had slept in the car at the edge of the Black Forest,
muffled up in travelling rugs they had purchased in
Freiburg. Puffy-eyed and irritable, both Brunner and
Lansky showed the minor ravages of their improvised
night's rest. Vanek, on the other hand, who could get by
with only cat-napping, looked as fresh as on the morning
when they had crossed the Czech border at Gmünd.

"We have no time or need for any more research,"
Vanek said. "Wohl lives alone. We know he is there

every evening. We have checked the immediate surroundings where he lives. We will visit him tonight."

Inspector Gruber of the Freiburg police took every possible precaution: without knowing what might happen, half-convinced that nothing at all would happen, he mounted a formidable operation. At Lanz's suggestion twenty men, all armed with automatic weapons, had thrown a loose cordon round the vicinity of Dieter Wohl's house—loose because they wanted anyone who approached the house to slip inside the net before they tightened it. So observation had to be from a distance and the nearest policeman was over a hundred metres from the building.

Six men were held back in a special reserve force, hidden inside a truck which had been backed into a field and parked behind trees. Communications were excellent; every man was equipped with a walkie-talkie which linked him with a control truck half a kilometre up the road to Freiburg and inside a field. Inside the truck the BND chief sat with Lennox, Inspector Gruber and the communications technician; a transceiver perched on a flap table linked them with the walkie-talkie sets.

To try and counter the distance problem—the fact that they had to stay well back from Wohl's house—Gruber had issued several men with night-glasses for scanning the house. His orders were specific: they must let anyone who approached reach the house, then close in on command from Gruber personally. Everything really depended on how well the men with the night-glasses were able to operate. And all traffic was to be allowed to pass along the road. Any attempt to set up checkpoints would have been useless: they had no idea who they were waiting for, whether in fact there was anyone to wait for.

"You really think someone is going to come and attack Wohl?" Gruber asked at one stage.

"I have no idea," Lanz admitted. "As I have explained

to you, there could be political implications behind this operation."

"An urban guerrilla gang?" Gruber pressed.

"Something like that . . ."

They waited as night fell, as the naked trees faded into the darkness. And with the coming of night the temperature dropped rapidly. Then they had their first hint of trouble: huge banks of mist drifted in off the Rhine, rolling across the fields in waves like a sea shroud, a white fog which seemed to thicken as it approached the house. Very soon the man nearest the house was in difficulties. It wasn't so much that he couldn't see anything; what he could see was deceptive, hard to identify. Lennox, who was growing restless, said he was going outside to take a look at things. It was at this moment that Lanz handed him a 9-mm Luger. "If you insist on prowling about outside, you had better carry this."

Several cars and a petrol wagon had already passed down the road, and each one was checked in and out of the section under surveillance by an observer at either end. In the truck Lanz and Gruber were careful about this as the reports came in—especially since the mist had arrived. "If one of those cars doesn't come out at the other end we're going to have to move damned fast," Gruber remarked. "This mist is something I could have done without . . ."

Worried, Lanz checked his watch. "I'm almost hoping no one comes," he said. "We could have left Wohl inside a trap."

Gruber shook his head. "Wohl took the decision himself when we consulted him," he said. "And remember, he's an old policeman . . ."

Behind the wheel of the black Mercedes he had hired at Kehl, Vanek was driving slowly as they came closer to Freiburg from the south. Ahead of him were two other cars in convoy. He could have passed them several times and Brunner, irritably, had suggested he should overtake. "I'm staying on their tail," Vanek told him. "If there are any patrol-cars about they're less likely to stop three cars travelling together. They're always interested in the car which is on its own. A policeman in Paris once told me that."

"There's a mist coming down," Brunner commented.

"I like mist. It confuses people."

"I think we're close now," Brunner said. "I remember that old barn we just passed."

"We are close," Vanek agreed.

"Three cars coming in," the policeman with the night-glasses at the southern end of the section reported. "At least I think there were three. It's so thick I couldn't get any idea of the makes . . ."

"Were there three or not?" Gruber demanded over the air. "I have told you before, you must be precise—otherwise the whole operation becomes pointless."

"Probably two . . ."

"Probably?" Gruber shouted over the transceiver. "I will ask you again. How many vehicles just entered the section? Think!"

"Two vehicles," the man replied.

"Something just went past," reported the man at the northern end of the section. "It's hellishly difficult to see now. More than one . . ."

Gruber looked at Lanz and then cast his eyes to the roof of the truck. "Sometimes I wonder why I became a policeman. My wife wanted me to buy a grocer's shop."

"It must be very difficult for them—in this mist," Lanz said gently. "I think they are doing very well."

Gruber turned the switch himself and leaned forward to speak. "Number Four. You said quite clearly there was more than one vehicle. Can you be sure of that?"

"Quite sure," Number Four replied. "There were two

travelling close together. Two cars."

"He's a good chap," Gruber said as he returned the switch to "receive." He rubbed the side of his nose. "So is the other man, to be fair. It's my own fault—now the mist has come I just wish I'd blocked off the road with checkpoints. We'd better leave it alone now."

"We'd better leave it alone," Lanz agreed.

When he left the truck Lennox made his way back to the road and started walking along it towards Dieter Wohl's house. He was worried about the mist but he didn't dare get too close to the building for fear of confusing the watching policemen. When two cars approached him, nose to tail, he saw a blur of headlights and pressed himself close against the hedge. As they went past he walked a short distance further and then stopped on the grass verge. He was now at a point half-way between the northern end of the section and the house.

Under his seat Vanek carried the 9-mm Luger pistol which Borisov had obtained for him. Vanek didn't expect to use a gun but he believed in carrying some protection and he was an expert at concealing a weapon. At the moment the pistol was held to the underside of the seat with strips of medical adhesive tape. He was now driving even more slowly, allowing the two cars ahead to disappear into the fog, but he kept the Mercedes moving until they had just gone past Dieter Wohl's house which was a grey blur in the mist. Then he pulled up. No point in giving the German warning, making him wonder why a vehicle had stopped outside his house on a night like this.

"You wait with the car," he told Lansky, "and keep the motor running. I don't think there'll be any trouble but you never can tell."

"Why are you nervous?" asked Brunner, who was coming with him. It was unlike Vanek to anticipate trouble—to refer to it openly.

"I'm nervous that Lansky will forget to keep the motor ticking over," Vanek snapped.

Why was he nervous, Vanek wondered as he got out of the car with Brunner. Some sixth sense kept telling him something was wrong. He stood on the grass verge, looking at the blurred shape of the house, glancing up and down the road and across the fields he couldn't see. Then he walked back to the house and towards the front door. Changing his mind, with Brunner close behind, he went to the side, opened the wire-gate quietly and walked round to the back of the house. The only lights were in two windows on the ground floor at the front; all the other windows were in darkness. With his coat collar pulled up against the chill, Vanek walked back to the front door. Brunner slipped out of sight to the side of the house. Vanek pressed the bell by the side of the door, his right hand inside his pocket where it gripped the Luger he had extracted from under the car seat. It was uncannily quiet in the mist.

He had to wait several moments before he heard a rattle as a chain was removed on the other side of the door, then the door was opened slowly and the huge figure of Dieter Wohl stood in the entrance. He was carrying a walking-stick in his right hand, a heavy farmer's stick without a handle.

"Good evening," Vanek said in his impeccable German. "I am Inspector Braun of the Criminal Police." He showed Wohl the forged Sûreté card Borisov had supplied and quickly replaced it in his pocket with his left hand. "A man has been found dead in the road two hundred metres from here in the Freiburg direction. May I come in and have a word with you?"

"Could I have a closer look at that identity card?" asked the ex-Abwehr officer. "The police themselves are always warning us to be careful who we let in . . ."

"Certainly . . ." Vanek withdrew his right hand from his coat and pointed the Luger at the German's stomach.

"This is an emergency. I don't even know you really live here. I'm coming inside so please move slowly back down the hall and . . ."

The German was backing away as Vanek took a step forward. "If it's as serious as that then please do come in, but I would be glad if you would put away . . ." Wohl was still talking when he wielded the heavy stick with extraordinary speed and strength. It cracked down on Vanek's wrist as he was still moving and the shock and pain of the blow made him drop the weapon. In acute pain, Vanek kept his nerve; whipping up his left hand, the palm and fingers stiffened, he thrust it upwards under Wohl's heavy jaw. Had the ex-Abwehr man stiffened, his neck would have snapped, but he let himself go over backwards and crashed down on the polished floor, rolling sideways to take the impact on his shoulder. Vanek suddenly realized that this was going to be a more dangerous opponent than Jouvel or Robert Philip. And Brunner couldn't get into the narrow hall to lend assistance because Vanek was in the way.

The Luger, sliding along the polished floor, had vanished. It turned into a dogfight. Vanek had age on his side; Wohl was enormously strong. The German, still gripping the stick, was clambering to his feet when Vanek crashed into him again to bring him down. Caught off-balance, Wohl toppled, half-recovered, then fell; clutching at a table to save himself, his hand caught a cloth, dragging it off with several porcelain vases which crashed to the floor. Falling backwards a second time, Wohl rolled again, taking the fall on his other shoulder. Vanek's legs loomed above him and he struck out with the stick he still grasped, catching the Czech a heavy blow on the shin. Vanek yelped, brought his fist down into Wohl's face, but the face moved and the blow was only glancing, sliding down the German's jaw. Behind them, Brunner still couldn't do anything in the narrow hall.

The two men grappled on the floor, rolling over, smashing into furniture, each trying to kill the other.

"I don't like it," said Lanz.

"Those two cars—which might have been three?" Gruber queried. "I'm moving in," he decided. He was on the verge of issuing the order to the truckload of six men waiting in reserve behind the copse of trees when another report came in: a bus and a petrol tanker had moved into the section from the south, travelling one behind the other. Cursing, Gruber delayed giving the order. "That's something we can do without," he rasped. "A bloody collision in the fog . . ."

"They always do it in a fog," Lanz commented. "One vehicle comes up behind another and hugs its tail. It gives them comfort so they ignore the risk . . ."

"I'm getting worried," said Gruber.

They waited until the policeman at the northern end of the section reported traffic moving past—he couldn't identify the vehicles—and then Gruber told the reserve truck to drive to Wohl's house. Twenty seconds later—too late to stop it—another report came in from the southern end of the section. A second petrol tanker had appeared and was now moving slowly into the section.

Wohl's hallway, normally so neat and tidy and cared for—the ex-Abwehr officer was a methodical soul—was a total shambles. Furniture was wrecked, pictures had come off the walls, the floor was littered with the debris of smashed porcelain, and there was a certain amount of smeared blood. Wohl's stick lay on the floor beside its dead owner; the German's skull had been cracked by his own weapon.

Vanek, still panting, left Brunner by the front door and went inside the living-room where a light was burning. The Czech had expected to spend some time searching for the war diary and manuscript but he found them

waiting for him on the German's desk; Wohl had been
working on his memoirs when the door-bell rang. Vanek
read only a few words of the neat, hand-written diary. *In
1944 the Leopard went everywhere accompanied by a
vicious wolf-hound called César . . .*

Stuffing the diary and the few pages of manuscript
into his pocket, he returned to the hall to look for the
missing Luger; on his way out of the living-room he
toppled a bookcase so it crashed to the floor, scattering
its contents. There was no question of making this death
look like an accident but it could still look like an attempted burglary which had gone wrong. He found the
Luger hidden under a low chest and went to the front door
where Brunner was waiting for him. "Something's coming," Brunner warned. As Vanek moved through the doorway a police truck appeared, stopping just beyond the
house. A second later something large loomed out of
the mist, coming very slowly. A petrol tanker. It began
crawling past the stationary police vehicle as men emerged
from it. Vanek raised the Luger, took deliberate aim,
fired three times.

The heavy 9-mm slugs penetrated the side of the
tanker with a series of thuds. Vanek began running
towards the Mercedes, followed by Brunner. Behind them
someone shouted, a muffled shout, succeeded by a muffled
boom. The petrol tanker flared, a sheet of flame consumed
the mist and behind the two running Czechs someone
started screaming and went on and on. Billowing black
smoke replaced the mist and a nauseating stench drifted
on the night air. Vanek reached the car where Lansky,
white-faced, sat behind the wheel with the motor ticking
over.

"What the hell was that . . ."

"Get it moving," Vanek snarled. "Slam your foot down
—if we hit something we hit it . . ."

The Mercedes accelerated, not to high speed but very
fast for the mist-bound road. Brunner, who had wrenched

open the rear door, was still only half-inside the vehicle when it moved off with the door swinging loose beside him. A few metres further along the road Lennox had heard the shots and then what sounded like an explosion. He was standing on the grass verge when the Mercedes's blurred headlights rushed towards him with the rear door still open and someone only half-inside the car. Behind it a police siren had started up. He fired twice as the car roared past him and both bullets penetrated Brunner's arched back. The Czech's body spun out of the open door and thumped down in the road as the Mercedes vanished in the mist, still picking up speed.

14

"This decaying American Republic whose power is fading . . . America, that cauldron of many nationalities which has not yet found a true identity . . . Withdrawing her troops from Europe when she no longer had the strength to dominate the world, she is now dissolving into chaos . . . One thing above all we must ensure! That never again must she be allowed to garrison Europe—to reassert her one-time control over us!"

It was President Florian's most vicious attack yet and it was made in a speech at Marseilles where the French Communist party is never far below the surface. A massive audience acclaimed the speech, showing the enormous support Florian enjoyed in the south where once, so many years earlier, a République Soviétique du Sud had almost been established at the end of the Second World War.

Afterwards there was a huge parade along the Canebière, the main thoroughfare of the turbulent French seaport where thousands of people broke ranks and tried to surge round the presidential Citroën. On the direct orders of Marc Grelle, who had flown to the city, CRS troops drove back the milling crowd, which later almost caused a confrontation between the president and the police prefect. "You spoiled the whole spontaneous demonstration," he raged. "There was no need . . ."

"The spontaneous demonstration was organized by the Communist party," Grelle said sharply. "And my reaction is you are still alive. Do you or do you not want me to protect your life?"

The sheer vehemence of the prefect startled Florian, who changed direction suddenly, putting an arm round Grelle's shoulders. "You are, of course, right. Nothing must happen to me before I fly to Russia. We have peace within our grasp, Grelle, peace . . ."

The Soviet convoy K.12 had now passed through the Dardanelles and was proceeding south across the Aegean Sea. It was proceeding slowly, at a leisurely pace which puzzled the naval analysts at NATO headquarters in Brussels. The team of analysts was under the control of a British officer, Commander Arthur Leigh-Browne, RN, and on Tuesday, 21 December—the day when Florian made his violent attack on the Americans at Marseilles—Browne circulated to all western defence ministers a routine report.

"K.12's most likely destination would appear to be the Indian Ocean, making passage in due course through the Suez Canal—except for the fact that the aircraft carrier, *Kirov*, is too large to pass through the canal . . .

"Other possible destinations are the newly-acquired naval facilities granted by the Spanish government at Barcelona . . .

"The factor we find most difficult to equate with either of the above two conjectures is the presence of the fifteen large transports (contents as yet unknown) . . ."

As Browne put it to his German second-in-command after the report had been sent off, "At the moment, it's all hot air. I haven't a clue what they're up to. We'll have to play the old game of wait-and-see . . ."

Guy Florian made his speech in Marseilles at noon. At the same equivalent time in Moscow an enlarged meeting of the Politburo which had been called unexpectedly was listening to a brief speech by the First Secretary. Among those present were the Foreign Minister of the Soviet Union and Marshal Gregori Prachko, Minister of Defence. It was these two men—forming a quorum of three with the First Secretary—who had earlier sanctioned the despatch of the Soviet Commando to the west.

Revealing for the first time to the enlarged meeting the identity of the Frenchman he called "our friend," the First Secretary went on to give details of the Franco-Soviet pact which would be announced while President Florian was in Moscow. "The President of the French Republic has, of course, under the French constitution, full powers to negotiate and conclude treaties with foreign powers," he continued.

It was clause 14 which was the key to the whole agreement. This clause stated that in the furtherance of world peace joint military manoeuvres would be carried out from time to time on the respective territories of the Union of Socialist Soviet Republics and the Republic of France. In simple language it meant that the advance elements of two Soviet armoured divisions now aboard convoy K.12 would be landed at French Mediterranean ports within the next few days.

"Where will they go to?" enquired Nikolai Suslov, the most intellectual member of the Politburo.

"I will tell you!" It was the immensely broad-shouldered, uniformed and bemedalled Marshal Gregori Prachko who replied. Prachko intensely disliked non-practical intellectuals and especially disliked Nikolai Suslov. "They will be put ashore at Toulon and Marseilles immediately Florian has announced the pact in Moscow. The date of his visit—23 December—has been carefully chosen. Over their famous Christmas the government ministers of the west all go on holiday, so they will not be behind their desks to react quickly . . ."

"But where will the troops go?" Suslov persisted.

"To the Rhine border with Germany, of course! As he gets up on Christmas morning to open his presents, Chancellor Franz Hauser will find himself facing Soviet troops to the east—and to the west. The whole of western Europe will fall under our control—including the powerhouse of the Ruhr—which will enable us to win any confrontation with China . . ."

PART THREE

THE POLICE PREFECT
OF PARIS

December 22–December 23

15

Any experienced policeman knows it: you can throw a cordon round an area, set up road-blocks, and three times out of four you are too late. Gruber set up a cordon and caught nothing but irate motorists and truck-drivers. The Mercedes, which had been hired in Kehl, was found a week later inside a copse at the edge of the Black Forest. Four of the six policemen who had been getting out of the truck when the petrol tanker detonated were lucky; most of the blast went the other way, travelling across open fields. The other two policemen were badly burned, one of them with first-degree injuries which required plastic surgery later. The petrol tanker driver died from the fumes which filled his cab before he could escape.

Lanz and Gruber searched Wohl's house, looking for the war diary which Lennox had seen, and found no trace of the diary or the manuscript. Brunner's dead body was taken to the police mortuary and examination of his clothing and pocket contents revealed very little. He was carrying a large sum of money—two thousand deutschmarks—and a French identity card in the name of Emile Bonnard. "Which will undoubtedly prove to be false," Gruber commented. Underneath his German hat and coat Brunner was wearing a French suit and underclothes. Apart from this there was very little to prove who he really was—until the preliminary results of the medical examination came through.

"My colleague has come up with something interesting,"

the medical examiner reported to Gruber who was sitting in a hotel bedroom eating dinner with the BND chief and Lennox. "He is a dental technician and according to him the dental work and teeth fillings were definitely carried out in eastern Europe—probably in Russia . . ."

Lanz phoned Marc Grelle direct from police headquarters at Freiburg. Strictly speaking, any such call should have been made to the Sûretè, but whereas Lanz knew Grelle well and trusted his discretion, he neither liked nor trusted the Director-General who was Commissioner Suchet's superior. As Lanz explained to Grelle, he had two reasons for informing him of this development. The assassin Lennox had shot dead—and Lanz was careful not to mention the Englishman in any way—was travelling with French papers in the name of Emile Bonnard. Also— and here again Lanz phrased it carefully—he had reason to believe the Commando had recently come from France and might well have re-crossed the border back into that country . . .

"You have solid grounds for saying an assassination Commando, possibly Soviet-controlled, is on the move?" Grelle enquired.

"Yes," Lanz replied firmly. "Without going into details, I'm pretty sure of it. And perhaps it would be helpful if we both keep in touch . . ."

Grelle had just put down the phone when Boisseau came into his office with a routine report. "Lesage has just called in. That Algerian terrorist, Abou Benefeika, is still holed up in the derelict apartment building in the Goutte-d'Or. No sign of his pals coming to collect him yet. We let him go on fermenting?"

"Continue the surveillance . . ." Grelle took a bite out of the sandwich he would have to make do with for his evening meal. Normally he dined at Chez Bénoit, an exclusive little restaurant in the old Les Halles district where you had to phone for a table; he was beginning to miss the place. "I have just had a call from Peter Lanz of the German BND," he informed Boisseau. "He played it very cagey but somehow he has found out that a Soviet assassination Commando is at work. This evening they killed an ex-Abwehr officer in Freiburg." He paused. "The name of the Abwehr man was Dieter Wohl . . ."

"One of the three names on Lasalle's list . . ."

"Exactly. So now it looks as though this Commando has been sent with the express purpose of wiping out everyone on that list—and they've done it, for God's sake. All avenues through which we might have seen a little light are closed . . ."

"The surveillance on Roger Danchin and Alain Blanc is producing nothing?"

"Nothing . . ." The prefect frowned as his phone rang. He checked his watch. 10 p.m. Only recently returned from his flight to Marseilles when he had accompanied the president while he delivered his most bitter anti-American tirade so far, Grelle was feeling very tired. Who the hell could it be at this hour? He picked up the phone, swallowing the last of his sandwich. It was Alain Blanc.

"No, Minister," Grelle assured him, "I have not dug up any connection between the president and Lucie Devaud as yet . . . We now know her father was Albert Camors, a wealthy stockbroker who died a few months ago and left her his apartment in the Place des Vosges . . . No, we do not know any more . . . Yes, she must have been illegitimate . . . No, no connection at all with the Elysée . . ."

Grelle shrugged as he replaced the receiver. "He worries about a scandal, that one. As I was saying, all avenues seem closed to us, so all we can hope for once more is the unexpected break. And yet, Boisseau, I feel that somewhere I am overlooking something—something under my nose . . ."

"Something to do with the Commando? Incidentally, we may as well cancel the alert on the man the German police shot in Freiburg. Did Lanz give you a name?"

Grelle consulted a notepad. "Emile Bonnard," he replied. "And I do not expect we shall ever see the other two men—Duval and Lambert. They have done their job. They will never return to France."

Carel Vanek and Antonin Lansky approached the checkpoint to cross back into France the following morning, Wednesday, 22 December, which was the deadline day Borisov had given them in Tábor to complete their mission. They were on their way to visit Annette Devaud. They came up to the passport control counter separately with half a dozen people between them and Vanek presented himself for inspection first.

"Papers . . ."

The passport officer took the document Vanek had handed him, opened it after studying the Czech's face and then compared it with the photograph. The name he had already noted. Vanek waited with a bored look on his face, chewing a piece of chocolate while he studied the extremely attractive girl waiting next in line. He grinned at her engagingly and after a moment's hesitation she smiled back at him.

"You have been to Germany on business?" the passport official enquired.

"Yes."

The official returned the passport and Vanek moved on, to be joined a few minutes later by Lansky. Vanek had presented the third set of papers he had brought from Tábor, papers made out in the name of Lucien Segard, papers which carried a photograph of him without a moustache. Only the previous night in Kehl he had shaved off the moustache in the station wash-room before accompanying Lansky to a small hotel where they had spent the night. Lansky had also used his third set of papers which carried the name Yves Gandouin. When frontier control officials have been asked to look out for men travelling under the names of Duval and Lambert it is only human for them to concentrate on people of those names, and to be anything but suspicious of different names.

Without having the least idea that their previous identities had been blown, Vanek had taken his decision the previous night after they had abandoned the Mercedes. "Twice we have crossed the French border using our present papers," he had told Lansky, "and twice is enough." He had then proceeded to burn the papers carrying the names Duval and Lambert before they walked to the nearest village and independently boarded a bus crowded with Christmas shoppers for Kehl. Inside Germany they were really in no danger: the only people who knew their names were inside France, and on the phone Marc Grelle had been reluctant to give Peter Lanz such information because of the delicacy of the investigation he was conducting.

Arriving back in Strasbourg, Vanek kept well away from the Hertz car-hire branch in the Boulevard de Nancy. "Never go back," was one of his favourite maxims. Instead, the two men took a cab to the airport where Vanek hired a Renault 17 from the Avis car-hire branch in the name of Lucien Segard. By 2 p.m. they were on their way to Saverne, which is only twenty-five miles from Strasbourg.

Alan Lennox had stayed up half the night at the Hotel Colombi in Freiburg talking to Peter Lanz. The German, who had been handed a copy of the *Frankfurter Allgemeine Zeitung* containing Dieter Wohl's letter just before he left Bonn—"I should have been shown it days earlier, but no one thought to read the correspondence columns" —was dubious as to whether Annette Devaud would still be alive.

"From what Wohl said to you," he remarked, "she would be a very old lady now—and if she is blind how could she recognize anyone? Even assuming she ever knew what the Leopard looked like . . ."

"There's nothing else left," Lennox said obstinately. "No one else left, perhaps I should say. What Leon Jouvel told me is very inconclusive—although he was convincing at the time. In any case, the poor devil is dead. I'm going back across the Rhine tomorrow to try and find Annette Devaud."

"Going back again over the frontier for the third time on false papers? I'm not asking you to do that . . ."

"Call it British bloody-mindedness—we're known for it. I just want to get to the bottom of this thing and find out who the Leopard really is. Wish me luck."

"I have a feeling you're going to need more than luck," Lanz replied gravely.

Remembering the atmosphere of intense police activity at Strasbourg station only thirty-six hours earlier, it took a certain amount of will-power for Lennox to hand his papers across the counter to French passport control and then wait while they were inspected. They were examined only cursorily and handed straight back; no one was interested in a man called Jean Bouvier. Probably the easiest way to pass through a checkpoint is to choose a time when someone else is being watched for.

Obtaining the address from Bottin, the telephone directory, Lennox left Strasbourg station and went straight to Hertz car-hire in the Boulevard de Nancy where he chose a Mercedes 350 SE. It was expensive but he wanted some power under the bonnet. By noon he was leaving Strasbourg, driving west for Saverne in the Vosges mountains. He had, of course, no idea that for the first time since he had embarked on this trip at the behest of

David Nash of New York he was two hours ahead of
the Soviet Commando.

It was Boisseau who heard about the newspaper cutting
of Dieter Wohl's letter to the *Frankfurter Allgemeine
Zeitung* sent to Paris by the French Secret Service agent
in Bonn. Oddly enough he was shown the photostat of
the cutting by Commissioner Suchet of counter-intelligence
whom he had made it his business to cultivate. Suchet was
under the impression that this gave him a private pipeline
into the préfecture, whereas the reverse was true; the only
information given to him by Boisseau had first been vetted
by Marc Grelle. It was late in the morning of Wednesday,
22 December, when Boisseau showed the photostat to his
chief.

"So there could just be a witness who never appeared
on Lasalle's list," Grelle mused. "That is, assuming she
is still alive, after all these years . . ."

"She is. I phoned the police station at Saverne. She's
living at a remote farmhouse quite a distance from Saverne
itself—high up in the Vosges mountains. This letter made
me go through the files again and there is one we overlooked. Annette Devaud was in charge of the Leopard's
courier network. The really interesting thing could be
the name . . ."

"Annette Devaud—Lucie Devaud . . ." The prefect
clasped his hands behind his neck and looked shrewdly
at his deputy. "All avenues closed, I said. I wonder. All
right, Boisseau, fly to Saverne. Yes, this afternoon, I
agree. In view of what has happened to the other witnesses should you not call Saverne and ask them to send
out a police guard?"

"She must be old—they might frighten her. And in
any case, since she was not on Lasalle's list why should
she be on the Commando's? Both Lasalle and the Commando must have been working from the same list—in
view of what happened. So where is the danger?"

"I leave it to you," the prefect said.

Driving across the flat plain of Alsace which lies between Strasbourg and the Vosges mountains, Lennox soon ran into atrocious weather. Curtains of rain swept across the empty road, adding even more water to the already flooded fields, and in the distance heavy mist blotted out the Vosges completely. He drove on as water poured down his windscreen and then the engine began knocking badly, which made him swear because he knew the mountain roads ahead could be difficult. It was his own fault: the Hertz people had been reluctant to let him have this car, the only Mercedes 350 on the premises for hire. "It has not been serviced, sir," the girl had protested. "I am not permitted . . ." Lennox had impatiently over-ridden her objections because he liked the car and now he was paying for it.

Driving on across the lonely plain, the knocking became worse and he knew he had been foolish. Squinting through the windscreen, he saw a sign. *Auberge des Vosges and petrol five hundred metres ahead.* He wanted in any case to check Annette Devaud's address—and to find out whether anyone knew if she was still alive. Through the pouring rain a small hotel with a garage attached came into view. Pulling up in front of the pumps, he lowered the window and asked the mechanic to check the vehicle. A few minutes later the mechanic came into the hotel bar with the bad news. He had found the defect: it would take a couple of hours to put it right.

"Can't you hurry it up?" Lennox asked.

"I am starting work on it now," the mechanic informed him. "I can hurry it up, yes. It will take two hours."

Lennox ordered a second cognac and two jambon sandwiches, which arrived as large hunks of appetizing French bread sliced apart and with ham inside them. Had the mechanic said three hours he would have been tempted to try and hire another car. He sank his teeth hungrily into the sandwich; two hours shouldn't make all that difference to the state of the world.

Annette Devaud, now spending the evening of her life at Woodcutter's Farm, had held one of the key positions in the Leopard's Resistance group in 1944: she had controlled the network of couriers, mostly girls in their late teens and early twenties, who had carried messages backwards and forwards under the very noses of the enemies. Almost forty years old, slim and wiry, she had been a handsome woman with a proud Roman nose and an air of authority which had rivalled that of the Leopard himself. Of all the men and women who had worked under him, the Leopard had most respected Annette Devaud, possibly because she was an outspoken anti-Communist. "At least I know where I am with her," he once said. And Annette Devaud had another distinction—she knew what the Leopard looked like.

Because he found it useful to build up the reputation of an invincible personality, the Leopard kept it a secret when he was shot in the leg during a running battle in the forests. The wound did not take long to heal, but for a short period he was bed-ridden. It was Annette Devaud who shared his solitary convalescence, nursing him swiftly back to health, and it was during these few weeks that she came to know exactly what he looked like.

Annette Devaud heard, but did not see, the celebrations of Liberation Day; she had gone blind overnight. No one was able to diagnose the cause of her affliction, although some thought it was the news of the death of her husband who had fought with General Leclerc's division. Then again it could have been the death of her nineteen-year-old daughter Lucie, who drowned when the Leopard drove his car into the river to avoid Dieter Wohl's ambush. This happened after Annette had nursed the Leopard back to health when he was shot.

At the end of the war, returning to her home, Wood-cutter's Farm, she remained there for over thirty years. The onset of blindness was an even greater blow than it might have been for some people; Annette had been a talented amateur artist who drew portraits in charcoal, and this too she put behind her as she adjusted to her new life. But in a folder she kept the collection of portrait sketches she had made during the war from memory. Among the collection were two life-like portraits of the Leopard.

Annette Devaud had endured another tragedy. Against her will, her daughter Lucie had insisted on becoming one of her couriers, and during her time with the Resistance the nineteen-year-old girl had taken as a lover an ex-accountant called Albert Camors. Out of the liaison a child had been born only six months before the Leopard drove Lucie Devaud into the river. Taking its mother's name, the child was called Lucie. Camors survived the war but quarrelled violently with the strong-willed Annette Devaud and he refused to let her have anything to do with the child. Prospering in peacetime—he became a Paris stockbroker—Camors brought up the child himself and never married.

A solitary but strong-willed child—reproducing in some ways the character of her grandmother, Annette, whom she never saw—Lucie grew up in a bachelor household and developed an obsession about the mother she couldn't remember. From her father she heard about the Leopard, about how her mother had died. Then, when she was almost thirty, Camors expired in the arms of his latest mistress and Lucie inherited his fortune and an apartment in the Place des Vosges. And for the first time she visited her blind grandmother.

The two women took to each other immediately and one day Annette, talking about the war, showed her grand-daughter the folder of sketches, including the two of the Leopard. Lucie instantly recognized the portraits, but in her secretive way she said nothing to the blind woman. Using the names of people who had belonged to the Resistance group—which Annette had mentioned—she began checking. With her father's money to finance the investigation, she employed a shrewd lawyer called Max Rosenthal to dig into the Leopard's background. And without saying anything to Annette, she removed the two portrait sketches from the folder and took them back to her Paris apartment.

It was Max Rosenthal who traced Gaston Martin, the Leopard's wartime deputy, to Guiana where he was on the verge of being released from prison. Lucie Devaud wrote a careful letter to the man Annette had mentioned, hinting to Martin that the Leopard had become an important political figure in France, and then waited for a reply. The letter reached Martin shortly after he had been released from prison and he took his time about replying to her.

It was during the opening of a Paris fashion show that Lucie played the macabre trick which finally convinced her she had uncovered the real identity of the Leopard. She had seen the animal in a rue de Rivoli shop which specialized in exotic presents costing a great deal of money. Purchasing the animal, she kept it in her apartment and then obtained a ticket for the fashion show in the rue Cambon. In a newspaper she had read that President Florian would be attending the show with his wife, Lise.

When Guy Florian arrived escorting Lise—he was attending the show to dispel rumours that they were no longer on speaking terms—the show had already started, models were parading, and Lucie Devaud was sitting in a front-row seat with her draped overcoat concealing the underneath of her chair. Florian and his wife sat down almost opposite her. The show was almost over when Lucie tugged at the chain she held in her hand and which led underneath her draped chair. A model had just walked past when the leopard cub emerged from under the chair, stood on the carpet with its legs braced and bared its teeth.

It was over in a moment. An armed plain-clothes security man, one of several sent to the show by Marc Grelle, caught the expression on the president's face, grabbed the chain out of Lucie's hand, tugged the animal and led it out of the salon, followed by its owner with her coat draped over her arm. Florian recovered quickly, made an off-hand gesture and cracked a joke. "I have had nothing to drink and yet there are spots in front of my eyes!"

Outside in the foyer Lucie took the chain from the detective without a word and left the building. The salon owner had been amused when she arrived with a leopard cub. "How chic," he had remarked to his *directrice*. "We should have one of the models parading with that animal . . ." Getting into her car, parking the leopard cub on the front seat beside her, Lucie drove back to the Place des Vosges. On the following day she returned the animal to the shop, which accepted it back at a much-reduced price.

So often a woman takes a decision on feminine instinct; so often she is right. Lucie Devaud was now certain Guy Florian was the Leopard. She had seen a certain expression in his eyes before he recovered, a sudden wariness and alarm as he stared back at her—as though when he saw the look in her own eyes he had understood. "Who the hell are you? You have found me out . . ." She knew there was no way she could be traced: she had paid for the leopard cub in cash and had applied for the salon ticket in a false name. It was while she was driving back to her apartment that she decided she would kill Guy Florian. The following morning the letter from Gaston Martin arrived.

Martin replied to her letter with an equally guarded communication. He said that he was interested in her theory and told her that he was returning soon by ship from Guiana. Could they meet when he arrived in Paris? Lucie Devaud wrote back immediately, suggesting that they met at a small Left Bank hotel called Cécile in the rue de Bac. Presumably she was not too keen on inviting an ex-convict to her luxurious apartment in the Place des Vosges— or possibly she was still displaying the secretiveness which was so much a part of her life.

On the night before Wednesday, 8 December, she wrote out a complete account of her activities and sealed the report in a package which also contained the two sketches of the Leopard produced more than thirty years before by her grandmother, Annette Devaud. Across the package she wrote in her own hand, *To be delivered to the police prefect of Paris in the event of my death.* In the morning she delivered the package to her lawyer, Max Rosenthal, with strict instructions that it must remain unopened. Reading in the paper about Florian's nightly walk from the Elysée to the Place Beauvau she had decided not to wait for Gaston Martin—even though the Frenchman was on the eve of arriving back in France. On Wednesday evening, waiting outside the fur shop in the Faubourg St Honoré, she produced her 9-mm Bayard pistol. But it was Marc Grelle who fired two shots.

The letter Lucie Devaud had written and deposited with her lawyer, Max Rosenthal, was not delivered to the police prefect of Paris. An extravagant man, who spent vast sums on gambling, Rosenthal was not prepared to gamble his career. When he heard of his client's attempt to kill the president he became frightened that delivery of the package might involve him. Lucie had always come to see him and given only verbal instructions; no written correspondence had passed between them; and she had paid his bills in cash—which he had not declared to the tax man. Confident that there was no discoverable link between them, he locked the package away inside a deed-box where it stayed until a year later when he died un-expectedly.

One of Lucie Devaud's more benevolent actions before she died as a would-be assassin was to persuade her blind grandmother to see an eye specialist. Perhaps medical technique had advanced in the intervening thirty years, or maybe the trauma which had induced the affliction had run its course. Annette Devaud was operated on during September—three months before Guy Florian was due to fly to Russia—and recovered her sight completely. She went straight back to Woodcutter's Farm from the hospital and started reading and drawing avidly, resuming her old solitary way of life but now blessed with the return of her sight. When she was told about the death of her grand-daughter by the man who brought her supplies she flatly refused to accept the circumstances surrounding Lucie's death. "It's all a ghastly mistake," she said firmly. "They must have mistaken her for someone else." This was the old woman the Soviet Commando was now on its way to kill.

16

Ignoring the downpour, Vanek drove at high speed along the deserted road from Strasbourg to Saverne. Beside him Lansky sat in silence as he chewed at the sandwiches they had bought at Strasbourg airport and drank from a

bottle of red wine. Once he pointed out to Vanek that
he was exceeding the speed limit. "Get on with your
lunch," the Czech told him. "We have only one final visit
to make before we start back for home. And there is a
limit to how long time is on our side. With a bit of luck
it will turn out that the Devaud woman died years ago,"
he added.

Imperceptibly—because he decided that Lansky was
right—Vanek reduced speed, but Lansky, who was watching the speedometer needle, observed what was happening
and smiled to himself as he finished the sandwich. To
some extent Brunner had acted as a buffer between the
two egotists, and Lansky, who was intelligent, decided
not to make any more provocative comments. They still
had a job to do.

"We'll have to check on the address of Devaud as soon
as we can," Vanek remarked, overtaking a vegetable truck
in a shower of spray. "So keep a lookout for a hotel or
a bar. If she's still alive and living in the same place the
locals are bound to know. In provincial France you can't
pee behind a wall without the whole village watching . . ."

"This time," Lansky suggested, "we needn't be too fussy
about arranging accidents. Just do the job and run, I say,
now we haven't got that old woman, Brunner, round our
necks any more . . ."

"I'll decide that when the moment comes," Vanek
snapped.

Across the plain there had been no sign of habitation
for miles. They were coming close to Saverne when Vanek,
peering through the rain-soaked windscreen, saw the sign.
Auberge des Vosges and petrol five hundred metres ahead.
He reduced speed. "This place should have a phone
book," he said, "and we're in the right area now." Turning
off the highway, he pulled in close to a battery of petrol
pumps. "Top her up," he told the attendant, "while we
go inside and have a drink . . ." Vanek believed that you
never could tell what emergency might lie ahead of you,

that it always paid to keep a full tank. As they got out
of the Renault a mechanic inside the garage was wiping
the windscreen of a Mercedes 350 he had been working
on.

Lennox checked his watch and walked out of the bar
of the Auberge des Vosges on his way to the wash-room.
Two hours exactly. The mechanic had just informed him
his car was ready and Lennox had paid the bill. Earlier
he had checked Annette Devaud in Bottin and there had
been no entry, but the barman had been more helpful.

"Funny old girl. Must be over seventy now if she's a
day. She still lives at Woodcutter's Farm, all on her own.
The locals don't see her from one year to another—except
the chap who delivers her supplies. Remarkable woman,
Annette Devaud. You know she was blind for getting on
thirty years?"

"I haven't met her yet," Lennox said carefully.

"Remarkable woman," the barman repeated. "Happened just at the end of the war—she went blind, just
like that. Some disease or other, I don't know what. Then
a few months ago a specialist takes a look at her and says
he can do something." The barman gave a glass an extra
polish. "A miracle happens. He operates and she can see
again. Think of that—blind for over thirty years and
then you see the world all over again like new. Tragedy
that—about her grand-daughter, Lucie. You know who
she was?"

"No."

"Girl who tried to bump off Florian the other week.
Must have been a nut—like that chap who shot Kennedy
in Dallas." The barman leaned forward confidentially. "I
live only two kilometres from the old girl and the few
of us who knew who Lucie was kept our mouths shut.
Even the police didn't catch on—the girl only came here
a few times. I'm only telling you seeing as you're going

to visit her—might give her a shock if you said the wrong
thing . . ."

Lennox was thinking about it as he went into the wash-
room and took his time about freshening up—the previous
night in Freiburg he had enjoyed only two hours' sleep.
It could only happen in a provincial French hamlet—a
conspiracy of silence to protect a local and much-respected
Frenchwoman. Over the basin a large mirror faced the
door and he was drying himself off when the door opened.
Lowering his towel he stared into the mirror and the
man standing in the doorway stared back at him. For
a matter of seconds their eyes met, then the man in the
mirror glanced round the wash-room as though looking
for someone and went out again.

Drying himself quickly, Lennox put on his jacket and
coat, then opened the door slowly. For a few seconds in
the rue de l'Épine at the entrance to Leon Jouvel's building in Strasbourg he'd had a good look at the face of
the man with the umbrella he had cannoned against,
knocking his pebble glasses down on to the cobbles.
He was still not absolutely sure—the man in Strasbourg
had seemed older—but not with the light from the street
lamp full on his face, he reminded himself. The passage
outside the washroom was empty. He walked down it and
glanced inside the bar.

The man who had come into the wash-room had his
back turned, but his face was visible in the bar mirror.
He was talking to another man, tall, dark-haired and
clean-shaven, a man of about thirty. The tall man, who
was idly turning an empty glass in his hand, looked over
his companion's shoulder and stared straight at Lennox
and then away. Lennox was even more sure now. There
had been three men in the Soviet Commando's car at
Freiburg. The man called Bonnard was dead, which left
two of them. And at the back of the war diary they had
taken off Dieter Wohl had been the address of Annette
Devaud.

At this moment Lennox cursed himself for accepting Peter Lanz's theory that by now the remnants of the Commando would be fleeing back to Russia. It had been a reasonable theory—at the time—because the third witness on Lasalle's list had just been killed, so why should the Commando linger? Lennox walked back into the hotel out of sight of the bar as though leaving by the front entrance, then he ran up a wide staircase which turned twice before reaching the upper landing. He waited at the top where he could see through a window to the road beyond.

The barman had disappeared behind a curtain when Lansky returned to the bar where Vanek was leaning against the counter. Picking up his drink, Lansky swallowed it as Vanek played with the glass in his hand. "That Frenchman I saw coming out of No. 49—Jouvel's place—the chap I bumped into, is in the wash-room here," he said in a quiet voice. "That's no coincidence . . ."

"Are you sure? Describe him," Vanek said casually.

Lansky described Lennox in a few words. "I'm quite sure," he said. "I'm trained to remember things like that —in case you've forgotten. We looked at each other in the mirror for a few seconds and we both knew each other. I could have dealt with him—the place was empty—but that would have sparked off the police and we don't want that at the moment, do we?"

"No, we don't. Incidentally, he's looking in at the bar now, so don't turn round . . ." The situation didn't surprise Vanek; sooner or later something was bound to go wrong—it had in Freiburg—up to a point. It was just a question of deciding how to handle it. "He's gone now," Vanek said. "I think we'll get away from here, too."

As they walked out of the front door a Peugot 504 with a single man behind the wheel was moving off to Saverne after filling up with petrol. The rain obscured the silhouette of the driver. "That's probably him," Vanek said. From the first-floor window Lennox watched them drive off in the direction of Saverne. Going downstairs he went back into the bar where the barman was polishing more glasses. Ordering another cognac, Lennox made the remark as casually as he could.

"Those two men who came in here after me—I thought I recognized one of them. Or are they locals?"

"Never seen them before—and don't want to see them a second time. I gathered from the tall one they're something to do with market research. They pick names of people and go ask them damned silly questions. I think they're on their way to see Annette Devaud . . ."

"Really?"

"Something to do with a campaign to increase pensions," the barman explained. "Was her husband alive, they wanted to know. How could they find Woodcutter's Farm? I just told them—I didn't draw them a map like I did for you." The barman grinned sourly. "And I didn't tell them Annette will chase them off her property with a shotgun as good as spit . . ."

Lennox finished his drink quickly and went out to where the Mercedes was waiting for him. If anything, it was raining even more heavily, and as he drove away from the hotel he saw in the distance thick rain-mist enveloping the Vosges mountains. There had been mist at Freiburg when the Commando killed Dieter Wohl and now there was mist over the Vosges. The association of ideas worried him as he pressed his foot down and drove well beyond the limit in his attempt to overtake the Renault.

Carel Vanek was a fast driver but Alan Lennox was a more ruthless driver. Risking patrol-cars—and the appalling weather—moving at over a hundred and ten kilometres an hour, the Englishman came up behind the Czech just beyond Saverne where the highway climbs into the mountains. For a moment there was a brief spell of shafted sunlight breaking through the clouds, illuminating the peaks of the Vosges, the shiny road ahead, and less than three hundred metres away Lennox saw the Renault arcing round a bend, sending up spurts of water from under its fast-moving wheels. Then it began to rain again, slanting rain which slashed down like a water curtain.

In the brief glimpse of sunlight Lennox saw the ground sloping away to the right beyond the road edge in a severe drop. He reduced speed a little, maintaining his distance behind the car in front. His opportunity came less than half a minute later as they still circled up the side of the mountain with the slope continuing down to the right. In the distance—where the road reappeared as it descended again—coming towards him, towards the speeding Renault, he saw the blur of a large truck. Lennox pressed his foot down, closing the gap until he was almost on the tail of the car ahead. Still climbing, the road straightened out as the oncoming vehicle, which he now realized was a huge timber wagon, came closer. He timed it carefully, gauging the width of the road, the combined width of the three vehicles, then he pulled out without warning and accelerated.

"Bloody maniac . . ."

Behind the wheel of the Renault Vanek, still keeping a lookout for the Peugeot 504, was startled as the car coming up behind him began to overtake seconds before the timber wagon passed them. Instinctively he steered nearer to the right-hand edge where rain-mist blurred the view, trying to give maximum possible passage to the crazy idiot who was overtaking at this dangerous moment. Behind the windscreen of the timber wagon's cab the driver blinked as he saw what was happening, but there was no room to give leeway.

"Watch it," said Lansky, suddenly alerted. "There was a Mercedes at that hotel . . ."

Lennox was alongside the Renault, squeezed into a

gap where there was no margin for the slightest error as
the timber wagon started moving past. Then it was gone.
Lennox turned the wheel slightly. The side of the Mercedes cannoned against the side of the Renault. The wet
road did the rest. The Renault skidded and went over
the edge.

The slope was less steep at this point on the mountain.
Vanek wrestled desperately as he felt the car go over
and down, losing speed as he released pressure on the
accelerator, allowing the car to follow its own momentum.
The wheels were slipping on a muddy slope, churning
up great gouts of mud which splashed over the windscreen, blotting out vision, so Vanek was driving blind
as he lost more speed, as the car went down and down,
skidding and sliding, twisting and turning while the Czech
fought to keep the vehicle on some kind of straight course.
Then, not knowing what lay ahead, he braked. The car
hit something. Then stopped.

"We're alive," Vanek gasped hoarsely.

"That's something," Lansky agreed.

When they got out into the rain they were half-way
down a long slope with the road obscured by mist where
they had come over. A grassy rampart had stopped them
sliding even further. A few metres beyond where the
Renault had stopped a muddy farm-track continued on
down the slope and went back up the hill towards the
highway. "It was that Frenchman I saw in the washroom,"
Lansky said. "I caught a glimpse of him behind the wheel
just before he hit us. He can't be the police or he wouldn't
have bounced us over the edge."

"We meet him again, we finish him," Vanek replied.
"Now we've got to heave this car round and then I'll try
and make it up the track. It's going to take time," he
added.

High on the mountain Lennox stopped the Mercedes close to the edge and looked down. He had to wait a minute until the mist cleared and then he saw the car and two small figures moving round it far below. One of them got inside the Renault and the faint sound of the motor starting drifted up to him. After a minute it stopped, the driver got out and both men started manhandling the vehicle. Disappointed, Lennox drove off. Hoping to kill them, he had gained only a respite.

The weather higher up was foul and he was forced to cut his speed. Clouds blotted out the mountain summits, a grey mist smothered the lower slopes and the world outside the car was a shimmer of dark fir forest in the gliding fog. The address Dieter Wohl had provided— Woodcutter's Farm, Saverne—was misleading, as are so many addresses in rural France. Annette Devaud lived some distance from Saverne. Using the map drawn on the back of a menu card by the barman at the Auberge des Vosges, Lennox drove on through the mist. At one point he passed close to a canal far below him in a cut where oil-skinned figures moved about on a huge barge. Turning a corner, he saw a crude wooden sign rearing above a hedge. *Woodcutter's Farm*.

The track, climbing above the highway and sunk between steep banks, was greasy mud and squelching ruts running with water. Several times he was stopped, his wheels churning uselessly, and now it was so overcast he had his headlights on. As he topped the crest of a hill the lights swept across the front of a long, steep-roofed farmhouse. The building, huddled under a looming quarry dripping with creeper, was the end of the road. Leaving the motor running, he got out into the wet. Lennox estimated he might have no more than fifteen minutes to get Annette Devaud away from the farmhouse before the Commando arrived.

The woman who opened the door held a double-barrelled shotgun which she pointed at Lennox's stomach. She told him she had seen him from an upper window and didn't admit strangers. Lennox started talking rapidly, getting a note of hysteria into his voice. "Can I use your phone? There's been an accident down on the highway and a woman's badly hurt . . ."

"I don't have a phone . . ."

"Then get some bandages, for God's sake . . ." Lennox was waving his hands about, gesturing. Knocking the barrel aside, he jerked the gun out of her hands. "Sorry about this, but shotguns worry me—they're liable to be feather-triggered. And there's no accident down on the highway, although there's liable to be one up here in about ten minutes—and you'll be involved in it." He took a deep breath. "Two men are on their way here to kill you . . ."

In one way Lennox was relieved. He had expected an infirm old lady, but the woman who had faced him with a shotgun was hardly infirm. Of medium height, her back erect, she had moved agilely when he took the gun away from her. Now she stood glaring at him, still a good-looking woman with a Roman nose and a firm jaw. "You don't look crazy," she said. "Why should anyone want to kill me?"

"Because you may be able to identify the Leopard . . ."

It took him well over fifteen minutes—much too long he realized when he checked his watch—to convince Annette Devaud that he might know what he was talking about. And during that time, standing in her old-fashioned living-room, he understood something he had puzzled over ever since the barman had told him she was still alive. If she was able to identify the Leopard—which he doubted—and if by some wild chance Leon Jouvel had been right, how was it that she had not seen Guy Florian's picture during the few months since her sight had been restored? In the newspapers, in the magazines, on television? She supplied the answers after she had told him about how she had once nursed the Leopard when he had been shot in the leg.

"Since I regained my sight, Mr. Bouvier, I read books . . ." She waved her hand towards the walls which were lined with books from floor to ceiling. "All these years I have had to make do with Braille—now I can read proper books! I was always a great reader from girlhood. Now it is my ambition to read all these before I die . . ."

"But the newspapers . . ."

"I don't believe in them. Never did. They're boring. Magazines? Why read them when you have books?"

"And television?"

"Don't believe in it. And I don't have a radio." Madame Devaud stood very erect. "I live here on my own and I love it. I have twenty-five hectares of woodland where I wander for hours. The world I saw during the war I can do without for ever. All my supplies are delivered by a man in the village, so I'm self-contained. I actually like it that way, Mr Bouvier . . ."

"But if the Leopard were still alive you would know him?"

"The Leopard is dead . . ."

"But if he weren't?" Lennox persisted.

"I think I would know him, yes. He had good bone structure. Bones don't change . . ."

He managed to persuade her to get into the front passenger seat of the Mercedes for one reason only. "If you drove the Renault with those two men inside it off the road," she pointed out, "then your own car should show traces of the collision." After she had slipped on a heavy fur coat he took her outside and she briefly inspected the dented Mercedes, then she got inside the car quickly. "We'd better hurry," she informed him curtly, "otherwise we'll meet them coming up the track. I thought you were telling the truth before I saw the damage—I'm a good judge of character, but you must admit I had a right to be suspicious . . ."

"I'm going to drop you off close to the nearest police station," Lennox said as he began descending the track. "I know somewhere we can hide and still see the entrance to the farm . . ."

She had wanted to bring her shotgun with her but he had put it away in a cupboard before they left the house. The Luger loaned to him by Peter Lanz was inside his coat pocket as they came closer to the highway, and he had turned off his headlights now, fearing that they might reveal the obscure entrance to the track if the Renault was coming up the highway. On his way to the farmhouse he would have missed the entrance himself without the map and the sign-board. Close to the bottom of the track the way ahead was masked by a wall of rolling mist. The mist was suddenly lit up, became a luminous gloss as headlight beams from the highway swept across it. The Renault had arrived only seconds before they were clear.

Lennox began depressing the brake prior to attempting the impossible—to back up the track the way they had just come. In the luminous glow blobs of moisture caught the lights and sparkled. The glow faded. Sweat was glistening on Lennox's forehead as he released the brake; on the highway a car's headlights had swept round the bend, flashing briefly over the entrance before the vehicle continued on up the highway. Risking the mud, he accelerated. "Stop at the bottom," Annette Devaud commanded. "If those men find the farm after we've gone they may damage it. So get rid of the signboard, please . . ." To humour her, Lennox stopped briefly, jumped out and gave the post one hard shove. There was a wrench of rotting wood breaking and the signboard collapsed backwards out of sight. It wasn't entirely to humour her: if the Commando couldn't find the farm they might linger, looking for it, and while they were searching Annette Devaud might be able to contact the police. Jumping back behind the wheel, he followed her instructions, turning to the left out of the track—which took them away from the Saverne direction—and then he turned left off the highway, thinking that it was a fork in the road. Instead he found himself driving up a similar mud-track which spiralled up and up round a steep rock-face.

"Where does this lead?" he asked.

"Back on to my land—to a high bluff where we can look down on the entrance to the farm . . ."

It had all happened so quickly. Not knowing the area it had seemed wiser to Lennox to follow her directions, and now she had led them up to some peak which was still not far enough away from the farm for his liking. "They'll never find us up here," Madame Devaud said confidently. "And we'll be able to see what's happening—I don't like to leave my home unattended . . ." At the top of the spiralling track which was hemmed in by dense fir forest they came out into the open where an old barn was perched on the craggy bluff. The building was derelict, its roof timbers rotting, its two huge doors lying abandoned on a carpet of dead bracken. Thick tangles of undergrowth circled the rim of the bluff. Lennox switched off the motor and the headlights and the clammy silence of the forest closed round them. She had led them into a dead end.

It was 3 p.m. when André the Squirrel alighted from the Alouette helicopter which had flown him to Saverne and was driven to police headquarters by a waiting car. At headquarters he collected three policemen and the car then proceeded up into the Vosges. During his flight from Paris Boisseau decided that he should perhaps have taken Grelle's advice about providing a police guard on Annette Devaud, so now he was taking men with him to leave at the farm when he had interviewed the only known survivor who had once worked with the Leopard. At headquarters he had made the suggestion that someone should

phone ahead to Woodcutter's Farm, only to be told that
Madame Devaud had never had a phone installed. As they
drove up into the mist-bound mountains Boisseau became
restless.

"Hurry it up," he told the driver, "I want to arrive at
the earliest possible moment . . ."

"Hurry? In this fog, Mr. Director-General?"

"Use the damned siren. Hurry . . ."

From the top of the craggy bluff behind the barn there
was, as Madame Devaud had said, an excellent view down
a sheer one-hundred-foot drop to the highway below and
to the entrance to the farm beyond. To the right of where
Lennox stood a thread of a path curled down a more
gently-sloping section and ended at a tiny summerhouse
perched on a rocky platform seventy feet or so above
the highway. Immediately below him the rock-face
dropped away dizzily. Beyond the derelict barn behind
him the Mercedes was parked with its nose pointing
towards the track they had come up; Lennox, disturbed
to find there was no way out from this eminence except
down the track, was on the verge of telling Madame
Devaud they were leaving. But first he was checking the
highway. Through the mist he could see a car coming
from the direction of Saverne, its silhouette still too
blurred for him to recognize the make of vehicle. He
glanced at his watch. 3.15 p.m.

Behind him Annette Devaud stood inside the barn,
leaning on a window ledge as she tried to see what was
happening. The car crawled closer, coming very slowly as
though lost, and then he felt sure it was a Renault. Crawling past the concealed entrance to Woodcutter's Farm—
now completely invisible because the signboard had been
removed—it continued up the highway until it was
below where Lennox stood and he was looking down
directly on its roof. Pausing for a few seconds, it turned
off the highway, vanishing from view as it headed up

the mud-track which led to the bluff.

"They're coming up here," Lennox called out to Madame Devaud. "Get round here as fast as you can . . ."

She hurried out of the barn and round the back of it and Lennox sent her down the thread of a path to the summerhouse. He waited for a second, watching her move down the path sure-footed as a goat before running round to the front of the barn, then he hid himself inside a clump of undergrowth close to the sheer drop and waited. In his right hand he held the Luger.

Vanek drove slowly up the track and beside him Lansky put on a pair of thin and expensive kid gloves. It seemed likely that he would have to throttle the old woman the barman at the Auberge des Vosges had told them lived alone. One kilometre back down the highway they had again asked for directions at the office of a sawmill. "One kilometre up the highway from here," they had been told. "Up an old mud-track . . ." Driving past the concealed entrance which led to Woodcutter's Farm they had turned up the next track. Turning a corner, they arrived on top of the bluff.

"Something's wrong—look . . ." Vanek nodded towards the Mercedes parked on the bluff. "I'll cover you . . ." They exchanged no more words as Lansky opened the car door very quietly and slipped out. Trained to operate as a team there was no need to say any more as both men grasped the situation; somewhere concealed on the bluff was the man Lansky had bumped into in the rue de l'Épine, the man who less than an hour ago had tried to kill them by driving them off the road. Inside the car Vanek waited, his own Luger in his hand, waited for any sign of movement while outside the car Lansky studied the lie of the land and noted that the open-ended barn was empty. Crouched inside the undergrowth Lennox couldn't see the man behind the wheel because the Renault had stopped on a rise and the car's bulk hid the second man. Lansky's sudden manoeuvre caught him off-balance.

The Czech sprinted the short distance across the open and disappeared inside the barn. Then, for a minute or two nothing happened, or so it seemed to Lennox. Inside the barn Lansky sought elevation, somewhere high up where he could look down on the whole bluff. Very quietly he began climbing up the inner wall of the barn, using the cross-beams along the wall as steps until he reached a hole where he could peer down into the Mercedes. The car was empty. He scanned the bluff carefully until he found the silhouette of a man crouching in the under-growth. Then he climbed down again.

With the body of the parked Mercedes between himself and Lennox he crept forward, pausing only once to make a gesture to Vanek. The Czech nodded. Lansky had located the target. Reaching the side of the Mercedes, Lansky opened the door-handle a centimetre at a time, then opened the door itself. He slid behind the wheel and reached for the ignition key he had seen dangling from his barn wall perch. To shoot him the Frenchman would have to stand up—and if he exposed himself to view Vanek would shoot him first.

Crouched a dozen or so metres behind the rear of the Mercedes, Lennox resisted the almost overwhelming impulse to lift his head, to see what the hell was going on. So far he had heard no sound since the second man had vanished inside the barn. Lansky, who carried in his head the precise location of the crouching man, paused as he touched the ignition key. This was going to have to be very fast indeed. And he was going to have to pull up in time or else the Mercedes would go over the sheer drop with the Frenchman. Either way the unknown man was dead: if he stayed where he was the car would topple him over the brink; if he exposed himself Vanek would kill him with a single shot. Then all four people on the bluff heard it—Madame Devaud waiting in the tiny summerhouse with her heart beating like a drum and the three men above her—heard the distant wail of an approaching police car siren. Lansky didn't hesitate. Turning on the ignition, flipping the gear into reverse, he began moving backwards at speed.

Lennox grasped what was happening instantly. Someone had got into his car. They were going to knock him over the edge. He timed it to a split second, standing up and exposing his silhouette at the moment when it was masked from the Renault by the speeding Mercedes heading straight for him. He had a camera-shutter image of the Mercedes's rear window framing the twisted-round head-and-shoulders of the driver. He fired twice through the centre of the frame, angling his gun downwards, then dived sideways, sprawling on the ground. Both bullets hit Lansky in the back and neither was instantaneously fatal. The spasm of reaction drove his right foot hard down on the accelerator. The Mercedes tore over the shrubberies and went on beyond, arcing into nothingness and then plunging down and down until it hit the highway one hundred feet below. The police patrol-car, with Boisseau inside and a local driver behind the wheel, was turning into the entrance to Woodcutter's Farm when the Mercedes landed. As the patrol-car changed direction the Mercedes burst into flames.

Vanek had heard the police siren and he reacted as he saw the Mercedes with Lansky inside disappear over the edge; he drove the Renault round in a tight circle so it faced back down the track. A few metres away he saw Lennox sprawl on the ground, then start to get back to his feet. Braking, Vanek grabbed the Luger out of his lap, took instinctive aim and fired. The Englishman was aiming his own pistol when the bullet hit him and he went down again.

Vanek drove down the twisting track at reckless speed but he managed to keep the vehicle under control. When he emerged at the bottom the blazing Mercedes blocked the road to his right, blocking off the patrol-car. He turned left and started driving west along the

deserted highway, his mind racing as he worked out what
he had to do next. The answer could be summed up in
one word: vanish. It was the death of his partner he had
just witnessed which gave him the idea. Climbing a steep
stretch of highway he came to a point where the road
curved sharply with a fence to his right and a warning
notice. *Dangerous corner*. Stopping the Renault just beyond the bend he got out and walked back to the recently-
erected fence. Beyond it the ground dropped away a good
two hundred feet to a rock-pile with a canal crossing the
field beyond. Vanek ran back to the Renault, switched
on the ignition again from outside the car, released the
hand-brake, slammed the door shut as the car started
moving backwards slowly, and then guided it with his
hand on the steering-wheel through the open window.

He had stopped the car on a reasonably level patch of
tarmac before the highway went into a further steep ascent
so it moved back quite gently for a few seconds as he
walked alongside; then the road began to slope down
and the car picked up momentum. Vanek had withdrawn
his hand from the wheel and the Renault was moving
faster when it hit the white-painted fence—erected only
to define the edge—broke through and dropped out of
sight. He heard it hit the rock-pile with a crunch of dis-
integrating metal but unlike the Mercedes it did not burst
into flames. Satisfied that he had given himself a temporary breathing-space, the Czech left the highway, climbing
up into the forest above and began moving back at a trot
towards the craggy bluff where Lansky had died.

17

Making his way through the woods, following the road below to guide him, Vanek arrived back at a knoll which overlooked the bluff in time to see Madame Devaud being escorted by a squad of men to a patrol-car. There had been a delay while she was guarded in the barn until more patrol-cars, summoned by radio, arrived with men who made a quick search of the wooded area surrounding the bluff. It was Lennox, still conscious and now inside an ambulance, who had warned Boisseau that these men were professional killers, that no chance must be taken with the life of Madame Devaud.

By the time Vanek reached the wooded knoll looking down on the bluff the convoy of patrol-cars was ready to leave. Using the small but powerful monocular glass he always carried, hidden behind a clump of pines, the Czech watched while Annette Devaud was escorted to one of the cars. The glass brought her up so close that he saw her head and shoulders clearly in his lens and he reflected that had he been equipped with a telescopic rifle she would be dead by now. Then, as though his thought had travelled down to them, the police escort huddled round her and she disappeared behind a wall of uniforms. The range was far too great for him to even contemplate using his Luger.

Crouching on his haunches, Vanek waited as the patrol-cars disappeared down the track, led by the ambulance, and later reappeared on the highway where the mist had

229

now dissolved. Even so, in the late afternoon light the cars were no more than a blur but it was the direction they took which interested him. Towards Saverne.

"The second killer went off the road and down to the edge of a canal," Boisseau reported to Marc Grelle over the phone from Saverne police headquarters. "Men should be arriving at the point of the crash about now. And the Englishman, Lennox, has appeared. It was he, in fact, who shot the first assassin, and was then shot himself . . ."

"He is dead?" the prefect enquired from Paris.

"No, he will be all right, but he will be in hospital for a few days. He has a message for you. A very cautious man, Mr Lennox—I had to show him my card before he would pass on the message through me. He says he believes Madame Devaud can identify the Leopard . . ."

"You have Madame Devaud with you?"

"I can see her from where I am sitting . . ."

Boisseau broke off as the Saverne inspector who had just taken a call on another line signalled to him. Listening for a moment, Boisseau resumed his call to Paris. "This may be bad news. The Renault—the assassins' car —which went off the highway has now been examined. There was no trace of anyone inside and it appears it may have been tipped off the road deliberately to throw us off the scent. One of the assassins is still at liberty . . ."

The motor-barge chugged slowly forward out of the mist towards Vanek where he stood waiting for it by the edge of the lonely canal. His breathing was still a trifle laboured from his exertions when he had come down the mountainside from the knoll, making his way through the woods until he cautiously crossed the highway and negotiated the lower slope which brought him to the edge of the canal. He had been walking along the deserted towpath —keeping well clear of the highway—when he heard the chugging motor coming up behind him.

Gesturing to the man in yellow oilskins and peaked cap behind the wheel at the rear of the barge, Vanek called out "Police" several times, then waited until the barge was steered close enough to the bank for him to jump on board. He showed the leathery-faced bargee his Sûreté card. "Are you alone?" The man assured him he was and pointed out he had already been stopped higher up by policemen who were examining a crashed car. "How far to the next lock?" Vanek demanded, ignoring the question. It was six kilometres. "I'll travel with you," Vanek told the man. "I'm looking for the murderer who escaped from that car . . . "

For several minutes Vanek stood behind the man, pretending to watch the fields they were passing through while he observed the way the bargee handled the controls. Idly, as though to pass the time, he asked one or two technical questions as the barge chugged on through a remote section of the canal fogged with drifting mist. Clearing off the mountains, the mist was now settling in the narrow gulch through which the canal passes on its way to the Strasbourg plain. "Your cap looks like a chauffeur's," Vanek remarked. "But then, fair enough, instead of a car you drive a barge . . ." He was still talking when he took out his Luger and shot the man in the back.

Before he threw him overboard Vanek took off his oilskin coat and put it on himself, then he donned the bargee's cap. He used a heavy chain lying on the deck of the barge to weight the body, bringing it up between the legs and over the shoulders. The barge, which he had stopped, was drifting gently as he heaved the weighted corpse over the side; pausing only to watch it sink out of sight under the grey, murky water, he re-started the engine and took up station behind the wheel. A few minutes later a bridge appeared out of the mist with a patrol-car parked in the middle and a policeman leaning

Blass

over the parapet. The policeman waited until the barge was close.

"Have you seen a man by himself as you came along the canal?" he shouted down.

"Only a lot of your friends checking a car which drove off the highway," Vanek shouted back.

The policeman waited, staring down from the parapet as Vanek, looking straight ahead, guided the barge through the archway and continued down the canal. A few minutes later the bridge behind him had vanished in the mist as he saw the faint outline of another bridge ahead. Vanek reckoned he had now moved out of the immediate area where they would be searching for him and in any case he had to leave the barge before he reached the lock. Passing under the bridge, he stopped the barge, hid the oilskin under a coil of rope and climbed the muddy path which took him up to a country road. The cap he had tucked away inside his coat.

Walking a short distance along the road away from the highway, he found a convenient hiding-place behind a clump of trees where he stood and waited. During the space of fifteen minutes he let two tradesmen's vans pass and then he saw a BMW saloon approaching from the direction of the highway. There was only one man inside and the vehicle stank of money. Stepping into the middle of the road, he flagged down the car, calling out, "Police, police . . ."

Again he showed his Sûreté card to the suspicious driver who protested he had been stopped on the highway. "I don't believe you," Vanek said, taking back his card. "How far away was that?" One kilometre away, the driver informed him. A man in his late fifties, expensively suited, he had an arrogant manner which amused Vanek. Producing the Luger, he made the man move across to the passenger seat and got in behind the wheel. He put on the cap which he had taken from the dead bargee. "I am your chauffeur," he announced. "If we are stopped by a police patrol you will confirm that. If you make one mistake I will shoot you three times in the stomach and you will die slowly."

It was not so much the nature of the threat as the off-hand manner in which Vanek made it that thoroughly frightened the BMW owner. The Czech drove off in the same direction—away from the highway. Five minutes later in the middle of a wood, convinced that he had driven beyond the range of police patrols, Vanek stopped the car to check the road map purchased at Strasbourg airport which had guided himself and Lansky to Saverne. He found he could now reach Saverne again by a different route, keeping north of the canal and the highway until he almost reached the town. "You'd better give me the car's papers," he said. "The chauffeur looks after things like that." The man, who had told Vanek he was driving back to Metz, omitting to mention he was a banker, handed over the papers.

"I'm going to leave you here tied up with rope." Vanek patted his pocket to indicate the rope. "In an hour I shall phone the Saverne police and tell them where to find you. I am a burglar and have no wish that you should die of cold." Getting out of the car with his prisoner, he shot him by the roadside and concealed the body behind some bushes. Returning to the BMW, he drove on by the roundabout route towards Saverne.

Boisseau had exerted all his considerable charm and powers of persuasion but he had made no impression on Annette Devaud's decision. Yes, she would travel to Paris and see the police prefect if it was all that important —and here Boisseau detected a certain excitement at the prospect. Possibly her nearness to death had made her think she would like to see the capital city once more. But no, she would not fly there in a plane if they paid her a million francs. And no, she would not travel there by road; car travel made her sick. She would only go to Paris if she went there by train.

From police headquarters at Saverne, where they had rushed her by car—and that was enough driving, she had informed them fiercely—Boisseau made repeated calls to Marc Grelle, reporting the latest progress, or lack of it. And it was Grelle who took the decision to bring her to the capital by train. "But you must take the most stringent precautions," he warned Boisseau. "Remember that three of the witnesses have been killed already, and they very nearly got Annette Devaud as well. Very special arrangements must be made—since at least one assassin is still at large." After talking to Boisseau the prefect personally called Strasbourg to put his whole authority behind the operation. If everyone co-operated, Annette Devaud should be safely in Paris by nine in the evening, little more than twelve hours before Guy Florian was due to fly to Russia.

Police headquarters at Saverne was marked on the map Vanek was carrying, so when he reached the town he had no problem finding his way there. Still wearing his chauffeur's cap, he sat erect behind the wheel of the BMW as he drove slowly along the street as though looking for somewhere to park. Four patrol-cars were parked nose to tail outside the station while uniformed policemen strolled up and down, guarding the building. One of them glanced at the BMW and then looked away; as Vanek had once said to Brunner, in the capitalist west the police respect affluence and nothing is more affluent than a chauffeur-driven BMW.

Vanek had another reason for feeling confident: during his conversation with the banker he had later killed he had elicited the information that the Frenchman was driving to Metz, which meant that at least two hours should pass before anyone started worrying about his non-arrival. As he drove on Vanek was now convinced

they were holding Madame Devaud under guard inside
police headquarters, that soon they would have to take
her somewhere else—perhaps back to her home at Woodcutter's Farm. Pulling into a side street, he reversed the
car so he could get away quickly, put a coin in the parking
meter and walked back to a near-by bar from where
he could observe the police station.

The security operation to protect Annette Devaud's life
was organized by Boisseau from inside the Saverne police
station. Using the phone, and with the full weight of
Grelle's authority behind him—"This concerns the safety
of the president of the French Republic"—Boisseau
issued a stream of precise instructions. Before the 17.14
Stanislas Trans-European express for Paris left Strasbourg
a special coach was linked to the train immediately behind
the engine. Stickers were plastered over the windows
indicating that this coach was *réservé*. One minute after
the express was due to leave the ticket barriers were
closed and gendarmes, who had previously hidden in the
luggage office, filed aboard the sealed coach with automatic weapons.

The express was five minutes away from Saverne, a
place it normally flew past at speed, when the gendarmes
filed out of the sealed coach and moved along the full
length of the train, closing all the window blinds.
"Emergency," the inspector in charge of the detachment
explained in a loud voice to a dining-car passenger who
had the temerity to ask what the devil was happening.
"We've had a warning of terrorist activity . . ."

Stanislas was losing speed as it approached Saverne
station which had been sealed off by the local police and
extra men rushed in from Strasbourg. As the express
pulled in to the station the atmosphere was eerie. To stop
anyone who might raise a blind—power-operated on the
TEE express, it only requires the touch of a button
—batteries of lights mounted on trucks were shone on

the side of the train as it stopped. Anyone looking out
would have been blinded by the glare. In the waiting-
room, Boisseau sat with Madame Devaud, muffled in her
old-fashioned fur coat, who was still calm and controlled
despite all the fuss. "Is it true I shall be having a whole
coach to myself?" she enquired. Boisseau assured her it
was true. He personally escorted her to the coach after
making her put on a pair of dark glasses—partly as a disguise, partly as protection against the glare of the lights.
As she moved along the corridor to her compartment the
train also began to move again.

A short distance from the station, out of sight of the
convoy of parked patrol-cars, the chauffeur of a BMW
was having a little trouble with his engine. With the hood
up he stooped over the motor, checking the wiring. The
express had just begun to move when he sorted out
the problem, closing the hood and getting back behind the
wheel. He drove off at speed, accelerating through the
darkness as soon as he had left Saverne behind, heading
for Strasbourg airport where there is a frequent Air Inter
plane service to Paris.

18

In Paris Marc Grelle believed he had found out how the
list of Lasalle's three witnesses had been passed back
to Moscow. As events had unfolded, as information came
in showing that a Soviet Commando was eliminating the
very people whose names had been on Lasalle's list,
the prefect realized that the coincidence was too great.

Someone in Paris in addition to himself had seen the list and had then caused it to be transmitted to Russia. The Soviet Commando had then been despatched to the west.

He started his discreet enquiries at the Ministry of the Interior, tracing the route his memo containing the list had followed. Grelle had, of course, sent his memo to Roger Danchin by despatch rider late on the morning of Tuesday, 14 December. François Merlin, the Minister's assistant, who liked the prefect, proved helpful. "We haven't heard from Hugon, our pipeline into Col Lasalle, recently," Grelle explained, "so I'm double-checking the security of our arrangements . . ." It didn't surprise Merlin that the prefect himself was making the enquiry: all Paris knew Grelle's quaint habit of attending to details personally.

Copies of the communications from Hugon were restricted to a very narrow circle: Grelle himself, Boisseau, the Minister and his assistant, Merlin. Pressed to go through the files, Merlin told Grelle that the confidential memo containing the names and addresses of the three witnesses had arrived at the Place Beauvau just before noon on Tuesday, 14 December. "I was in the office when he read it," Merlin remarked. "A few minutes later Ambassador Vorin arrived for a private word with the Minister before going on to the Elysée. By then my chief had dealt with the memo . . ."

"Dealt with it?"

"He had a copy of your memo sent to the President's office at once. I took it down myself and handed it to a despatch rider who was just leaving for the Elysée. On my way down I met Ambassador Vorin who had just arrived and was waiting to see Danchin. The Elysée, of course, sees everything that concerns Col Lasalle," Merlin explained.

The prefect grunted and drank the rest of the cup of coffee Merlin had provided. "Do you think I could have a word with the monitoring section?" he suggested.

Among the cluster of radio masts which rise up from the roof of the Ministry of the Interior in the Place Beauvau is the antenna used for monitoring radio signals transmitted by foreign embassies. At 4 p.m. on 14 December the technician on duty inside the monitoring unit recorded a long signal emanating from the Soviet Embassy at 79, rue de Grenelle. The tape-recording of the signal was handed to the Russian section who went through the routine motions of studying the coded signal—routine because no one expected to be able to unravel the stream of ciphers.

The Russians use the one-time code, which is unbreakable. Codes are broken by discovering a pattern; only a fragment can unlock the key. But when each element of a code is linked to a particular book—often a novel (in the past the Russian encoders have favoured Dickens)—there is no way to break the code without knowing which of the thousands of books published over the past hundred years has been used. And as the same book is never used twice it is literally a one-time code which is employed.

It was cryptographer Pierre Jadot who had studied the signal transmitted, and he immediately recalled the incident when Grelle asked him about any Soviet signals transmitted on that day. "I made my usual routine report in a memo to the Minister," he said, "and I remember suggesting that one section of the signal could have been a list of names and addresses . . ."

"You are sure about that?" Grelle asked casually.

"By no means—it is no more than an educated guess. And there is no way of cracking the Soviet codes."

"Can you give me any idea of how long it might take the Soviet encoder at this end to prepare that signal for transmission? Even a guess would be helpful."

Jadot took down a file, extracted his copy of the signal and studied it for a few minutes. "At a guess—it can be no more than that—I would say between one and two hours. Probably nearer two hours . . ."

Thanking Jadot, the prefect left the Ministry and called at the Elysée on his way back to the prefecture. Again he asked to see the visitors' register, and again he concealed what he was really looking for by glancing at several pages. Then he drove straight back to his office and called in Boisseau. It took him only a few minutes to explain. "The point is Leonid Vorin, the Soviet ambassador, left the Elysée to return to his embassy at 1.45 p.m. Allowing for the traffic, he must have got back say half an hour later—at 2.15 p.m. That gave the Soviet encoder just under two hours to prepare the signal for transmission which began at four o'clock—which fits in with the time Jadot estimated it would take. A signal which may well have contained Col Lasalle's list of names and addresses . . ."

"Which brings us back to the men who knew about the list and who saw Ambassador Vorin," Boisseau replied gravely. "Danchin and . . ."

"The president," Grelle added. "I have the feeling that daylight is beginning to break through this business."

"Or the blackest night," Boisseau commented.

It was six o'clock in the evening when Alain Blanc came up to Grelle's office at the préfecture looking grim and despondent. The *Stanislas* express with Annette Devaud on board was now racing through the night on its way to Paris. At Charles de Gaulle Airport mechanics were busily servicing the Concorde which would fly President Florian to Moscow within a few hours. Blanc came into the office with a savage expression as he closed the door and flopped into a chair.

"You've heard about the Soviet convoy, of course?" the Minister of National Defence enquired. "It is now inside the Sicilian Narrows and its destination could be either Barcelona or even Lisbon."

"What is worrying you, sir?" the prefect asked quietly.

"Everything!" Blanc threw up his hands in an expressive gesture. "The Russian convoy. The persistent rumours of an imminent *coup d'état* in Paris. By whom, for God's sake? And half an hour ago I hear for the first time that the president made a secret flight to Germany on Monday—to the French army GHQ at Baden-Baden!"

Grelle stared at the minister in astonishment. "You didn't know he had flown to Baden-Baden? He didn't inform you? The Minister of National Defence? I thought you knew—I made the arrangements myself with GLAM . . ." GLAM—Groupe Liaison Aérien Ministériel—is the small air fleet which is reserved for ministerial and presidential usage. "What on earth is going on?" the prefect asked.

"That I would like to know myself," Blanc said grimly. "And I have just heard also that our two armoured divisions in Germany, the 2nd and the 5th, are moving through the Ardennes on their way back to France, which will leave no French troops on German soil. When I phone the Elysée to request an immediate appointment I am told that the president is busy with the Soviet ambassador . . ."

"And he leaves for Moscow tomorrow."

"Precisely," Blanc snapped. "Recently he has been acting as though I don't exist—a total change of mood and method I cannot even begin to understand. It is almost as though he were trying to provoke my resignation. He may succeed—I may have to resign . . ."

"Don't do that," Grelle said quickly. "We may need you yet. You've discussed this with other ministers?"

"They are supine!" Blanc exploded. "They think he is God and they are the apostles! I am the only one who has started to ask questions, to demand what the hell is going on. I tell you, I shall have to resign if this goes on . . ."

"Don't do it. We may need you desperately," Grelle repeated.

Only a few minutes after Blanc had left Grelle was told he had another visitor waiting to see him and he asked his secretary to repeat the name, sure she must have got it wrong. But no, it was Commissioner Suchet, his old enemy of the counter-espionage service. Apologizing for calling without an appointment, Suchet squeezed his gross bulk into a chair and came straight to the point. "These *coup d'état* rumours are coming from the Red Belt suburbs—from Billiancourt. Certain agitators are very active today saying that soon the people may have to defend the Republic. Coming from that scum, it's a great joke, but I'm not laughing—I'm worried stiff. An hour ago some of my agents uncovered an arms dump at Renault. I thought you ought to know. Someone must act . . ."

Grelle took decisive action at once, first phoning Roger Danchin to obtain his approval, then issuing a stream of orders. Guards were trebled on all public buildings. A special detachment was sent to key points like the telephone exchanges and the television transmitters. Tough CRS troops were drafted from the barracks outside the city into Paris to guard the bridges over the Seine. With a minimum of fuss Paris was moving into a state of siege. Then at 7.30 p.m. Grelle made what appeared to be a routine visit to the Elysée to double-check security ready for the drive to the airport the next day.

Arriving at the palace, it didn't particularly surprise Grelle to discover that Soviet Ambassador Vorin was not only not there; he had not been anywhere near the Elysée since the morning. Someone had been instructed to keep ex-paratrooper Blanc away from the palace until Florian's departure on the following day. Admitted to the palace by an usher who opened the plate-glass doors for him, the prefect wandered towards the back of the building, opening and closing doors in what appeared a random way.

He was looking for Kassim, Florian's dog.

He found him outside in the walled garden where the dog spent so much of its time—and where the president was accustomed to strolling with Leonid Vorin when the Russian visited the Elysée. At Grelle appeared the Alsatian barked and romped forward through the dark, jumping up to his full height and perching his forepaws over the prefect's shoulders while it panted happily in his face. Grelle reached up and fondled the animal for a short while round the studded collar which encircled its powerful neck. Then he gave Kassim a hard slap to make him get down and went back inside the palace.

From there he walked quickly to the near-by rue des Saussaies and up on to the fourth floor of Sûreté headquarters. The electronics expert he had earlier sent there from the préfecture was waiting and he gave him certain instructions before returning to the Elysée to collect his car and drive back to his office. It had been easier than he had expected, and this was one decision he did not inform Boisseau about. One career at stake was quite enough.

The prefect had just attached a tiny transmitter to the inside of Kassim's studded collar. The words of anyone who spoke close enough to the dog would be relayed to the receiver linked to a tape-recorder inside the locked room at the rue des Saussaies, only a few dozen metres away from the Elysée Palace.

19

So far Vanek had avoided travelling by air. At airports individual passengers can easily be checked, searched, but to reach Paris ahead of the express carrying Annette Devaud he had no alternative. As he bought his ticket from Air Inter and made his way to the departure point the Czech carried nothing incriminating. He had tossed the Luger pistol into a canal on his way to the airport. The BMW was now standing in the airport car park. And he had thrown the bargee's cap into the canal after the Luger.

When he bought his ticket he paid for a return fare: he had no intention of returning to Strasbourg but for airport personnel there is something normal and reassuring about a return ticket. He had no trouble passing through the security checks, partly because by now he was no longer alone. Waiting in the departure lounge for the Air Inter flight, he observed an attractive girl of about twenty-two who was obviously on her own; he further observed as she took off her glove to light a cigarette that she wore neither an engagement nor wedding ring.

He lit her cigarette and sat beside her, looking anxious. "I do hope this flight for Paris isn't late. It's my sister's birthday and she expects her present . . ." He prattled on, instinctively choosing the right approach. Most women were happy to chat with Vanek if it wasn't too obvious a pick-up; the reference to a sister was reassuring, clearly indicating a man who treated women with respect. They went through the security check together. Vanek holding her small hand-case, joking with her, and everyone thought they were a couple.

On the plane he sat beside her, found out that her name was Michelle Robert, that she was personal assistant to an executive with a tyre firm whose headquarters were at La Défense. Before they were half-way to Paris he had extracted her phone number. And somewhere over Champagne their Fokker 27 aircraft overtook the *Stanislas* express carrying Madame Devaud to the capital.

The TEE express was due to arrive at the Gare de l'Est at 9 p.m. Vanek, who had phoned the railway station from the airport to check its arrival time, caught the 6.30 flight from Strasbourg which landed him at Orly Airport at 7.30. Fortunately, Michelle Robert was being met by a friend, so he got rid of her without any trouble. Mistrusting Paris traffic, Vanek used the Orly-rail system to reach the city and then he changed to the Metro. He calculated that with a little luck he should reach the Gare de l'Est just before the express arrived.

The express from Strasbourg reached the Gare de l'Est at 9.6 p.m. Normally the ticket barrier is open—tickets have been examined aboard the train—and people just walk off, but on the night of 22 December the barrier was closed and no one was permitted near the platform.

"It is an outrage," one passenger aboard the express fumed. "My wife is expecting me . . ."

"There is a terrorist alert. You must wait," the inspector informed him. And in that much of a rush, he thought cynically, it can only be your mistress who awaits you.

The superintendent Grelle had personally despatched to the station had sprinkled the concourse beyond the platform with armed plain-clothes detectives. One man, equipped with a sniper-scope rifle, waited in a window overlooking the platform. And some of the detectives who lounged about the station even had suitcases filled with files they had grabbed from their offices to provide weight. The door to the sealed coach was opened and a circle of plain-clothes men gathered at the foot of the steps. There were no uniformed gendarmes in sight. "Nothing conspicuous," Grelle had warned. "Keep it as normal as possible."

With Boisseau in front, Madame Devaud climbed down from the steps and the crowd of plain-clothes men closed round her. Boisseau separated himself from the group, going out on to the concourse and standing idly while he lit a cigarette, his coat hanging open so he could reach his revolver at a second's notice. This was the moment he feared most—getting her from the train to the car. The group moved across the concourse, moving slowly at Madame Devaud's pace. It went on into the exit hall, then outside to where a car door had already been opened. Several passengers were stopping now, beginning to take notice. It was impossible to cover up completely.

Boisseau heard a car door slam shut and sighed with relief. Moving quickly out of the exit he climbed inside another police car and pulled the door shut. "I want sirens all the way," he told the man beside the driver who had radio communication with the other cars. "We jump lights where we can . . ." The radio man transmitted the message and the motorcade moved off. There were four vehicles. One in front. Then Madame Devaud's. A third vehicle—to ram any car which tried to intercept. And Boisseau bringing up the rear. It was 9.9 p.m.

Vanek ran up out of the Metro and into the main station of the Gare de l'Est. He dropped to walking pace as he saw the *Stanislas* in the distance and when he got close he was in time to see the last passengers coming through the open barrier. It was 9.15 p.m. He had been badly delayed on the Metro but there had been nothing he could do about it; getting off and finding a taxi would only have taken longer. He waited for a few minutes by a bookstall—on the off-chance that they were going to take off the Devaud woman when all the other passengers had disembarked—and then he went to a phone booth to call the Paris number.

"Salicetti here . . ."

"I have nothing for you . . ."

"I have something for you," Vanek snapped, "so stay on the line. The previous order you specified will now have to be fulfilled in Paris—I am speaking from the Gare de l'Est. I need the firm's address."

For the first time since the phone calls had begun the cold, anonymous voice at the Paris number was unsure of itself. There was a brief pause. "You had better call back at half-hour intervals—ten o'clock, ten-thirty, and so on," the voice replied eventually. "I have no information at this moment . . ."

"I shall need more samples," Vanek said tersely.

The voice recovered its poise; it was ready for this contingency. Salicetti must go to the Bar Lepic in the Place Madeleine giving the firm's name, Lobineau, to the proprietor, who would hand him a baggage storage key. The samples were in a public locker at the Gare du Nord station. And would he be sure to call back at half-hourly intervals? At 10 p.m., 10.30 . . . Vanek slammed down the receiver. Bloody hell, what a primitive arrangement. Things were managed with greater finesse when he was in Paris. He took a cab to the Bar Lepic, collected an envelope, left a five-franc tip to make the transaction look normal to anyone who might be watching, and took another cab to the Gare du Nord.

Using the numbered key he found inside the envelope, he opened the luggage locker at the Gare du Nord and took out a hold-all bag covered in tartan cloth, which again was stupid: it was too noticeable. It was a very long bag, the type used to carry around tennis racquets. But the contents inside showed that someone had used his head: a French MAT sub-machine-gun with a wire

stock, the magazine folded parallel to the barrel to make
it inoperative, and a spare magazine; a Smith & Wesson
.38 revolver with spare rounds; and a short, wide-bladed
knife inside a clip-on sheath. Vanek crossed the deserted
hall to the opposite battery of lockers, chose an empty
one, slipped the hold-all inside, shut the door, inserted his
coin and turned the key. He had no intention of carrying
weapons until it was necessary—especially since he had
noticed during his two cab-rides intense police activity in
the streets. There were also truck-loads of CRS bully-boys
parked at strategic points. But Vanek had also noticed
that cabs were still moving normally about the city; no
one ever notices the Parisian cab-driver who is as much a
part of the scenery as the Louvre.

Vanek, who had not eaten anything since the snack-
lunch in the Renault on the way from Strasbourg to
Saverne, would have liked to snatch a sandwich and a
cup of coffee. He looked at his watch and swore. It was
almost ten o'clock; time to make the next phone call.
Using one of the station phones, he dialled the number.
He had hardly announced it was Salicetti speaking when
the voice broke in, as abrupt as ever.

"Rue des Saussaies. Now! You know where I mean?"

"Yes . . ."

Vanek broke the connection first this time. So they had
taken Madame Devaud to the Sûreté Nationale headquarters, the fortress of the capitalist police system. Collecting the tartan hold-all, Vanek went out into the
street beyond the Gare du Nord, ignoring the official
taxi pick-up point. He wanted to make a careful choice,
selecting a certain type of cab-driver for the next stage
of the operation.

The police prefect of Strasbourg, who was not especially
well disposed towards Marc Grelle—unlike the prefect
of Lyon—was disturbed about the elaborate arrangements
made to transport Madame Devaud to Paris. When he

had tried to elicit further details from Grelle on the phone he had been told brusquely, "This concerns the safety of the president and I am not at liberty to go into the matter further . . ." Annoyed—and determined to cover himself —he phoned the Ministry of the Interior in Paris where he spoke to the Minister's assistant, François Merlin. "Grelle was very cagey on the phone," the Strasbourg prefect complained. "I gathered this Devaud woman was an important witness in some case he is working on . . ." He was going off the line when he spoke again. "I insist the Minister hears about this."

The efficient Merlin immediately dictated a memo which was put on the Minister's desk where it lay undisturbed—and unread—for over an hour. It was 8.45 p.m. before Roger Danchin, who had been attending a long meeting to check on the security for the presidential motorcade drive to the airport the following morning, walked back into his office. "An important case Grelle is working on?" he queried with Merlin when he had read the memo. "Devaud is a reasonably common name but it could be something to do with the attempted assassination case. I must tell the president . . ." He lifted the phone which would put him direct through to the Elysée.

At 9.15 p.m., summoned by an urgent phone call, Ambassador Vorin arrived at the Elysée, and his visit was duly recorded by the duty officer in the visitors' register. Florian already had his coat on and, as was his custom, led the Soviet ambassador out into the walled garden where they could talk undisturbed. The Alsatian, Kassim, ready for a breath of fresh air like his master, came with them, sniffing around in a shrubbery as they conferred in low tones. Vorin's latest visit was very brief, lasting only a few minutes, and he was then driven back at speed to the Soviet Embassy in the rue de Grenelle.

The method of communication between Vorin and Carel Vanek was carefully arranged so that no link between the two men could ever be established. Arriving back at the embassy, Vorin immediately summoned the Second Secretary and gave him a message. The Secretary, who would normally have made the call from a phone booth inside the nearest Metro station, returned to his own office, locked the door and dialled the number of an apartment on the Left Bank near the Cluny Museum. "The deeds of the Devaud property will be found at the rue des Saussaies. Have you got that?" The man at the other end of the line only had time to say yes before the connection was broken.

The apartment near the Cluny was occupied by a man who had never attracted the attention of the police. Equipped with Danish papers under the name of Jurgensen, he was in fact a Pole called Jaworski who did not even know that the calls he received came back from the Soviet Embassy. It was 9.50 p.m. when he took this call. At 10 p.m. he passed on the information when Vanek phoned him again from the Gare du Nord.

They took Annette Devaud to a room on the fourth floor of Sûreté headquarters in the rue des Saussaies where Grelle was waiting for her. He could have interviewed her at the préfecture on the Ile de la Cité but he still thought it wise to keep up the fiction that this concerned the Lasalle *affaire*, and this operation was officially conducted from the Sûreté. To avoid upsetting Danchin, he had even phoned his assistant, Merlin, at eight o'clock to tell him a witness was on the way from Alsace whom he would interview at the rue des Saussaies. Merlin had mentioned this to Danchin before the Minister phoned the Elysée. Alone with the first live witness he had been able to lay his hands on, Grelle talked for a few minutes to put Annette Devaud at her ease. Then he explained why she had been brought to Paris.

"And you really think that after all these years you can identify the Leopard?" he asked gently.

"If he's alive—as you say—yes! I lost my sight for

thirty years before that doctor carried out his miracle operation. What do you think I saw in my mind's eye all those years when the world was only sounds and smells? I saw everyone I had ever met. And, as I told you, I nursed the Leopard through an illness." Her voice dropped. "And later he was responsible for the death of my only daughter, Lucie . . ."

As Grelle had foreseen, he felt horribly uncomfortable. Although Madame Devaud did not realize it—and it was Boisseau who had mentioned the point when phoning from Saverne—the prefect was the man who had been compelled to shoot Lucie Devaud. "It was many years ago," he reminded her, "since you knew the Leopard. Even if he is still alive he may have changed out of all recognition . . ."

"Not the Leopard." Her pointed chin jutted upwards. "He had good bone structure—like me. Bones don't change. You can't hide bones . . ."

Grelle was so determined to test her that he had devised an odd method of identification. Remembering that Boisseau had mentioned over the phone that she was an amateur portrait artist, he had brought into the room Identikit equipment. He explained to her how the system worked, asked her what she would like to drink, and was so amused when she requested cognac that he joined her. He started by helping her with the Identikit, and then let her get on with it by herself. She was obviously enjoying the new game.

Starting with the outline of the head, she began to build up the face of a man. The hairpiece came first. Grelle opened several box-files of printed hair pieces and helped her select several. Soon they were arguing. "You've got it wrong," she snapped. "I told you he brushed his hair high on the forehead . . ." The face began to take shape.

The eyebrows she found quickly, but the eyes gave her trouble. "They were very unusual—compelling," she explained. She found the eyes at the back of the file and then worried over the nose. "Noses are difficult . . ." She chose a nose and added it to the portrait. "That's the nose. I think it's his most characteristic feature . . ." It took her five minutes to locate the mouth, ferreting in a fresh file, trying one and then another before she was satisfied. Pursing her own mouth, she screwed up her eyes as she completed the Identikit while Grelle watched with an expressionless face. "That's the Leopard," she said a few minutes later. "That's the way he was."

The prefect stood up, showing no reaction. "Madame Devaud, I know you don't like television, but I would like you to watch certain programme extracts I had made earlier this evening. They are recorded on what we call cassettes. You will see three men briefly—all of them older than the face you built up on the Identikit. I want you to tell me which—if any—of these three men is the Leopard."

"He has changed a lot then?"

Grelle didn't reply as he went to the television set and switched on. The first extract showed Roger Danchin broadcasting at the time of the riots a year earlier when he had appealed for calm, warning that mass arrests would follow any further demonstrations. The set went blank and then Alain Blanc appeared, confident and emphatic, telling the nation why more had to be spent on the defence budget.

Madame Devaud said nothing, reaching for her glass of cognac as the image faded, to be replaced by Guy Florian making one of his anti-American speeches. As always, he spoke with panache and sardonic wit, gesturing vigorously occasionally, his expression serious, but smiling the famous smile as he closed. The screen went blank. Grelle stood up and went over to switch off the set.

"The last man," Annette Devaud said, "the man attacking the Americans. He hasn't changed all that much, has he?"

Carel Vanek chose his cab with care, standing on the sidewalk with the tartan hold-all at his feet. He avoided any vehicle with a youngster behind the wheel, but he didn't want an elderly driver either; older people can panic, acting on impulse. He was looking for a middle-aged driver with a family to think of, with the experience to make him cautious. He yelled at an approaching cab, waving his hand.

"It's a place off the Boulevard des Capucines," he told the driver. "I'm not sure of the address but I'll recognize the street when I see it. A side-turning off to the left . . ."

He settled back in the cab with the hold-all on his lap. What he had said to the driver was true: he didn't know the name of the street but he had walked down it several times three years earlier, a street which was narrow, dark and unlit at night. There was very little traffic about at that hour and Capucines, a street of expensive shops, was almost empty on the chilly December evening, despite the closeness of Christmas. The driver went slowly to give his passenger a chance to locate the street.

"Turn here!"

Vanek had opened the window behind the driver wider to speak to him and he stayed leaning forward as the cab turned and entered a narrow, curving street. The walls of the high buildings on either side closed in on them and the street was as deserted as Vanek remembered it. Capucines was only a memory now as the cab cruised deeper inside the dark canyon while he waited for further instructions. Vanek strained his eyes to see beyond the windscreen, one hand inside the hold-all. Soon they would be near to the far end, moving out into a more-frequented area.

"Here we are. Stop!"

The driver pulled up, set his brake and left the engine running. Vanek pressed the muzzle of the Smith & Wesson into the back of the driver's neck. "Don't move. This is a

gun." The driver stiffened, sat very still. Vanek shot him
once.

It was 10.45 p.m. when a patrol-car drew up outside the
entrance to the Sûreté headquarters on the rue des Saussaies. Boisseau himself came out of the building first and
looked up and down the quiet street. There was nothing
in sight except a lone taxi-cab coming from the direction
of the Place Beauvau. Boisseau held up his hand to stop
them bringing Madame Devaud out and waited. Two gendarmes stood on the sidewalk with him. The driver was
behind the wheel of the waiting patrol-car, his engine ticking over.

Grelle had decided at the last moment to use only one
car to take Madame Devaud to a hotel the Sûreté used
for guarding important witnesses; a single car is less conspicuous than a motorcade. Also it would be able to move
very fast at this hour when the Paris streets were deserted.
Grelle himself, standing back inside the arch with Madame
Devaud and three detectives, was waiting to see her departure. The cab came towards the entrance slowly and
Boisseau noted it was not for hire. So far as he could
see the back was empty; the driver was obviously going off
duty. The cab cruised past and the driver took one hand
off the wheel to stifle a yawn.

Watching its tail-light, Boisseau made a beckoning
gesture and the small procession emerged from under
the archway. The three detectives crowded round Madame
Devaud, moving at her deliberate pace. They reached
the sidewalk. Inside the archway Grelle lit a cigarette, a
walkie-talkie tucked under his arm. He would be in con-
stant touch with the radio-controlled vehicle until it
reached its destination in the seventh arrondisement.
Madame Devaud had moved across the sidewalk and was
about to enter the car.

"Don't worry—it is only a few minutes' drive," Boisseau
assured her.

"Tell him not to drive too fast. I didn't enjoy the journey from the Gare de l'Est at all."

"I'll tell him. It will only be a few minutes," Boisseau repeated.

Vanek, wearing the cab-driver's cap—he had great faith in headgear as a medium of disguise—reached the Place des Saussaies which is round the corner from the entrance to Sûreté headquarters. He had been cruising past the archway at intervals—many cabs take this short-cut at night—completing the circuit round the large building and coming back again. Now he turned in a tight circle and drove back against the one-way system. Boisseau was about to help Madame Devaud into the car when he saw the cab returning at speed. He shouted a warning but the cab arrived at the worst possible mo-ment—while the huddled group, bunched together, was trapped in the open.

Vanek held the wheel with one hand while he cradled the sub-machine-gun under his right arm, his index finger curled inside the trigger-guard. He fired a steady burst, the weapon on automatic, the muzzle held in a fixed position, so he used the movement of the vehicle to create an arc of fire, emptying the whole magazine before he went past them, still driving the wrong way and dis-appearing into the Place Beauvau.

Grelle, by himself and free from the group, was the only one who even fired at the cab, and one revolver shot smashed the rear window. Then he was using the walkie-talkie, which put him straight through to central control, already organized for the president's motorcade drive to Charles de Gaulle Airport the following day. Via Grelle, the cab's description, including the smashed window and the direction it had taken, was circulated within one minute to every patrol-car within a five-mile radius. Only then did Grelle turn to look at the tragic scene on the side-walk.

The two gendarmes had run off after the cab. Boisseau,

shielded by the open car door, has escaped unscathed, but the three detectives lay on the ground, two of them moaning and gasping, the third very still. They had to lift the two men gently to get at Madame Devaud who lay face down, and when they eased her over they saw where the assassin's bullets had stitched a pattern across her chest.

"Armed and dangerous . . ."

All over Paris patrol-cars leapt forward, moving inwards on a cordon pattern laid down by the commissioner in charge at central control. In a way he welcomed the emergency on the eve of the president's departure: it gave him a chance to check the system. The cordon closed in like a contracting web, its approximate centre-point the Place Beauvau, and with sirens screaming patrol-cars rushed along the big boulevards. The commissioner at control was moving into action his entire force, repeating time and again the warning.

"Armed and dangerous . . ."

They found Vanek quite close to the Sûreté. His cab was spotted crossing the Place de la Concorde on the Tuileries side. Patrol-cars converged on the vast square, coming in over the Seine bridge, from Champs-Elysées, Rivoli and the Avenue Gabriel. A blaze of lamps, empty only seconds earlier, the Place was suddenly filled with noise and movement, with the high-pitched screams of sirens, the swivel of patrol-car headlights. Vanek braked by the kerb, jumped out with the sub-machine-gun and ran for the only possible refuge. The Tuileries gardens.

At this point in the Place de la Concorde the pavement by the kerb has a low stone wall beyond it. Beyond that lies another pavement and beyond that a high stone wall rises up to a lofty balustrade with the Tuileries park beyond like a huge viewing platform overlooking the entire Place. Vanek started running for the entrance to Tuileries at ground level, saw a patrol-car pull up, block-

ing him off. Jerking up his weapon, he emptied the second
magazine and everywhere policemen dropped flat. Throwing down the gun Vanek jumped over the low stone
wall, ran across the second sidewalk and began hauling
himself up the wall, using projecting stones like a ladder.
To his left and below him a flight of steps went down and
underground. He had almost reached the balustrade;
once over it he would have the whole park to hide in.
Behind him he heard shouts, the screams of half a dozen
more patrol-cars rushing into the square. He whipped one
leg over the balustrade. The park beyond was a dark,
tree-filled vastness, a place to manoeuvre in.

They caught him in a crossfire. Two gendarmes to the
right on the sidewalk below, another group of three to
the left as he hung above the world below him. There was
a fusillade of shots as the gendarmes emptied their magazines, very loud in the Place because all the patrol-cars
had now halted. Vanek hung in the night, one leg draped
over the balustrade, then his limp hand lost its grip and
he slipped over, falling as they went on firing, crashing
down into the deep staircase well where a large notice
proclaimed "Descente Interdite." Descent Forbidden.

20

"A woman who can positively identify me as the Leopard
has arrived in Paris. Her name is Annette Devaud. Apparently they brought her in under heavy guard aboard the
Stanislas express . . ."

A dog barked, a deafening sound on the tape. The

familiar, so recognizable voice, spoke sharply.

"Quiet, Kassim! I don't see how there is time to intercept her. I can personally take no action which will not arouse the gravest suspicion . . ."

"Why did you not add her to the Lasalle list earlier?" The second voice, husky, accented, was also quite recognizable.

"She went blind at the end of the war—so I assumed she was harmless. My assistant phoned the police chief at Saverne just before you arrived—apparently she had an operation recently which restored her sight. This is the most appalling mess, Vorin, coming at the last moment . . ."

"Mr. President, we may be able to do something . . ."

"I added her to the list later—when Danchin sent me his routine report with the *Frankfurter Allgemeine Zeitung* letter which mentioned her name. Your people were supposed to have dealt with the problem . . ."

"Something went wrong . . ."

"Then you cannot blame me!" An argument was developing; the well-known voice was sharp, cutting. "It is imperative that you rectify your error . . ."

"Then I must leave at once for the embassy, Mr. President. We have reached a stage where minutes count. Do you know where they will take the Devaud woman?"

"To the rue des Saussaies . . ."

Alone in the fourth-floor room at Sûreté headquarters, Marc Grelle switched off the tape-recorder which had been linked to the tiny transmitter inserted inside Kassim's studded collar. He had played it twice, standing while he listened to it with a frozen expression, concentrating on the pitch of the voices. It was a futile exercise—replaying the tape—because the timbre of Guy Florian's voice had come over with such clarity the first time. In any case the words spoken were diabolically conclusive.

Staring at the opposite wall, the prefect lit a cigarette, hardly aware of the action. For days now the terrible truth had thrust itself into his mind and he had refused to accept the evidence. Gaston Martin had seen three men enter the Elysée, one of them the president. The surveillance on Danchin and Blanc had revealed no evidence of a Soviet link contacting either man, but Florian met Soviet Ambassador Vorin almost daily. And so on . . . Staring at the wall, smoking his cigarette, Grelle felt a sense of nausea, like a husband who has just found his wife in bed with a coarse brutal lover.

Extracting the tape from the machine, he put it inside his pocket. Picking up the phone he asked for an outside line and then dialled a number. Still in a state of shock he made a great effort to keep his voice cold and impersonal.

"Alain Blanc? Grelle here. I need to see you immediately. No, don't come to the préfecture. I'm going straight back to my apartment. Yes, something has happened. You will need a glass of cognac before I tell you . . ."

The 2nd and 5th French Armoured Divisions, stationed in the German Federal Republic and commanded by Gen. Jacques Chassou, were already on the move. The German authorities had been informed, the consent of the government of the Duchy of Luxembourg had been obtained— all at very short notice. Within hours the advance elements of the two divisions had crossed the Luxembourg frontier and were moving into the Ardennes on their way back to France. At 10 p.m., just before he flew to Sedan, Gen. Chassou opened the secret instructions which had been personally handed to him by President Florian when he made his lightning visit to Baden-Baden on the previous Monday.

"For the moment you will not return to Germany at the conclusion of the exercise. Once over the Sedan bridges you will proceed on into France . . . You will halt in the general military area of Metz . . . transport parks have been prepared . . ."

Handing the secret communication to his assistant, Col Georges Doissy, Chassou told him to make the necessary adjustments and then flew off to Sedan. Doissy, who had once served under Col René Lasalle, immediately realized that this order would leave Germany isolated, with only a token British detachment alongside the German Army facing Russia. He thought about it for a few minutes, then he remembered President de Gaulle's advice to the recently elected President Kennedy. "Listen only to yourself . . ." Doissy picked up the phone and asked the night operator to put him through urgently to the Minister of National Defence, Alain Blanc.

At 10 p.m. on 22 December, Commander Arthur Leigh-Browne, RN, the British officer in charge of the NATO analyst team watching the Soviet convoy, K.12, issued a routine report. "If K.12 continues on her present course, at her present reduced speed, she can make landfall at Barcelona by changing course again some time within the next twelve to eighteen hours . . ." Being a precise man, he added a rider. "Theoretically she could also make landfall on the south coast of France, at Marseilles and Toulon . . ." Following the normal practice, a coded signal of his report was despatched to all NATO defence ministers.

Abou Benefeika, the Arab terrorist who had come within seconds of destroying the El Al airliner at Orly, tried to make himself more comfortable as he rested his head against the "pillow" of bricks in the basement of the abandoned building at 17 rue Réamur. The fact that he had folded his jacket and placed it on top of the bricks did not help him to sleep, nor did the rustle of tiny feet he kept hearing; the rats also had taken up unofficial tenancy in the condemned building.

During the day Benefeika had crept out of his hiding-place to purchase food and drink from the local shops, and

because this district of Paris was a ghetto peopled by
Algerians he was not too worried about breaking cover.
Absorbed as he was in his task, on the lookout only for
uniformed police, he failed to notice two scruffily-dressed
men who followed him everywhere with their hands in
their pockets. Returning to his squalid hideaway, he ate
and drank while outside one of the scruffily-dressed men
climbed up to the first floor of the building opposite. Using
his walkie-talkie, Sergeant Pierre Gallon made his routine
report. "Rabbit has returned to his burrow. Observation
is continuing . . ."

"Then I must leave at once for the embassy, Mr. President. We have reached a stage where minutes count. Do
you know where they will take the Devaud woman?"

"To the rue des Saussaies . . ."

In his apartment on the Ile Saint-Louis Grelle switched
off the tape-recorder and looked at Alain Blanc who sat
in an elegant chair with his legs crossed and a glass of
cognac in his hand. The Minister's expression was grim: it
was the third time the recording had been played back
for his benefit and he now knew the conversation word
for word. He drank the rest of his cognac in one gulp
and there were beads of sweat on his high-domed forehead. He looked up as Grelle spoke.

"Within two hours of that conversation—I phoned the
security officer at the Elysée and Vorin arrived there at
9.15—Annette Devaud was brutally murdered by the
assassin we later trapped in Place de la Concorde," the
prefect said. "There is no room for doubt anymore that
the man who . . ."

"I recognize Florian's voice," Blanc broke in impatiently. "Vorin's too. There is no room for doubt at
all." He sighed. "It is a terrible shock but not so much
of a surprise. For days now I have been wondering what
was going on—although I never suspected the appalling
truth. These rumours of a right-wing coup which seemed

to emanate from near-Communist sources. Florian's sudden and quite inexplicable journey to Baden-Baden . . ."

Blanc stood up and hammered his fist into the palm of his other hand. "Oh Jesus Christ what have we come to, Grelle? I have known him since he was a young man at the Polytechnique after the war. I organized his rise to power. How could I have been so blind?"

"Caesar is always above suspicion . . ."

"As I have just told you, I had a phone call from Col Doissy at Baden-Baden before I left to come here—saying that the 2nd and 5th divisions will proceed to Metz and stay there, which leaves Germany naked. With the American Congress in its present isolationist mood Washington will not even threaten to press the nuclear button— Moscow has its own button. The United States will only react if the American mainland is in danger. All this stems from the fiasco in Viet Nam and Cambodia. You know what I think is going to happen within the next few hours?"

"What?"

"I think Florian will announce in Moscow tomorrow the conclusion of a military pact with the Soviets—remember, the president can conclude such a pact himself. You've seen that report which just came in from Brussels —I think Florian will further announce joint military manoeuvres with the Russians. The ports of Toulon and Marseilles will be opened for the landing of Soviet troops aboard convoy K.12."

"Then something must be done . . ."

"Germany will wake up to find herself encircled— Soviet divisions to the east of her, Soviet divisions west of the Rhine. On French soil! I think Florian will fly back from Moscow later tomorrow and if there is any reaction here he will say there has been an attempted right-wing *coup d'état* by Col Lasalle and half of us will be behind bars . . ."

"Calm yourself," Grelle advised.

"Calm myself he says . . ." Blanc was showing great agitation, his face covered in nervous sweat as he moved restlessly about the living-room. "Within a few days we may even have the Soviet flag flying alongside the tricolour!" Accepting the refilled glass from Grelle he made as if to swallow it in a gulp, then stiffened himself and took only a sip.

"We have to decide what to do," Grelle said quietly.

"Exactly!" Blanc, after his outburst, suddenly recovered his natural poise. "It is quite useless consulting other ministers," he said firmly. "Even if I called a secret meeting they would never take a decision, someone would leak the news, it would reach the Elysée, Florian would act, call us right-wing conspirators, declare a state of emergency . . ."

It was Grelle who brought up the precedent of President Nixon, pointing out that whatever the solution the public and the world must never know the truth. "Nixon's actions were a bagatelle, hardly more than a misdemeanour compared with what we are talking about. Yet look at the shattering effect it had on America when he was exposed. Can you imagine the effect on France—on Europe—if it is ever revealed that the French president is a Communist agent? No one would ever be sure of us again. France would be demoralized . . ."

"You are, of course, quite right," Blanc said gravely. "It must never become public knowledge. Do you realize, Grelle, that leaves only one solution?"

"Florian must be killed . . ."

Along the German-Czechoslovak border between Selb and Grafenau there was a sudden burst of Soviet aerial activity in the early hours of 23 December, at first thought to be connected with large-scale manoeuvres and winter exercises being carried out by the Warsaw Pact countries. Later Soviet Foxbat aircraft were reported to have crossed and recrossed over the frontier and Chancellor Franz

Hauser was dragged out of bed at 2 a.m. to assess the situation. At 3 a.m. he ordered an amber alert which mobilized forces along the disturbed frontier and certain back-up groups.

At 2 a.m., pacing round his living-room, Grelle was barely more than a moving silhouette in the smoke accumulated from the two men's cigarettes. "I have imagined myself as an assassin," he said. "When I planned the security cordon I plugged up loopholes by seeing how I would have gone about the job of making an attempt on Florian's life tomorrow. I don't think anyone can penetrate the cordon."

"Perhaps I could," Blanc suggested quietly. "It has to be just between the two of us—only in that way can we ensure it will always remain a secret. If I had a gun—while I was waiting with the other ministers drawn up at the airport waiting for him to board Concorde . . ."

"Impossible!" Grelle dismissed the idea with a contemptuous gesture. "Everyone would wonder why you of all people had done it. And I have told the security squads that if anyone—even a minister—produces a revolver he is to be shot instantly." He stopped in front of Blanc's chair. "To make my point I have even told them that if I produce a revolver they must shoot me."

"Then it cannot be done . . ."

"It can be done by only one man."

"Who is?"

"The man who devised the security cordon, of course. Myself."

Before returning to his Ministry in the rue Saint-Dominique, Blanc made two more efforts to speak to Florian. When he phoned the Elysée from Grelle's apartment the operator told him that the president could not be disturbed, "except in the event of world war . . ."

Blanc then drove through the night to the Elysée to

find the wrought-iron gates—always open before and
barred only by a white-painted chain—closed, sealing
off the courtyard beyond. Blanc leaned out of the window.
"Open up at once," he demanded. "You know who I am,
for God's sake . . ."

The officer in charge came out of the pedestrian entrance to apologize, but he was quite firm. "The president
issued the instruction personally. No one is to be allowed
in tonight—except . . ."

"In the event of world war. I know!" Blanc jumped out
of the car, pushed past the officer and went through the
side entrance. Running across the cobbled yard and up the
seven steps he found the tall glass doors locked. Inside
the lobby another official who knew him well shook his
head, then made a scissors gesture across his body. Blanc,
who a moment before had been livid, stood quite still and
lit a cigarette. The scissors gesture had decided him. A
simple act by an official of no consequence at all, but it
crystallized the whole position for Alain Blanc. The
president had sealed himself off inside a fortress until
he flew to Russia in the morning.

Arriving back at his Ministry, Blanc went straight down
to the emergency communications room. "Get Gen.
Lamartine," he ordered. "Tell him not to dress—I
need him here five minutes from now . . ." There had
been tension among the seven uniformed officers on duty
on his arrival, but in the few minutes he had to wait for
General-in-Chief Lamartine his ice-cold manner defused
the tension. Lamartine arrived grizzle-faced and with a
coat thrown over his dressing-gown.

"You look like a mandarin in that dragon-embossed
robe," Blanc remarked. "I'm issuing certain instructions
and may need your authority to confirm them. I'll explain
later—we have a minor emergency and the president has
issued orders he must not be disturbed. Very sensible—he
has a long trip tomorrow. Now . . ."

This was the old Alain Blanc speaking, the man who

had planned Guy Florian's rise to power, who had kept his nerve in every political crisis. With Lamartine at his side, he proceeded methodically, informing the underground communications bunker at Taverny outside Paris —the bunker designed to operate under conditions of nuclear warfare—that until further notice they could act on no orders from any quarter without his countersignature. "From any quarter," he repeated. "I have Gen. Lamartine by my side who will confirm what I have just said . . ." Putting his hand over the receiver he saw that Lamartine was hesitating. "Get on with it," he said sharply, "I haven't got all night . . ."

Inside ten minutes Blanc had frozen the movement of all the French armed forces—not a single tank, plane or ship could move without his express sanction. Blanc had also spoken to French headquarters at Baden-Baden and Sedan—and his orders were that once through the Ardennes the two armoured divisions were to turn round immediately and move at speed back through the Ardennes to Germany. To ensure the order was carried out he had removed Chassou, Florian's general, from command and replaced him by Gen. Crozier. Chassou was placed under close arrest by the military governor of Metz.

Seated by his side, Lamartine confirmed each order, not sure of what was going on, but it was impossible even for Lamartine to suggest approaching the Elysée—which had been sealed off. Blanc, the master manipulator, was turning Florian's weapon of isolation against him. By three o'clock the job was done. The crisis would come in the morning if the president heard of what had happened while he slept.

Now quite alone in his apartment on the Ile Saint-Louis, Marc Grelle, haggard and unshaven, still wearing his polo-necked sweater and slacks, smoked and studied a series of reports and diagrams. They showed all the security precautions he had mounted to protect the president during his coming motorcade drive to the airport. As he had done so often before, Grelle was checking for a loophole, some open door he had omitted to close through which an assassin might walk. He wished he had Boisseau by his side, but this was one operation he could only work on alone. Occasionally he glanced at the framed photograph of a woman perched on a near-by grand piano, a photograph of his late wife, Pauline.

Some ambitious officials in France take good care to marry rich wives; money can advance a career. Grelle had married a girl whose family was of very modest means, and then out of the blue, shortly before she had been killed in the motor crash, Pauline had inherited a small fortune from a relative she had not even known existed. "I'd love to buy an apartment on the Quai Bethune," she had said one day. "It's the only extravagance I've ever craved . . ." Shortly afterwards she had been killed.

As police prefect Grelle had automatically been provided with an apartment inside the préfecture, but after Pauline's death he had purchased this place; not so much because he wanted it, but he thought she would have been happy to know he was living there. His eyes strayed more frequently to the photograph as he went on struggling with the problem; he was wondering what she would have thought of it all. At 4 a.m., suddenly aware that the room was choking, he got up and opened the window, then he stood there looking across the Seine, breathing in fresh air to alert his brain. He had still not found a loophole.

21

No airport in the world was ever more heavily guarded than Charles de Gaulle Airport on the morning of 23 December. The presidential Concorde—looking in the half-light of near-dawn like a huge, evil bird—waited on the tarmac, already fully fuelled for its long flight to Moscow. In a few hours, at 10.30 a.m. precisely, the aircraft would lift off at a critical angle of forty-five degrees, its vulture-like head arched as it headed for fifty thousand feet.

And already the presidential pilot, Captain Pierre Jubal, who had got up from his bed in his expensive flat in Passy at 5.30, had arrived at the airport the French often call Roissy because it was built near the village of Roissy-en-France. Driving himself the twenty-five kilometres from Paris to the airport, Jubal had been stopped three times at checkpoints along Autoroute A 1, the highway over which the presidential motorcade would pass later.

"This bloody security," he snapped to his co-pilot, Lefort, as he got out of his Alfa Romeo, "this bloody security is insane. Do they really believe someone is going to take a potshot at him?"

Lefort shrugged. "In a bar last night I heard someone say Florian will never reach Roissy alive."

The airport had been closed to all civil aircraft from midnight, an unprecedented step even for the protection of a head of state. "It's that police prefect, Grelle," Jubal grumbled as he walked towards the waiting aircraft. "He's power-mad. Look at all that . . ."

He waved his hand towards the huge circular building which is the centre-piece of the world's most advanced airport. Silhouetted against the growing light, uniformed men of the Air Transport Gendarmerie patrolled the roof of the building with their automatic weapons. The two men passed a scout-car mounted with a machine-gun. Surrounding the circular building are the seven satellites, the separate modernistic departure centres where passengers board their aircraft after travelling on underground travelator belts. Jubal gestured towards the roof of a satellite where the same sinister silhouettes patrolled. "The man's a maniac," he growled.

"There has already been one attempt on President Florian," Lefort reminded his superior. "And, as I've just told you, in a bar last night there was a strong rumour . . ."

"You shouldn't have been in a bar last night," Jubal rapped. "You should have been in bed like I was, getting my kip . . ."

"With Jacqueline?"

As the pale early morning light spread over the plain in which Charles de Gaulle Airport stands, Concorde was emerging in stronger silhouette, looking more than ever like a rapacious bird crouched for take-off. In three hours she would be on her way, climbing towards the stratosphere, taking the president of the French Republic on his historic flight to Soviet Russia.

Just before 9.30 a.m. on 23 December the city of Paris was like a frozen tableau where shortly the curtain would rise on great events. Every intersection leading on to the route the presidential motorcade would follow had been closed on Grelle's orders. At every intersection truckloads of CRS troops waited with the engines running. Behind every intersection "dragon's teeth" of steel chain had been thrown across the incoming roads, blocking off any vehicle which might try to rush the presidential convoy.

Crowds lined the route, kept well back from the road by a maze of crash barriers erected by gendarmes in the middle of the night with the aid of arc-lights mounted on trucks. The crowds were strangely silent, as though expecting something dramatic and tragic to happen. Some of them had tuned in transistor radios to Europe Number One; Col Lasalle was expected to make yet another broadcast shortly. Occasionally, as they waited on that crisp, clear December morning—only two days away from Christmas—they looked behind to the rooftops where police patrolled the skyline like prison camp guards.

At other times the crowd stared above into the sky, which was also guarded. Over the route a fleet of helicopters flew backwards and forwards at a height of one hundred feet, their engines thumping, disappearing out of earshot and then returning again. And all these elements in the vast cordon—on the ground, on the rooftops, in the air itself—were linked by radio to central control at the préfecture on the Ile de la Cité. Boisseau was the man in direct control of the huge operation, waiting in the office Grelle had loaned him for the first radio report to come in. "He has just left Elysée . . ."

Blanc was sitting in his car inside the Elysée courtyard, one of a whole convoy drawn up to follow the president once he had left, his wife Angèle by his side, when he saw a car drive half-way into the palace entrance before it was stopped. He stiffened. Gen. Lamartine was getting out. Some bloody fool of a security officer had permitted the general to browbeat his way through the cordon. Blanc looked through the rear window at the steps and saw that Florian had just come out, was pausing as he saw Lamartine arguing with the security chief. "I'll only be a minute," Blanc said to his wife and slipped out of the car. In the vehicle ahead Roger Danchin was twisted round in his seat, wondering if it was something which concerned him.

Lamartine had left the security man, was hurrying across the yard to the steps while everyone stared. Florian descended into the yard, was met by Lamartine as he started to walk to his car. The general was talking animatedly while Florian walked slowly, listening. Lamartine's face froze as he saw Blanc coming towards him. He's told him, the minister thought, told him everything—to cover himself, the shit.

"What's all this about, Alain?"

Florian was half inside his car and spoke over his shoulder, then he settled in his seat and left the door open, looking up at Blanc who bent down to speak. One minute—two at the most—would decide it. "We had a little problem last night," the minister said crisply. "They wouldn't let me inside the palace, so I dealt with it myself."

"You are planning a *coup d'état?*"

There was a look of cynical amusement on the long, lean, intelligent face, an expression of supreme self-confidence. At that moment Blanc was more aware than he ever had been of the magnetic personality of this man who had wrongly been called the second de Gaulle. He leaned forward as Blanc remained silent, made as though to get out of the car, and the minister's pulse skipped a beat.

"You are planning a *coup d'état?*" Florian repeated.

"Mr. President."

That was all Blanc said. Florian relaxed, closed the door himself and told the driver to proceed. Blanc went back to his own car, not even glancing at Lamartine who stood like a statue, sure now that he had destroyed his career. "All for nothing," Blanc told his wife as he settled back in the car. "Lamartine is an old warhorse—I think we may soon have to put him out to grass . . ."

He was talking with only one part of his mind as the

first car, full of CRS men, left the courtyard and turned into the Faubourg St Honoré, followed by the presidential vehicle. So much confidence bottled up inside one man! Florian had decided it was too late for anyone to stop the wheels of history he had set in motion. Blanc, his closest friend, had issued instructions during the night which could be interpreted as high treason. No matter, he could deal with that when he returned from Moscow. Had a certain American president some years ago had the same feeling of invulnerability—even though his actions had been minor misdemeanours compared with those of Guy Florian?

The route the motorcade was taking to Charles de Gaulle Airport had been carefully worked out by Marc Grelle personally. It must pass through as few narrow streets as possible, to eliminate the danger of a hidden sniper firing from a building. Turning out of the Elysée to the left, it would follow the Faubourg St Honoré for a short distance, turn left again down the Avenue Marigny and then enter Champs-Elysées. Once it reached this point it was broad boulevards all the way until it moved on to Autoroute A 1 and a clear run to the airport.

"He has just left Elysée . . ."

At central control André the Squirrel was able to see the motorcade's progress at various selected points where hidden television cameras watched the crowd for hostile movement. With the microphone Boisseau was now holding in his hand he could be "patched" through to any radio-equipped sub-control centre along the route, even warning them of something which caught his eye. On the television screen he watched the motorcade moving down Avenue Marigny; the CRS vehicle in front, the president's car next, followed by twenty-three black saloons containing cabinet ministers and their wives. The sun was shining brilliantly now—there had been a complete weather change late the previous day— but Boisseau, watching the long line of black cars passing, had the macabre feeling he was observing a funeral procession.

Boisseau was sweating it out. A professional to his
fingertips, his only concern now was his immediate duty—
to get the president safely to Roissy. The Leopard investigation had temporarily faded out of his mind; during
the past few hours the prefect had not even mentioned the
subject. His expression tense, Boisseau continued watching the television screen. He was waiting for the moment
when the motorcade would turn on to the autoroute,
which soon moved into open country, and here it would
be impossible for an assassin to conceal himself.

"Just get to Porte Maillot," Boisseau whispered. "Then
you are away . . ."

Suddenly he became aware that he was gripping the
mike so tightly that his knuckles had whitened. Inside
his car, Alain Blanc also realized he was clenching his
fist tightly. Like Boisseau he understood that once the
president reached the autoroute he would be safe. Blanc
found himself peering out of the window, glancing up at
the windows of tall apartment blocks, looking for something suspicious, something which shouldn't be there.
How the hell was Grelle going to manage it? The motorcade seemed to crawl up the Champs-Elysées.

It seemed to crawl to Boisseau also as it reached the
top of the great boulevard, rounded the Arc de Triomphe
where Napoleon's victories seem to go on for ever, and
then started down the Avenue de la Grande Armée which
is also lined with tall apartment blocks on both sides.
"Get to Porte Maillot," Boisseau whispered to himself
again, glad that he was alone in the office. Everything
which had happened in the past few weeks had emptied
out of his mind: Boisseau was in charge of the president's
security. The responsibility weighed on him heavily.

Alain Blanc was now beginning to give up hope that
anything would happen. Grelle had obviously failed, which
was hardly surprising. Perhaps his nerve had failed which
would be even less surprising. Still looking up at the

apartment block windows, Blanc took out a handkerchief and mopped his damp forehead. For a different reason he was under as great a strain as Boisseau. He frowned as he heard the thump of an approaching helicopter's engine, flying very low, then he pressed his cheek against the window trying to locate the low-flying machine. The crowd, still strangely silent, as though they too felt they were watching a funeral procession, craned their heads to stare at the helicopter which was flying straight up Champs-Elysées from behind the motorcade. Passing over the Arc de Triomphe, it headed down the Avenue de la Grande Armée, scattering pigeons from the rooftops with the raucous clatter of its engine. Then it passed over them and flew off into the distance. Blanc sagged back in his seat. "Really, there was nothing we could have done . . ." Inadvertently he had spoken aloud and his wife glanced at him in surprise. Then the lead vehicle, followed by the president's, began turning. They had reached Porte Maillot.

At 10.25 a.m. Captain Pierre Jubal sat with his co-pilot, Lefort, behind the controls of Concorde five minutes before take-off time. On the tarmac outside in the blazing sunshine the entire French cabinet stood in line, waiting for Florian to board the plane. Near-by stood squads of Airport Gendarmerie, their automatic weapons cradled in their arms. From where Alain Blanc stood the view beyond Concorde went straight out across the plain, interrupted only by a tiny cluster of distant buildings which was the village of le Mesnil Amelot perched at the edge of the vast airport. The sun caught a minute spike which was a church spire, a tiny rectangle which was an abandoned factory. Then the president was walking past his cabinet ministers, smiling his famous smile.

"He has the presence of a king," Danchin murmured to the minister standing next to him. "France is indeed blessed at this time of her great power . . ."

About to board the aircraft, Florian seemed to remember something. Swinging round, still smiling broadly, he went back and shook hands with Alain Blanc. "Alain," he said warmly, "I will never forget all you did for me in the past . . ." Only Blanc noticed the emphasis he placed on the last few words, like a chairman saying goodbye to the director he had just dismissed from the board. The execution is delayed, Blanc thought as he watched Florian going up the mobile staircase, but it will be carried out the moment he returns.

At the top of the staircase Florian turned, waved his hand, then disappeared. The jets began to hum and hiss. Technicians near the nose of the plane ran back. The incredible machine began to throb with power. Watching the scene on television in Paris, Boisseau mopped his own forehead.

Earlier, before the motorcade turned out of the Elysée, it was helicopter pilot Jean Vigier who spotted the small black car moving at speed away from the centre of Paris. He saw it first below him, driving along the Boulevard des Capucines. Intrigued—it was the only vehicle moving along the deserted boulevard—he changed course and picked it up again beyond Opéra. Impressed by its speed, by the sense of urgency it conveyed, he continued tracking it.

What started as a routine check turned into something more alarming as Vigier followed its non-stop progress; the car was moving past road-block after road-block without stopping, without any check being made on it. Worried now, Vigier continued his aerial surveillance on the rogue vehicle while he radioed central control. "Small black car passing through all checkpoints without stopping . . . now located at . . ."

Receiving the message, Boisseau took immediate action, telling an assistant to phone the police station at 1 rue Hittorf, which was the nearest checkpoint the car had passed through. The assistant returned a few minutes later. "It is the police prefect inside that car—that is why they are letting him through the checkpoints. He radios each one as he approaches it . . ." Boisseau wasted little time on speculation; his chief was clearly checking something out. Sending a message back to helicopter pilot Jean Vigier, "Driver of black car identified—no cause for alarm," he forgot about the incident.

Inside the car Grelle was now approaching the Goutte-d'Or district. Again he radioed ahead to the next checkpoint to let him through, and then he did something very curious. Pulling in by the kerb in the deserted street, he changed the waveband on his mobile communicator, took out a miniaturized tape-recorder, started it playing and then began speaking over the communicator, prefacing his message with the code-sign. "Franklin Roosevelt. Boisseau here. Yes, Boisseau. Is that you, Lesage? Interference? Nothing wrong at this end. Now, listen!" The tape-recorder went on spewing out the static he had recorded off his own radio set in his apartment, garbling his voice as he went on speaking.

"Rabbit has been seen . . . Yes, Rabbit! Walking down rue Clichy five minutes ago. Take your men and scour the Clichy area now. Don't argue, Lesage, he's got away from you—just get after him! When you find him, tail him—no interception. I repeat, no interception. He may lead you to the rest of the gang . . ."

Having given the code-word for the operation at the beginning of his message, Grelle was satisfied that Lesage would carry out his order immediately. Driving on again, he passed through the next checkpoint and then turned into the rue Réamur where Rabbit, the Algerian terrorist Abou Benefeika, was still waiting for his friends to come and collect him. Getting out of his car, he approached the derelict entrance to No. 17 with care, but the rubber-soled shoes he was wearing made no sound as he entered the doorless opening with his revolver in his hand. A

stale smell of musty damp made him wrinkle his nose
as he stood in the dark hallway listening. He was even
more careful as he made his way down the staircase leading to the basement.

He waited at the bottom to accustom his eyes to the
gloom, and gradually the silhouette of a sleeping man
formed beyond the doorway into the cellar, a man sleeping
on his side and facing the wall. Switching on his pocket
torch the prefect found a wire stretched across the lower
part of the doorway; following it with the beam of his
torch he saw it was attached to a large tin perched on a
pile of bricks. Any incautious person who walked through
the doorway would bring down the tin, alerting the
sleeping terrorist. Grelle stepped over the wire, still using
the torch to thread his way among a scatter of old bricks
as he approached the sleeping terrorist. Bending down, he
picked up the magnum pistol close to the man's inert
hand. Then he wakened him.

Grelle drove out of Paris through the Porte de Pantin
and continued along route N3; then, just before reaching
Claye-Souilly, he turned due north through open countryside. The Algerian terrorist, Abou Benefeika, was
crouched on the floor in front of the passenger seat Grelle
had pushed back to its fullest extent. Covered with a
travelling rug, which had apparently slipped on to the
floor, he was crouched on his haunches facing the door
with his back to Grelle who occasionally lifted the revolver
out of his lap and pressed it against the nape of his neck
to remind him of its presence.

Abou Benefeika was partly relieved, partly terrified.
The civilian who had woken him up with a gun in his
face, warning him to keep quiet, had told him he had
come to take him away, to get him out of the country.
"Your friends ran for it." Grelle told him savagely, "so
I have been left to see you don't get caught. The police
are closing in on this district, I suppose you know?" Grelle

had warned him to get his head down and keep it down. "This is a stolen police car so you'd better hope and pray we can get past the road-blocks they've set up. I have the identity card of the detective I shot to take this car, so we should be able to manage it. But if I have to shoot you to save myself I shall do so . . ."

Benefeika, cooped up in the basement with the rats for days, was in a demoralized state. He didn't trust the man who had woken him, but he was encouraged when Grelle passed through police road-blocks without giving him up. What other explanation could there be except the one this man had given him? Beyond the Porte de Pantin there were no more checkpoints for a while, but the occasional prods with the muzzle of his rescuer's revolver encouraged Benefeika to keep his head down. In the back of the car another travelling rug was draped over the floor, but it was not a man who lay concealed beneath this covering.

The visit to the rue des Saussaies at 5 a.m. had been hazardous. The guard who let him inside the building had assumed Grelle was going up to the room on the fourth floor where some mysterious project was carried out—the room, in fact, where a man waited for the next call from Hugon, Col Lasalle's treacherous deputy, Capt. Moreau. Grelle did proceed to the fourth floor, going first to the office which had been set aside for his use, the room where he had interviewed Annette Devaud. He was only inside for a moment while he left a pack of cigarettes on his desk. He then went to the strong-room on the other side of the building, unlocked the door, slipped inside and locked it again. He was now inside the outer office, facing the strong-room door.

Grelle proceeded with great care. Using gloves, he took the key to the strong-room door and pressed it into a key blank he had brought with him. He deliberately made a poor job of it, shifting the key so the impression was out of true. Afterwards it would be assumed someone had made a fresh and perfect blank, providing the means to furnish themselves with a duplicate key. Still wearing the gloves, he dropped the imperfect key blank on the floor and pushed it out of sight under a filing cabinet. Within a few hours teams of investigators would tear the room to pieces, would locate every speck of dust inside the place. Then he opened the strong-room door.

The SAM missile launcher was wrapped in protective canvas, laid on the floor against the wall. Beside it, inside a smaller roll of canvas, lay the two *strela* rockets. He made one bulky package of both, using the larger roll of canvas and fastening a strap he had brought round it. Leaving the strong-room, he locked it, went out into the corridor and re-locked the outer door. The difficulty now would be getting the large roll out of the building. He was bound to encounter a guard at the exit, if not inside the building.

To avoid the patrolling guards, whose routine he knew, he went a long way round, walking through endless corridors and down back staircases. The damned building was a rabbit warren he had often cursed in the past but this time it could be his salvation. He went down the last staircase, then he crept back up it as he heard the footsteps of a guard in the passage below. He waited. The footsteps faded and silence returned to the decrepit interior. He walked down the staircase quickly, reached the bottom and slid the canvas roll inside a cupboard which had remained empty for years. Walking across the hall, he opened the outer door quietly.

The guard was leaning against a wall and Grelle thought he had dozed off standing up, but it was too much of a risk to try and sneak past him. "Thomas!" he called out in a loud voice. The man straightened up with a jerk and there was a tremor in his voice. Grelle was not a man who regarded any kind of slackness lightly. "Yes, Mr. Prefect?"

"I've forgotten my cigarettes. Run up to Room 407 for me, would you?" Grelle handed Thomas a key. "There's a fresh pack on my desk . . ."

Grelle listened to the retreating footsteps from the bottom of the staircase, took the roll out of the cupboard, carried it across the courtyard and laid it on the floor of the rear of his car. Then he spread out a travelling rug over it. He was waiting in the hall when Thomas returned with the cigarettes and the key. "Thank you, Thomas." He gave the man a cigarette. "Be sure that wall doesn't fall on you . . ." He left Thomas staring nervously after him, fairly confident that he would omit to mention to his superior that Grelle had called. Driving back to his apartment on the Ile Saint-Louis, he locked the car away in the garage and went upstairs to shave.

Beyond Grelle's windscreen the tiny village of le Mesnil Amelot was in sight, a silhouette of a cluster of houses, a church spire and an abandoned factory building. Beside him on the floor Abou Benefeika was sweating; they had just passed another checkpoint. Leaving them behind at the Porte de Pantin, the prefect had run into them again as he approached the perimeter of Charles de Gaulle Airport, checkpoints which he had ordered to be set up. At the last one, still some way from the village, he called across quickly to a guard. "Keep your eyes open for strangers. I have received a report there could be trouble round here . . ."

"You are going on into the village, sir?"

"I'll probably stop well this side of it—to watch the take-off . . ."

He drove on while Benefeika, huddled under the rug, marvelled at the audacity of this fake policeman. Several times he had asked where they were going and Grelle had been curt. "To a place where there is transport to get you out—and that's all you need to know . . ." Coming close to the village, Grelle glanced at his watch.

10.20. Jesus Christ, it had taken him longer than he had estimated. In ten minutes Concorde would be airborne.

Over to his left the plain stretched out in the sunlight beyond the wire which enclosed Charles de Gaulle Airport and he thought he could see the waiting Concorde. As he had hoped, the village street was deserted; everyone had crowded into their neighbours' houses overlooking the airport where they waited for the presidential plane to take off. Grelle turned the car sharply, driving round the back of an abandoned factory building into a large yard.

"A helicopter will land here and take you off inside one hour," Grelle informed the Algerian as he hustled him at gun-point out of the car. "In the meantime you will stay quiet . . ." Taking him inside the building, Grelle prodded him up a crumbling staircase and into a small room on the second floor where the window was barred. He bolted the door with Benefeika on the inside. Only recently, checking every aspect of security surrounding the president's departure, the prefect had driven all round the airport perimeter and had stopped at le Mesnil Amelot; intrigued by the old factory, he had walked all over it. Having locked away Benefeika, Grelle took the heavy canvas roll out of his car and lugged it up on to the roof. There was still no one about and only the church and the graveyard faced the derelict factory. Next he checked his watch. 10.27.

In Paris at the préfecture Boisseau was extremely irritated when an assistant told him there was an urgent message from Lesage, the detective in charge of the team watching the Algerian terrorist, Abou Benefeika. "For God's sake, at a time like this," Boisseau fumed, then he remembered his chief's knack of keeping his eye on half a dozen things at once. "Put him through," he snapped. He listened for less than a minute and then exploded.

"You fool! I gave no orders to pull out. You say the

voice was badly distorted but it gave the correct code-sign? It wasn't me! You've been fooled by someone in the terrorist cell. Get back to the building at once and search it. I can tell you now you'll find him gone!" Boisseau turned his attention again to the television image which showed the president going up the steps of the mobile staircase, turning to wave, then disappearing inside Concorde. "In no time at all he'll be airborne," he remarked to his assistant.

Characteristically, in the manner of a Pierre Trudeau or a Jack Kennedy, Guy Florian went through the passenger section of Concorde to the control cabin. He proposed to sit there while the plane took off, to watch how the pilots handled the controls. "Sit down," he told the flight deck staff. "I'm just another passenger now . . ." He grinned boyishly. "But important enough to sit with you while you take her up. If you have no objection . . ."

At 10.30 precisely the huge machine began moving down the runway to reach the main take-off area, travelling some distance before Jubal turned the aircraft and pointed her along the main runway. There was a moment's pause while he waited for the control tower to give him formal permission, then he set the plane in motion. From where Alain Blanc stood it still looked like a venomous bird of prey, a beautiful machine but something evil and predatory. The whine and hiss from the enormous power of the engines came across to the cabinet ministers as they stood in a dutiful line, waiting. The sky was now absolutely clear, the sun shining brilliantly. No other aircraft could be seen—the sky had been emptied for the departure of President Florian. Far down the runway the plane changed direction, climbing suddenly at an acute angle, its vulture-like head and neck arched with its body, trailing in its wake a stream of dirt.

At 10.31 on the rooftop of the abandoned building Grelle was sprawled on a sheet of oilskin he had brought to protect his clothes. Hugging the missile launcher hard into his shoulder, the way Buvon had explained when he told the prefect at Orly how the weapon worked, Grelle was staring through the telescopic sight. Only a blur to the naked eye, Concorde came up close and clear through the sight, so close he could read the words *Air France* painted along its side. He was sweating profusely. In the president's entourage aboard the moving plane were men he knew well, men he liked and respected. Grelle's mouth was tightly compressed, his teeth clenched.

She climbed like a triumphant bird, nose and neck arched, her huge bat-winged body arched, climbing at that severe angle which is so awe-inspiring—and terrifying —seen from the ground, or the rooftop of an abandoned factory. One thousand feet . . . two thousand . . . climbing. This is always the critical moment—when a huge aircraft laden with fuel has to keep on going up and up without pause because there is now no point of return and you keep going up towards the stratosphere—or there is oblivion.

"For France . . ."

Grelle squeezed the trigger.

The rocket sped up from the rooftop. Grelle was running one flight down to the room where the Algerian terrorist was still waiting for the chopper to come and take him to safety. In the empty sky above Charles de Gaulle Airport there were only two occupants—the ascending rocket and ascending Concorde. There was instant panic among the radar operators tracking Concorde's course. Another object had appeared on their scanners. An incredibly small object, streaking across the screens at supersonic speed, moving so fast that only one operator was able to shout.

Guy Florian was speaking from the flight deck over the radio, relaying a message which was being transmitted as people gathered around television sets in Paris bars to watch the climbing Concorde. "This historic mission I am making to Moscow will further the cause of world peace so that our grand-children . . ."

The Russian-made *strela* missile impacted with Concorde at the control cabin. The head and neck of the plane—which enclosed the control cabin from where Florian was speaking—broke off from the body. As the fuel detonated there was a tremendous b-o-o-m. In the streets of Paris twenty-five kilometres away people stopped as though they had been shot. From the ground the assembled cabinet ministers saw a terrible fireball flare as the fuel ignited seconds after the control cabin had gone spinning off into space. The fireball consumed half the body while the rear half fell away and plumed into a second fiery dart which plunged into fields thirty kilometres away. As the dart settled a great column of black smoke rose vertically into the clear morning sky. A fragment of tail landed a score of metres away from the cabinet ministers and they scattered. Up to that moment they had stood there in silence, motionless with horror. It was Alain Blanc who recovered first, slipping away to his car. "Drive like hell back to Paris," he ordered.

The entire village where the missile had been fired from was sealed off. Grelle personally directed the operation. Patrol-cars converging on the village overtook the police prefect as he was driving *towards* le Mesnil Amelot, and he led the way into the village where the inhabitants were now in the street staring skywards in a state of shock. The cars pulled up and Grelle was the first to jump out.

"Back into your houses . . . everyone off the street . . . there may be shooting at any second . . ."

The village was sealed off within three minutes as more cars arrived, as Grelle ordered a house-to-house search and warned his men against getting trigger-happy. "I saw something streak into the sky from this village," he told the inspector in charge of the detachment. "Me too," the inspector replied excitedly. Over a car's radio Grelle got in touch with Boisseau. "Keep the streets of Paris clear. No crowd must be allowed to assemble. Use the CRS troops if necessary. Someone may try to organize an insurrection."

Having attended to Paris, Grelle resumed control of the house-to-house search. It was 10.55 a.m. exactly—he had checked the time by his watch—when he heard the inspector running down the street, shouting his head off. They had found the Algerian.

Abou Benefeika was on the rooftop of the abandoned factory, sprawled on his back, his eyes open as he stared sightless at the sky, his own magnum pistol in his hand, with one bullet fired, bearing his own fingerprints. He had apparently shot himself through the right temple. The SAM missile launcher lay close by next to a spare rocket; later, when they checked the weapon, it also carried his fingerprints.

On 7 January the great bells of Notre Dame rang out for the state funeral of Guy Florian—part of his body had miraculously survived intact—and heads of state from all over the world attended the occasion, including the titular president of the Union of Soviet Socialist Republics. Alain Blanc, newly elected prime minister, led the mourners.

On the previous Christmas Eve Marc Grelle handed in his resignation as police prefect of Paris to Alain Blanc, who had also temporarily taken over the post of Minister of the Interior. The two men remain closeted in private for over an hour. Grelle then immediately issued a statement to the press. "Failing in my duty to protect the life of the president of the French Republic, I have resigned and will go into immediate retirement." Georges Hardy,

Grelle's old friend and police prefect of Lyon, took over as police prefect of Paris.

On 8 January, the day after the state funeral of the president, which Grelle had watched alone on television in his apartment on the Ile Saint-Louis, the ex-prefect drove Alan Lennox to the airport for his flight back to London. Still convalescent and heavily bandaged, Lennox had insisted on going home at once after making a lengthy deposition of his activities in France to André Boisseau. The deposition made no mention of the Leopard and Boisseau, who carried out the interrogation personally, never referred to the Resistance leader once.

After seeing the Englishman aboard his flight at Charles de Gaulle Airport, Grelle started the drive back to Paris alone. In his breast pocket he carried the photograph of his wife, Pauline, which he had extracted from the frame in his apartment. His last words to Alan Lennox before leaving him had been nostalgic. "For years I have looked forward to retiring to a certain village in the Dordogne—the fishing there is good . . ." But Grelle had devoted most of his life to preserving and upholding the law; nor had he any illusions that the steps he had taken to cover his tracks would stand up to intensive investigation. He had only sought to buy himself a little time. If he was not available for questioning then, in due course, Boisseau could issue his report confirming that Abou Benefeika was responsible for the president's death. He hit the crash barrier travelling at 140 kph.

Over five hundred people attended his funeral. And as at the funeral of Guy Florian, Alain Blanc, later to become the next president of France, was the chief mourner. On top of the coffin was draped Marc Grelle's black uniform embroidered in silver, which is reserved for official occasions. "It struck me," André the Squirrel remarked afterwards, "that he would have preferred them to drape slacks and a polo-necked sweater . . ." The Prime Minister was one of the pall-bearers, and as he walked slowly with a corner of the coffin perched on his shoulders there were people who said later that never before or since had they seen Alain Blanc so distressed.

> *"This is Helen MacInnes*
> *at the top of her form."*
> —JOHN BARKHAM

AGENT IN PLACE

by Helen MacInnes

2-3127-5 $1.95

AGENT IN PLACE—the spellbinding new novel of suspense adventure—is a magic blend of betrayal and intrigue set against the colorful backdrop of New York, Washington, and the Riviera.

AGENT IN PLACE begins with the theft of a top secret memo and explodes into violent shock waves that rock agents all over the world. For Tony Lawton, British agent, masquerading as a wine merchant, hunting down the traitor becomes a real challenge. But for well-known journalist Tom Kelso and his beautiful wife, Thea, the affair has unleashed a very special terror. "The hallmarks of a MacInnes novel are as individual and as clearly stamped as a Hitchcock thriller."
—*The New York Times*

FAWCETT CREST BESTSELLERS

AGENT IN PLACE *Helen MacInnes*	2-3127-5	$1.95
THE WOMAN SAID YES *Jessamyn West*	2-3128-3	$1.95
THE STONE LEOPARD *Colin Forbes*	2-3129-1	$1.95
SWORD OF VENGEANCE *Sylvia Thorpe*	2-3136-4	$1.50
THE MAGNOLIAS *Julie Ellis*	2-3131-3	$1.75
THE GOLDEN UNICORN *Phyllis Whitney*	2-3104-6	$1.95
THE PEACOCK SPRING *Rumer Godden*	2-3105-4	$1.75
MAKING ENDS MEET *Barbara Howar*	2-3084-8	$1.95
STRANGER AT WILDINGS *Madeleine Brent*	2-3085-6	$1.95
THE TIME OF THE DRAGON *Dorothy Eden*	2-3059-7	$1.95
THE LYNMARA LEGACY *Catherine Gaskin*	2-3060-0	$1.95
THE GOLDEN RENDEZVOUS *Alistair MacLean*	2-3055-4	$1.75
TESTAMENT *David Morrell*	2-3033-3	$1.95
TRADING UP *Joan Lea*	2-3014-7	$1.95
HARRY'S GAME *Gerald Seymour*	2-3019-8	$1.95
IN THE BEGINNING *Chaim Potok*	2-2980-7	$1.95
THE ASSASSINS *Joyce Carol Oates*	2-3000-7	$2.25
LORD OF THE FAR ISLAND *Victoria Holt*	2-2874-6	$1.95
REBEL HEIRESS *Jane Aiken Hodge*	2-2960-2	$1.75
CSARDAS *Diane Pearson*	2-2885-1	$1.95
WINNING THROUGH INTIMIDATION *Robert J. Ringer*	2-2836-3	$1.95
CENTENNIAL *James A. Michener*	V2639	$2.75
LADY *Thomas Tryon*	C2592	$1.95

Send to: FAWCETT PUBLICATIONS, INC.
      Mail Order Dept., P.O. Box 1014, Greenwich Conn. 06830

NAME _____

ADDRESS _____

CITY _____

STATE _____ ZIP _____

I enclose $_____, which includes total price of all books
ordered plus 50¢ for book postage and handling for the first
book and 25¢ for each additional. If my order is for five books or
more, I understand that Fawcett will pay all postage and handling.